HATE CATS TRAGEDY

JAMES WALLACE BOWEY

HATE CATS TRAGEDY

ABOUT THE AUTHOR

James Wallace Bowey was born in 1993. He is the only son, and the youngest of four. James was a shy and timid child growing up. He found it extremely difficult to engage in conversation with new people. He could, however, talk to himself for hours at a time, finding it the safest way to have a conversation. Going through school to college and other occupations, he was able to improve his confidence in talking to others.

Writing was never a path James would have thought to go down. Yet having a slightly uncontrollable imagination, it seemed the perfect platform to share his thoughts.

What started as a hobby for the first two years, became an obsession over the next two, and something he had to see through. He was able to find out a few things about himself along the way.

ACKNOWLEDGMENTS

Thank you to family and friends who showed interest and support throughout.

Thank you to my mother, father, and three sisters – to my sister Naomi Bowey who designed the cover art.

Thank you to my editor Joanna Booth at Book Helpline.

Lastly, a special thank you to author Stuart R. Brogan, who inspired me to start writing in the first place.

You can find me on Twitter at @JWallaceBowey.

ONE

Adam was awake. He had been awake for a while. With his head resting on the pillow, he stared at the digital clock on the bedside table. The clock read 6:58. He never had liked the look of digital clocks. Never knowing how close to the minute the time was, by hiding the seconds. The soulless rectangular shell made of cheap gray plastic with sharp corners. Finally, the need to add more to it than was necessary. He had heard that some clocks even made coffee when the alarm went off. Adam's alarm was going to go off at seven. It wasn't going to make him coffee. He had known he would get up before the alarm. His eyes were wide open and his heartbeat mimicked the tempo of a blues drummer as it pulsed with an unbalanced rhythm. He didn't feel like this often.

The clock blinked to 6:59. Adam slowly moved his arm out from under the covers, and carefully pushed the button on top of the clock. His hand was shaking. It was difficult to press the correct one. With his hand still on the clock, he took a deep breath. Held it for a few seconds, and then readied himself for the day ahead.

He reluctantly lifted his body, and slowly slipped his legs out of the covers and onto the floor. The cover dropped off him completely. He closed his eyes. A smile began to grow on his face because he knew when he looked over his shoulder, he would see an angel. He opened his eyes and turned. There she was with her heavenly glow, still asleep with her back toward him. Even though he could only see the back of her, his smile became more prominent. He had to bite down on his lower lip to resist the temptation of waking her up by feeling the soft brown skin of her naked back, or running his fingers through the long hair on her head, dark as the void, flowing onto her neck.

He took another deep breath and stood up. He gently pulled the cover back over the sleeping angel. He didn't want her catching a cold. He moved away from the bed and strolled over to the window. It was an overcast morning and New York had been awake for hours already. He could sense the busyness radiating from behind the pane of glass. He pulled himself away.

He had an important day ahead of him. So, he figured a shower would calm his nerves. This meant passing through the aftermath of the mess that had been left over from the night before. The last remaining drops from the empty bottle of whiskey toppled over on the table, formed a small puddle on the glass table surface, and one glass sat next to it. Clothes covered the floor like a minefield. There was Adam's suit; a dark gray jacket and matching pants lying brazenly on the floor, a fair distance from each other. Adam's underwear was near the bed while the woman's was on the arm of the couch. Seeing those, Adam smiled and let out a soft chuckle.

Walking slowly past the couch, he saw her dress stuffed in between the cushions. He gently tugged the dark-green silk dress from the cushions and slowly laid it down across the back of the couch. Before letting go, he ran the fabric between his fingers, bringing his hand to his nose to smell the sweet perfume. He saw movement from under the bed sheet out the corner of his eye. He looked over, thinking he had woken her. She was still asleep, just shifting into a more comfortable position.

Adam finally got to the bathroom and climbed into the shower. He stood naked, wet, and motionless, thinking over what the day would bring him. He had not thought this day would ever come and certainly had never planned for it. In any case, it was long overdue. The cold water flowed off his face, making all the hairs on his body stand up. Adam had many scars etched all over his body. Cuts, tears, and holes. Some were clean, precise incisions, others looked like they had been torn with brute force. Most were faded and would need to be seen up close to be noticed. A few, however, were very prominent. A long horizontal scar engraved its memory across his lower abdomen. As the water ran down his body, it avoided his many scars. It moved around them like there was a force field blocking the path. Before leaving the shower, he rubbed the larger of a pair of star-shaped scars imprinted on the left side of his chest.

He cleaned his teeth and flattened his dull blonde hair that changed to a dark shade of brown in a different light. After a subtle sniff of the angel's perfume bottle on the basin, he shaved the minuscule amount of stubble he had on his face, revealing a half-inch scar on the underside of his chin.

Adam had a young face. He looked like he was in his early twenties. Pale, rough skin, slender cheekbones, and tired green eyes. Yet the style of clothes he wore made him look older.

Feeling that a black or gray suit would be too boastful and bring unwanted attention to him, he decided to wear a brown suit today. He got dressed with a tremendous amount of care. Any onlookers would mistake him for having a lack of personality. Adam probably would have agreed, as he didn't know who he truly was. He was hoping to find out today.

He tucked his shirt into his pants, pulled a thin pair of black braces over his shoulders, polished his shoes, and did up his tie with mild frustration. It took him three attempts to get the knot right, for his angel would normally help. He buttoned up his waistcoat, yet left the jacket open, so he could get to his watch. It wasn't in his pocket.

With a perplexed look on his face, he moved his hand from pocket to pocket, not knowing where it could be. Then it popped in his head. He walked over to the table by the couch. He could see the silver full Hunter pocket watch through the bottle, rippled and distorted. He carefully picked it up, letting the chain hang down.

The watch had seen better days. The casing didn't close properly and when opened, the hinge barely held together. With so many scratches, the engraved script was barely visible. But Adam knew what it said. *To Adam. Always in my heart. From your loving wife.* Even though it was falling apart, the mechanisms inside moved the hands freely without any disturbance. It also included a second hand. Adam looked at the watch with comfort in his eyes, like it was an old friend. But as he clipped the chain to his waistcoat and graciously dropped it into his pocket, the watch became a part of him. He closed his eyes for a few seconds in repentance, a tremendous weight bearing down on him.

While wearing the suit, Adam could pass as a man in his early thirties, which was something he approved of. He walked over to the front door, picked up his keys, half a pack of cigarettes and a lighter from the small bowl on a table near the door. He checked to make sure the angel was still asleep while he silently opened the drawer of the table, grabbed a small velvet box, and quickly placed it in his jacket. Before leaving, he smiled, seeing the photo frame on the table of them dancing together.

Adam lived on the third floor. He took the stairs down instead of the elevator. Being encased in metal wasn't very appealing. He slid his hand down the banister keeping a firm grip, as he carefully took each step. When he got to the second floor, he pivoted smoothly around and continued on. Finally getting to the first floor, he gave the mailbox a quick glance. It was empty. He knew it would be but he liked to check anyway.

The sun was trying to burn through the clouds, yet the breeze was still cold and able to blow Adam's jacket apart as he stepped outside. He took a cigarette from the inner pocket and placed it in his mouth. He got his lighter and lit the cigarette with his left hand while buttoning up his jacket with his right. He put the lighter back and used both hands to smooth any wrinkles in his jacket. He hopped down the several steps of the porch and proceeded to head down the street.

He passed his car parked next to the curb. It was only a few years old and wasn't something that would catch anyone's attention. His destination wasn't that far away, only a couple of blocks. He was happy just to walk. Even though it was early, the cars passed by him at speeds that made him feel uneasy. Like he was holding them all up just by being there. He tried to relax and press on.

Still distressed, he almost walked right past his stop. It was an old apartment building that had been converted into an office. The exterior has been well-maintained, but time still showed its mark. The red brick had turned brown and the mortar was beginning to crack. Adam raised his foot, stubbing his cigarette out under his heel, and then threw it into an open trash can.

He walked up the stairs. As he approached the door, he noticed a plaque mounted beside it. It had been updated from the one he remembered. It was a permanent fixture set next to the door. He sighed in relief seeing the name hadn't changed. *Dr. Joanna Chambers.* He smiled while reading the engraved words on the smooth polished brass. He took another moment to himself before twisting the handle and going in.

The interior of the waiting room had changed. Medical

posters covered the painted sky-blue walls. It felt cold and isolated like a hospital corridor. A young woman he didn't know sat behind the desk. Her dirty blond hair was tied back and her thin-rimmed glasses pushed up on her nose. He walked slowly up to her. She gave him a quick look but didn't stop typing on the computer.

"I have an appointment," he said, his voice cracking as this was the first thing he'd said all day.

She reluctantly stopped what she was doing, and moved her attention over to him. "Okay, let me see. It's Adam, yes?" she said with a quick yet quiet voice.

Adam nodded.

"You didn't put a surname but that's okay. Dr. Chambers should be here shortly. You can wait in her office if you like," she said, already snapping her attention back to the computer screen and rapidly tapping the keyboard.

"Okay. Thank you," Adam nervously replied. Leaving the woman to her own devices, he walked across the waiting room floor and entered Dr. Chambers' office.

A wave of nostalgia swept over him and for a brief moment, he felt like he was stepping in for the first time again. The room hadn't changed at all. The rich color of mahogany furniture still stained the room. The painting of the three horses running in a field still hung over the fireplace, and the chairs were still in the same position as they had been so long ago.

He walked over to the one he'd sat in, up against the window. The brown leather had faded from the sunlight. The arms were worn and cracked from all the nervous people sharing their secrets. Adam made his way past the chairs and over to the desk. He brushed his hand across the surface while looking at the various items scattered across it. There was a photograph of a young lady in a graduation gown and cap, which hadn't been there before.

Dr. Chambers opened the front door and greeted the secretary. "Good morning," she said, covering her mouth as she yawned.

"Morning. I got your email. Your first appointment is waiting for you," the secretary replied.

Dr. Chambers nodded and curiously walked to the door of her office.

Adam was so deep in thought he hadn't heard the front door open. Startled by the sound of the office door handle moving, he stopped what he was doing. He put his hands in his pockets and faced the door. It crept open and Dr. Chambers peeked her head inside.

When she saw Adam's face, her curiosity merged into astonishment.

Adam met her gaze. "Hello, Joanna," he said softly.

Joanna slowly walked toward him.

With each step she took, Adam's calm and collective posture flipped. He squirmed like an insecure little boy. His hands moved from his pockets to pull the bottom of his jacket. He hadn't seen her for such a long time, but she was still clearly recognizable. She was wearing a beige dress and matching blazer. She was slim with tired-looking skin, and her hair now grayer in comparison to the brown it once had been. He never would have admitted it, but he felt pity for her. Time had taken hold of her exterior and most likely burrowed its way deep inside. His feeling quickly subsided before she could notice.

When she was close enough, she reached out with her shaking hand to softly touch his face. Adam turned his head away in shame. Joanna quickly placed her hand on his cheek and firmly pulled to meet his eyes again. Her eyes welled up and lips quivered.

"Is it really you? How?" she asked.

"It's been a long time," Adam said in a soft tone.

Joanna's face tightened up from his complete disregard for her question. "It has," she replied politely, biting her lip through frustration.

Adam moved past her. He brushed his hands through his hair and scratched the back of his head.

Joanna flicked the tears from the corners of her eyes. She walked around her desk and opened the bottom drawer. She dug through stacks of papers to find a crumbled half a packet of cigarettes that had been stowed away, left behind from another patient. She didn't care about the stale tobacco or the harshness of the smoke that filled her lungs. She was just feeling the intoxicating nostalgia through her body. Now composed, with nicotine in her veins, she walked back around and perched herself on the edge of her desk.

"You have some explaining to do," she said, this time demanding a response.

"I know and I'm sorry for doing this to you. But I need your help again," Adam said.

"I don't remember being much help to you the last time you were here." Joanna exhaled a puff of smoke. "When was that? About twenty years ago?" she continued, knowing full well how long it had been.

Adam scratched the back of his head, wondering if it had really been that long.

"Twenty years. Give or take a few days."

Joanna put out her cigarette in an ashtray resting on the corner of her desk. "Well, let's hear it."

Adam pulled out his watch and stared into the crystal. The hands, always ticking forward. "Do I deserve to be alone or can someone like me change?" Adam slowly walked toward Joanna. His body trembled and his eyes turned bloodshot.

Joanna pushed further onto the desk until she was almost sitting on it.

Adam's voice gave off a searing pain, like it physically hurt him to speak. "My name is Adam." He paused and swallowed before speaking again, this time with a deep southern drawl. "I was born William Lake in 1843 and I'm unable to die."

TWO

On September 4, 1843, in Green Lake, Mississippi, Mary and her husband Arthur gave birth to a healthy baby boy. They called him William.

Arthur and Mary lived on a small cotton farm. They were both short and slightly plump. Mary's motherly, loving eyes overwhelmed her other facial features. Arthur's features were round, matching his belly. Always leaning slightly forward, he used his weight for momentum. With Mary taking care of baby William and their older son Marshall, Arthur would take care of the fields.

The cotton farm had been passed down from Arthur's father; a man who baby William never had the chance to meet. The farm wasn't very large and didn't turn much profit each year. Even though it brought a comfortable living to Arthur and his family, he was driven to earn more. He had a few hired hands for security to watch over the dozen African American slaves.

With the profit not satisfying him, Arthur became strict and very short-tempered. Unfortunately, his attitude would stay with him when he got back to the homestead.

On good days, he would talk politely to his family. Love and passion would show in his eyes and voice as they sat at the dining table. On bad days, they would eat supper in silence, except for Arthur's hateful ramblings about the slaves, thinking they should be working harder. Love changed to hate and passion turned to loathing, all aimed toward the slaves and the rest of their kind. His ideals would rub off on the older son Marshall, and eventually to William. No matter what mood Arthur was in, William would respect him and fear to disappoint.

William spent most of his young life learning how to run the farm; watching everything his father and brother did. They would preach orders from the top of their horses, while he stayed silent on his. He was quite a timid boy growing up. Marshall, on the other hand, was a strong capable young man. He would get into fights. Some he started, and other times it was somebody else. On rare occasions, he would be protecting William. No matter what, he would always win. He'd lose once he got home and saw his father. Marshall bullied young William himself to try and toughen him up. He'd call him names, and make him do his work as well as his own. William didn't mind. No matter what, he knew deep down his brother would always be there for him.

By 1863, William, who had once been a scrawny shy boy, had turned into a strong, cocky twenty-year-old. He was nothing in comparison to the strength of his brother, who had turned into a mountain of a man and shadowed over him. His brother had traits similar to a Neanderthal—wild dark hair, wide forehead, and bushy eyebrows. Even though William hadn't touched the delicate flesh of a woman, he was much better talking to them. He would never have traded his confidence for his brother's physical prowess, even if that meant being teased daily. They watched over the slaves from atop the comfort of their horses. Their routine consisted of patrolling the field, while the slaves gathered cotton. Their naked backs simmered in the burning sun.

May 9, 1863.

"Get back to work!" Marshall yelled to one of the slaves who had simply stopped to wipe the sweat off of his brow.

"You heard him, nigger. Speed up," William interjected, trying to maintain a gravelly and frightening voice.

The sweat dripping from the worker's face turned cold. His soul stolen from out of him, he quickly pulled open the bag from his shoulder and with the other hand gently pried the leaves away to get to the cotton inside. He never said a word.

Marshall and William took large gulps of water from their canteens and poured it onto their heads, quenching themselves from the heat of the beating sun. They trotted around the field while the slaves continued to work in silence. They didn't get to drink until their work had been done.

As the day was coming to an end, Marshal and William cantered to the front of the farmhouse and leaped off their horses.

William stretched his back and legs with an aching groan.

Marshall fanned himself down with his hat.

Like most days, they had worked extremely hard.

"Boy! Come here, boy!" Marshall yelled to the young slave boy who tended to the horses. "Take the horses back to the barn. Quickly now."

"Yes, sir," the boy whimpered. He wrapped the reins around his wrists and started running.

"Make sure they get plenty of food and water!" Marshall yelled again.

"Yes, sir," the boy replied. The horses were twice the height of the boy. He was barely able to keep up with them galloping. He managed to keep a tight grip on the reins though.

Marshall and William chuckled as they saw the boy struggling to control the horses.

"Haha! They haven't got the capability to lead," Marshall muttered, patting William on his back with a heavy thud. "Race you to the door," Marshall said, immediately pushing William to the ground, and flicking dust into his face as he began throwing his bulky legs into a jog.

"You son of a–" William shouted as he bounced back up to catch him.

"Don't talk about our mother like that!" Marshall shouted, smiling and panting while he said it.

William was right on Marshall's heels. He pounced, wrapped his arms around Marshall, and tackled him to the ground, but to no avail.

Marshall quickly overpowered him, clambering back up and taking the final few steps to the front porch. "You may be faster than me, little brother, but you ain't as strong as me," he said, standing victorious with arms in the air.

"Whatever you say, big brother," William said, clambering back to his feet with a sore-loser look plastered on his face.

"I do say. In fact, I'm smarter and better looking than you too," Marshall gloated, being just as much of a sore winner.

Trying not to take any notice of Marshall, William dusted himself off and went inside. They took no notice of the young, dark-skinned girl sweeping the porch.

They scraped their boots off on the mat before stepping any further in, then walked through the hallway and into the living room. The only sounds that could be heard were from their mother sobbing, and the ticking of the long, cased clock in the far corner.

Their father raised a letter so they both could see. The wax seal had been broken.

"It's time for us to do our part, boys. We leave in the morning," he said, his cold stare unflinching. Marshall nodded and began eagerly tapping his foot.

William didn't utter a word. He wasn't paying any attention to anything his father was saying, he just kept trying to read what the letter said. He never would have mentioned it, but he had no desire to go to war. His father kept moving his hand, making the letter difficult to read. The few words William could make out made his eyes well up and brought up a terrifying feeling in him that sunk deep to his core.

By the governor of Mississippi, John M Fletcher asks for volunteers to join the Confederate forces.

Country. Duty. Resistance. Enemy.

The sound of his pounding heart overwhelmed his mother's sobbing and the clock's ticking. He could see his brother and father talking but couldn't hear the words coming out of their mouths. They turned their heads to look at him. He could see Marshall's mouth move, yet still couldn't fathom what he was saying. Marshall firmly put his hand on William's shoulder. He jumped and his ears popped back into existence.

"You ready for this, little brother?"

William kept his hesitation short. He didn't want to be called a coward, and, more importantly, didn't want to disappoint. He took his emotions and buried them as deep as he could. Mustering all his confidence, he said one word. Knowing it would seal his fate and he would be heading to war. "Yes."

William didn't have much sleep that night. So many thoughts rushed around in his head. He may have been a ruthless and brazen man to the slaves when out in the fields, however, he knew that standing up against an enemy that had the same level of power would be a terrifying thing.

He dreaded the sight of the sunrise and stayed tucked safely in bed for as long as possible. Yet he couldn't stop time, and the morning inevitably came around. He begrudgingly crawled from his bed and peeked out the window. His father was ordering the workers to load the horse and cart. He slowly got dressed but then suddenly heard Marshall shout from outside, "William, get down here!" and he picked up his pace. Tying his boots into a loose knot he grabbed his hat before leaving his room.

He stopped in front of the hallway mirror. He checked over his face, tucked in his shirt, and placed his hat on his head. Then he made his way outside and over to the cart.

His father constantly hollered at the workers.

"Hurry up, boy!" he yelled, pushing the slave boy out of the way as he finished loading the cart with supplies. "Say goodbye to your mother, William, and let's get going," his father said, rearranging his belt so his Colt revolver fitted comfortably.

His mother was hugging Marshall who towered over her.

"Please, Mother. We will be back before you know it," Marshall said while rolling his eyes. He slowly pulled away and walked to the cart.

"Take care of your brother," she said.

He raised his hand, nodded, and smiled, then took the space up front next to his father.

William approached his mother, trying to keep a brave face. She saw straight through it. Tears started to run down her face. William quickly went in for a hug. He felt her arms wrap around him and squeeze tight. He couldn't hold in his emotions any longer. Tears began to trickle from his face onto his mother's shoulder.

"Let's get a move on, William!" his father shouted.

She helped clear the tears from his eyes. It was nothing his father or brother needed to see. She smiled and he smiled back. No words were spoken.

Now composed, he walked over to the cart. He gazed out into the field, seeing the workers looking back at him. His fear turned to a burning rage. *Why do they get to be safe?* he thought to himself. They were staying on his father's land while they could be going off to die. Words began to spiral around in his head. *Lazy, selfish, worthless, disgusting.* He took a deep breath and he jumped on the back of the cart.

"Let's go," Arthur said with a flick of the reins. He looked back as his wife. The slightest smile could be seen on his face as he took his hat off to her.

It was a long journey to Jackson. They took turns steering the cart and resting in the small space in the back. On the fourth night, William was trying to sleep in the back of the cart. He was having trouble relaxing due to the shaking on the dirt road. He could hear his father and brother talking to each other at the front. His father was talking about policies and how the Confederacy would come out on top. Marshall would say the occasional joke and they'd cry with laughter. William wanted to join the conversation but just lay in the back quietly. Marshall was a lot closer to their father than he was.

Dawn came. The cart hit some uneven terrain, which spooked William. He quickly sat up and looked forward, seeing the town of Jackson in the distance. Butterflies started moving in his belly. The closer they got, the more people they saw evacuating the town. There were hundreds of women and children carrying as many of their belongings as they could.

They rode the cart as close to the town as they could. They ended up tucking it away behind a barn just outside of town. The sheer number of locals trying to leave made it impossible to take it any further.

William hopped off and started taking off their belongings.

"Leave all of that, William. No one is going to steal anything," Marshall said with concern in his voice as he watched all the townsfolk scurrying past.

William, feeling like a fool put everything back and draped a cover over it.

They made their way into town with their father at the front. Arthur firmly pushed through the evacuees to get to the Confederate soldier directing people out of town. He didn't look much older than William, yet held more confidence in his gray uniform as he encouraged people to leave.

Arthur approached him. "I'm Arthur Lake. Where can I find Mayor Fletcher?"

The man frowned. Not stopping what he was doing, he sternly replied. "What? The mayor left days ago. If you're here to assist, go to the front of the town hall. There, you can get your weapons and be sorted into a unit." He walked away before Arthur could reply and continued with his job.

Arthur was insulted, thinking a more formal welcome would have been done for him. He snapped out of his formal mindset and signaled his sons to follow again.

When they got to the town square, they saw volunteers lining up to get their equipment. They made their way through men who'd already got theirs and joined the end of the line.

William could hear a man shouting the same words over and over again. "Name, jacket, rifle, supplies. Next!" He never asked any other questions or said anything else. It was their turn. William's butterflies frantically flapped their wings.

"Next!" the man shouted.

Arthur walked up and signed the sheet of parchment for all three of them. Without hesitation, Marshall grabbed his jacket and began checking over his rifle.

Arthur tilted his head back at William. "Go on then, Son."

William cautiously walked over to the pile of jackets on the floor and picked one up. It was a dull gray and far too big for him to wear comfortably. He put it on and tightened it around his waist as best he could. The color of his skin started to match the jacket as he walked over to collect his rifle. It was an early Springfield model that had definitely been in battle before. The hammer was loose and the iron sight had worn away. His stomach churned, holding the cold wood in his hands.

He kept walking while trying to sort out his weapon.

An officer grabbed him by the arm. "You're with me, boy," he said. Not waiting for a response, he dragged William into his unit. Standing in a mass of almost a hundred men, William looked around. He was hoping to see his father or brother join him. Everyone looked the same. He was having trouble telling any of them apart through the forest of gray.

"Listen in, men!" shouted the officer who had grabbed him. "It's simple. Defend the town until the evacuation is complete. We'll be placed in the western field. In case you don't know, it's that big green thing," he said with a smug grin.

The men surrounding William started to chuckle and, again, not wanting to be judged, William made a convincing smile.

The officer continued to bark orders. "The enemy has the high ground, so we'll let them come to us. We'll fall back behind the cobbled wall of the field if needed. That's all, men. Get everything sorted and be ready to move out."

Everything was moving so fast. Without realizing it, William was marching out into the open field in three ranks. He stood on the front rank, second in from the right-hand marker. The field sloped up away from Jackson, making it difficult to see anyone advancing.

"Halt!" the officer shouted in a more cautious tone.

The unit stopped moving, and voices began to murmur from within. Some of them started to twitch as they heard movement up ahead.

The officer strained his eyes to see further. Then they appeared, all marching in formation. Soldiers in matching dark blue uniforms. Their unit was twice the size of the one William was, unfortunately, standing in.

William started looking around within his rank to get confirmation on what to do next. He then peered over to the unit fifty feet to the right of him. He could see the large figure of his brother. He couldn't see Marshall's expression but could sense his determination. His brother's unit raised their weapons and then William's officer commanded them to do the same.

He raised the rifle, pulling it into his shoulder, and rested his cheek on the side. The wood was cold and sent a shiver down his spine.

"Hold!" yelled the officer, with a long and drawn-out screech.

The bluecoats kept moving closer and closer. William could almost see their faces. He was shaking and panting as he looked down the sight. He aimed at the man in blue directly in front of him. He wasn't sure if that made the man lucky or not. Suddenly, the bluecoats stopped. Then a roar from the officer. "FIRE!"

With a swift pull on the trigger, a deafening sound and a cloud of smoke appeared in front of them. Disoriented, William mirrored the man to the left of him. He took a knee and started to reload his next shot. The second rank raised their weapons and fired over William's head. As the shot went off, he looked up at the enemy and saw men drop to the ground. Yet the two volleys barely made a dent in their ranks. Just like the first, the second rank took a knee. The third raised their weapons and the bluecoats did the same.

A rapid popping sound echoed in the distance, followed by a blanket of smoke. Blood sprayed onto William's face, and the man he was mirroring slumped to the ground. Like a ripple effect, others began to mirror him. Before the diminished third rank fired, the officer with a trembling voice commanded all to stand and fire on his order.

William failed to wipe away the blood from his face. He stood up and again raised his rifle. His stomach sank as he saw the blue coats do the same and knew they would fire first.

Their volleys tore the unit apart with a cloud of red mist. Something sharp hit William's chest, making him stumble. Using the rifle for stability, he looked down. A small hole had appeared in his coat. Too confused to be scared, he softly touched the wound and felt warm blood oozing out onto his fingertips.

The order from the officer to fall back was muffled through William's ringing eardrums. The dazed William pulled himself up and started running back toward the cobbled wall. There was so much going on around him that he just concentrated on getting to the wall one step at a time. Trampling over the dead men from his unit, he felt like he was lucky not to have joined them. The survivors were only a few feet away from the wall.

"Fire!" shouted a distant, stern, ghostly voice.

The men around him dropped to the ground, and without a doubt, a round hit William straight in the back and came cracking out of his chest. He stopped in his tracks, and out of the corner of his eye, the same thing happened to the smug officer. He was bewildered as to why the officer fell straight to the floor, yet he remained standing. It felt like a lifetime to William before he started to move again. He decided to sit down and die. He walked the last few feet to the wall and tumbled his way over. Leaning up against the jagged stone, he waited quietly and calmly for the inevitable.

William didn't feel fear or pain anymore. He marveled over the blood that slowly stained his gray jacket. He looked around at the scenery before him, thinking it was the last thing he would see. Brave men still fought behind the wall; others dragged the wounded and the dead to the town square. He took a deep breath. He would be joining them soon. He started to think about his brother and father, and about where they might be.

William craned his neck to the left and just ten yards away was Marshall. He was holding his own behind the cobbled wall, with the same determination as before. William kept staring. He didn't have enough energy to shout his brother's name.

Marshall cursed at the enemy. He fired shot after shot, picking up fallen soldiers' weapons, and not wasting time on reloading. He ducked behind the wall as a volley came in. Marshall lost his fighting spirit and a cloud of absolute dread covered his face when he saw his baby brother lying in his own blood. "William!"

No longer concerned for his own safety, Marshall foolishly stood up to run to his brother's side. The second he was above the sanctuary of the wall, though, a shot collided with his head. A gaping hole consumed one side of the face of the self-proclaimed better-looking brother. He no longer looked like Marshall. He barely looked human.

"Marshall!" William's hearing came rushing back when he screamed, and a sickening boost of energy rushed through him. Gripping the damp crimson grass, he crawled toward his brother's lifeless body. Tears ran down his face as he screamed his brother's name, hoping he'd answer back. William kept crawling. A black haze started to form over his peripheral vision. He stretched out and grabbed Marshall's warm hand. Pulling himself closer, William rested his head on his brother's chest. He softly repeated his brother's name, until the haze covered his eyes completely. He thought death had finally claimed him too.

With the evacuation complete but the town lost, all the gray coats had started to retreat and fled back to wherever they'd come from. Only men in blue remained in Jackson. Plus, one other.

A veteran soldier stepped over the deceased, jabbing them with his foot as he went. He stopped, standing over the apparently dead William, who was still resting on his brother. The soldier could see the boy was still breathing. With one hand gripping his sidearm, he gave William a swift kick.

"Get up, boy."

William's eyes opened and he quickly jumped up as if he had overslept in the morning. William kept his chin pinned to his chest. The only thing he could distinguish on the soldier was the insignia on his uniform. *Sergeant.* William could sense the veteran's war-torn eyes inspecting him up and down.

"Did you know him, boy?" the sergeant asked, giving Marshall's body a gentle tap with his boot.

William nodded, trying his best not to cry. "He's my brother."

———

The veteran moved his attention back to William. Mistaking the blood on him for his brother's, his gaze softened. William was no soldier, just a boy who should not have been there in the first place. "Take off the jacket, boy. Go home."

———

William slipped off the jacket. He took one final look at his brother and curiously walked past the veteran.

None of the other blue coats who swarmed the town took any notice of William passing through. They were too busy torching buildings and gathering the dead. William made his way to the barn where the cart was. He just wanted to get out of there. Something on a dead gray coat caught the light and shone into his eyes though. He looked back to see if anyone was watching him before walking over to the item in question.

He stood at the feet of the unrecognizable body. The face had been destroyed; shredded skin clung onto bone. The left leg and left arm were missing and bloody boot prints covered the chest. His heart sank when he saw the Colt revolver still comfortability tucked into the belt. William turned away and he covered his mouth. It took everything he had left not to scream. He checked again if anyone was looking. He grabbed the blood-stained Colt from what remained of his father, concealed it under his shirt, and then sprinted to the cart.

It was such a good sight, seeing the cart still tied up. The horse reared when William approached, still distressed from the sounds of the battle before. Going over to the horse, William rested his head on its side and softly ran his hand across the smooth brown hair on its back. William finally broke and burst into tears at the realization of the deaths of his father and brother. He buried his face into the horse's side to muffle the sounds of his whimpering.

After a few minutes, he quickly stood up straight and began patting down his shirt like he was on fire. Checking over it, he stuck his fingers into two small holes. Failing to stay calm, he ripped off the shirt. He looked down at his pale skin covered in smears of dried blood. He could see two bullet-wound scars. There was one on the left side of his chest and a much larger one in the center. Both were shaped like stars. He didn't know how it was possible. He should've been dead.

He wiped the tears from his eyes and went to the back of the cart. He pushed the sack and crates that contained food, clothing, and cotton to trade out of the way. All of which had been foolish to bring in the first place. He took another shirt from his duffel bag and put it on. He tucked the clean shirt into his belt, adjusting the Colt as he did so. He climbed into the front of the cart, and with a frantic whip of the reins, the horse started to move. It was going to be a long and quiet journey home. The only things he left behind were the corpses of his father and brother, and a torn blood-stained shirt with two holes in it.

William's mind was vacant during the ride back. He didn't eat or sleep, only ever stopping for the horse. William listened to the cart's wheels rolling across the dry ground. He barely controlled the reins. The horse was just following the path on its own.

The cart hit a rough patch of dirt at the bottom of an inclining slope, which disrupted William from his trance. He had a look around to get his bearings. He was reassured when he realized that just on the other side of the slope was his home. The horse was exhausted but carried on climbing the slope. It dragged the creaking cart behind it, which was lighter at least.

The ground level out at the brow and the remaining sunlight blinded William's eyes. Rolling down the other side, William let go of the reins completely. He shielded his eyes from the orange glow of the sunlight. The horse struggled to stay ahead of the cart with it pushing down the slope. As the pair of them descended, William could finally see the dark silhouette of his house.

Riding ever closer to the house, he could see a shadowy figure standing on the porch. He stopped the cart where it had been when he'd left and jumped off. His vision was blurry, head spinning, and his emotions started to rise again.

He approached the house and stepped into the shade. His eyes began to distinguish colors again. From the brown of the wood, the light yellow of the curtains in the window, and finally, the black skin of the young girl standing at the edge of the porch. William stopped. What had been the happiness of hoping to reunite with his mother turned to utter rage. She wasn't what he wanted to see.

The girl was wearing a faded floral dress. She couldn't have been more than fourteen years old and she was the only one who was allowed in the house. Though she had been on the farm for over three years, William had never cared to find out her name, only ever calling her girl. She stood there terrified. Arms by her side and head pinned to her chest.

William turned his face away. "Get me my mother," he said, gritting his teeth.

Looking down at her feet, she gave a quick nod and scurried into the house.

William paced around in a small circle. He was able to calm down as soon as the girl was out of his sight. Taking some deep breaths, he closed his eyes; almost finding peace within himself. He heard the soft voice of the person he had wanted to see in the first place.

"William."

He looked at his mother who was scanning around to see her husband and older son. "Mother," he replied. Tears began to run down his face while he tried to explain what had happened.

She shook her head. She realized what had happened. She opened her arms in a ready embrace and ran over to him.

Finding sanctuary between her arms, William closed his eyes tight. He finally felt himself again, and for a brief moment, it was like nothing had changed. Softly swaying and slowly spinning, William went from facing the house to facing the field. He slowly reopened his eyes and looked out onto the cotton. Rage set in again, seeing the slaves in the distance. *Why do they have it so easy?* he thought to himself, comparing them to him and what he had been through. *So selfish.*

William sat at the side of his mother's bed, watching over her. Two months had gone by in a flash since the day he'd died. His secret was eating him up from the inside. He had never told his mother what had actually happened. She had gone through enough with the loss of her husband and son, and now an illness was taking hold of her. He didn't want her worrying herself about something he couldn't even understand.

Mary had become an empty shell. Skin, muscle, and fat loss gripped her frail frame. She was no longer the caring and devoted mother she once had been. The mechanism in her mind had stopped turning. She was just able to pull off her jade stone wedding ring and hand it to William. She mumbled inaudible ramblings. The only words William could decipher were, "Take care of."

After she passed, William buried her outside. He covered the grave with stones and marked it with a wooden cross facing east, so the sunrise would be the first thing she would see. After a few days, he added two more graves. Both covered in stones. Both marked with crosses. Both empty.

Sadly, because of all that had happened, William's respect and views on life became sour. He got rid of all the security, and he kept the slaves in line on his own. His father had taught him well. He knew what to do. Now, as he rode his horse, patrolling the field, his canteen of water was replaced with liquor and he kept a firm grip on his father's Colt at all times. Other than barking orders to the workers, he said nothing to no one. After work, he went back to the house alone. He repositioned the young girl to the fields. He no longer had any use for her inside.

Weeks became months and the outside word William occasionally heard was that the war was coming to an end, with the bluecoats ending up on top. The thought of slaves having freedom sickened him to the core but also brought concern. There would be no use of a farm if there was no one to tend to it. William's patrols got shorter and eventually stopped altogether. He would either look out the window from his room or sit on his mother's rocking chair on the porch.

Even though William kept his distance, the workers continued without him. They could feel the presence of his eyes still on them, like a vulture stalking a wounded animal. He decided to get rid of the slaves before the inevitable concession of the south and the abolishment of slave ownership.

At the end of that working day, as the slaves were storing the cotton into the barn, he finally showed himself.

William stepped out of the front door and choked on the fresh air that filled his lungs. Stepping out of the shade of the porch, his eyes strained to adjust to the orange evening sunlight. He stumbled toward the barn, still tipsy from the copious drinking throughout the day.

One of the male workers caught a glimpse of William

walking toward them. He sharply clapped his hands, signaling to the others. They stopped what they were doing and sorted themselves into a straight line; men on the left and the women on the right. The nine of them stood there, hands down in front of them, and heads tilted toward the ground like they were praying.

In terrifying silence, William stood before them. He'd never had so much power. He'd never had it when his father and brother were alive. Loosely holding on to the Colt tucked in his belt, he took some deep breaths, soaking up the fear coming off of them. He took a moment to glare at each of them separately in disdain. He stumbled, catching the eyes of the girl in the floral dress. Their eyes stayed connected for several seconds. There wasn't any fear in her eyes, only pity. He pulled his eyes away from hers. Trying his best not to break character after falling off his pedestal, he walked back to the middle and faced them all. He hadn't spoken a word to anyone for quite some time. His voice sounded dry and scratchy as he spoke a single sentence. "I want you all gone in the morning." Quickly checking to see if they all heard him, he turned and made his way back to the house. He purposely avoided eye contact with the girl in the faded floral dress.

Morning came. It would have been around the time when the slaves would head into the field. Yet now they gathered the few belongings they owned. All they had to do was walk past the house, up the hill, and they'd be free.

William was on the porch, slumped in his mother's rocking chair. He had half a bottle of whiskey on the floor and the Colt balanced on the armrest. He gormlessly looked at the free men and women leaving his property. Trailing at the back of the group was the girl in the floral dress. Again, she caught William's attention. He didn't understand why she seemed different from the others. Perhaps it was just the consumption of alcohol making him soft. Nevertheless, he lifted himself up and sharply issued his final order.

"Girl!" he shouted, flicking his head at her to come closer to him.

She stopped. Pulling down on the sides of her dress, she looked over to the others for guidance. They stopped and waited, but couldn't do anything else. She turned and walked over to William, stopping before she stepped on the porch.

With his eyes glued on her, William blindly leaned down to grab the bottle of whiskey. To not be obscured by the bottle, he twisted his head to keep one eye on the girl as he took a large swig. He spilled part of the amber liquid on his chest when he took the bottle away from his lips.

Resting the bottle on his lap, he pulled himself up in the chair. He proceeded to open his mouth. He wanted to know her name but no matter how hard he tried, the words wouldn't come out. Glancing at the other former slaves and back at the girl, he wondered what they were all thinking, yet didn't want to find out. He slumped back in the chair and flicked his head again, getting her to move on. Taking swigs from the whiskey bottle and using his foot to rock softly back and forward, he watched them climb the ridge. He only moved when the girl in the dress went out of sight.

It was a couple of minutes to six o'clock in the evening. The last ounce of sunlight glowed through the living room window. The room had started to grow cold as only embers remained in the fireplace. William was sitting on a chair pointed toward the long-case clock in the corner of the room. The Colt rested heavily in his lap, and an empty bottle of whiskey lay on its side on the floor. William breathed deeply while he concentrated on the second hand. The second hand began its final rotation to six o'clock. William's heart started pounding out of his chest and shivers pulsed through his body. Breathing quicker and louder to get more oxygen in his veins, he lifted the Colt and pressed it firmly under his chin. The rough cold steel of the end of the barrel nicked his smooth skin like a cut-throat razor. As the second hand approached the twelve o'clock position, William clenched his teeth, determined not to wake up this time. At the first strike of the clock, William snapped his eyes shut and with the following four strikes, flinched in the chair. As soon as the sixth and final strike touched his eardrums, William pulled down hard on the trigger.

It was a couple of minutes past six o'clock in the evening. Conscious, William sat confounded amidst his blood. Looking around the room, a large spray mark of blood was across the rear wall and reaching all the way to the ceiling. Small splinter-like pieces of bone were scattered around the floor. Running his fingers through his hair, he felt stubble growing from his scalp, beginning to cover a newly formed bald spot. He brought his hand down to stroke the bottom of his chin, only to feel a small scar where the barrel had cut him.

His bottom lip quivered and pools of tears flowed from his eyes. He dropped the Colt on the floor and curled up into a ball on the chair, whimpering in sorrow. He was truly alone. The longcase clock continued to tick, while the handle of the Colt soaked up the blood from the floor.

THREE

As hard as it was for Adam to share this with anyone, he was relieved he no longer had to bear his secret alone. He nervously twitched in the chair, waiting for Joanna's reaction.

Stunned at what she had just heard, Joanna lunged for another cigarette. Her hands trembled so much; she couldn't get her lighter to spark. Adam took out his and lit it for her. After inhaling a large dose of nicotine, Joanna was able to relax. Thinking the circumstances over in her head, she tried to find a logical explanation for seeing a man who hadn't aged a day since the first time they'd met twenty years ago. She wanted to doubt but something deep inside her made her believe him. She was almost speechless, and only able to let out one single word. "How?"

Adam was disappointed with her response, clinging on to the hope that he would get some kind of miracle breakthrough answer. Burying his accent in the back of his throat, he replied, "I'm over a 150 years old. If I knew that, I wouldn't be here."

———

Joanna shook her head and smirked, remembering how stubborn he had been when they'd first met and how she would need to take a different approach. "You didn't go by the name Adam the last time we were together," she said, casually taking another puff on her cigarette.

———

"I've gone by many names in the time I've been around," he replied, firmly rubbing his hands up and down his thighs.

"And during that time, you didn't think to tell anyone?"

Adam looked down at the floor and sighed. "What could I have done? I had no one left. Besides, no one would've believed me." He paused, catching his breath. "I came close once. But I'm getting ahead of myself." Adam cleared his dry throat. Sharing was harder than he'd thought it would be.

———

Joanna observed him for a moment, reading his body language. She noticed he was digging his fingers into his thighs, certainly hard enough to inflict pain. In her twenty-three-year-long career, she had never come across someone so hating and disgusted of themselves. Thinking if she was ever going to get through to him, she would have to let him go at his own pace. "It's alright. Take your time," she said with a genuinely sincere tone to her voice.

Adam squirmed in his chair again, creating a horrible leathery squeak. Running his fingers through his hair, he took another deep breath.

"Even if someone would've believed me, I didn't want to talk. I had lost everyone I cared about." He turned his head, breaking eye contact with Joanna. "I lost everyone who'd cared about me."

After letting Adam sit in silence a few more minutes, Joanna spoke in a more direct tone. "Can you continue with your story? I want to hear the rest."

He looked back into Joanna's eyes. "I'm scared."

"Of what?" she asked.

Adam stuttered nervously as he imagined the horrific acts he had done. "That you ain't gonna like me. You're gonna hate me." Tears started dripping from his face as he let his imagination run wild. "You're gonna fear me." Breaking down, he buried his head in his lap.

Joanna got up and knelt in front of him, placing her hand on his shoulder. "Listen to me." She lifted his head by his chin, getting him to look her in the eyes. "I'm not going to fear you," she said, shaking her head. "You've just got to trust me. Like I should have trusted you the first time we met."

"I was an asshole." Adam chuckled.

"Yes, you were," Joanna replied. Glad to see a smile through all the tears. "But you joked about this and I didn't believe you. For that, I'm sorry." She wiped away his tears and reassured him. "I can't help you if you don't talk to me. That's what you're here for, right?"

He nodded.

Joanna stood up and went back to her chair. "So, talk," she said, leaning back, legs crossed, and hands resting on her higher knee.

Adam also leaned back in his chair, using the palm of his hands to dry his damp face.

"What did you do next?" Joanna asked.

"Nothing," replied Adam, exhaling his emotions.

"Nothing? You didn't try and kill yourself again?"

Adam nodded, breathing heavily out his nose. "Yes, but not for a very long time."

FOUR

1867. With no one left in William's life, he planned on living the rest of it in complete isolation, only ever seeing a courier he had organized to bring supplies from the nearest town once a month. The supplies mostly consisted of alcohol, tobacco, and dried meat, which would all be consumed by the end of the first week. After converting a small patch of the cotton to grow crops and exchanging all but one horse for some dairy cows, he would trade cotton and milk as partial payment for the supplies.

The courier would change every few years. William didn't talk to them much and got very tired of their preposterous rumors they'd all like to rant about. The stories always started the same way.

"Have you heard about the man who invented pictures that move?"

"Have you heard about the man who invented a box that can talk to anyone in the world?"

"Have you heard about the man who invented a cart that drives itself?"

William didn't care what was happening in the world. He just wanted to secure himself inside his limbo. He would thank them for the supplies and they would be on their way.

William spent most of his time tending the crops, milking the cows, riding his horse, and occasionally he would labor in the cotton fields. The blistering heat in the field exhausted William. Cuts and scratches toughened his hands as he pried the cotton from the bushes. Only collecting in a month what the slaves could have done in a couple of days. As he worked in the field, never once did he think it had been hard for the slaves.

He familiarized himself with his Colt, oiling it regularly and cleaning the barrel through. Some days he would go out hunting birds or any other vermin running round. He got quite good at it. Closing one eye, squeezing the trigger softly, and aiming where the animal was going to be rather than where it was. He had pheasant stocked up for weeks, which was good for he didn't like the taste of snake.

His family had almost become a distant memory that he yearned for occasionally. He'd fantasize over the good times, when they would sit around the dinner table while they enjoyed a meal and pleasant conversation with each other. Or when he and Marshall would muck about and drive his father up the wall. He would push all notions and reasons of why he was still alive to the back of his mind, so as not to fear what the future held for him.

The best part of living now was riding his horse and watching the sunset; a bottle of whiskey in hand and a small piece of chewing tobacco wedged into the corner of his mouth. Days blurred into months and months into years. He was lonely at times and still had a lot of hate buried inside him, yet William felt content with how he was living his life.

William woke up screaming in a cold sweat as he was reimagining the battle in Jackson. His father's and brother's decaying corpses flashed in his head, and he could feel the gunshot pierce his skin.

He rubbed his face and fanned himself down when he realized he was in his room. He got out of bed and opened the window for some clean air. He let out a relaxed sigh as the fresh morning breeze rushed into the room. It was almost sunrise, but still, an hour or so before he would routinely wake up. He couldn't bear the thought of going back to sleep, not with the dream still vivid in his head. So, he figured he'd start his day early.

He got dressed and walked out of his room. Making his way down the stairs, he passed through the hallway. The mirror on the wall caught his eye. He didn't know how long he had been unintentionally avoiding his reflection. He thought that he must have forgotten to cut his hair and shave for several years. He had grown a full mop of hair and a slightly ginger beard. He looked down at what he was wearing. His pants were ripped at the knees. His white shirt had become a sickly yellow and had worn through at the elbows and cuffs.

He had a sudden realization that he looked no better than a common slave. Deciding he needed to do something about it, he headed toward the bathroom. He tore off his shirt. He was never going to wear it again. Picking up his cut-throat razor, he grabbed tufts of hair and started slicing it off. Putting cream on his face, he very carefully shaved his beard, wiping off the mixture of cream and hair onto the tattered, torn shirt. He washed his face and took another look in the mirror. Inspecting every inch of his face, he noticed that, for however many years it had been, he hadn't aged a day.

He looked exactly as he had when he'd left for Jackson. The understanding that this was going to be his life from now on with no sign of end made his skin crawl and blood curdle. Without thinking or breaking eye contact with his reflection, he pushed the sharp blade of the razor into the palm of his hand. He swept the blade across and his flesh curled back on itself. He clenched his hand into a fist, wincing at the wound, and feeling it burn and sting. Sweet cherry blood oozed out from between his fingers. For several minutes, he watched his blood fill the sink. He listened to each drop as it joined the pool and watched the ripples pulse out to the edge.

The time between each falling droplet became further and further apart, and the throbbing sensation began to die down. A droplet hung at the bottom of his clenched fist, not heavy enough to fall. He opened his hand and looked at his palm. It was smeared with dry brown blood and a freshly healed scar. Frustration boiled in his eyes. He clenched his hand into a fist once again and hurled it at the mirror shattering it completely. The broken glass fell into the sink, splashing into the lukewarm liquid, and then sank to the bottom. William walked back up to his room, not coming back out for the rest of the day.

William carried on existing. He barely took any notice of the courier not making its deliveries. Without them, he had no perception of time. The cows and the horse had long since perished. He spent most of his day killing time in the cotton field.

William grew strong lifting sacks filled with cotton. He was easily carrying 150-pound sacks over each shoulder without even breaking a sweat. With no way to exchange it, he stored the cotton in the barn. Once full, he closed and barred it shut with a large plank of timber. Feeling slightly hollow, now he had one less thing to do, he left the field to rot. Besides himself, the only things living were the crops. Ironically, William rarely ate anything he grew. He was never hungry.

The high, burning sun boiled the sweat on the back of William's neck. He took a step back from tending the crops, had a stretch, and drank some water from his canteen. Using his hand to shield his eyes from the sun, he could see something coming over the ridge. He could just make out the silhouette of a cart, but the dust it was kicking up shielded the driver.

William became nervous. He quickly stopped what he was doing and walked back to the house, keeping one eye trained on the approaching dusty shadow. He stepped onto the porch and leaned against the support. His right hand lightly gripped the handle of the Colt tucked in his belt behind his back.

His grip got tighter as the cart stopped in front of the house. When the dust finally subsided, he saw a scrawny old man sitting at the front of the cart. He had a patchy gray beard and his thin hair peeked its way out from under his hat. William still had his hand on the Colt, yet his nerves started to settle. He knew the old stranger wouldn't be a threat if he caused any trouble.

William lifted his chin. "Who are you?" he said, his bark cracking under the lack of use.

With a crooked cigar held in his mouth by whatever remaining teeth he had left, the stranger cheerfully replied. "Me? Well, I'm Thomas. But I think you mean what am I doing here?" He turned and stuck his hand into the back of the cart.

William stood up straight and adjusted his footing.

The startled old man quickly raised his hands, one of which was holding onto a scrap of paper. "Easy, boy. I'm not looking for trouble," he said, as he softly waved the paper at William.

William settled down again, finally releasing the Colt and nodded at the man to continue.

Thomas dropped his hands and started scanning over the paper. He then began reading it aloud, putting his personal twang on the words. "I'm from the finest courier service of the state of Mississippi, and here to apologize for the unexpected stoppage of your orders due to the war."

William's eyes widened and interrupted Thomas's speech. "What war?"

"God damn, boy, have you been hiding under a rock this

entire time? It was the biggest war the world has ever seen." Thomas looked back down at the paper and continued.

William listened but the information went straight over his head.

"I'm here now to see if you would like to continue with your contract as stated, of two crates of whiskey, one pouch of tobacco, etc., etc., every two months."

William interrupted again. "Every two months? It was every month."

"Afraid not. It clearly states here every other month," Thomas replied, getting annoyed at William's incompetence.

William couldn't comprehend how long he'd been hiding away for. "What year is it?" he said, losing the sternness in his voice.

"1919. You slow or something, boy?! Do you want to start up your delivery again or not?"

William went pale, not knowing what to believe. Had he been hiding away all that time, or was the old man just playing a trick on him? William's attention switched to the cigar wangling in Thomas's mouth.

"Alright, there, boy? I haven't lost you, have I?"

William made eye contact with him. "You got a spare cigar?"

Thomas nodded and put his hand into his shirt pocket and pulled one out.

William stepped off the porch and walked over. "Thank you," William said as he took the cigar and a box of matches. He puckered his lips, inhaled for several seconds, and then blew out a damp cloud.

Thomas sat on the cart, twisting his neck around, taking in the surroundings. "So, where's the old man?" he asked.

William lost in the enjoyment of the smooth cigar, looked back at him confused.

"The old man, William Lake. He's got to be about eighty

years old by now," Thomas said, looking at the paper again for the customer's name.

William sucked on the cigar again and had a revelation. He could be someone else. He exhaled the smoke from the cigar and with confidence replied, "He's dead. Died about two years ago. He was my grandfather." William had never met his grandfather, so he didn't think it was such a terrible lie. "I came here about six years ago to take care of him. It didn't feel right to leave when he died." Taking another prolonged draw on the cigar, he had just enough time to think of a new name. William reached out his hand. "The name's Ethan."

Thomas looked down at him and took his hand.

"Pleasure to meet you. But you're telling me that you have spent the last six years cooped up here?" Thomas said, astounded.

William, now going by the name Ethan, flicked his eyes up to the left as he thought of something to answer him with. "That's correct. I apologize for the way I acted at first. It was the old man. He didn't like strangers coming round. Always paranoid for some reason. Force of habit." Ethan was surprised how easy it was to fabricate a new life, and how gullible the man was.

Thomas sat there for a few seconds before speaking. "Well, God damn, son! You need to get yourself out there, boy. The whole world is going along without you. Christ! It could have ended and you wouldn't have known a thing." Thomas shook his head and relit his cigar.

Ethan finished off his own and skipped it across the ground. He gazed around the farm. There wasn't much left that resembled its former beauty. The field had dried up and the house was in tatters. There was no family to make it feel like home. He looked back at Thomas and nodded. "You know what? I think you may be right. So, no, I'm not gonna need your delivery service."

"Well, I'm glad. Now I must get back with the information about the termination of your contact," Thomas said with a cheerful grin. He gave Ethan another cigar and a small salute. He steered the cart around and headed back up the ridge.

Ethan smoked his new cigar, watching Thomas until he went out of sight. He thought to himself, there was only one thing he should do before leaving the farm. Give William Lake one last chance to die.

Ethan sat complacently on a small stool in the living room. The fire was burning, filling the room with warmth, and the majestic sound of the longcase clock kept in time with the crackling embers. Ethan was using his razor to cut long strands of fabric from a bedsheet. He had a satisfied grin on his face as he braided the strands together. He wasn't really sure why he felt like he had to go through with what he was about to do. He thought it was like some kind of ceremony, to have a proper goodbye. Or hoping at the slight chance it might actually work.

He tied loops at both ends of the rope, one larger than the other, and then stood up from the stool. The rope draped over his shoulder as he picked up the stool and walked to the center of the room, underneath the cross beam. Standing on the stool, he chucked the rope over the beam and threaded the large loop through the small one, and gave it a strong tug. Feeling content with his decision, he squeezed his head through the large loop and pulled it tight making the fabric dig into his neck. He closed his eyes, took one deep breath, and reopened them. "Goodbye, William Lake," he said softly and stepped forward off the stool, knocking it over as he went.

When the rope went taut, Ethan immediately regretted the decision. A sudden jolt stopped his drop, and a loud crack came from his neck. The searing pain from the braided sheet ripped into his skin, and his limbs seized up and twisted uncontrollably. He looked almost peaceful as he slowly spun around, listening to the clock ticking, embers spitting from the fire, and the soft sound of wheezing from his vein-pulsing face.

The few minutes he hung there felt longer than the entire time he had been in isolation. He slowly regained control of his limbs. Contorting his arm, he gradually reached down to his pocket. His hand shook vigorously as he dug into his pocket and grabbed the cut-throat razor, making damn sure not to drop it. Flicking out the blade, he raised it over his head and frantically started slashing at the rope. The rope creaked and groaned as it gave way and Ethan's dead weight fell to the floor.

The floorboards made the same sound his neck had as he slammed on them. He pried the rope away, which had sunk so deep into his neck it couldn't be seen. Finally free, he was able to take a massive gasp to fill his lungs up with oxygen. He grabbed the back of his neck with both hands, feeling the unnatural alignment of bones. A cramping pain started to emerge from within his neck, he burst out laughing when he felt the bone pop back into place with a muffled clunk. *Well, that was a fucking stupid idea,* he thought.

He was slightly disappointed that it hadn't worked. But at least William Lake was gone for good.

FIVE

Ethan had butterflies in his stomach again as he arrived in the town he hadn't been to in sixty years. He was wearing the best shirt he had, which wasn't saying much, a worn pair of boots and he had a small amount of money stuffed into his pants pocket. The only other thing he was wearing was a handkerchief tied around his neck to hide his gruesome week-old scar. He had noticed that it had already started to fade. He had no means of transport. The journey was long enough to even make him thirsty. Putting his fingers under the handkerchief, he scratched at the irritated skin and headed into Jackson.

He stood in the middle of the road, looking at his surroundings. A lot had changed since he was last there, which was very disorienting for him. To make matters worse, he started reimagining the battle again. The sounds of volleys and screams reverberated in his ears. Visions flashed through his mind of his brother running toward him and the disfigured corpse of his father. His skull felt like it was going to burst. He squeezed his head between his hands in an attempt to hold it together. Ethan thought that it might not have been such a good idea to come back to this hell of a town.

A high-pitched horn suddenly jolted Ethan back from his nightmare. He quickly jumped backward out of the way of the most peculiar thing he had ever seen. The contraption looked like a cart but there were no horses pulling it. A very sharply dressed man at the front, with a top hat and a thin, waxed mustache gave Ethan a disgruntled look.

Still amazed that the silly rumor he'd heard had turned out to be true, he kept staring at the machine. Until he saw the beautiful young lady in the back who was graciously waving a fan and keeping a curious eye on him. He had a cheeky little boy's grin on his face as he gave her a small wave. She smiled back at the foolish boy, then hid behind her fan to conceal her blush. The spectacular machine left Ethan's sight. "I've got to get me both of those," he said under his breath.

His butterflies dissipated and his thirst came back. Thirty feet away, he saw two water fountains side by side. Standing in front of them, he inspected them both. After a few minutes, he decided to drink from the fountain that was more maintained. Putting his lips down near the spout, he twisted the handle to get the cool liquid into his throat. Slurping it up, the water ran down his chin and soaked into the handkerchief.

Feeling refreshed he took another look at his surroundings. It all seemed quiet and peaceful, with only a few people walking around. Looking at the reflection in the nearest window, he could see the general store across the street. He needed to get a trim and some new clothes, especially if he was ever going to impress a lady. Not knowing where anything was, he decided to enter the store.

A bell rang as he pushed open the door, and the middle-aged man behind the counter looked at Ethan.

Smirking at what Ethan was wearing, the man welcomed him into the shop. "Howdy, partner," he said, chuckling to himself.

"Hello," Ethan replied knowing full well he was commenting on the handkerchief.

The man kept a close eye on Ethan as he browsed the contents of the store. The only thing that caught Ethan's eye was a dark brown baseball bat, on the top shelf behind the storeman. The bat reminded him of the time when he and Marshall played stickball when they were kids.

"Can I help you with anything?" the storeman said, leaning on the counter.

Ethan still hadn't got used to interacting with people, and he stammered before replying. "Uh, you got any cigars?"

"Afraid I sold the last to the pompous English fellow with the top hat and stupid mustache. He's set up an automotive shop around the corner. I got cigarettes if you'd like?"

Ethan now wondered if the man commented on the attire of everyone who came into his store. Not wanting to sound like a fool, he accepted the offer of the cigarettes.

The man turned around and took a pack of cigarettes off the shelf and placed them on the counter. He looked Ethan up and down. "You need matches with that?"

Ethan nodded and before the man returned with the matches, he took the money he had out of his pocket and placed it on the counter. Ethan waited nervously, watching the storeman squint as he inspected the money given to him. After a few uncountable seconds, the storeman shrugged, accepted the money, and gestured the change to Ethan's hand.

With a silent sigh of relief, Ethan took the change and put it in his pocket. Having things going better than he expected, he grew in confidence.

"I'm new in town. Is there anywhere here I could get a drink?"

The storeman raised one eyebrow. "This is a dry state, boy, ever since the prohibition. It's coming up to a year ago now."

"Uh." Ethan's confidence evaporated, and what the man had just said went over his head.

The storeman leaned back on the counter; the corner of his

lips sloped down. "It's illegal to sell or produce alcohol now. I think it was the best decision they could have taken," he said, straightening back up, chest puffed out, and arms crossed.

Ethan silently thought the man was stupid and so was the prohibition policy.

"Thanks for the cigarettes," he said with a smirk. He grabbed the cigarettes and matches and headed to the exit. The bell rang again as he opened the door and walked out.

Ethan stood outside the store and wondered what he had just purchased. He opened the packet and took out a cigarette. Confused by the small, long stick, he slid it across his nostrils to smell the scent, but there was nothing. Holding it between his lips, he sparked up a match and ignited the tip. The taste of burned paper was unpleasant and so was the aroma that flowed into his nostrils. He screwed up his face but persisted with the unsatisfying replacement for a cigar. He continued his walk through the town.

The sun was beginning to set and the town was empty, but still, he kept a cautious eye out so he didn't get in anyone's way again. Looking around, he saw a closed building that said *Theater* blazoned across the front in red writing. He took a right turn at the end of the street and saw seven automobile contraptions parked up across the road. He looked around before crossing, fearing he would still interfere with something. Seeing the coast was clear, he scampered across the road to get a closer look at the spectacular machines.

The seats inside looked more comfortable than any feather mattress he had ever lain on. His eyes followed the wave of the front wheel arch all the way to the rear. He bent down to see his reflection through the dark blue metal surface. As he was about to touch the shine of the ornament on the bonnet with his finger-tips, a voice crept up behind him.

"1919 Paige roadster."

Ethan pulled his hand back like he had just been told off by his mother for grabbing another slice of pie. Standing up and facing the voice, he saw it was the mustache man from before. "Excuse me," he replied, once again confused at what someone was saying to him.

The man pointed his bony index finger at the machine and said again, "1919 Paige roadster." He paused to light up a cigar, and after a few puffs into Ethan's face, he continued with a smug grin, "It's very expensive."

Ethan breathed in the cloud of smoke from the cigar that should have been in his own hand. He knew he couldn't possibly afford the machine, and even though he had spent all that time in solitary, understood when he wasn't welcome. Figuring it was getting late he decided it was time to make his way back home.

Without losing prowess, Ethan took a large drag on his nearly burned cigarette. "Good day to you," he said, exhaling the fumes back into the man's face and then walked away. Passing back round the corner, he flicked the remains of the disgusting thing onto the floor. He started the long journey home and contemplated that his first experience back into civilization hadn't been as good as what he had expected.

It was two weeks before Ethan journeyed into Jackson for the second time. He planned his time better than the previous trip. The general store had just opened when he finally arrived. His feet were blistered and he was dying of thirst. He stumbled his way to the water fountain and filled his stomach with the cool liquid.

Out of the corner of his eye, he saw people entering the theater. He felt left out as he took the last bit of change out of his pocket, knowing he wouldn't be able to afford entry inside. His focus turned to his worn boots. The leather was cracked and he could feel the sharp stones pierce through the soles into his feet. He knew he needed a way to earn some money. He glanced over to the general store he had visited, thinking the storeman might have some information for him but decided not to go through with it because he did not want to have another conversation with the obnoxious man.

He walked down the street and took a left. The street wasn't as maintained as the others. The houses were shabbier, with most of the windows boarded up. Thinking there wasn't going to be anything useful to see, Ethan decided to turn around. Yet after a couple of steps back, he heard a sound. It sounded similar to the horn of the automobile, but this was more gracious and smoother to the ear.

He had never heard music such as this before. It flowed from high to low like the tide, the tempo swapping between the sea and a river. Ethan closed his eyes while the soft sound consumed his body with warmth. He slowly reopened his eyes as the beautiful sound drifted away. He spun around in circles hoping to find where the music was coming from.

Two men walked around the bend. They were making such a racket about the problems with their business, it made it impossible for Ethan to concentrate on tracking down the enchanting music. Disappointed upon losing the sound, his attention was uncontrollably pulled toward the two men who had disturbed him.

"We're ruined if we can't sort out this delivery!" one of them shouted to the other.

"Don't you think I know that already? I'm trying my best to sort something out. Besides, I don't see you doing anything to save our skin," said the other.

"Don't go blaming me. You're the one who said no boll weevils would get to our cotton. Now we're full of the goddamn pests!"

Ethan knew right then and there, he had an opportunity to make some money. He walked over to the men, who were still too busy arguing to take any notice of his approach. Both men were short and overweight, their bellies overhanging their belts. The slightly thinner man, which wasn't saying much, had a permanent frown fixed on his face.

"Excuse me," Ethan said, standing only a few feet away.

The men completely ignored him, still too busy blaming each other for their endeavors.

"Hey!" Ethan snapped.

Both men turned to face him and began to sweat.

Now that he had their undivided attention, Ethan gave them his proposal. "I hear you're in need of cotton? How much are we talking?"

"What's it to you?" snapped the scowling man.

"Shh," said the larger, and more timid of the pair, while giving his friend an elbow to his side. He then started to explain their predicament. "We've got a big problem with boll weevils. They destroyed our crop and now we're behind on our delivery."

Ethan nodded. He had already heard all of this from across the street. "How much do you need?" he interrupted.

"Five tons."

Ethan tried to fight his twitching grin. "I think I can help you with that. I've got a farm south of here with all the cotton you need. For the right price."

"Bullshit!" barked the scowler. The other man wasn't able to silence him this time. "There is no way you have a field that isn't infested just like everyone else's."

"I'm not a liar, sir. The cotton is picked and has been sleeping in a barn for quite some time—free of insects and weather. If you'd like proof then I'll take you to see it for yourself." Ethan's top lip twitched again. He didn't like being called a liar.

"There we go. I knew we would sort this mess out," the larger man said, rubbing his hands and looking awfully excited. "You take the truck and the boy to the pure white nectar, and I'll sort out his payment. Good day to you." He patted his friend on the back and scampered away before his friend could react.

The scowler let out a loud sigh.

Ethan was quite deflated himself. He would have preferred to have gone with the more joyful of the two men.

"Well, then. Guess we'll go and get this nectar of yours." The man grunted and started walking. "Come on. Let's get this over with."

Following right behind him, Ethan's nerves started to rise as he saw another one of the spectacular machines. He stopped short and watched the man hop into the truck. He gave Ethan an impatient wave for him to get in. Ethan hesitated before opening the door and climbing up inside the monstrous machine. Ethan's nerves didn't let up after the door closed behind him and he was encased in metal.

"So, which way are we going?" the man asked.

"Uhm, just turn right and keep heading south," Ethan replied, keeping his hands in his lap, afraid to touch anything. He jumped out of his skin when the engine of the machine roared, and then was pushed back into his seat when it pulled away. His head began to spin as he saw the scenery fly past the window.

The man was still annoyed at being on the wild goose chase. He didn't care to notice how unsettled Ethan was.

After a few minutes, Ethan was finally able to relax and was relieved that he wouldn't have to walk home again. Looking at the man out of the corner of his eye, he could tell he wasn't up for conversation. But he reluctantly introduced himself as Johnathan Cale midway through the journey. Ethan's eyes drifted down to Cale's hands holding the steering wheel. He watched his feet rise up and down to the rhythm of the engine. Ethan silently started to predict Cale's next motion, with a fair amount of success.

· · ·

Astonished that it only took a few hours to get back to the farm, Ethan felt slightly diminished from not wanting to get out of the truck.

Cale looked out into the cotton field, shaking his head and gripping the steering wheel tight.

Ethan couldn't waste any time. He had to get Cale face to face with the sacks of cotton.

"Stop just near that barn," he said. He quickly hopped out of the truck and marched toward the barn doors.

However, Cale couldn't help himself, and prematurely opened his mouth. "I knew it. I knew this would be a waste of time. Look at this pile of waste."

Ethan was getting tired of hearing his big mouth and wanted to shut it for him, but the look on the man's face when he opened the barn would be much sweeter.

He took away the plank, lifting it like it was a feather, and flung open the doors.

Johnathan Cale stared into the barn, full to the brim with sacks of cotton. Exactly the same expression Ethan had when staring at the young lady with the fan. Finally, Cale was at a loss for words.

Being right had never felt so good for Ethan. Feeling smug he pulled the top sack out and untied the string.

Cale leaned forward onto his toes to peer over Ethan's shoulder, the most physical thing he had done in days. Ethan grabbed a clump of the white gold and lifted it up to Johnathan's fat face. After ripping it apart and rubbing it between his fingertips, he spoke to Cale in such a manner that he wouldn't doubt him again.

"No boll weevils in my cotton, Mr. Cale."

Sweat started to spew out of Jonathan's creased forehead. He took a large gulp from his stretched-out throat. "I can see that and what fine quality cotton it is. My partner and I would be happy to purchase it from you."

Ethan had him where he wanted him and began to put his father's bartering skills to use. "Hold your horses. I want double the standard rate," Ethan said, hiding the fact he had no clue what the going rate was.

"That's impossible. There's no way my partner and I can afford that. We could probably raise it a quarter."

Ethan looked at Cale's trembling hands and the fear that glowed in his eyes. He knew if he held his guns, he would get what he wanted, and it would definitely cost the two men dearly.

Cale deserved a punch in the jaw for the way he had been acting. Yet Ethan had proven his point that he wasn't a liar and the fact that he was just as lucky to run into them as they were to him. He made the deal more reasonable. "I'm not interested in selling just five tones. I need it all gone. If you do that, I'll let it go at the standard rate. If you get some men, you can scavenge the field. Gotta be some cotton still ripe out there. I'll fill up the truck now. You can come back anytime for the rest. I'd also appreciate a lift back to town and payment for the five."

Cale grabbed his chest and let out a massive sigh of relief, then offered his hand with appreciation. Ethan respectfully accepted.

The journey back to town was cheerful. Cale seemed to be a completely different person, happily conversing with Ethan.

"Me and my partner were lucky you came by. It's impossible to get rid of those insects once they start breeding. Now, the only thing we can do is to burn the crop and hope to be back up next year. At least with your help, we might stand a fighting chance." Johnathan asked Ethan where he was from and how his farm wasn't riddled with weevils.

Ethan used the same lie that he used on the old courier Thomas, which Jonathan soaked up completely. Still intrigued by the truck, Ethan asked for some basic advice on how to control the machine. How to use the brake and the gas and the need to switch gears. All the pieces of the puzzle were coming together.

They arrived back in Jackson and parked up in the same spot. They could see Johnathan's partner already waiting for them.

"You look happy there, Johnathan."

"Mighty, mighty happy," he said with a smile reaching ear to ear as he clambered his heavy frame out of the truck.

The jolly man had a confused expression slapped across his face. "So, it's all sorted then?"

"Yes, yes, it's all sorted. Have you got the boy his money?"

He nodded and took the envelope out of his jacket and handed it over to Ethan.

"That's for five tons. I'll personally make sure you get the rest when we collect the other cotton," Jonathan said, reassuring Ethan.

The now not-so-jolly man crooked his neck and whispered in Cale's ear, "The rest?"

"Oh shh! We've got enough cotton for this deal and the next. And with the problems we're having, I don't think giving the boy a little extra is going to be a problem." He gave Ethan another handshake and Ethan returned it with a smile.

The other man stood there still confused, yet also shook Ethan's hand.

"Good day to you both."

"And to you," Jonathan replied, escorting his dazed partner away.

Ethan peered into the envelope and started laughing. "That was easy." He had made a lot of money and there was more to come. Lucky for him, he knew exactly where to spend it.

Ethan knelt down, mesmerized by the shiny blue paint. Seeing his reflection, he noticed that he definitely needed a change of attire. He kept admiring the beauty of the machine, and to stall for more time sparked up a cigarette. Sucking in the harsh smoke, he eventually got the attention he was waiting for.

"1919 Paige roadster. Very expensive," the salesman stated in his pompous English accent as he repositioned his top hat.

Ethan smoked his cigarette and the man polished off his cigar stump. They stared each other down for several seconds until Ethan pulled his eyes away.

The man sniggered as he walked away.

"Will this cover it?" Ethan shouted.

The salesman spun back around, gripping the stump with his teeth.

Ethan stood there with his arm stretched out, and gently held between his thumb and index finger was a large stack of notes folded in half.

The man froze. His eyes bulged out of his sockets, and the cigar stump started to singe his mustache.

Within an hour of receiving his payment, Ethan had purchased an automobile and several new outfits. He changed into his new attire before exiting the clothes store. The dark gray lounge suit was a little loose on his waist, but he didn't mind. It was too hot to wear a jacket. He had also rolled his shirt sleeves halfway up his forearms for practicality and from the habit of working on the farm. Finally, he lost the tie that came with the suit as he had trouble tying them. His mother used to tie them for him. He couldn't wear it anyway; he still had the handkerchief on to conceal his neck.

How he looked wasn't important to him, he felt smart. Like he was one of the important visitors that his father would have round for dinner on special occasions; purely there for business but, nevertheless, his father would always have the best dishes and wine out to also show some class.

He was gently resting his new clothes in the trunk of the

automobile that he couldn't wait to drive home in when he heard a familiar voice call out.

"Well, I'll be. If it isn't young Ethan from the farm."

Looking up, he saw the courier Thomas hobble across the road.

"Glad to see you made it out of the graveyard, boy," he said, clutching his bad leg.

"I decided to take your advice," Ethan replied with a large smile of appreciation.

Thomas glanced over at the shiny vehicle and looked Ethan up and down. "And doing quite well for yourself it seems."

Ethan smiled again. "Yeah, I'm doing alright."

With his old man charm, Thomas said his farewell. "Well, I'm glad you're back on your feet and putting your mark on this world. I'd wish you good luck but it doesn't look like you need it. But if there is anything I can help you with, I'd be mighty obliged to do so. Good day to you." Thomas tipped his hat and Ethan gave him a wave goodbye.

As he closed the trunk and Thomas brushed past onto the path, he smelled a strong spice coming off of him. Ethan's eyes widened with excitement. "Thomas!" he shouted, then carefully looked around to see if anyone was in earshot of their conversation. "Any chance you know where I can get some liquor?"

With a large grin letting his few teeth see the sunlight, Thomas let out a sigh, and joyfully replied, "I'm starting to like you more and more, boy."

A wooden crate with an array of bottles and jars filled with the finest moonshine from Mississippi, made a high ringing sound as they bumped against one another on the passenger seat.

Ethan headed home accompanied by the crunching sound of the gears from his newly and poorly learned driving capability. He howled at the top of his lungs as he thundered over the bumpy road and chucked up dust from the rear. He felt like he was the fastest thing alive.

He relaxed in the rocking chair on the porch. With an open jar of moonshine in one hand and a cigarette in the other, he marveled at the beautiful machine basking in the dimming sunset. He was delighted at how his second day had played out compared to his first. He sipped on the fermented juice, and boy did it pack a punch on the way down his throat. Then between sips, he inhaled on the cigarettes that he had finally got a taste for. The next thing he wanted to do was go to the theater.

Ethan looked slightly overdressed to be in the theater. Nevertheless, he looked rather dashing in his suit. Centered in the middle aisle, he was laughing hysterically at a peculiar-looking man on the screen. Charlie Chaplin was his name and he was up to some strange antics at the zoo. Ethan smoked like a chimney, and sipped on his moonshine from a small canteen he had concealed in his inside pocket. He was snickering and cackling at the short man's tomfoolery, without any consideration for the other patrons in the room.

Stepping back out onto the street and holding his ribs in pain from all the laughter, he took a deep breath to calm himself down. Suddenly, the same young lady he'd seen a few weeks ago, walked out of the theater and took his newfound breath away. He thought she was drop-dead gorgeous, with her long blonde hair flowing down both sides of her neck into soft curls, and resting gently on her pale yellow dress, the delicate skin of her face and subtle curves of her petite figure, and lastly, her eyes. They were the lightest blue Ethan had ever seen, similar to a cloudless summer sky. She stood demurely with her hands together. But as he stared at her beauty, he could see her tightening her grip.

He raised his gaze to her slender neck and watched it twitch and spasm. When their eyes met, Ethan spoke. "Hi there," he said with a soft smile.

"Hello," she replied avoiding any more eye contact and keeping a straight face.

Ethan hadn't talked to a woman for a long time, especially not one as beautiful as her. Butterflies began to flap in his stomach. "Did you enjoy the moving picture?" he said.

She looked at him with a frown. "I would have, however, a loud young man was spoiling it," she said changing her frown into a blushing smile.

He could tell she was interested in him, but he would have to peel one layer off of her at a time. He moved in a little closer. "What's your name?"

She raised her hand to her mouth to cover her chuckling.

Maybe not, he thought as he started to turn red himself.

"You're not from around these parts?" she said.

"Well, I am new in town, if that's what you mean. Is it that noticeable?" he replied, keeping the facts to himself.

"Oh, I'm so sorry. I didn't mean to offend you," she said sincerely. "It's just if you were from around these parts, you would know of my father, and, therefore, know my name."

"Why's that?" Ethan asked.

"Everyone knows my father. He didn't take kindly to you purchasing one of his favorite vehicles. Or 'a perfect example of quality engineering,' as he liked to put it." She giggled.

"Is that so?" Ethan chuckled, glad he was able to get under the skin of that pompous English man.

"Indeed. No one speaks or acts like that around my father. It was the only thing he talked about when he arrived home."

After all this time, Ethan hadn't lost his charm. He stared for a moment. He could have stared at her forever. "What is your name?"

"Abigail," she answered, gesturing her hand toward Ethan with her palm facing down.

He gently shook her delicate hand with two fingers and thumb. "Delighted to meet you. I'm Ethan."

"Pleasure," Abigail replied, fluttering her eyelashes.

Letting go of her hand, Ethan took out a pack of cigarettes from his jacket. Taking one for himself, he then offered the open packet in Abigail's direction.

She pinched her lips together and shook her head.

Ethan quickly pulled his hand back so as not to offend her. "I'm sorry. Do you not smoke?"

"No, it's not that. It's just my father wouldn't approve of it."

"Well, we wouldn't want to annoy him anymore, would we?" he said with a grin. "I like your accent by the way."

"Thank you. I like yours too. People speak so differently here," Abigail replied, shifting her gaze toward her father's former automobile.

Ethan walked over to it and leaned on the bonnet. "Would you like to take a ride?"

Again, she shook her head and sighed. "My father wouldn't approve."

Ethan could feel the frustration in her tone. Putting his cigarette in his mouth and striking up a match, he blew out a large puff of smoke. "Do you always do what Daddy tells you?"

Abigail shook her head again; this time with a mischievous grin.

Abigail sat in the passenger seat, a cigarette in her hand, and her long blonde hair flowing in the wind. Ethan pressed the accelerator to the floor and looked over at her. He watched her succulent lips as she smiled and closed her eyes while the breeze caressed her cheeks. His gaze dropped to her legs, resisting the urge to touch them. Putting his attention back to the dirt track, he yanked the steering wheel to stay on route. Abigail shrieked with laughter and continued with her daydreaming.

Pulling up at the house, Ethan noticed Abigail's enjoyment turn to caution.

"You live here?" she said, with a wobble to her voice.

"Yeah. Is that a problem?"

"Well, do you know what happened here?"

"Happened here?" he repeated, confused about where the conversation was heading.

"Well, what people say is that, after the Civil War, the youngest son of the house was so ashamed, he took his rage out on the slaves, working them ten times as hard, taking their clothes and never feeding them." She glared out into the cotton field, lowering herself down in her seat. "I've heard stories of how he worked them in the field until they dropped down dead. Then the cotton would do the rest."

Ethan looked mildly intrigued by the story. "Then what happened?"

"When all the slaves were all dead, he went insane. He killed his mother and left her in her bed-chamber. Then he took his own life. People have been avoiding this place for years."

Ethan thought it through in his head for a moment. "So, everyone here died?" he asked.

Abigail turned around and gave him a nod in return.

With terror on his pale skin face from her ghost story, he leaned in toward her and positioned his mouth next to her ear. "Then who told the story?" he whispered and burst out into hysterics.

Abigail sulked in her seat, crossed her arms, and pursed her lips. "Well, I don't know! But where does any story come from?" she shouted.

Ethan patted himself on his chest and buried his laughter. "Look, I appreciate the story and I don't know where they emerge from either. But in my opinion, nothing in life is so dramatic or exciting." As soon as the words left his mouth, he realized what he had said wasn't true.

He'd forgotten the past several decades, like it was all merely a dream. It couldn't have been a dream. He had the scars to prove it.

"So, what is the truth?" Abigail asked. She then bit down on her lower lip as she watched Ethan stare up into the sky.

"Loneliness," he muttered then cleared his throat. "Anyway, we don't have to go inside the scary haunted house." He turned on the ignition and slowly drove into the barn.

"You have horses?" Abigail's voice sparked up with excitement.

"Afraid they are all long gone."

"Oh, shame." Abigail's voice lowered again. "Horses are such beautiful creatures. I've always wanted to learn how to ride them."

Ethan looked around the barn. He had forgotten how big it was inside. He was finally able to see most of it now that half the cotton was gone. "Maybe I'll get some," he said, looking back over at Abigail. "Horses I mean. I'll teach you how to ride if you like."

Abigail sucked on her lips and began to smile. "You'd do that?"

Ethan nodded. "For you, I would." Ethan became wide-eyed. Not really sure what to do, he simply smiled nervously at her.

***

Abigail mirrored him with a blushing smile, and her heart fluttering. This was her first time being completely alone with a boy, especially one as handsome as Ethan. She could tell he was strong under his smart suit, but thinking no matter how well he cleaned himself up, he would still have a roughness about him. *A fighter*, she thought. Someone who wouldn't control her but would protect her when needed. She wanted to kiss him.

Ethan felt terrified, not wanting to misunderstand the situation. He watched Abigail. *Abigail is such a lovely name.* She flicked her hair over her shoulder to show her neck, and nervously screwed up a fist full of her dress in her hand, raising it higher and higher as she did so. Ethan took a deep breath trying to slow down his heartbeat. He grazed her cheek with the back of his hand.

Abigail accepted the proposition, leaning in and pressing against his coarse skin. Her cheek was warm and an urge pulsed through Ethan's body. Opening his hand and placing it on the back of her head, he leaned in for a kiss. Their lips touched in synchronization. The sweet taste of her succulent lips was extraordinary. Ethan couldn't wait to embrace her in his arms any longer.

They made love there and then in the barn, their bodies full of lust. Their pure untouched flesh intertwined in a sea of cotton. After the radiant incarnation, Ethan drove back to town as fast as he could. Abigail mentioned she couldn't be late home. Her father wouldn't approve.

A few days passed. The rest of the cotton was delivered, and the second half of the payment went in Ethan's pocket.

Cale and his business partner were ecstatic. They'd even brought a photographer to mark the special occasion. Ethan had never had his picture taken and was reluctant at first. But feeling like he'd been too quick to judge Cale, he was obliged to do so. The blinding flash was unsettling, yet once it was done it was like he was finally a part of modern society. He gazed out into the dead field, thinking he could honor his family and revitalize the farm.

Abigail kept playing on his mind, he was so anxious to see

her again. There was only one place he could think of to find her. It was a shame he saw someone else.

Ethan sat in the theater, barely paying any attention to the moving picture. He twisted his neck around trying to see if Abigail was there. He walked out of the theater disappointed, and his throat scratchy from all the cigarettes he'd been smoking, mostly out of boredom. With his canteen dry as a bone, he strolled his way over to the water fountain. He closed his eyes, slurping up the cold water from the spout.

Suddenly he sensed a shadow go over his face, blocking out the sun. He opened one eye and peered over, hoping to see Abigail's beautiful face. His other eye snapped open and his pupils dilated with rage, as he saw a colored man drink from the shabby water fountain beside him. He tried to stay perfectly still, but he couldn't stop his body from trembling. The water hit his closed lips while he strained to look out the corner of his eye at the man.

After a few moments, he finally stood up straight facing the dark-skinned man, who was still drinking from the fountain too engrossed to notice Ethan shadowing over him. He was dressed in a black suit that had started fraying at the sleeves and collar. He couldn't have been any more than twenty years old, with his shiny dark skin and short thick hair peeking out from under his tilted black hat. After filling his stomach full of fresh water, he dipped his fingers under the slowly flowing waterfall and rubbed his burning forehead. He then, unfortunately, saw the fierce-looking stranger gazing right through him.

Ethan couldn't bear to look the man in the eye, as he wouldn't be able to contain the hatred for his skin. Ethan wanted to tear him apart.

The man was terrified, uncertain about his fate. He gave Ethan a wide berth as he scurried across the street. Not wanting any trouble, he kept his chin pinned to his chest and turned left at the end of the road to the unmaintained street.

Ethan was able to calm down, once the boy was out of sight. Looking back at the two fountains, he finally saw two small planks nailed to the bases. *Whites only* on the pristine fountain and *colored only* on the other. He scanned around and the signs now stood out like a sore thumb. *Whites only* on the general store. *Whites only* on the theater and the clothes store. Without any thought, he followed in the boy's footsteps to confront him.

When he turned the corner everything became clear, and the only thing he could see was darkness. The darkness of the men, women, and children's flesh, trying to live their lives peacefully. Everyone was wearing poorly fitting, and patched-together ragged clothing. On the right side of the street, he could see a group of men repairing the colored-only theater with whatever materials they had to spare. Across from them was an elderly woman sewing a patch into a dress, while she rocked in her chair. Women took care of babies that all had empty bellies, and older children played in the street, avoiding the broken glass from the shattered windows.

Ethan saw none of this, however, too blinded by the color of their skin. To him, the street looked exactly like all the others. He saw men with tools they shouldn't have, raising children they didn't deserve, and smiles that hadn't been earned. Fear brewed from within himself, more than ever before. His head felt like it would erupt again as he tried to make sense of the situation. How in the world could this have happened, when he had lost everything that he held dear? But colored folk hadn't suffered at all, living their free lives like proper members of society while he was being punished by continuously existing in the world.

SIX

A few more days had passed. He was uncertain how many. It was difficult for Ethan to keep track of time. He sat on the bonnet of his motor vehicle, close enough to hear the priest talk.

"We are gathered here today to celebrate the life of one individual Thomas Mathews, who now serves God in heaven."

Ethan stopped listening to the priest and pondered his own thoughts. *God.* Ethan scoffed and turned his nose up at the notion of such an ideology. He had lost all faith after what had happened to him. He had prayed for hours at a time, even into the early hours of the morning while living in his solitary life, hoping he would be released from his not so-mortal coil, with never a whimper from the all-powerful almighty Christ our Lord. "Fuck God," he muttered under his breath.

Still, he didn't want to disturb the ceremony, for Thomas's sake, or be branded a heretic in front of all the white townsfolk who were attending. He had only met Thomas a few times since he'd come to the farm but was truly sad that he had passed. He was the one who had told him to leave his isolation and had been able to supply him with alcohol in this ridiculous prohibition.

The thing that was bothering Ethan the most, was how Thomas had died. He had forgotten that people grow old, and how he would never experience it. He flicked his cigarette to the ground and anxiously lit another. Everyone he had cared for or would care for would eventually leave him, and he would end up alone. It wasn't a conclusion he liked but knew he would have to get used to it and the sooner the better. Thinking it was for the best, he pushed it from his mind and buried his true feelings.

When the priest was finished and Thomas was laid in the cold earth, the crowd started to disperse. Ethan was confused by the sour looks he was getting from everyone who walked past him. His mood changed when he saw the radiant glow on Abigail's face in the sun. He smiled and she returned the favor. However, before he could speak, her father grabbed her forcefully by the arm and pulled her away. Ethan watched in annoyance but didn't intervene. It was her father's right and Ethan respected it. Ethan's eyes were fixed on her unhappy face, as her father dragged her away.

"Come, Child. You've gotten yourself into enough trouble. I should never have brought you here," he muttered, leaving Ethan's sight.

Ethan was alone, just like he said he would be. It wasn't going to be as easy as he thought. He got into his automobile and planned to go home. Driving down the main road out of Jackson, he caught a glimpse of the young black man who had come back to drink from the colored-only fountain. He had a cheerful smile and had put the unpleasant confrontation with Ethan behind him. Again, he, unfortunately, didn't notice Ethan's presence looming over him. Ethan became jealous of the dark man's smile that he rightfully deserved, and how he should have been holding Abigail in his arms. Determined he would wipe the smile off of the black man's face, he pulled over, straightened his jacket, and walked into the general store.

Ethan firmly pushed open the door. The bell rattled away, startling the storeman.

"Well, howd–"

"How much for the bat," Ethan interrupted, still with the cigarette held between his lips. He pointed at the bat on the top shelf.

The man looked and smugly said, "Well, that's bee–"

Ethan rolled his eyes; he didn't have time for stupid games. He grabbed a handful of notes out of his pocket and firmly placed them on the counter. "There, give me the bat."

Their roles had switched. The storeman couldn't get a grip on Ethan's newfound attitude. He quickly turned, raised his heels, and took the dust-covered bat off the top shelf. He blew the dust off and the shine started to show. Holding the barrel, he presented the handle to Ethan.

Ethan snatched it off of him and marched to the door. He had wasted too much time already. Flinging the door open, the bell frantically rang again on its cord. Intrigued, the storeman walked from behind the counter and pressed his nose against the window.

Walking with determination across the street, Ethan looked around for any observers, but no one was in sight. The unsuspecting man was still quenching his thirst. Ethan flicked his cigarette onto the ground and approached him. The man choked on the water as Ethan grabbed the back of his jacket and threw him to the ground.

Landing on his backside disoriented, he looked up at his attacker.

Ethan pointed the bat at him. "Niggers like you, need to earn their water," he said with venom in his tone.

The man shielded his face with his arms and waited for the blow that was coming next.

Ethan gripped the bat with both hands and prepared to swing it with all his might. Ethan wouldn't ever doubt his ability again.

The bat slammed into the side of the colored-only fountain. The cover cracked into chunks and the water pipe exploded, soaking Ethan and the helpless colored man on the ground. He yelled out as he kept pummeling the fountain until he knew it couldn't ever be repaired. When the water started sputtering from the pipe, Ethan finally lowered the bat, resting the tip in the puddle that surrounded him.

Taking in some relaxing, deep breaths, he slowly strolled back over to his vehicle. He felt like he had finally done something meaningful. He placed the bat on the passenger seat and slowly pulled away. He didn't care to look at the man, still lying in the pool of water that he had intended to drink.

The storeman had the perfect view from his window, he saw everything that happened. Once it was all over, he had a large, crooked grin on the left side of his face.

Ethan managed to light his cigarette with his damp matches as he drove home. He was calm. His hands steadily held the steering wheel. What just happened was already a distant memory. He inevitably made it home, not remembering the journey back. He stepped out of the car and took the final drag on the cigarette. The embers burned his fingertips for several seconds before he was willing to let it go. As his skin felt the heat, he knew what his next plan of action was going to be.

Marching into the house, he stripped off his damp clothes and then opened the small door under the stairs. Inside was a safe that hadn't been opened since he'd said goodbye to himself. Spinning the dial and twisting the handle, he saw three items inside. The first was his mother's ring. The second was the deed to the house, still with his father's name on it. He would have to sort it out eventually but now was not the time. The other object was his already-loaded Colt.

· · ·

On one insignificant day back in Jackson around noon, Ethan sat on the bonnet of his car. He was smoking and skipping stones across the street, feeling blue like a little boy without anyone to play with. His arm was wound up and ready to hurl another pebble, when a young teenage black boy minding his business turned the corner. Where he was going wasn't of any importance to Ethan, nor was he shying away from the fact he was staring at the kid.

The boy slowly walked on, pressing his shoulder against the side of the buildings to maximize the distance between Ethan and himself.

Ethan kept his vulture-like gaze fixed on the boy, waiting for the most mundane reason to react to him. Alas, with a small twitch of his eyes to get a glimpse of Ethan, he fell into the snare.

"What the fuck you looking at, boy!" Ethan snapped, trickling the pebbles to the ground. Ethan walked over to the small boy and with a gentle shove, knocked him to the ground.

The boy's bottom lip started to quiver, but then he started to frown like he was tempted to get up and retaliate. Ethan could see the boy's arms and legs, preparing to get back up. For the briefest moment, he felt the slightest respect for the boy; because of the thought of standing up and facing his enemy. For that reason, he thought he should warn the boy about the consequences of his next decision. Ethan spread his arms out wide and opened up his hands, to show the boy the pure white flesh of his palm, like it was a guardian angel. "What you going to do, nigger?" he said slowly, showing the differences between them.

The boy understood and only his quivering lip remained.

"Smart move. Now run back to your nigger ma and pa because I don't think they want to be burying their little boy today." Ethan's creepy smile squirmed around on his face as he sparked up and walked to his car. He watched as the boy sobbed back to the dark skin street. Thinking he had only wasted five minutes of his life, he agreed with himself it had been a very entertaining five minutes.

Jonathan Cale was across the street. He looked like he was in a rush for something. Luggage filled his truck to the brim.

"Mr. Cale!" Ethan shouted, waving his hand. He didn't respond. Ethan quickly proceeded across the street. "Mr. Cale!" he shouted again. It was impossible for Cale not to have heard but he continued with what he was doing. "Mr. Cale," Ethan said, standing right behind him, frustrated by the ignorance.

He finally turned around, not looking happy to see him. "Oh, hello there, Ethan," he said pretending that he hadn't heard his yelling. "What can I do for you?" He continued to occupy himself with his truck and avoided getting into a proper conversation.

"You going somewhere?" Ethan asked.

"Yes," Cale replied. "My partner and I did better with all that cotton than we ever would have expected. I've decided to move up north with the family." He hopped his heavy posterior into the driver's seat and rolled down the window to carry on. "Besides, what's starting to happen here isn't what I want for my family."

"What do you mean?"

Cale shook his head. "What you did to that boy over there." He paused in disappointment. "It's not something I agree with."

"The boy? You mean that nigger? I'm just putting them back in their place. It's the right thing to do. Someone's gotta do it."

Cale looked hurt by the thought, thinking Ethan was better than that. "You're right." He nodded. "Someone's gotta do something, but sadly I'm not the man, and unfortunately, this town only has you." Cale let out a big sigh, relieved he had got it off his chest before leaving. "You gave me and my partner a good deal on the cotton. Good enough for me to leave this place, and I'll never forget that. I just hope you can do a kind service for some other folk. Have a nice life, Ethan." He closed his window and before Ethan could react, pulled away, leaving Ethan standing in the road with dust covering his feet; completely alone.

Everyone Ethan had got to know or had started to care for had left him, exactly like he'd thought they would. The thing he couldn't understand was why. A broken mind can come up with very irrational and delusional conclusions to make sense of the events unfolding, and that is precisely what happened. He figured that people weren't leaving him, they were leaving because of the scourge of black skin spreading through the town.

The dream of bringing the farm back up to working conditions drifted away as fast as it had come. For the next two weeks, he watched the black community from afar, like a lion stalking its prey. He was waiting for the prime opportunity to strike. He smiled when he saw it.

A group of black men shook each other's hands with appreciation at the completion of the colored-only theater.

It was early in the morning in the dark-skinned street. An elderly colored woman sat on her chair sewing and humming a tune.

A 1919 dark blue Paige roadster came speeding into the road and parked up adjacent to the theater. A man in a gray suit but without a tie and who went by the name Ethan stepped out and put his back against the newly refurbished building. He glanced to his left and then to his right with a smile on his face. Then he pulled the Colt from within his belt and fired a shot into the air. The firearm was certainly out of date, yet was still capable of having the desired effect of bringing everyone's attention toward him.

He waited a moment for the creatures to nervously gather up

across the street. Whispers and murmurs came from the group of men and women but stopped, once Ethan opened his mouth.

"You may already know who I am. You may not. It doesn't matter." He started walking the length of the theater back and forth, explaining his motivation. "You see, I don't like you people. If you can even be called that. It's everything about you. The way you look. The way you talk, walk, smell. I don't like how you all drink water." Pausing to look at everyone's reaction, he was happy not to see any smiles.

He also noticed the crowd of white folks gathered up at the edge of the black community, but couldn't tell what their expressions were. He then continued with his preaching. "Frankly, your kind disgusts me. And I'm here to make sure you know you're not welcome anymore. Now, you can stay but my advice is to go back to whatever dark dirty hole you came from. Or things are gonna get much worse around here for you folks."

Women held the arms of their men, stopping them from crossing the street as tears ran down all their faces.

Ethan lit a cigarette and leaned into the car, picking up his last bottle of moonshine. He positioned himself back in front of the theater like a performer on stage, listening to the tears and screams. He pulled off the handkerchief that had been an annoyance to him ever since he'd put it on. The pale white skin of his neck was shown to the sun with no visible scar. He tied the handkerchief to the bottle with a small loop. Taking a drag from the cigarette, he used it to ignite the handkerchief and whispered to himself, "Only way to get the boll weevils out now is to burn them." With anger branded on his face, he released the flaming bottle through the window of the colored-only theater.

The men and women screamed in horror watching their creation go up in a red blaze. An elderly colored woman sat in her chair.

The dress she was repairing was screwed up in her lap, still with the needle and thread attached. She shook in terror as she recognized the man surrounded by fire. She knew him only as William Lake.

SEVEN

"If you don't like how this is going, you best stop listening. It only gets worse from here," Adam said, nervously looking down at his feet. He was anticipating Joanna's reaction after hearing about the horrible acts he had committed.

Joanna took her time before speaking so she didn't sound judgmental. That would be the last thing Adam needed in his time of despair. She wasn't surprised and felt slightly foolish for not anticipating that this sort of thing would have been a part of him, especially during that time. It was hard to keep all her emotions in check.

When she had been at university, one of her favorite subjects had been American history. She'd enjoyed studying the policies and transgressions throughout the years. Now she was sitting next to a man who had lived through all of it, selfishly thinking how easy the final exams would have been if he had been sitting beside her. Even now in her later years, she was still willing to learn more. People always fantasize about meeting a famous person from history; to get opinions and perspectives on different subjects. Although Adam wasn't historically famous in any way, the feeling still excited her.

By no means did Joanna agree with the racism that Adam's past life had executed. But even in her life, she could relate. She had seen it growing up in New York and had even passed judgment herself from time to time. Fortunately, her father had taught her to judge people on their character and not the way they looked.

He had been a tranquil man, a loving husband, and a gracious father to Joanna. Yet she could tell he had been missing something; always searching for some distant memory in the clouded parts of his mind. He had been extremely proud of Joanna before his time had come and she had been of him. He had helped her become the woman she was today, and taught her not to pass judgment, especially when someone was being completely honest. Looking at the boy sitting in front of her, she knew that he was sorry about the decisions he had made so long ago. All she had to do now was to convince him to do the same.

She cleared her throat. "It was a different time back then," she said.

"That doesn't give me the right to be like that," he said sharply back at her.

"True but that was the way you were brought up. In a time when that was the norm. It made you short-tempered, violent, and judgmental. But it was a very long time ago."

Adam looked back down at his feet and with a lack of conviction nodded in agreement.

Joanna took out two cigarettes and handed one over to Adam. The twenty years she had been smoke-free started to seem meaningless now but the circumstances called for relief. As the pair of them sat there enjoying the intoxicating fumes, Joanna wanted Adam's opinion on a specific matter. "So did you stay on your own the whole time."

"What do you mean?" he asked with smoke escaping his mouth.

"Well, I'm pretty sure there were other people back then who had the same beliefs," she answered, still only hinting. After a few seconds, he understood what she was referring to.

———

Adam straightened himself back in his chair, slightly annoyed at why she didn't just ask. "The Ku Klux Klan," he said, sarcastically back in his southern accent and then swiftly burying it again. "What do you want to know about them?"

"It was a very large society that you had something in common with. Are you saying you didn't join them?"

Adam scoffed at the notion. Like an old man listening to modern music being broadcast on the radio. "No, I did not!" he said firmly.

"Why?"

Adam knew she wasn't going to quit until he went into proper detail. With a deep breath that failed to calm him down, he spewed out his rant. "I wasn't going to be caught dead in their stupid white hooded get up they used to prance about in. Don't get me wrong, I liked the work they were doing, but I wasn't about to spend the rest of my endless life, walking around like a ghost with a bunch of religious fanatics."

"Fanatics, you say. You don't believe in God?"

"Not anymore." Adam shook his head.

"And why is that?"

He leaned in; his top lip twitching in frustration. "If God existed, he would have killed me during the war."

———

Joanna thought his opinion of the KKK was interesting in a hypocritical and selfish way. He was not going to hide his face for his beliefs. Joanna had started to become enticed to hear the rest of the story and asked him to carry on. "So, what did you do next?"

Adam looked up at her. His cheekbones prominently stood out from his slender face as he sucked on the old cigarette she handed him. "I went to war. Things would be a lot different this time around."

EIGHT

With the passing years, the numbers in the black community noticeably decreased. The reason was unknowable. Certainly, the slight chance they would have a more civilized life up north with less discrimination was worth leaving their homes for. The egotistical Ethan liked to think he had a major role in their migration out of Jackson. In his eyes, the only black people left were the stupid, stubborn, old, and feeble, which weren't worth his time.

The tension between Germany and the rest of the world had every skin color on edge. In 1939, the world went to war for a second time. Ethan wasn't going to sit there and do nothing like he had the first time around. With his superior ability, he didn't have an ounce of fear. As young men started getting conscripted, he knew it was time. He certainly couldn't wait for his papers to come through, as no one had any evidence that he even existed. To their knowledge, he was still William Lake and that he would be close to celebrating his 100th birthday. That meant he would have to volunteer and sign up himself.

. . .

Ethan parked his pride and joy in the barn and covered it with a tarp, concealing the shine of the blue metal from the elements. Taking one last look at the silhouette of the beautiful machine, he pulled the barn doors shut and wrapped a large chain and padlock to the doors, assuming a dark skin wouldn't pass up the chance to take it for a spin. He gave the chain a strong yank to ensure it wouldn't budge before walking to the house.

Every time he walked into the house, he expected to hear someone call out his real name. He envisioned his mother preparing supper and the smell of roast beef in the air. His father and Marshall chatting around the dinner table, with an empty space laid out for him. Taking his seat, he observed what they were doing. His mother dished out the food as the pair kept talking. He watched them for several minutes. It was nice to be a family again.

Suddenly, he realized he could see their lips moving but there was no sound coming out of their mouths. He felt ashamed. It had been so long since he'd heard their voices, that no matter how hard he tried, he couldn't imagine what they would have been talking about. Before coming back to reality, he savored the moment for a few seconds longer; watching his mother serving food and his father and brother in silent conversation.

He wiped the tears from his eyes as he sat in the dark, dank dining room alone. He knew he had let them all down and if he wasn't capable of thinking of any other occasion they'd had together, other than sitting at the fucking table, then he would force himself to forget them initially.

Jumping up from the chair and with long strides, he took himself toward the safe under the stairs. Neither William nor Ethan thought they had any luck. But if there was one thing they wished for, it was to never come back to this place again. Not feeling confident he would get such a blessing; he gave himself something to come back to. Opening up the safe and taking out the deed to the farm, he forged both signatures onto it. *William*

Lake, Ethan Chaplin. Then he added a third. Not much thought went into the name. It was just the first thing that came into his head. Besides, he could always change it if he liked. The last signature read Matthew Cale.

The newly appointed Matthew Cale traveled by bus to Camp Moore in South Georgia. With a new name and new place, he figured a different manner of speaking would be appropriate. He was able to speed up his speech and conceal his southern drawl. After a fair bit of practice, no one batted an eyelid with the new way he spoke.

When he finally arrived, the camp generously took away his clothing and supplied him with a uniform and a freshly shaven head to go with it. Matthew didn't know who he was anymore and the complete change of appearance took away the last thing that had anchored him to the past.

As he entered the accommodation, he felt like he had stumbled into a hall of mirrors. Replicants of himself walking around. All wearing green, shaven heads and white faces. He thought if he didn't know who he was, maybe they didn't know either.

As he traversed the dorm toward an empty bunk at the end of the first row, the recruits already stationed there went quiet. Even though Matthew was physically strong, his slim figure made him feel inadequate compared to the other men who were eyeing him up and down. The average age of the recruits was nineteen, yet his young face made him look like a child surrounded by men. He was lacking the confidence he'd had back in Jackson, making him an easy target to mock.

He crept to the corner bunk and placed his spare uniform, phys kit, and washing supplies on the top bed.

"That's my bunk!" shouted one recruit from the cluster.

Matthew said nothing as the young man emerged from the group. He was one of the oldest there, being in his mid-twenties.

He had the matching haircut and a small scar splitting his right eyebrow into two. He was about two inches taller than Matthew, clocking in at a whopping six foot four and an extra thirty pounds of muscle to go with it. He gave Matthew a menacing look.

Matthew couldn't understand why he no longer had the impervious spark that he had in Mississippi and didn't feel confident in standing up to the man, who had a strong resemblance to his brother. Without any resistance, he picked up his belongings and placed them on the bottom bunk.

"Lay off the boy, Fletcher, before he shits himself," said another recruit, followed by a chuckle from the rest of the rabble.

Matthew kept his head down as he packed away his belongings, but kept listening to what was being said.

"Fine. I'll lay off the kid for now. Besides, he has to get through the run in the morning," Fletcher said, his eyes still trained on Matthew, and another chuckle rattled from the group.

The front door swung open and the sergeant walked in. He was tall and thin. Thick and rough skin covered his gaunt face. Short gray hair peeked out from under his cap.

"Quit the laughter, boys, and lights out!" he shouted.

They wiped the grins off their faces, frantically got out of their uniforms, and clambered into the beds.

The sergeant flicked off the lights and gave his orders in complete darkness. "Reveille at seven. You get your breakfast and then you're straight into the mile. Good night, gentlemen."

Matthew lay there looking up at the top mattress that was caving in from the intimidating mass of Fletcher. Matthew took a couple of quiet but deep breaths, pondering what he'd got himself into. He closed his eyes and tried to get some sleep and prepare for tomorrow's events.

Matthew had spent numerous nights sleeping and had grown tired of the mundane task. Sometimes he skipped it altogether. He was still human, however, and eventually would feel the fatigue scratch at his eyeballs. This night was one of those occasions when he yearned for a bed and the blessed peacefulness of the dark. Knowing how nothing went his way in his life, it didn't surprise him that as soon as he laid his head down on the pillow and closed his eyes, the sun had risen and it was time to get out of the soft cocoon.

He heard the rustling of all the other recruits scrambling out of bed. They were like a herd of gazelles pushing into one another as they got dressed and tried to get to a sink to shave. Sitting on the edge of his bunk, Matthew massaged the itch from under his eyelids. It wasn't an effective way to wake up compared to the thundering sound and rushing breeze of Fletcher hurling himself off the top bunk, clipping Matthew's shoulder as he slammed his large feet on the floor.

Fletcher looked over his shoulder at Matthew. "I'll look back at you on the mile, boy," he said, cackling, then walked across the dorm to the washroom with a heavy thud from his heels.

Queuing up at the canteen, Matthew was gobsmacked at the amount of food being served to him. Never once in his life had he seen such a mountain of bacon and egg on one plate. Though he wasn't that hungry, he polished off his serving and enjoyed every mouthful of the splendid meal.

The sergeant walked in, trying his hardest to sieve out the best candidates that would do well on the mile. It wasn't looking very promising, as all he saw was a rabble of young men with their mouths full of sausages and beans. With a disappointed look on his face, he snarled, "Outside in ten minutes!" They quickly wiped their plates clean with slices of bread and hustled outside five minutes early.

They lined up into three ranks outside the canteen entrance.

"Left turn!" the sergeant shouted then looked at them in amazement when they couldn't perform a simple order correctly.

Some of them turned with a delayed response or hesitated, waiting to mimic the action of the man beside them. The sergeant bit down angrily on his bottom lip, seeing several men had turned to the right, then witnessed the shocking realization settling on their faces when they figured they got the order wrong and were staring into the eyes of their fellow recruit.

When they finally settled, he barked his next order, "Quick march!" and then continuously hollered, "Left, right, left, right, left." The sergeant thought they resembled newborn calves, learning to walk for the first time, and tripping over their own feet as they tried to get in step. "There will be no singing on my march!" the sergeant hollered and quickened his pace to get to the front, not wanting to see the brutal mockery they were making of the march.

After ten minutes of the poorest degree of marching the sergeant had ever witnessed, he finally shouted at the top of his voice, "Halt!"

The recruits, not anticipating the order, crumpled to a stop, pressing their noses and chins into the back of the men in front.

"Listen up. You see that flag at the top of the hill there? That's the mile!" shouted the sergeant again. The men strained their eyes squinting at the small, flickering silhouette at the top of the hill in the distance.

Even the sergeant had one eye closed as he pointed his index finger at the microscopic shape. He retracted his arm back to his side and continued to give his order as he walked toward a light military vehicle. "That's where you're going. You have ten minutes. Don't be late. At the sound of my horn, move out." He hopped into the front seat of the vehicle.

It didn't have a roof or any doors, and the front window rattled as he pulled away, flicking dry dirt up into the recruits' faces.

Matthew thought the sergeant would be extremely jealous of him if he ever saw his roadster. It put a smile on his face, which was quickly taken away when Fletcher barged to the front of the pack, pushing Matthew to his knees.

"You just ate the sarge's dust. Now get ready to eat mine, boy," Fletcher sniggered with hate in his eyes.

Matthew was getting quite sick of his attitude but still didn't say a word. He just pondered why Fletcher hated him so.

The cab was half a mile out when it finally blasted its horn. The men sprang to action, flailing their arms and legs. Matthew pulled himself up and started running to catch up with everyone else. Then they all made their way up the long steep, winding track of the hill called the mile.

After two minutes in, the cluster of recruits had started to separate, showing the different levels of fitness. Fletcher powered on at the front with several others trailing behind. Some men had already cracked and were down to a slow walk, with their arms on their hips or above their heads, gasping for air.

Matthew was also struggling. Sweat poured from his brow, slid down his cheeks to the bottom of his chin, and then finally dripped onto the dirt path in front of him. His pace was all over the place, and he was stumbling around like a drunk.

As the muscles in his stomach began to seize up, beautiful little flashes of light started to appear in his sight. Matthew's blinking started to slow, poised to close, and grab onto the peaceful darkness. With his wheezing breath, he reopened his eyes and at the right time, as he'd almost gone straight off the track and into a tree. When he got his position back on track, he caught sight of Fletcher. Matthew didn't want him getting the satisfaction of beating him and could already hear the taunting coming out of Fletcher's lips. He gritted his teeth and widened his steps.

It was no use. Five minutes in, Matthew's heart pounded out of his chest. His stomach churned so much he was close to seeing the sausage, egg, and beans again. His legs were jelly, vision wobbly, and his brain throbbed against the inside of his skull. He stopped. He couldn't go on any longer. He wanted to lie down and sleep, even if it meant letting Fletcher win. Matthew exhaled all the air he had, letting the pain consume him.

With a loud snort, his body sucked in all it could through his nostrils and filled his lungs up to the maximum. The wheezing stopped and he opened his mouth to get an extra portion of oxygen. The red blood cells flowed through his veins. His pupils started to dilate when a surge of adrenaline pulsed from within. He pushed off his back leg and launched into each stride. His calf muscles got stronger with each new push. His pace got wider and faster to the point for a brief moment, he wasn't touching the ground. As his stomach muscles relaxed and reformed, he knew gaining so much energy and strength so quickly wasn't a normal occurrence.

With veins protruding from his neck, he flew past Fletcher. "Eat my dust, bitch," he said, feeling extremely satisfied with his appropriate choice of words.

Fletcher had started to suffer and couldn't react quickly enough to Matthew's bravado. Cramping and groaning, he continued to trudge his bulking body up the slope.

The sergeant was leaning back in the driver's seat, parked next to the flag. He was reading a paper and smoking a cigar. Apart from the gentle ambient sound of the leaves on the trees waving in the breeze, the only other sound was the ticking of a stopwatch placed on the passenger seat.

The sergeant loved this part of the training. Being able to just sit back and relax in the peace and quiet for the ten to fifteen minutes it would take for the recruits to arrive. He didn't feel guilty at all. He had done his fair share of running around when he was in training, and in his later years, it felt like he never stopped moving. Thankfully, no one had ever got to the top of the mile in under thirteen minutes and he would be able to finish reading his paper and smoke his cigar.

The sergeant, still relaxing in the cab didn't hear the sound of footsteps approaching, until the culprit was already upon him. He spun sharply in his seat to face the intruder and was shocked to see Private Cale standing there. He curiously picked up the stopwatch, and his eyes bulged out of their sockets as he saw the clock read 9:43.

Matthew glared at him while a soft sadistic grin tried to emerge. With every exhalation, a subtle growl rumbled in his throat, like something in his mind was refusing to release the endorphins that flowed in the current of his veins.

The sergeant walked over to Cale, still stunned by how he had accomplished such a time. He stood toe-to-toe with him and stared right into his eyes. His brow was tense as he inspected Matthew's blood-rushed face. "You look familiar, boy," he muttered.

Cale didn't reply and just continued to tremble with adrenaline.

The sergeant's brow softened when he saw several drops of sweat fall off Cale's forehead and splash onto his shiny polished boot. "Good job, Private," the sergeant said, giving Cale a gentle nod and handing Cale the last inch of his cigar for his efforts. Then he made his way back to the cab.

———

Matthew was finally able to relax. He stood next to the flag, polishing off the last few puffs of the cigar before the other recruits arrived.

The stopwatch read 16:22. The sergeant tapped his foot in time with the ticking, as the stragglers of the group dragged their broken bodies the last few feet. Fletcher's beady eyes glared at Matthew. Matthew slowly rocked from side to side like he knew something that everyone else didn't. They were all standing as a rabble, some with their hands on their knees, and others collapsed on their backs due to exhaustion.

The sergeant put the stopwatch in his pocket and faced them. "That was the most pathetic thing I have ever seen!" he shouted with a grizzled look on his face. Gazing over the men, he then spoke with a more relaxed and upbeat tone. "But good, you made it."

Puzzled looks appeared on the faces of the recruits, as they craned their necks from the ground to look up at the sergeant. They felt proud as they received the approval, yet couldn't shake the feeling that there was a catch.

Matthew started clenching and unclenching his fist repeatedly, keeping his blood pumping. He smiled when he heard the next order the sergeant spouted.

"Alright, everyone! Get back to camp. Have a shower then you've got a presentation."

As soon as he finished speaking, Matthew launched off at maximum speed, welcoming the endorphins back into his veins.

The rest of them looked at each other confused and deflated. The thought of having to run back down the hill sounded unbearable.

The sergeant hopped back into the driver's seat and looked back at them. "Well, what you all waiting for? Get going!"

They were sitting in rows of chairs inside an emptied-out dorm, listening to the sergeant talking. Clean from their showers but still aching from the so-called mile.

Matthew was slouched back in his chair in the middle of the group, only pretending to pay attention to the sergeant's speech. He kept on talking about teamwork and taking care of each other. *Bullshit* was the best word to describe teamwork, Matthew thought. Peering out of the corner of his eye, he examined the men to the left and right of him. He knew he would never need anyone's help but his own. He was faster than all of them and was convinced he was stronger than them all as well. The ability to not die just seemed to be a bonus. By this point, Matthew thought in his selfish mind, that he would only need to look after himself.

December 11, 1941.

America goes to war. Everyone was huddled around the radio in the dorm, listening in to the updates on the tragic event that occurred at Pearl Harbor almost a week ago. Matthew was lying on his bed across the room, just about managing to hear the scratchy voice on the radio.

He liked having his own little space. It was bigger now, from men transferring and Fletcher moving to the closest bunk to the washroom. Matthew had his bunk and the one next to him to himself, the way he liked it. Not from the lack of the other recruits trying, bar Fletcher. However, anytime they tried to talk he would only reply with brief answers, stopping the conversations from continuing. After several months, they stopped bothering altogether.

He did speak when he had to. When training or doing tasks he would certainly give his input. He would communicate, help anyone who had fallen behind, and he even took charge in some situations. Even Fletcher, with his unwillingness, would still listen to Cale's orders. But when they all came back to the camp, had their meals, sorted their kit, or just had some free time, he'd be on his own.

The sarge barged through the door. "Everyone outside now! Now! Now!"

They all jumped up from their beds and chairs and ran out of the dorm in mixed dress. Some stragglers were left behind trying to tie their boots while the sarge shouted in their ears.

Standing at attention in ranks of three, they listened to the sergeant's meaningful words.

"I know you all heard what happened."

They all stood silent.

"War is a terrible thing. But it is the choices and decisions you make, which can save the life of the men standing next to you, and your friends and family back home. Do you understand what I am saying?"

"YES, SERGEANT!" they shouted in harmony.

The sergeant looked at the strong men who he'd be deeply proud to serve with in this dire time. Composing himself, the sergeant went back into his performative manner. "Right then. Training stops now! Time to prepare for war. Twenty push-ups, go!"

Matthew breezed through the push-ups, and everyone else followed suit, only beginning to suffer during the last few. They hopped back to attention.

"What camp are you at!" the sergeant shouted.

"Moore, Sergeant!" they replied in unison.

"More? You all want more? Is that it. Then get back down and give me another twenty," he said, trying his best to hold in his smirk.

When they finished pressing their faces into the dirt, they formed back into ranks and started marching. They marched unflinchingly with perfect symmetry, unrecognizable to the rabble they had been eighteen months previously.

With a synchronized stomp of their boots, they halted at a very familiar spot of the mile. They had gone up and down it so many times, they could have done it blindfolded. Spreading out, the other recruits gave Cale some space. Although it was a bitter pill to swallow, even Fletcher stepped back from him.

"Go!" the sergeant shouted, then walked to his jeep. He would overtake them a few hundred feet ahead.

Matthew reached the top of the hill and saw the sarge looking at him unsurprised.

The sergeant had stopped looking at his stopwatch six months previously when the young private had passed the seven-minute mark. Fletcher would be the next to arrive, but not for at least another five minutes. This left the sergeant and Matthew a moment to talk.

He stuck out his hand holding a cigarette and gestured to Cale.

Matthew walked over eager to get his hands on the cigarette. He wasn't out of breath at all. He barely felt anything anymore from the runs. What used to be a pounding urge that made him feel alive, had turned to a numb tingle, like pins and needles from lying on his arm for too long. He ignited the cigarette and while taking a drag, wished he could feel how he used to; so invincible. He wished there was a way to feel like it all the time.

"I received your letter to transfer," the sergeant said. "82nd-airborne. Feel like jumping out of planes now, boy?"

Cale shook his head. "I've never even seen a plane, Sarge." Exhaling two streams of smoke from his nostrils, he continued, "It's just I don't feel anything here anymore. Maybe falling from the sky might give me some meaning to my life." Matthew's stomach churned. It was the most honest thing he had said to anyone for a very long time.

The sergeant nodded with a puzzled look. He could understand what he meant, but it wasn't the attitude he expected to hear from a young lad.

"Well it was a pleasure to meet you, Private Cale," he said, then shook his hand.

"Likewise, Sergeant."

Matthew packed his belongings and headed out of the dorm. He gave gentle nods goodbye to his fellow recruits, and some even gave him unexpected handshakes as he passed. When he approached the door, Fletcher slid in front of him, blocking the exit. They stared at each other silently for several unsocial seconds.

"You've got some kind of problem with me, haven't you?" Matthew finally said.

Fletcher shook his head, gritting his teeth. "I ain't got no problem with you." He leaned in close so no one else could hear. "There's something about you. It's not quite right," he said with twitching eyes, inspecting every detail on Matthew's face. He stood back up straight and buried his emotions. "I hope I never see you again. You're fast. I don't want to know how strong you are," he snarled, then moved out the way.

Matthew didn't think much of Fletcher's ramblings. *Some people just hate for no reason,* he thought to himself.

North Carolina. 82nd airborne. Paratrooper training.

Two miles became eight, and 7:00 am in the morning became

5:00 am. From working on the farm to now, Matthew's body had changed. His muscles pushed out from under his skin, giving him a bulkier frame compared to his slim past self.

He had finally figured out more about his unique ability. After ingesting alcohol, he never did have a sore head in the morning like the other paratroopers complained about. Or the feeling of stale alcohol in his stomach, wanting to eject itself back up from where it came. He could drink anyone under the table, with nothing more than a slight dizziness. Smoking didn't have an effect, and he never lost weight when he didn't eat, or gain any when he did indulge in the meals he liked. Dessert was his favorite.

The impurities in his body would leave before he could even feel them. He would lie in bed contemplating what the point was if nothing had any risk. Fortunately, he was training for the riskiest thing he could ever do.

NINE

June 3, 1944. In the late hours of the night, Private First Class Cale walked out of his tent. The air was cold in England compared to back home. Hunching over to keep warm, he lit a cigarette and quietly patrolled around the encampment.

He still hadn't aged a bit but his face was weathered more so than usual. Heavy bags were engraved under his eyes, his skin pale and rough from the cold and the minute amount of stubble piercing through his skin was sore and irritating.

He looked up at the clear sky. He stared up into the bright stars so hard that they lingered in his vision for a few seconds after he brought his head back down. Flicking the ash from the cigarette and seeing the orange glow float to the ground suddenly go dark, made him think of the first time he'd fallen from the sky.

Going up to the heavens in the basket of the barrage balloon had been terrifying. Having his theoretical life in the hands of a few wires keeping him in the air, shook him to his very core.

He was bunched up with a handful of other men in that

small space and every move they made swayed the basket from side to side. Occasionally, an arsehole recruit found it funny to jump while suspended a thousand feet up, making the basket bob up and down like a ship at sea. Standing with his toes hanging off the edge of the basket peering down at the earth he had never left before, was even more sickening.

He looked at the men still on the secure ground; so insignificant compared to the open landscape. He wondered what would happen if he stepped off without a chute, and let his weight slam back to earth. *Surely that would do the trick.*

But when Matthew gazed out in front to see the curvature of the world, all his fears and temptations evaporated and carried off with the wind. It was hard to believe that a hundred years ago, the only way to have seen this, would have been in his dreams tucked sweetly in bed. While at peace, he took a step forward and floated down on a parachute just like the beautiful orange ash.

Getting to the end of his cigarette, he stubbed it out on the heel of his boot and put it in his pocket. He heard movement to the left of him, between the gap of two tents. Feeling curious, he walked slowly through the narrow path, making as little noise as possible. Moving closer in he saw a baby-faced English soldier sitting on a supply crate with his legs close to his chest trying to stay warm.

The English soldier was so deep in his own thoughts he didn't see Cale approach him and only reacted when he spoke.

"You alright there, kiddo?" Matthew whispered.

He turned and a small gasp jumped from his mouth as he saw Cale emerge from the shadows. He looked him from top to bottom, scanning over his uniform, clueless over the different colors and symbols compared to his own. His face lit up in amazement, thinking Cale was some kind of war hero just at the sight of him and how he carried himself. Towering over him, broad shoulders and back up straight, projecting his strength without effort.

Cale smiled slightly, finally seeing the first person who looked younger than him in a long time.

"I'm fine, sir. Sorry, sir," the boy whispered in his squeaky voice.

"I ain't a sir, boy," Cale said smiling and shaking his head. He sat down next to the kid, who quickly shimmied over. Cale pulled out two cigarettes and handed one to the boy without giving him a choice.

Cale had got quite a name for himself for being stingy with his cigarettes, never giving any to anyone who asked. He would always answer the same way. "I haven't got enough. Sorry." Never trying to sound believable. Deep down he thought, why waste something on someone who was going to die? But this time he figured it might help the boy.

"Thank you," the boy said nervously, taking in a small puff trying his hardest not to cough.

Cale just sat there facing forward, looking into the darkness, squinting to see the tent ahead.

"Are you American?" the boy asked, still nervous.

"Yep," Cale replied.

"What's that symbol mean?"

Cale sighed, thinking that giving the boy the cigarette was enough and he could go on his way again. Looking at the boy, he pointed at the patches on his arm and spoke more welcomingly. "I'm in the 82nd airborne. Paratrooper."

The boy nodded with a blank look on his face.

"I jump out of planes, kid. You?"

"Uh, 3rd infantry division," he said shrugging.

Cale nodded as he had been briefed of the operation ahead and knew where this boy was being placed.

"Can I ask you a question?"

Cale looked over at him. "Haven't you been doing that already," he said smugly. "Go ahead, ask away," he said, caving in.

The boy leaned in closer to Cale; the night concealing his excited gaze. "What's it like? To jump out of a plane I mean."

Matthew rested his head gently on the tarp of the tent behind him and started to drift back to his first jump out of a plane.

The Douglas C-47 was a monstrous thing to behold. How humans could have invented such an amazing thing was unfathomable to Matthew. *Man had conquered the earth. Now they would conquer the sky,* Matthew thought while lying back in his seat in the plane rather than sitting since he was buried under all the equipment attached to him.

The thunder of the engine and the scenery moving slowly past the window made Matthew grow restless. The sound of the wind crashing into the metal rattled his brain. The feeling tripled as the wind came through the open door, echoing and bouncing around in the floating tube.

The plane turned blood red from the jump light. Pulling themselves up, they all hooked onto the guide rope. Standing in a line, Matthew thoroughly checked over the man in front and gave him the all-clear, praying that the man behind would do the same for him. Without warning, the plane went from blood red to a blinding green.

Looking forward, he saw men disappearing out of the plane quicker than he could blink. The men in front became fewer and fewer, and without noticing, his feet were shuffling forward. It was almost Matthew's turn. He glared up at his clip thinking if he was going to forget one thing, that wouldn't be it. He approached the doorway and saw a glimpse of the ground through the different shades of gray of the clouds hovering below.

The commander shouted in his ear, "Now!" and Matthew stepped out.

For the briefest moment, he felt like he was walking on air and that gravity was just a myth people had made up, to stop anyone from sprouting wings. He felt at peace. *Is this what heaven feels like?*

His smile was wiped off his face when the concrete wall of air collided with him, spinning him around and around. Or so he thought. He couldn't focus on anything; which way was up and which way was down? He even contemplated that he wasn't in the air anymore and his consumption of alcohol had caught up with him. Then he felt the sudden jolt of the parachute bring him back to his bearings. He held on tight and rested his cheek on one of the straps to say a silent thank you as it cradled him to the ground. He landed in the training field and ran the green blades of grass through his fingertips.

The couple of minutes he'd been in the air, felt longer than his entire life on earth.

Matthew stubbed the cigarette out on the side of the crate he was sitting on and again put it in his pocket. He wasn't going to make a mess in someone else's backyard.

The boy copied him, rubbing the outside of his pocket as he hadn't extinguished the flame probably. Keeping his hand on his pocket, he changed the subject. "Have you, have you killed anyone before?" he stuttered.

Cale stared forward into the darkness, his vision blurry, not focusing on anything. For whatever reason unknown to him, he decided to tell the truth. "Yes. Maybe. Hard to say. Both sides were shooting everywhere. But the man in my sight fell to the ground a split second after I pulled the trigger."

The boy slumped his shoulders in disappointment. He pictured Matthew standing with a gun in one hand and carrying a wounded soldier over his shoulder while firing at an entire platoon of Germans. "Oh," he said, not knowing how to respond to reality.

Matthew could see it wasn't the answer he'd expected and thought he could enlighten him, or at least prepare him for what was to come. "I've seen a lot of dead though." He leaned in a little closer to the boy making sure he was listening. "No matter how many you kill, boy, you'll see twice as many dead."

"This isn't how I imagined it," the boy muttered.

"How did you imagine it?" Matthew chuckled.

The boy shook his head. "I don't know. Smaller, fewer people. Everything went by so quickly. I was painting when I got my conscription letter. Now, I'm here."

Matthew scratched his head. Not knowing how to answer, he replied in the only way he knew. He took out another two cigarettes and handed one over.

The boy puffed on the cigarette more confidently.

As Matthew ignited his own cigarette. He saw the boy's hand appear out of the darkness and into his line of sight.

"I'm Thomas," he said with a smile finally on his face.

Matthew looked into the boy's eyes that were like a cloudless summer sky, yet with a hint of green.

He knew how this story would go. "It was nice knowing you,

kid," he said, exhaling, then quickly got up from the crate and left the way he'd come.

He regretted wasting the two cigarettes on the kid. Whatever advice Matthew had given to the boy, it had just been undone.

Morning, June 5, 1944. Matthew and the rest of his unit sat in a hangar, listening to the commander shouting their objective. Matthew wasn't paying much attention. He had heard the same speech more times than he could count. He understood what he was to do and knew he could achieve it. He passed the time by looking at the maps and markings of the other units' orders.

Utah and Omaha were the sections of Normandy beach the Americans would be landing on. *Suicide,* he thought. He knew he wasn't a military genius, but the experience he did have made him question their decisions. Back in Jackson, he had been defending. *Best to stay put, and let the enemy come to them.* This time he was attacking and unlike in Jackson, the defender had the high ground.

In this modern-day where they have grenades and automatic weapons, the men on the beaches wouldn't stand a chance. He thought it was ironic. If he hadn't transferred he would have been storming those beaches and probably would have been the only one who would have made it out alive.

Matthew and his unit geared up. Layers upon layers of pouches and straps, and topped off with his parachute. Then one last sack tied onto his front carrying his weapon, ammo, and equipment. He had two weapons on his person—the beautifully crafted Colt M1911 pistol and an M1 Carbine rifle. As he secured the bag to his chest and gave it a shake, he recited the attributes of the weapon to himself. *M1 Carbine; effective accuracy up to 200 yards. Firing thirty caliber rounds in a fifteen-round clip. Fitted with an iron sight and a folded stock. And fire rate of...* His mind went blank. It was on the tip of his tongue but he couldn't quite squeeze the number out of his mouth. Frustrated, he settled for *as fast as I can pull the fucking trigger.*

It was crazy how far weaponry had improved. From the long, bulky musket he'd been given in the Civil War, such that he could barely get off two shots per minute, to the Thompson submachine gun. He yearned to have it in his possession. If he'd had a Thompson back in Jackson, the north wouldn't have stood a chance.

The propellers of the C-47 started turning. Matthew stood in the queue, waiting to climb aboard. Out the corner of his eye, he saw the English soldiers moving to some trucks. He assumed they were heading closer to the coast, but he couldn't be certain. What he did know was what they were going into. He felt sorry for them; something he hadn't felt for anyone in a long time.

He caught a glimpse of Thomas. His shoulders were slumped and he was dragging his boots in the crowd of men all wearing the same brown uniform. Without thinking, Matthew stepped out of line.

"Cale, where are you going?" shouted a handful of men from his unit.

Not looking back but gesturing his hand for them to wait, he started running toward Thomas. No one else could run with all that weight and restricted movement, yet Matthew did it with ease. He barged past other soldiers like they weren't even there.

He grabbed Thomas by the back of his collar, pushing him out of the line on his toes.

Disoriented Thomas yelled out. "What are you doing! Get your hands off me!"

Matthew took him just out of earshot of everyone else.

Thomas calmed down slightly when he saw who it was. "It's you. I got to get on the truck," he spoke nervously again.

Matthew bent down looking him dead in the eyes. "Listen to me." He could see Thomas's eyes looking over at the other soldiers getting on the truck. He grabbed his head, forcing him to look at him. "Listen to me, Thomas. You get to the back of the boat. I don't care how you do it, just push your way through. When the door drops, stay low and wait until they finish firing. Then, climb over the side." He pulled at the straps on Thomas's waist, making them slack. "Drop your gear quickly. Swim fast."

Tears started running Thomas's face as he nodded.

Giving him a swift nod back, Matthew firmly rubbed away the tears and helped him onto the truck. Thomas looked back as the truck drove him away.

"The name's William," shouted the American.

It grew cloudy. Or was it just that Matthew was closer to the heavens? It was hard to tell. He could hear the rain smash on the plane like a hurricane. The plane shook with turbulence, wobbling the men's heads.

The twenty-four had all trained the same, yet had different ways of coping with stress and fear. Matthew sat second in from the tail. He glanced over at Smith who sat across from him. Matthew hadn't talked to him much. He was newly married with a little baby boy. His eyes were closed and there was sweat on his brow. He was taking in deep breaths, trying to remain calm.

To Matthew's right sat Jameson or was it Johnson? Matthew couldn't remember. A confident young man. Maybe not so confident today as he kept fidgeting in his space, tugging on his straps and chain-smoking his entire ration of cigarettes.

Finally, to the left at the rear of the plane, was Harper. The oldest man in the unit, excluding himself. Matthew liked Harper. He would talk to him the most. He'd been married for twenty-two years, with four children, two girls, and two boys. He'd got a letter a couple of weeks back, saying his oldest son just got drafted. Concealed in the darkness, Matthew could hear Harper muttering to himself peacefully.

"God, take care of my wife and children in these dark times.

Let them be shielded from the death and destruction in the world. Let them grow old and bear children of their own in a better world while I wait for them."

Matthew was confused. Why didn't he just pray to be safe himself? Matthew knew he would be safe. He didn't need to breathe to stay calm, smoke away his fears, or bargain with a worthless God. But looking at Harper in the darkness, he noticed he wasn't bargaining. He already believed it. His children would grow, get married, and have kids of their own and he would die.

The innards of the plane glowed red and the sound of gunfire echoed in the distance. The turbulence got progressively worse as they all clambered to their feet. Clipping their hooks to the guideline, Matthew checked over Harper's chute and the man whose name he couldn't remember.

A sudden burst of turbulence hit the plane from the side, making everyone stumble.

"Three minutes, boys!" shouted the commander at the front.

Matthew placed his hand on the cold steel of the plane to aid himself back onto his feet. Fear erupted from within him as he felt vibrations, creaks, and groans from the body of the plane. *The plane is going to go down.* He knew it in his gut. It wasn't a fear of dying, he had. Matthew couldn't die. Being stuck in a husk of twisted metal and dead bodies, unable to move, unable to think, and with no means of escape though; that would be worse than any death.

Matthew knew what to do. He pulled himself up straight and unclipped himself from the line. Words of confusion traveled forward in a ripple until they reached the commander.

The commander peered back through the red light, seeing Matthew standing straight with his cord wrapped around his arm.

"Private Cale! What are you doing! Get your hook back on the rope!"

Red-faced and sweaty, Matthew shook his head and nervously

shouted back, "We're not gonna make it, sir! We need to get out n–."

He was cut short by the turbulence that threw everyone onto the roof of the plane, crashing into the hard steel. The man whose name he couldn't recall died instantly from the impact. A shot beckoned from the dark void below, hitting the left engine and sending the plane into a volatile tumble.

Matthew grabbed onto anything he could as bodies, legs, and arms spun around inside the plane like a tornado. Their lines became intertwined together, making it impossible to escape. Smith fell out of the open door, but with his line still tangled, he just slammed into the outside of the plane repeatedly. The pilot and copilot terrified for their lives tried their best to get the plane under control. The commander's limp body fell into the cockpit, compressing the pilots to the glass and pushing the controls down.

Wails and screams bellowed from the soldiers ensnared in the cobweb of ropes and hooks. Broken limbs and contorted bodies made it impossible to escape their torturous fate, as the plane plummeted and spiraled toward the ground.

Matthew frantically clung onto a jagged piece of metal at the tail. He looked down at the men he had trained with for the past few years. All had been wiped out in a matter of seconds. His invisible scar started to burn, seeing the battered purple face of Harper with his cord wrapped around his neck. Matthew hoped his deal with God had been worth it.

The metal he was clinging to started to give way. This was his only chance.

He looked down and picked the clearest route through the maze of wires and bodies. He still wouldn't fit through the space with all his equipment attached. He was going to get an answer to his question. He unclipped the satchels from his front and his chute off his back, watching them fall and be tangled in the snare. He readied himself and put his training into action.

Letting go, he tucked in his arms, kept his legs together, and fell through the hanging graveyard.

The wind sucked him out the door like a ragged doll, spiraling around and around on his back. The deafening whistle as he fell from the sky drowned out the gunfire. Without a chute, he clamped his eyes shut anticipating the horrific pain or peaceful death to come while the cold wind stroked his face.

TEN

Wet, cold, and darkness. That was all Matthew could comprehend. Unable to move. Unable to breathe. He felt like he was back in his mother's womb, waiting to emerge. He tossed and turned the best he could to break free from whatever frozen hell he was in.

Finally, he was able to pull his head free into the light. He had fallen from the heavens and had been plunged deep into a dank bog. With his head out of the brown water, he spat out his mouth full of grime and earth. He pried his arms out of the sludge and clawed his way free from the bog onto the firmer ground beside him.

He lay on his front. His stomach convulsed, regurgitating whatever was rotting inside him. He struggled to get air into his lungs, still caked in a layer of filth. While learning how to breathe again, he looked up at the gray sky he'd fallen from, contemplating how long he had been buried in the wet dirt. Was it minutes, days, or could it have even been years? For all he knew, the war might already be over. But not knowing for sure, he pulled himself up onto his numb feet and proceeded with what he was trained to do.

He found himself a concealed ditch with bushes surrounding all sides and a tree growing overhead. Now, not concerned with being spotted, he tried to clean himself up the best he could. He made a small fire underneath the tree, stripped out of his wet clothes, and laid them down near the heat. Laying his pale bare skin on the ridge of the ditch and smoking his one and only salvageable cigarette to take the taste of swamp out of his mouth, he started stripping down and cleaning his Colt.

Now with his Colt in firing condition and his clothes dry, he was ready to move out. He had no clue where he was, so he just started walking in whichever direction felt comfortable. There wasn't much he could do. He just hoped to find someone or something that could help him. It was mundane walking through the woods, especially for him. He had nothing to keep his mind occupied, no one waiting for him when he got home, and nothing to fear where he was.

After all the years of being quiet in training, he now just wanted someone to talk to. Another voice to make him feel human. Again, the feeling of desperation that his abilities were meaningless went through his mind, as he put one foot in front of the other. Pushing through the thick brush in a direction he didn't know was starting to get to him. The dried mud on his clothes scratched and itched at his skin, making the journey even more tedious.

He kept his head pointed down, looking at his feet and began counting his steps. *One, two, three... ninety-six, ninety-seven.* Losing his footing on the uneven terrain made him lose count and start all over again. *One, two, three.*

The sun had started to set while Matthew was still walking and counting his steps, *Three hundred and fifty-four, three hundred and fifty-five.*

He stopped still as something appeared in front of his feet.

Crouching down to get a closer look at the ground, he finally figured out what it was. Footprints. His footprints to be exact. "Fuck!" he shouted sharply. His voice bounced against the trees. Standing up straight and failing to stay, calm he shouted again, "Shit! Fuck. God damn it." Kicking the fallen leaves around him, he suddenly went quiet, hearing the sound of twigs snapping.

Matthew turned around petrified. He looked closely through the trees to see where the noise had come from. Another twig snapped from a different direction, or did it? Sounds echoed through the woods he was surrounded by, making it impossible for him to know for sure. He kept spinning around to watch all directions, making himself dizzy. Then he heard it. A voice, speaking a language he had never heard before but he knew what it was. *German.* He dropped to his knees and pulled out his Colt, and with his best guess looked in the direction he thought the voice had come from.

Kneeling low to the ground, breathing slowly, and peering through the tree line, he waited quietly. His finger rested on the polished trigger. The voice got louder and clearer.

"Ruhig!"

Matthew turned sharply to the right, seeing a soldier in a dark gray uniform appear a hundred feet ahead. He was walking sluggishly in an unpredictable pattern with his weapon slung around his shoulder. He hadn't seen Matthew. His uniform still caked in mud made Matthew more concealed compared to his clean German opponent.

He stayed silent and observed the German soldier who was still looking down at his feet as he walked. It was almost like he too was counting his footsteps.

The German stopped and gestured with his arm behind him and shouted, *"Hier drüben!"*

Matthew was confused. He leaned out to look past the trees obscuring his vision.

Another soldier appeared and then a third. Walking up to the first, they started talking to each other.

"*Was ist es?*"

"*Fußabdrücke. Neun von ihnen vielleicht zehn. Einer von ihnen ist verwundet.*"

If Matthew was going to act, this was his chance. All bunched together and preoccupied, he could finish them all before they even raised their weapons. Lining the first man up in his iron sight, he was ready to push off his back foot and rush the other two. As he was about to pull the trigger, the first German gestured back again.

Matthew quickly huddled against the nearest tree. He peeked out with more frustration than when he had been walking in circles. He looked past the three Germans and saw them emerge. Over twenty more men clad in dark gray, weapons drawn and ready to fire.

Matthew's breathing became frantic. He could easily kill three unsuspecting men. Hell, he could kill ten without breaking a sweat. This wasn't because of the fear of dying, he couldn't die. No, this was a fear of being taken alive. He had heard the rumors of what they did to their prisoners, and he didn't feel like sharing the same fate for eternity. So, he decided to put the first part of his training into practice. Run.

Matthew ran as fast as he could. It was hard to get up any speed as he weaved in and out of trees and across the uneven terrain. The jagged branches ripped through his sleeves and tore into his skin as he shielded his face. He heard the Germans shouting behind him. He was not concerned about staying quiet. After what felt like forever running away, he finally saw an opening out of the thick brush.

He was almost free when his foot got snagged under a tree root. He fell face-first onto the ground, freeing his foot in the process, but not before hearing a loud crack from his ankle. He bit down on his tongue, resisting the urge to scream in agony. He could already hear sticks snapping from under the German boots. Looking down at his own, his right foot was twisted out at a forty-degree angle. He tried to move his toes but to no avail. He didn't have time for pain nor the time to let it heal. He swallowed his suffering, pulled himself up, and, without hesitation, continued running as before.

Breaking free of the woods and stepping out into a meadow, the knee-high grass shone in the sunset. Feeling the Germans' breathing on the back of his neck, Matthew kept running to the far side where the trees became thick again. He didn't notice the track he was leaving behind as he pushed through the tall grass or the sound from his ankle bones grinding together. He made it into the trees just as the Germans appeared from the woods behind. Thinking he might be safe, he thought he would change direction to get them off his trail. Yet before he could turn, something tackled him to the ground. It wouldn't have been so easy to take him off his feet if his injury wasn't making him unstable.

Disoriented as something lay on top of him, his heart went cold as he pondered how the Germans had caught up to him so quickly, loping ahead and luring him into a trap. What was going to happen at the camp he would be sent to? Would they find out his ability? Experiment on him? Slice open his brain to see what made him tick. Matthew started to panic at the horrible thoughts in his head, he tossed and turned to get a clear view of his assailant. When his attacker was finally in view, he wondered if being captured would have been better.

The American soldier who lay on top of him raised his index finger to his large lips and spoke softly, "Shhh."

Matthew didn't care. He was too fixated on the darkness of the soldier's skin. Matthew had a ferocious look in his eyes as he stared back at the dark-skinned man whose sweat was glistening in the setting sun. *Why is there a nigger here?* he thought.

Knowing the Germans were fast approaching, he kept his cool and with ease simply lifted the man off of him with one hand.

They both crawled until their backs hit a tree each. They were hidden from the Germans walking through the grass. Matthew pulled out his Colt and kept an eye on both the Germans and the man who'd jumped him. They had nowhere to go. Even with a second man with an M1 Garand, it would still be a risk to confront the twenty well-armed men—even if the second man was expendable.

Again, but with less of a surprise, more twigs started to snap. A large sinister grin appeared on Matthew's face as ten other American soldiers peeked through the trees, fully armed and ready to fire and with a more respectable skin tone. Matthew turned back to face the approaching German infantry with confidence, grinding his teeth in excitement. He felt like he was back in Jackson, but this time he knew he would win this battle. Without any order or acknowledgment of his fellow soldiers, he peeked out from behind his cover and calmly fired at the closest German.

The German's lower jaw collapsed from the impact of the shot. The other Germans in confusion raised their weapons in all directions. A moment later, the percussion orchestra of automatic and semi-automatic weapons emerged from the tree line. The sound radiated out in an arc across the field, then changed into a soft thud when it collided with the unfortunate German soldiers.

Some of the Germans fired back blindly, in a brave attempt to suppress their opponents. Yet their shots just embedded themselves into the thick bark of the shielding trees. Except for one that found its way into Matthew's side. With the sting of the round sinking into his flesh, he pulled himself up and advanced on the several remaining German soldiers. Limping on the heavily blood-soaked grass, Matthew picked off the survivors one by one and emptied his Colt into the wounded. As he entered the center of the field and saw the last remaining German fleeing back from where he came, Matthew quickly pried a rifle from a bloody corpse. He didn't think to go over the characteristics of the weapon.

He blinked, trying to focus on the weapon he had just picked up, but it was no use. He glared down to see a musket in his hands, and the body he'd taken it from was nowhere to be seen. He slowly looked around but the dead, the blood, and his allies had all vanished. He stood alone in the middle of the field, entwined in long grass with a soft breeze brushing the nape of his neck.

The colors were vibrant and too bright to stare at for long. It was almost like he had stepped into an oil painting. He tipped his head back down to see himself dressed in Confederate gray. The uniform was immaculate; handcrafted with an extraordinary amount of care. The gold buttons soaked up the sunlight, the fabric pressed to perfection, and not a stitch out of place on the gold embroidery that covered the sleeves. This uniform was only fit for a god and Matthew relished it.

He snapped his head to the left when he saw something move in the corner of his gaze. It was a man fleeing for his life. Matthew could hear his heavy breathing and the sound of the grass crumpling under his feet. No matter how fast the man could run, he wouldn't escape Matthew's wraith.

Matthew raised the primed musket, pulled back the hammer, and with both eyes open he fired and followed through with the shot.

The German fell to the ground and Matthew found himself back into what he mused was the real world. Strange occurrences had started to affect him less and less, therefore, he carried on with his next plan. Occupied with scavenging ammunition and weapons from the dead and finishing off any remaining wounded who had got this far, Matthew didn't hear the allied soldier approach him.

"Private!" shouted the man.

Matthew hunched down, rummaging through the pockets of the dead, and took no notice of the voice. "Private!"

After searching several more bodies, Matthew's eyes lit up when his fingertips touched the top of what he was looking for inside a blood-soaked front pocket of a dead German. The look of glee jumped onto his face as he wriggled out an almost full pack of cigarettes. "Yes," he whispered to himself in delight, opening up the packet and igniting one without hesitation.

"PRIVATE!" the man hollered.

Matthew finally took notice of the voice.

Talking with his lungs full of smoke, he smugly replied, "Private Cale First Class, 82nd airborne division."

The surprised look on the man's face became apparent when Matthew turned and stared at him with a blank expression.

"Sergeant," Matthew said with a subtle nod, looking into the eyes of the man who had taken him through infantry training.

The other soldiers gathered around and listened in to the conversation.

"It's good to see you, Private, but where did you come from?" Sarge said.

"I was with the first wave of airborne to drop. Our plane went down. I'm the only one who made it." Murmurs of doubt came from within the group of soldiers.

Matthew scolded them; his eyes bulged out of their sockets. He could sense what they were talking about. *Deserter? I'm the best chance these men have got to get home alive,* he said to his ego.

"If you've got something to say then say it," he said, spinning around to look at them all.

"No one is saying anything, Cale," the sergeant replied, defusing the situation before it started. "It's just." He paused and scratched his stubbly cheek. "It's been nine days since the initial assault. The guys, me included, were just wondering where you've been all this time."

Matthew's gut twisted into a knot. Again, he had lost days without knowing. This time spending it in a shallow wet grave. "Well, I can't really say. I lost all my gear in the crash. I didn't have a map, and so I just kept walking. Now, here I am," he promptly said.

"Well, lucky we came across you," Sarge said.

"Lucky you did," Matthew replied, changing the meaning of the statement and taking a quick glance at the black soldier.

"Right, everyone, move out," the sergeant ordered. Everyone dispersed, bar one whose face was also very familiar.

"Fletcher," Matthew said, feeling smug by the fact he was coping with the war better than him. Fletcher said nothing. He just stood there with sloped shoulders and a nervous facial expression, clutching onto his Thompson machine gun. He walked off and joined the other men.

The sergeant looked down at the blood on Matthew's jacket. "You hurt, Private?"

Matthew could already feel the wound closing with a numb sensation.

"Not my blood, Sarge," he said with conviction, gripping his German rifle in his hands. "Ready to move when you are, Sergeant."

Sarge moved off to lead his men.

Matthew took one step forward to follow, then realized what he needed to do. He turned his foot inside and rested all his weight onto his ankle until he heard the bone crunch back into place. He clenched his jaw, holding in the pain. The pain switched to anger as he walked off staring at the back of the black man's head.

"Sergeant!" Fletcher shouted, back from behind the tree.

"What is it, Soldier?" he replied as he approached.

"It's Marcus, sir. He didn't make it." Fletcher's eyes began to well up.

The sergeant knelt down to console him, placing a hand on Fletcher's shoulder and whispered in his ear. "I'm sorry, Fletcher, but there's not much we can do for him here. He was a good soldier. He did it well to make it this far." He gave Fletcher a firm pat on his back and carried on.

Fletcher wiped away his tears, leaned over Marcus's body, and gracefully unclipped his dog tag. His eyes burning red, he looked up to see Private Cale looming in the distance.

It was amusing for Matthew to watch the boy so strong, now sat broken, whimpering over someone he barely even knew.

Fletcher's pupils contracted and he clenched his fists. He grabbed his weapon and quickly scurried off to join the front of the group.

Matthew, like a vulture, walked over to the body. He dropped his German weapon and picked up Marcus's rifle that lay beside him. "I need this more than you," he said with an unsympathetic tone. *M1 Garand, effective accuracy up to 500 yards. Firing 30-06 caliber rounds in an eight-round clip.*

Matthew trailed to the back of the group, keeping a watchful eye on the black man. *Why was he here? What is he up to?* These were questions he needed answering for the safety of the other men.

One of the soldiers started whistling a soft tune, drawing Matthew's attention away. He was a scrawny kid, barely an ounce of meat on him. Confident and eager to prove himself, he kept bouncing up and down with his tune.

"Peters! What did I say about music, boys?" the sergeant hollered.

"Sorry, Sarge," Peters replied, then shortened his step until he was level with Matthew. "How is it going? The name's Peters. I've got to say, it was mighty impressive how you ran out under fire back there."

"Cale. Nice to meet you, Soldier," he said, eyes fixed back on his target.

Peters kept blabbering on to Cale, which went through one ear and out the other. After a few minutes, he took the hint and started walking ahead again.

Cale grabbed his arm and yanked him. "Peters." He leaned in close so no other could hear. "Who's the nigger?" Cale asked, gesturing with a flick of his head.

"Who? Private Hallis? We lost our interpreter a week ago. He's our replacement."

Cale nodded. "Good to know," he said then pushed Peters forward again. *Hallis. That's the nigger's name*, he thought with rage. *He shouldn't be here. Hell, if all his kind were here then we wouldn't have to be here.* He smiled. This kind of delusional thinking kept Cale occupied for several hours until they stopped to make camp.

The nine soldiers sat in a circle, hidden by the trees. A small fire had been made in the middle for warmth. Cale sat further out, messing up the neat circle. He wanted a clear view of them in his vision, especially Hallis. They weren't taking much notice of Cale even being there. As they chatted away to each other, he listened in to their conversations.

"How many Krauts you killed?" Peters said to another soldier who looked up in thought and counted on his fingers.

"Uh, six for sure," he replied.

"Impressive. What about you, Fletcher?"

Fletcher shook his head. "Not sure."

Peters asked the next man in the circle.

"You couldn't count that high if I told you," replied one of the older men in the group. He was a short, bulky fella, whose lips always pointed down, even when he smiled. Pops was what they called him. He chuckled and the others followed. Even Cale smiled at the concept.

Peters asked the sarge, who was lightly resting his eyes, the same question. "What about you, Sarge?"

The sergeant opened his eyes and stared at the fire. "I don't know. I have killed. I know that for certain. But every man I kill is just another widow I create. A child growing up without a father. Or taking a child from their mother." He looked up at the soldiers all listening intently. "We've just got to get the job done. The less I kill, the more I save, and a bigger part of me gets to move along with time. Don't worry though. I will protect the lives of my men before anything else."

"Thank you, Sarge," the men replied with admiration.

"Family is the most important thing in the world. Keep that in your mind while you're here and you'll see them again."

The impact his words had on the men could be seen on their hopeful but morbid expressions. Changing the subject, the sergeant saw Hallis sitting quietly. "What about you, Hallis? Got any family back home?"

Cale lifted himself up. He wanted to hear what Hallis had to say for himself. He had to be in his early thirties. He was a tall slender man. His uniform didn't fit him probably. The cuffs were cut off an inch before covering the wrist.

Hallis was nervous about getting a question directed to him. None of them had been horrible but he could tell they had been keeping their distance. "Uhm, yes, sir. Wife and newborn baby girl, sir," he said short and sweet.

"What are you hoping to do when you get out of here?"

Hallis started to relax in front of the group, answering in more detail. "Well, sir. I have some plans. But all I want is to kiss my wife and hold my daughter for the first time. Sir."

Cale had heard enough of the man's rambling. He tipped the contents out of a German canteen he had looted behind his back. "Hey! You like water, nigger? Fill this up," Cale barked and tossed the canteen at Hallis's feet.

Hallis slumped back and looked at the sergeant for advice.

The sergeant turned his gaze toward Cale. "Right, I think it's time for you all to get some sleep. I'll fill that, Hallis," the sergeant said, taking hold of the canteen. "Everyone get their heads down. I'll keep the first watch."

Murmurs of annoyance came from the men.

Cale didn't care, just so long as Hallis had stopped talking.

One by one, they took turns taking guard while the rest of them tried to get some rest. No matter where they lay, the ground was cold and damp. Sticks and rocks dug into their backs, and insects crawled across their faces. Yet still, they slept like they were sleeping on feather mattresses.

"Jerry!" hollered the soldier on guard, firing a burst of his rifle.

Everyone jumped up from their uncontrollable slumber, grabbed the weapons, and began scanning the area for movement.

The trees were dense and the night was dark. They could barely see a hand in front of their faces. "Soldier, fall back," the sergeant shouted to the man on guard.

Huddled against the trees or laying low on the ground, the men waited for the sergeant's orders.

"Hold your fire, men. Wait for my signal!" he said. His voice was solid and unwavering. It went quiet. Only the ambient sound of the trees creaking could be heard. Cale forced his eyes through the thick void, softly holding on to his weapon. His breath steady, he listened and waited for the intruders.

He caught a glimpse of movement in the distance and fired off several shots into the darkness, absorbing the full force of the recoil.

"Hold your fire!" the sergeant ordered.

Cale didn't listen. He sprung up and ran toward his target. He wasn't going to run away again.

"Cale! Cale! Get back here, Private!"

The sarge's voice faded more and more the further Cale went. Weaving in and out of the trees, he ran at his top speed. He jumped over the dead body of the man he had fired upon, tackling his second victim. The amount of force that Cale projected broke the man's back in an instant. Cale knelt on top of his neck to finish the job while firing at the other fleeing soldiers. The iconic sound of the M1 Garand clip ejecting from the top made a piercing ring in his eardrums.

"*Ami!*" shrieked one last German, holding his ground, and barely visible in the void.

Cale launched his empty rifle at him knocking him over.

The German fired his weapon into the air.

Cale ran over and disarmed him with a swift kick to the hand. Then he sat on top of him and repeatedly pummeled his face with his bare hands.

"Cale! You alright?" the sergeant asked as him and the rest of the unit approached. He stood speechless seeing Cale crouched down in the middle of five dead men, his hands caked in blood. Cale said nothing in return. He just stayed there rubbing the blood between his fingers and picking the hair and skin from under his nails.

"Hey, come look at this," Pops said, pointing down at the ground and flicking open his lighter.

The others were all at a loss for words. The horror on the men's faces shimmered with the glow of flame, seeing the caved-in face of a German soldier. It didn't look remotely human. It was just a pile of crushed skull fragments and brain matter.

"How did he do that?" Pops whispered.

The sergeant pulled his attention back to Cale. "Private! Soldier!" he shouted, finally getting a response.

Cale's eyes were hollow like a rabid animal's. No joy or hope, just relishing in the violence and anger before him. "The rest went that way," he said, calmly pointing his blood-soaked fingers in their direction. "They couldn't have gone far; we can leave in the morning. We'll run into them sooner or later."

The sergeant stayed silent.

Cale stood up and made his way back to the campsite. The men gave him a wide berth as he passed. He stopped short next to Peters. "There's another five for my list."

ELEVEN

Morning came and they became the hunters, following the tracks that had been made last night. Cale marched forward with the others struggling to keep up. He wasn't walking in circles nor was he counting his footsteps. He wasn't thinking much of anything. He just knew one thing; he wanted to kill again. Nothing came close to the feeling of taking another man's life. It was so permanent. The only thing that couldn't be taken from him.

Cale was right. They hadn't gone far. Two miles after breaking out of the woods, they came across an abandoned farmhouse. There was no sign of movement through the broken windows. They waited and watched far enough away for the sergeant to make the next plan of action.

They had been waiting for half an hour. Cale was starting to get impatient. *I could have done it on my own by now.* Staying low, he walked over to the sergeant. "What's the plan, Sarge?"

The sergeant ignored Cale's presence and turned to face everyone. "Right, here's the plan. We are three miles from the closest camp," he said, looking at his map. "We came from the north; camp's south. If there's no one in the building, they're long gone by now. But we have to check and make sure." He sighed. This was the hardest part. He wanted to make the right decision. Attack the enemy, who were better positioned, try to take them prisoners, or simply walk away? All choices risked the lives of his men.

The sergeant pointed at Pops and two others. "You three. I want you to go through the main entrance. Pops, you take the lead. Peters and Hallis, I want you to circle around and go in through the back."

"I got another idea, Sarge," Cale intervened.

"Not now, Private. I hope your German is up to scratch, Hallis. If you can, you give them one chance to surrender and avoid any more bloodshed. Alright, men. Get ready. Everyone else will keep guard outside. Fletcher, I want you to keep your eyes on the front door like a hawk."

They prepared themselves to move out. They took off any extra gear and made sure their weapons were ready to fire.

"Sarge, if I may," Cale said, not really giving him an option. "If I go through the back, I'll take them all out. If they try to run, they'll run into you," he said without a shred of doubt.

The sergeant shook his head. "Plan's already set. As long as everyone follows the orders, everything will go alright."

Cale didn't like his answer. He raised his voice back at the sergeant. "You going to risk people's lives by depending on this nigger?" he said, pointing at Hallis with dried blood still under his fingernails.

"Private Cale!" the sergeant snarled and walked right up to

him. Their noses were an inch from each other. "You defile the corpses of fallen soldiers, and you disobey my orders. Now you disrespect my men. You're making this very difficult to control. This is all our war."

Cale admired the sergeant for standing up to him but didn't listen to a word he said. Cale walked off like a spoiled brat not getting what he wanted.

The sergeant wiped his brow. "When you're ready, men."

The five soldiers entered the farmhouse. The rest waited quietly, watching the front door and windows.

Cale watched, frantically tapping his foot. "Fuck this!" he shouted. He wasn't going to go along with the sergeant's plan any longer. Standing up, he started to take off any gear he didn't need. "I'm not going to just sit here and do nothing." He placed his rifle on top of his gear and marched over to Fletcher. Without saying anything, he grabbed the Thompson he had strongly desired. Fletcher tried to resist, but Cale gave him a firm shove, putting him back on his ass and losing his grip on the weapon. Cale's eyes were scorched with violence; nothing was going to stop him from getting what he wanted.

Fletcher started to tremble.

"Pathetic," Cale muttered under his breath and started to approach the house, checking over the beautiful Thompson as he went. *Thompson submachine gun. Effective range, 160 yards. Firing .45 rounds in a twenty-round magazine.*

"Cale! Stop right there! That's an order, Private!" screamed the sergeant, lifting up his pistol as he did so.

"You going to shoot me, Sarge?" Cale said with a complete lack of emotion. The sergeant lowered his weapon and Cale continued toward the house. "I'd like to see you try," Cale said to himself with a smile.

He pressed his back against the wall next to the door. He

spun around and with a swift kick, smashed the door off of its hinges and stepped into the dilapidated living room. Pops and the other two soldiers spun around, pointing their weapons at the unsuspected intruder.

"Cale, what the fuck are you doing here?" Pops whispered.

Another bang rattled from an unguarded door as a German soldier barged out and another sprung up from behind a knocked-over table. They both sent out a hail of bullets at their enemy. The first two American soldiers dropped to the floor. Pops took several extra rounds before eventually falling himself.

Cale didn't falter, shrugging off the rounds that hit him in his legs, arms, and chest. He sprayed the Thompson from his hip in an arc across their stomachs. Their insignificant bodies collapsed to the floor, accompanying Pops and the other two American soldiers.

Cale stood over Pops' body, attempting to feel some remorse for the man. "He was never going to make it," he said. He was taken aback by the fact he had spoken in his southern accent. His confusion was cut short, however, when a round whizzed past his head, grazing the top of his ear and taking a chunk of flesh with it. Cale reoriented himself to face his new adversary.

The man stood with pale lifeless skin. He had slicked-back hair, yet if he let it grow, he would have had long thick locks the color of wheat. Standing half foot taller, Cale had to crane his neck to look him in his deep blue eyes.

The Aryan smiled and graciously placed his pistol gently on the dining table, then brandished a large six-inch knife from his belt.

Cale brazenly dropped his weapon, still with enough rounds to easily dispatch any soldier. *This will be fun.* Turning side on to the Aryan and raising his guard, he gave him an inviting nod. With a menacing grin, the Aryan lunged forward too quick for Cale to react, slashing him on his forearm. He taunted Cale with his blade and cackled to himself.

Failing to grab the blade again, Cale received a deep gash to his fingers. This was followed up with several more swipes, delivering cuts to his chest and stomach.

Cale took a step back, covered in open wounds that would have dropped any other man. He remained calm and steadfast, rejecting the notion of pain. The Aryan lunged his blade once again, producing a severe laceration under Cale's arm. Blood sprayed out onto the Aryan's face and across the floor. Still, Cale didn't react. He simply kept his gaze fixed on his now panting adversary. He could see those deep blue eyes beginning to waver.

The Aryan tossed his useless knife to the floor, let out a desperate scream, and charged.

Cale readied himself for the impact, adjusting his footing.

Wrapping his arms around Cale's waist, the Aryan used all his might to slam him onto the floorboards. He tugged one way and then the other, trying to move Cale's smaller frame, but his body wouldn't budge.

Time to end this, Cale thought, simultaneously delivering a swift knee to the man's face.

He staggered back, blood pouring out of his newly broken nose. He made a fist and threw it at Cale, who simply batted it away with his palm and punched him in the ribs. He stumbled further backward, coughing up blood as he retreated into the kitchen.

Cale advanced. "Face me, coward," he said to the fleeing German, who was scrambling over the dead. Cale went for his finishing blow.

The Aryan quickly grabbed his discarded knife and plunged it straight into Cale's side. Smiling at the thought he'd been victorious, he twisted the blade in deeper.

Cale blinked. He looked down and saw only the handle protruding. He could feel the tip scratching his liver. He pried the man's hand off the handle, breaking his wrist like a twig. The man screamed in agony and terror as Cale pulled out the large blade and placed it firmly on his neck.

"*Was bist du?*" he said through his weeping.

Cale had a hunch about what the man had said. He pulled him up by his collar and the Aryan flinched when Cale leaned in. "I'm disappointed in you." Cale pushed the man as hard as he could. The farmhouse shook on its foundation, and the wall cracked as the Aryan flew into it. His body went limp, falling face-first to the floor. Cale stretched out the blade in his hand, slitting the already dead man's throat as he fell, letting gravity do the work.

He placed the knife next to the pistol on the table and picked up his Thompson. Dust sprinkled from the ceiling. Cale approached the staircase, tilting his head. He could hear the subtle sounds of nervous breathing. He knew that they knew he was there. With each step going up, he pressed his heel, making sure the floorboards creaked. *Whoever's up there must be shitting themselves,* he thought, imagining some poor sod hiding in a corner.

A young German soldier with a bloody bandage around his head stood nervously pointing an MP40 at a wounded black American soldier. They could hear screams and gunfire from the floor below. His face was pale, body shivering and heart pounding as he heard the floorboards creak. He prayed silently, hoping it would be someone friendly.

A white American soldier appeared, looking very relaxed under the circumstances. Standing calm with his weapon pointing down, he waited for the German to respond.

"*Ich wollte nicht, dass das sie tötet!*" he shouted, rattling his gun at Hallis, who was lying on the floor.

Cale scoffed. After all the commotion downstairs, he had forgotten Hallis even existed. Cale kept his eyes trained on the young German as he talked to Hallis. "You speak German. What did he say?"

Hallis groaned through the pain of the wound to his stomach. "He said, it wasn't his idea to attack. He didn't want to kill anyone."

Cale glanced to his right. He became irritated when he saw the fresh body of Peters collapsed on the floor with his head caved in.

"*Amerikaner!*" the German shouted erratically.

Cale snapped his head back.

"*Du lässt mich jetzt gehen. Oder krank töten die nigger!*"

Cale's head perked up. "What did he say?" he said, again talking to Hallis without looking at him.

"Let him go." Hallis paused to catch his breath. "And he'll let me go free."

Finally, Cale turned his gaze and acknowledged Hallis's existence. "That's not what he said."

Hallis's skin started to go white from the loss of blood. He then lost a part of his soul when he interpreted the words of the German. "You let me go now or I'll kill the nigger," he said coughing up blood.

Cale's disgusting grin was priceless from getting what he wanted. Taking a satisfied breath he started to speak, too fast for Hallis to interpret. "You're shit at bargaining, you know that? You see, I don't give a shit about that nigger on the floor. So, what the fuck makes you think I'd give a shit about you?" He paused for his own dramatic effect. "You're going to die here, boy, but I'll give you a chance to leave." He dropped the smile off his face and directed his speech to Hallis. "Tell him to shoot me."

Hallis stayed silent.

"Say it!" Cale snapped.

Still, Hallis remained silent.

"Say it or I'll shoot you!" he shouted pointing his Thompson at Hallis.

"*Erschieß ihn,*" Hallis mumbled.

"Say it again!"

"*Erschieß ihn.*"

"Keep fucking saying it. I want him to shoot me."

"*Erschieß ihn!*" Hallis shouted louder, tears running down his face. *What have I got myself into? This is too big for me.*

The German trembled in his boots, flicking his target between Hallis and Cale after each of them spoke. *Worauf habe ich mich eingelassen? Das ist mir zu groß.*

"Private Hallis! I'm ordering you to tell him to shoot me." Cale peered down the iron sight ready to fire. "This is your last chance. Do something in your worthless God-damned life. Tell him to shoot me, nigger!"

126

"*Erschieße ihn um Himmels Willen!*"

The German fired.

Hallis covered his ears and closed his eyes.

Cale felt the rounds tear through his flesh. The cold air filled the holes in his chest and stomach. It was slow but it wasn't painful. He could see the anguish on both of their faces as he fell to the floor on his hands and knees. He was almost at peace. Sadly, the inevitable happened when the German's weapon was empty.

Hallis opened his eyes and uncovered his ears. They both waited for the smoke to settle. They remained silent as they watched Cale groaning on the floor.

He pulled himself back up onto his feet, wheezing from the shots that had pierced his lungs. Staring at the two men with their bewildered faces, he thought to himself, *What have they got themselves into? This is too big for them.*

He took a step closer to them and raised his weapon. "You missed," he said, swirling the taste of iron around in his mouth with his tongue. He fired the two rounds he had left in his Thompson directly into the German's heart. Cale stepped over to the man to make sure he was dead. Satisfied with what he saw, he turned his attention to Hallis.

Cale looked into Hallis's eyes. A smile started to grow on Hallis's face. Cale didn't return the gesture. Without saying a word, Cale pulled out his Colt and slowly pulled on the trigger.

The other men waited with the sergeant, not knowing what to do. They got up from the mud when they saw Cale strutting out of the farmhouse. He made his way over to the sergeant and handed him five dog tags. Annoyed by the sergeant's silence, Cale spoke. "You sent them in there. Your choice. Your decision. You killed them." He chucked Fletcher back his weapon and picked up his own. "Ready to move when you are, Sarge!" he said as if nothing had happened.

Everyone started to move out. They didn't notice Cale's wounds. He had taken another shirt from one of the white American soldiers whose name he had already forgotten.

TWELVE

Adam's story had taken a very dark turn. Joanna sat uncomfortably in her chair, unsettled at what she had just heard. Adam was a very different man from the one she had first met. He was impatient and short-tempered. After hearing about Adam's past, it seems she didn't know him either. She knew Adam hadn't shared everything yet, nor the reason why he was showing remorse.

"Four men died because of me. Then I murdered a fifth," he said, looking down at his feet.

She understood about having to kill during a time of war. But taking Hallis's life was something completely different. She was at a loss for words. She had never come across something as serious as murder before. "Why?" she asked.

"I refused to think about why. I hid the truth from myself." He felt ashamed and scratched at his face. "He knew my secret and he was black. That's what I kept telling myself."

She leaned in close but slightly cautiously. "I still don't know why you're telling me this. Why are you here?"

"I'll get to that. In time." Adam was more open in sharing now. He pulled at the chain of the pocket watch and looked at the second hand flicking forward. "Time is the one thing I have plenty of."

He had only been telling his story for an hour. The day was going slow. Time always goes slow for Adam.

It was difficult for Adam to recount the events after Normandy. He traveled for some time. He certainly didn't want to go back to Jackson, Mississippi, hearing the prohibition was still going strong. "Ridiculous thing to even start," he quoted from memory. But even when he was able to get his hands on liquor, it would never compare to the excitement of battle.

Luckily for him, it didn't take long for another war to appear. "There's always a war," he said with sympathy for humanity. "There haven't been many years of peace in this world." He sparked up a cigarette, offering one to Joanna who declined.

"People must love killing, I guess," she said, not liking how true the sentence sounded.

Adam exhaled. "Some people are even good at it."

The Korean war was next for Adam. "Jerries, niggers, gooks. It didn't matter to me. As long as I had a gun in my hand, I was happy." Again, he quoted from his violent past, hating himself as he said it. "Do you know what it's like to kill someone?" he asked.

Joanna shook her head.

"I know the feeling." His nose and top lip started to curl as he continued. "It's like listening to music and then pulling the power cord. You can remember the beat, the drop, and the hook in your head. But you'll never actually hear it again. Then it all starts to fade away, like what's that song. I can't remember how it goes."Adam noticed how uncomfortable Joanna had become. "I'm sorry. I've lived for a long time. Too long. Things get a bit hazy." He paused for a moment, checking if Joanna was okay. "I am right though. Killing. Silence. The world would be a more musical place without killing."

"Would you like to continue?" Joanne asked with her nerves settled.

Adam nodded, stubbing out half a cigarette.

"So, what was next?" she asked.

Adam sighed and tapped his middle finger on his temple. "Like, I said. There's always a war."

THIRTEEN

1964. Matthew. Marcus. Peter. The man who couldn't die nor grow old used many names throughout his time at war. He spent the tedious time between war traveling, state to state. Eventually, he made his way to New York City, where he now sat in a chair inside a recruitment building. He was grateful that no one seemed to ask any questions about his cloudy past. *They've got more important things to be dealing with,* he thought. He couldn't wait to get back out there again, so he made sure to be on his best behavior. Blocking out the black men in the room from his mind, the man who had gone by many names tried to focus on finding another.

He scanned his eyes over the propaganda mounted on the wall. *Fight for your country,* the man said in his head, reading the words off one of the posters. The words were colored red, white, and blue. He grunted in disfavor of the quote.

After the first couple of years of war, he had forgotten he was even fighting as a country. He hadn't cared about his country for a long time, it hadn't done anything for him. Now, he only fought for himself, using his ability to kill. Killing was the only thing that made him feel alive. The time between the wars was a war upon itself. He was forced by law not to partake in the only thing he was good at.

Fight for family! Fight for freedom! read the poster above his head. Again, he didn't care for the inspiring slogan, barely even remembering what the words meant.

Family. A slow damp drawling voice emerged from within his mind. He flinched in his chair. *What was that voice?* he thought.

You have no family. Freedom. No one can take your freedom away from you. The voice was making the man dizzy. He rubbed at his eyes and brushed back his hair that had grown too long.

To keep his mind steady, he observed the two white men sitting across from him and listened in to their conversation.

They were both young with shaved heads. One was slumped in his chair, eyes closed, legs crossed, and arms folded. The other was sat up straight, rapidly tapping his thighs.

"Hey!" said the excited one, tapping the slumped man with his elbow.

"What is it, Jenkins?" the other replied.

"I heard about this soldier who fought the gooks."

The slumped man sighed, opened his eyes, and turned to listen.

"The unit was completely outnumbered. They were forced to retreat. It was every man for himself." Jenkins kept flinging his arms around and shifting the tone and pitch of his voice. "But this one man charged right at the enemy, dancing and weaving through their bullets. He killed over thirty men, and most with his bare hands."

"Yeah, yeah," the other retorted. "It's just a story."

"A true story. I heard it from a guy who saw it happen. The man was able to save his whole unit, and I'll tell you another thing."

The slumped man rolled his eyes as Jenkins continued.

"You're gonna hear a story like that about me in this war," Jenkins said, holding his head high.

"Yeah, well, if that happens, I'll be clapping and cheering as you run toward a bunch of Vietcong shooting at you," the other said, turning his head away and shutting his eyes.

Jenkins slumped in his chair. "Jeez. I was just telling a story."

Story. The man who couldn't die started talking to himself. *Just a story. No one can dodge bullets and I wasn't trying to save anyone.* His attention was drawn to the poster that rested above the two men. It was outdated and hadn't aged well. The corners had ripped, and vertical and horizontal creases lined it where it had been folded. They had encased it in a frame to preserve what was left, but that didn't protect it from the sun. The man did agree with its slogan, bar one word: *Want.*

The strange voice rose again from the deep corners of his mind. *Want. No. Need. They need you.*

His brain felt like it was going to explode. The voice crawled under his skin, tugged at his organs, and nibbled at his flesh.

"You there. You're next," the recruitment officer said, pointing his finger. "State your name."

With a slight pause, the man who had gone by many names answered, "Sam Jenkins."

The officer escorted Sam into the examination room. "Take a seat there, boy."

Sam followed his instructions. The officer walked to the other side of the small room, meeting up with a nurse who carried on with the examination.

Oh, there's another one of those things, said the voice, as Sam saw the contrast between the nurse's flesh and her white gown.

"Mr. Jenkins, you didn't write much on your documents," she said, flicking through his paperwork. She wrote his name at the top, which he had left blank. "Besides not putting a name, you didn't put down where you're from."

"I'm from here," he interrupted.

"Very well." She jotted down his vague answer.

Sam looked at her hourglass figure from head to toe.

Mmm, she might actually be beautiful if it wasn't for her skin, the voice muttered again moist and sticky. Sam tried his best to ignore it.

"What about next of kin?"

"None," he said, short and sweet.

"None? No relatives? You don't have anyone close to you?"

Sam shook his head. "Nope. None." He wasn't about to share anything with her kind.

She flicked through his paperwork again. "What I'm getting from your documents is, you have substantial knowledge about weaponry and that your fitness is…" The nurse raised her eyebrows and brought the paperwork closer to her face. "Well, let's just say it's impressive."

"Let's." Sam was getting tired of the insignificant questions.

"For your occupation, you put soldier."

"It will be after you sign my papers," he said, leaning forward and twitching his lip.

The nurse took a step back. "Well, let's not get ahead of ourselves. Please, could you stand over there and unbutton your shirt? Just going to go through some health checks."

He quickly took off his shirt and chucked it on the chair he'd been sitting on. He rolled his shoulders back and stood at attention as the nurse took another step back into the small room. Sam assumed she'd stepped back in awe of his magnificent stature, but after several seconds the silence became unnerving. Sam took a peek down to see what she was staring at.

He had so many scars on his body. Too many to count. They weren't all noticeable, but Sam could see them very clearly. Bullet holes covered his torso like constellations. Cuts enveloped his skin, spreading onto his arms and hands. *I'm no better than the poster,* he thought, staring at the silver skin on his knuckles.

"What…what happened?" the nurse whispered.

"Like I said, I'm a soldier."

The nurse cleared her throat, "Uh...you can put your shirt back on now."

Sam quickly replaced his shirt, misaligning the buttons. "Are we done here?" he said, taking a seat.

"I've just got one last question." She scanned the paper with her finger. "Your date of birth."

Sam was at an impasse. He tried to work out the numbers in his head, but nothing would stick. Making up an age, he then worked back to get the year he would be born. Looking in the nurse's eyes his mind was in bits.

"Excuses me, Mr. Jenkins. Your age."

"Twenty-six," he blurted out. "I'm twenty-six."

The nurse waved the officer forward. He bent down and she whispered in his ear.

"Is there a problem?" Sam started to clench his hands into fists as they weren't taking any notice of him and wasting his not-so-precious time.

"Mr. Jenkins, I'm afraid we can't accept yo—"

Sam's hearing went muffled. Heat ruptured from his core, boiling his blood. Then the mysterious voice came roaring back. *How could this happen! What the fuck is this world coming to! They need you. They need you!*

Sam stood up, sliding the chair into the wall.

The nurse hid behind the officer.

Sam chuckled, seeing the officer raise his hands prepared to defend himself. "Pathetic," Sam muttered and stormed out.

The nurse followed him out into the waiting room. "Mr. Jenkins, please."

Sam stood in the middle of the room. The puzzled faces of the real Jenkins, his friend, and three black men, watched the situation unfold.

Sam could hear the voice speak to him and he repeated what

it was saying out loud. "You gonna pick these three niggers over me?" He looked back at the nurse in disgust.

"Please, Mr. Jenkins." the nurse said. "If something's bothering you–"

"Shut the fuck up, nigger! You're gonna lose this war without me."

When Sam stepped out onto the New York City street, the strange voice went with him.

FOURTEEN

Without war, Sam's life had no meaning. At least now he had some company though. The damp southern drawling voice had become a part of him, entwined into every part of his mind. He kind of liked it. It was someone who agreed with him.

How could this happen? Why are you being punished?

But that was just the start of it all. By 1965, a civil rights act came into effect. *Civil! There wasn't anything civil about it. Now niggers could go where they pleased.* Everywhere Sam looked, he could see their dark faces. Anyone fine about it was just a pathetic black sympathizer. There was no way he could have anticipated these events.

With the money he'd earned from the wars, Sam bought himself a single bedroom apartment on the second floor, in lower Manhattan, and a cherry-red Mustang GT. *V8 engine, 271 brake horsepower.* He had no clue what the numbers meant or even knew if he'd got them right. He just liked saying them. It was a menacing machine, yet nothing could compare to holding the smooth wooden grip of a Thompson machine gun. The occasional times he drove it reminded him of a simpler time. Neither

Sam nor the voice would have ever thought they would find something more thrilling than killing.

1970.

Early morning. What the day was, Sam couldn't even hazard a guess. He was leaving his apartment to go where he didn't know. He passed the front door to the other apartment on his floor. He could hear incomprehensible hollering and a baby crying. A pain crept into his heart making it tight. He just pushed it aside. He always felt pain. He walked past the door and down the stairs. He couldn't care less about other people's problems.

He let his feet move through the busy city, smoking as he went. Even with the gray cloud covering his vision, he could still see the amazing city. The colossal buildings, the moving cars, and the women; the gorgeous women. He wasn't subtle as he stared at any walking past him who he found desirable. Some even returned a smile. He was a handsome man, though he thought he was the best there was and ever will be.

"Hey! Hey you."

Sam looked around, wondering where the voice was coming from. He knew it wasn't the one in his head.

"Hey! You there." A man stood in an alleyway, just far enough back that the sun didn't hit him. "Come over here," he said, waving his hand.

Sam walked into the alley, feeling the warmth disappear from the back of his neck. He wasn't concerned about any danger. *Nothing can hurt you*, said the voice.

"Yo, man, how are you doing?" the happy chap asked. He wasn't much older looking than Sam. Buzzcut hair, a soul-patch beard. Dressed in a brightly colored red shirt, large gold rings, a chain necklace with a cross attached to it.

"What do you want?" Sam replied.

"What do I want? The question is what do you—"

Sam had already lost his patience and started to walk away.

The man dove in front of him. "Wait. Wait. Wait!" he squealed. "I think we got off on the wrong foot. I'm a business-man. The name's Jack. I just wondered if you would like to do some business."

The man could talk. Sam's interest increased slightly. "I'm Sam. What're you selling?"

"Well, that's what I like to hear. I've got stuff that can make you feel invincible. I've got stuff that can make you feel invisible and a few little things that can simply take the world's weight off your shoulders."

The man sure knew how to sell his mystery product.

"Invincible. What's that?" Sam was intrigued. It was hard enough to kill him already, but he wasn't going to pass up the chance for a little extra.

"Well, then." Jack looked around before taking out a small folded piece of brown paper. "Ever done drugs before, boy?"

Finally, Sam understood what the guy was talking about. "We had morphine during the war. Never had a reason to use it."

Jack cackled, "Yeah, I bet you didn't. Anyway, if it was morphine you were looking for, heroin would be your best bet. It will make you feel like you're falling from the sky." Jack lifted the paper pouch, waving it from side to side. "But this. This is yeyo. This is the base. This is snow. This makes men want to be you and women want to be with you," he said, his smooth voice rolling out the words. He peeled back a flap of the paper.

Sam's eyes flared, seeing the pure white powder. His inner voice was excited. Sam looked back at Jack. "What's it do?"

Jack smiled. It was the make-or-break moment. The words needed to be perfect to finalize the deal. Jack checked Sam up and down. "This… this will turn you into the fastest man on earth."

———

Yes!

Cocaine. Cocaine made Sam feel good. Really good. There was nothing he couldn't do when he was on it. His blood rushed through his veins and swirled around his head. He was feeling stronger than ever before, and even his scars began to sink further back into his skin.

He spent his time congregating in bars. He slicked back his hair and his new attire consisted of all black. Women wanted to be with him, especially as they snorted the white, powdered substance off of his fingertips. The feeling of sliding his hand up the side of a woman's dress was intensified. He could sense every fiber of the material and their silky-smooth skin underneath. Their hearts beat in time with whatever music was playing. The sweet taste of saliva as he kissed their lips. He didn't have a preference on who he lay with—blondes, brunettes, redheads—so long as their skin was as pale as the powder in his veins.

Lying with them was the easy part. The difficult part was getting inside the bars in the first place. He'd always get looks from the doormen for his young face, but a few folded notes shut any doubting lips. Occasionally, egotistical men would attempt to prove their dominance over the young man but it would always end in failure for them. Sam would stay calm and collected when they tried to talk down to him, and if they ever pushed him aside, he would push back ten times as hard. He'd send them flying across the dance floor. Most of the time, that would be the end of it. The men would walk away with their tails between their legs, embarrassed at being caught off guard by Sam's strength. On the rare occasion a man was really stupid, they would wake up in hospital not knowing how they'd got there.

After several months, the doormen wouldn't intervene with anything Sam was involved in. His fault or not, they didn't want to end up like the men on the floor. Once that started, he never had to bribe his way into a place again. When the sun rose, the bars closed, everyone slumbered, and Sam would slide the succulent heroin into his bloodstream.

Heroin. Heroin made everything stop. He was still able to function; unlike others he had witnessed. It warmed his body with an inch of heat, like an extra layer of skin. It kept him in the moment, not thinking of the past or the everlasting future. He was simply at peace like he was falling from the sky. While he was on this other concoction of chemicals, he could hear the whispers of the mystery voice, talking softly in the back of his head. It was nice having the constant company. They'd have long silent conversations with each other. Their opinions and thoughts were aligned. He knew what the voice would say and the voice knew how he would reply.

Weeks and months passed. While walking the city streets, Sam saw a dark-skinned man walking on the other side of the road.

Freedom. No one can take your freedom.

"But I can take theirs." Sam crossed the street and proceeded to follow the man. It never occurred to him to ask the voice who it was.

FIFTEEN

Sam kept his pace short and his steps silent while he stalked the man. No one other than Sam would have noticed the man's existence. He moved his slightly overweight frame with a slight skip to his step. Sam couldn't have seen it, but the man had a glint in his eyes. A soft smile lay gently on his face as he thought about something warm and familiar.

It was a shame Sam had found the man who was lost in his own little world. The only glint Sam could see was from a metal pipe sticking out of a pile trash bags. He picked up the pipe. Rust covered the entire length of it. The end he chose for the hilt was sharp and jagged. The other end had some kind of fitting attached to it, making it heavier. It was nothing compared to the slugger he'd once held, but it would work for what he desired. Holding it down by his side, he continued following his soon-to-be victim.

Sam followed the black man a few more steps. Once he was adjacent to an alleyway, he attacked. Grabbing the man by the back of his neck, Sam swung the metal pipe at his leg. Sam felt a vibration in the pipe when it connected with the man's knee, followed by a crack and a deafening scream. The cocaine in Sam's blood made the scream louder. He threw the man into the alley-way, to get away from the agonizing noise.

He dropped the pipe to the ground and covered his ears until the ringing subsided. The injured man lay face down on the damp ground, groaning as he grasped his dislocated knee. Sam crouched down and delicately rifled through his pocket, avoiding contact with the man's disgusting skin. He pulled out the man's wallet, and standing back up, he started checking through each compartment.

The man attempted to get back onto his feet, pushing himself up with his scuffed palm on the rough, wet ground.

"I would stay down if I was you." Sam chuckled, knowing he himself could never be in the situation that had befallen the man. "Your life isn't worth…" Sam paused to count the wrinkled notes he'd found in the wallet. "Sixteen dollars," he said with a devilish smile.

The man stayed dead still, yet continued to groan.

Sam crouched back down, leaning over the man's head. "Maybe you should risk your life. You ain't worth half that," he said, his demonic gaze burning into the back of the man's skull. With no reply from the man, Sam stood back up again, tossing the empty wallet onto his back. "Smart choice. You just saved your own life, boy." Sam stuffed the money into his pocket. "Don't feel bad about losing the money. Just think of it as some sort of freedom tax." Still no response from the man. "See you around, boy."

The man went silent, having passed out from the pain.

Sam twirled around and left the alleyway, leaving the now unconscious man alone. *It was so very nice of you to leave him alive.*

The nightlife awoke. The city lit up. A sea of colors, bright and vibrating. Black skin still looked black, soaking up the lights.

Sam's, the women's, and the other men's skin shone. Their flesh blue, green, and orange, reflecting the neon lights like a mirror. The females' skin contrasted with their dresses. Sam's concept of colorful was a suit of solid black with no tie. His appetite had started to subside. His collar felt loose around his neck. He may not have known it, but something was missing from the ensemble. He walked past the long line waiting for entry into the club with red neon lights above. He couldn't remember the name of the place. He thought all the eyes of the people waiting were fixed on him, but truthfully they weren't taking much notice. The bouncers stepped aside and opened the door for Sam.

The club was loud and bright. The lights inside flashed, and the glitter and sequin dresses swayed as the women danced. It wasn't Sam's scene. If he didn't have any alternative motives, he would have felt out of place. He stood in the middle of happy faces enjoying each other's company and dancing.Sam couldn't imagine dancing; never having seen the appeal of it, or having the knowledge to go with it. Drugs, alcohol, and women; that was why he was there. He could feel everyone's pulse move through the air. The smell of female perfume lingered on the hairs inside his nose; any other space was laced with the toxic white powder.

The cocaine made the colors on the dresses come alive. They swirled and spiraled into each other, like a rainbow being pulled into a vortex. Sam felt like he would be sucked into the colorful vortex if he lingered too long next to them. Brushing past the swaying bodies, he found a space at the bar. Clinging on to the underside on the bar, he steadied himself. The whole counter rocked in turn with the music. He bought a double dark brown whiskey and took a large swig. It burned the roof of his mouth, then followed down his throat. He figured he needed more cocaine in his system to counteract the effect of the heroin in his blood. He patted the outside of his pocket.

You're all out, said the voice. A small amount of disappointment could be heard behind the gravelly speech as it matched

Sam's expression. *Wait, look over there*, the voice sparked with excitement.

Sam scanned the club, past all the dancers.

Over there! The voice became infuriated at Sam's incompetence.

Sam saw what the voice was looking at. It was the first man who had given him the powerful substance.

Jackie. It couldn't be seen, but if the mystery voice had a face, it would have had a long sinister smile on it.

Sam let go of the bar, poured the rest of his drink down his gullet, and pushed through the crowd.

Jack was sitting in a cubicle talking to a small group; a mixture of men and women. None of them took any notice of Sam when he approached. He butted in with no regard to politeness.

"Hey, Jackie!" he shouted to be heard over the loud music.

The group paused their conversation and looked at the intruder.

"How's it going, Jackie?"

Jack sat on the outside of the cubical closest to Sam. Noticing the man was looking at him, he scratched the back of his head and swiveled his eyes. "It's Sam. Isn't it?"

"Yeah, that's right. How are you, Jackie?" Sam blurted out of his gurning jaw. His speech was slurred and inconsistent. He offered out his hand.

Jack reluctantly accepted the obligation. "Good, thanks. It's Jack, by the way."

"Yeah, whatever." Sam didn't care. He had finished the introduction and wanted to get straight to the point. Sliding onto the other end of the cubicle, the already-seated had no choice other than to shuffle over. Annoyed by Sam's arrogance, they turned their heads away. They continued with the interrupted conversation, leaving Jack to deal with him.

Jack rubbed his soul-patch beard with his thumb. "So, what can I do for you?" he said, wanting to get the matter finished as soon as possible.

Sam leaned across the table. "You got any coke?"

Jack noticed a thick wad of notes folded underneath Sam's left hand. "Straight to the point. That's what I like about you." Jack became more relaxed. When Sam had first approached, Jack had assumed he just wanted a freebie. Countless times, Jack had to deal with men he had done business with, who then wanted a free hand out or overstayed their welcome. Even though the club's atmosphere was filled with sweat and smoke, it was a breath of fresh air to see someone eager to do business. He would never pass up such an opportunity. However, his hunch told him to not rush into anything. Tugging on his gold cross necklace, he could sense Sam had a dark secret inside.

"How'd you like this place?" he said.

"It's alright, I guess," Sam replied after a quick whip around, rapidly tapping his knuckles on the table.

"Yeah, I like this place." Jack nodded in agreement. "I'm gonna own it someday. I'm gonna have my fingers in as many pies as I can," he said, stretching out his fingers mimicking his words, his heavy gold rings catching the light.

"Your point being?"

"My point is, where are your fingers gonna be?"

He's threatening you. Slam his fucking head into the table and take what you want!

Sam liked the sound of it, but he figured he would just humor Jack instead. "Haha! My fingers will be attached to my hand then inside a woman, maybe two. My nose will be filled with the cocaine you're about to sell me."

They both chuckled. Sam's was slow and artificial.

"Well, then, with that settled, how much would you like?" Jack pulled ten folded pieces of brown paper out of his pocket, his rings catching on the seam on his jacket. He shuffled them one at a time into the other hand like he was counting coins. "So, how many would you like? One, two, three?"

"I'll take them all." Sam began to dish out his money.

"Woah, steady on there, cowboy. No need to be greedy. Besides, I gotta keep some for myself."

Sam's insides started to grow cold. He needed this fix soon. His palms were sticky with sweat. He swallowed the saliva building up in his mouth. He stayed as calm as he could. "I'll take whatever you can spare."

No! You said you wanted it all! screamed the enraged voice from within his head.

Sam ignored the voice, pushing it further back to the deepest part of his mind. It was difficult keeping the unnatural force at bay but he was able to manage long enough for Jack to respond.

"Well." Jack tapped one of the packets on the table. "I guess I can give you six. That should last you a while." He stacked them into a small unstable tower and slid them across the table. "Don't worry. No need to hide it away in this place."

Sam picked them up slowly. He was eager, but not so much as to let Jack see his hand tremble. He passed Jack the notes in his hand. The top note was now damp from soaking up his sweat.

He wasted no time, placing four packets in his pocket and opening the other two. Keeping his hands and head steady, he leaned back in the chair and slowly started funneling the content into his nose.

"Jesus, take it easy," Jack said as Sam poured the second packet into his other nostril. "You gonna kill yourself if you keep that pace up, boy."

Sam closed one nostril with his finger and followed it with a strong sniff. He then repeated the process on the other. The substance tasted sour, lying dormant at the back of his throat. With another strong snort and a large gulp, he cleared the blockage and pulled it down into his stomach.

Ohh... that's much better, the voice sighed with relief.

Sam's eyes exploded. His irises became consumed by the dark void of his pupils, leaving only a thin ring of green. Sam's head violently snapped back to Jack who quickly pulled back from the table, banging his head against the headboard.

"I highly doubt that," Sam whispered, only letting Jack hear. His southern accent had unburied itself once again. Sam gave Jack a clenched, evil toothy grin.

Jack nervously chuckled. "You're crazy."

Sam looked down at the table. His reflection stared back at him through the polished surface. "I think you might be right." His accent was gone as quickly as it came. His eyes started to move independently from one another. The excess light stung his corneas. With a slow delay, they realigned themselves and saw her.

She was at the bar, and in the same place where Sam had just stood. Her curly inferno-red hair just covered the nape of her neck. Her tight dress, white with a diagonal black stripe caressing her small figure, ended so high up her thigh that Sam could almost look straight up. Without taking his solid black eyes off her, he stood up. "See ya, Jackie."

"It's Jack, asshole," Jack replied, annoyed as he rejoined the rest of the people at the table.

Sam floated across the dance floor. Dancers crashed into him, but they only took themselves off their feet. Finally, he got to the bar. Time had almost come to a halt as he gazed at the gorgeous woman. He placed his hand on the bar, every vein and tendon screamed out of his skin. She didn't take any notice of his presence as she elegantly held her martini with her fingertips and took a small sip.

He observed her thin lips stick to the glass. Her slender face tightened as she put the drink down and pushed it away. Sam leaned in, his dilated eyes still fixed on her.

"Hi there," he said.

She didn't respond.

"What's your name?"

Again, she didn't react to Sam's introduction. She looked over her nails and tucked one of her red curls behind her ear. Opening up her handbag, she took out a small silver tin. Prying off the lid with her nails, a puff of white powder came out.

There was more cocaine in the small tin than all of Sam's brown packets combined. The corner of his mouth began to collect saliva.

She scooped a small pile onto the nail of her little finger and gently sniffed it up her nose. Giving her nostril a gentle rub, she packed her belongings away with haste and finally turned to look at Sam. She didn't say anything. Her slender face mirrored Sam's simple smile. She softly stroked the side of his cheek, then brushed past him out of sight.

The cocaine in Sam's blood blocked his emotion. He didn't know how to feel; whether to be annoyed or embarrassed. He picked up her drink and placed his lips where hers had been. He downed it in one and peered into the empty glass. He felt rage or was it frustration? He crushed the glass in his hands. Shards of glass sank deep into his flesh. His intoxication masked the pain. "Fuck," he muttered through his gurning.

He went home early that night, alone. *Just an off day,* he kept saying to himself. Taking a detour home, he was able to get something to help him sleep. He had several people to help him with his glutinous habit.

Walking past the neighbors' front door, a pain crept into his heart. He was distracted by the muffled yelling coming from inside the apartment. He passed the pain off as a side effect of the concoction of drugs and alcohol rushing through his system.

He made himself comfortable in his bed. His suit was screwed up in a ball in a corner of the room. Lying naked under the sheets, he tied his belt tight around his arm. Finding his largest vein, he punctured his scar tissue with the syringe filled with the blissful syrup. Before Sam could pull the needle back out, his head went limp and fell backward onto the pillow. A black haze grew over his eyes until they were completely covered. Sam was left alone in the darkness, but he wasn't truly alone.

It was dark. A void. The darkest place Sam had ever witnessed. He could feel himself standing upright, but he couldn't see his legs. He waved his hand across the empty space where his legs were supposed to be. His hand was nowhere to be seen either. "What can I feel?" he said silently; his ears not receiving his voice. He blinked his nonexistent eyes. "I don't understand." Still no sound.

Strangely, he didn't feel alone. He felt a warm sticky breath hit the back of his neck. The smell of which flowed into his absent nose. The putrid smell, full of disease and decay. He wanted to vomit; to purge the horrific odor from his body. There was no hope. He had no stomach nor a mouth to do such an act.

The warmth started to consume him from within his core spreading outwards. The pain was excruciating. Puncture wounds pierced his inconceivable body. He knew his bones were not there, yet he felt them crack, twist, and contort. His skin started to soften and tear like wet paper. A burning tightness attacked his neck. Finally, when he thought the pain couldn't get any worse, a force from within his skull erupted. Sam's mind was scattered, lost in a deep black ocean, drowning in a current of pain. Sam could only distinguish one other thing, the strange voice whispering a single word, "William."

· · ·

Sam awoke from his torment. The sun glared in through the gap in the drapes. *How long was I out?* he said to himself. He pried the needle out of his arm and climbed off the bed. His limbs were heavy and weak. "Was that all just a dream?" he asked, glad to be able to hear his own voice. He shook away his negative thoughts, not wanting to concern himself with the ridiculous notions going on in his mind. He took a hot shower and soaked his aching muscles. He got dressed but left his jacket crumpled up on the floor.

He left his apartment and closed the door behind him. He didn't lock it. No need. He had nothing of worth inside. Before he could look, the neighbors' door slammed shut. He was about to walk past when something unexpectedly stopped him in his tracks.

Looking down at his feet, a cat was brushing up against him. The tabby cat was a scrawny little thing, yet extraordinarily affectionate to Sam. It rubbed the side of its mouth across the fabric on Sam's shin. Its tail was crooked like it had been in a scrap with another feline or hit by a car. Sam lowered his brow and gently shook his leg. "Shoo."

The stray scurried down the stairs and out of the small gap of the open front door. Sam didn't need a cat for company. He snorted a pinch of cocaine, lit a cigarette, and headed down the stairs. If anything was going to change Sam, a cat wouldn't be it.

SIXTEEN

"So, when do you and I meet?" Joanna said, unprofessionally butting in.

"Have you listened to anything I've just said?" Adam replied.

Wide-eyed, Joanna composed herself. "Look, many people suffer from drug addiction, and I've witnessed many people who have overcome those addictions." Joanna adjusted herself in her chair and decided to indulge in her addiction again. "Besides, you didn't seem to have an addiction when I first met you."

Adam breathed in Joanna's second-hand smoke as he spoke. "That's true. The drugs made time blurry. Hard to remember anything. But I don't think the drugs were the problem."

Joanna continued smoking, silently reading into what he was saying. She figured he was making excuses. She had heard it countless times from other patients, all trying to shift the problem away from their addictions.

"I know what you're thinking," Adam said, interrupting Joanna from her train of thought.

She turned her attention back to him, waiting for him to elaborate.

He spoke bluntly. "I know the drugs were scrambling my brain." His voice suddenly became uncontrollable and shaky. "But I heard that voice in my head long before I ever touched that stuff."

Joanna could see how disturbed Adam was. "Do you still hear the voice?"

"No." Adam's lips did the motion but no sound came out. His eyes began to well up. "But I can feel it. It's inside me. Under my skin," he whispered as quietly as he could. He pushed away the pools of water and wiped his runny nose.

Joanna's pulse started to race. Whatever had made Adam sob was unsettling. His skin turned pale, and the hairs on his arms stood upright. Whatever could scare a person like him, must have been truly terrifying. She hesitated. She wasn't sure if she wanted him to carry on. She dug her nails into the arms of her chair and pulled back as far as possible. She gritted her teeth. "Continue."

"I shouldn't have lived this long. No one should. Your mind starts to play tricks on you." Adam squirmed.

"Adam, what happened next?"

He took a deep breath, taking in the last of the second-hand smoke in the room. "I looked into the mirror, and saw a monster."

SEVENTEEN

Sam's obsession took over. He ate through his nose and slept by piercing his veins. The war in Vietnam was spiraling down like he said it would. It didn't concern him anymore. His only priority was to maintain his fix. It was getting difficult. Every day, he had to increase his dosage, and each time, the lasting effects grew shorter. It got increasingly hard when he began to run out of money.

1976 or 1977.

Sirens echoed and reverberated between the tall buildings in central Manhattan. Black smoke bleached the afternoon sky.

Sam emerged from a concealed alleyway to witness the commotion. The building across the street was engulfed in fire. The blood-red flames clawed out of the shattered windows, fighting back against the firemen. The water had no effect on the burning inferno. The glare of the fire reflected into Sam's dilated eyes and lit up his face. There wasn't an ounce of fat left on his person. His gaunt face; a skull wrapped in white leather. Black indented eye sockets and his dry thin skin absorbed the heat from the flames.

He looked down, counting twenty-six dollars in his boney hands. He stuffed them into his pants pocket and looked back at the fiery blaze. It had started to get an audience. *Good. Less attention on you,* said the inner voice, or was it him? He wasn't sure anymore. They were indistinguishable from each other now.

He shifted his attention to the crowd. Most just wanted to be nosey and see the action. Others were seeking medical assistance all covered in soot. It was hard to identify their natural skin tone. It occurred to Sam that besides a nurse, he had never visited a doctor. A minor side effect to never dying, he supposed.

The remaining people in the crowd were trying and failing to console each other. *Maybe they've lost someone.* His eyes moved back to the burning building. *No one could last long in there.* He smirked, remembering what he was. *Maybe someone needs help.*

He imagined what it would feel like being burned so severely. The intense heat drying the moisture throughout his body. The smell of burned flesh as his skin cooked. Then he pictured the reaction of the crowd as they saw his charred body step out of the building. *Oh. The horror on their faces.* His twitching eyes looked down at his hands. *Would it last? Maybe they would lock you up? Pay to see the disgusting freak. Not worth the risk.*

"Fuck that." Brushing the falling ash from his jacket, he walked at a fast pace away from the commotion. A black man lay unconscious in the alleyway.

Just like it had happened many times before, Sam started to crave his dirty habit. He wiggled his dry tongue around his gums. He walked over to the bedside table as his head began to itch from the inside. He pulled open the drawer. *Empty!* His blood went cold. He could have sworn he'd put his stash in there. There was no way he had used it all.

He bent down and stuck his hand in to feel the back of the drawer. He was getting desperate. He pushed everything off the top of the table. Empty cigarette packets, used syringes, and empty whiskey bottles littered the floor. Sweat started to excrete out of his forehead. He emptied the drawers in the kitchen. Unused knives, forks, and spoons smashed onto the counters. He overturned his mattress and leaned it against the wall. Shouting came from next door, making his head pound. He crawled on his hands and knees scouring the floor in the hope that he would find what he desperately needed. The muffled shouting got progressively louder.

Sam grabbed his ears in pain. "Shut up. Shut up. Shut up!"

The shouting wouldn't stop. He had to get out of there. He crawled through the trash he had created and pulled himself up by the doorknob.

The bustling nightlife was making Sam twitch. Moving lights, moving cars, moving people; they made him feel sick. It would have been impossible for him to vomit. He hadn't eaten anything for months. His cigarette couldn't calm him. Nothing other than his fix could help. He stumbled his way through the city, passing two black men chatting beside a doorway.

They paused their conversation, seeing the state Sam was in. "Smoking will kill ya," one said jokingly.

Sam was furious, he flicked his half cigarette at the talking man's face. "Not quick enough, boy!" he spat.

He carried on, scuffing his feet on the side, and scratching the back of his head like he had caught fleas from the men. He quickly lit another cigarette. He would have confronted the man, but he had more important things spinning around his scrambled mind.

He wasn't having any luck getting what he needed. *What the fuck is wrong with everyone!* He'd been to several dealers, and none of them had any or they refused to sell to him. It didn't help that he owed them money, and smacking them around didn't help either. He barged past people getting in his way. He didn't know where he was going. He was just following his stinging feet. His thin skin was rubbing against the side of his shoes.

Jackie. Sam snapped his head over. He didn't look any different, just more jewelry, a fuller beard, and wearing a purple shirt. He was concealed in a back alley away from prying eyes.

"Hey, you!" Sam shouted, marching over to him. "Hey, Jackie!"

Jack looked at the approaching man. His face not sparking up its normal flare. "What can I do for you?" he asked, he wanted to get it over with. He didn't listen to Sam's poor excuses. Jack had heard them all before and he wasn't about to change.

"Anyway, any chance you got any stuff?" the withdrawn Sam stuttered, scratching at his irritated skin.

"Nah. I ain't got anything for you," Jack replied, dismissing Sam's plea.

"What? Why not?" Sam's patience and consciousness were hanging by a thread.

Jack smirked. "I've got my hands everywhere." He paused. "My ears too."

Sam didn't understand nor care about what he was getting at.

"Word gets around quick nowadays. I'm hearing rumors about someone who looks a lot like you causing trouble."

Sam tried to use his wheezing voice to get Jack into doing business. "Rumors only ever tell half the story, and I know nothing about that, Jackie."

Jack's entire face tightened. "My name's not fucking Jackie. Now get the hell out of here before I change my mind."

It suddenly occurred to Sam that Jack didn't know what he was capable of.

Who the fuck does he think he is? Barking orders at you, gargled the voice.

Sam's thread snapped like a guitar string. "What you gonna do about it?" Sam asked. His body and face had stopped shaking.

Jack chuckled and twisted his body to the side.

Sam saw straight through his smiling poker face.

Jack went for a swing. He didn't get time to be shocked or surprised by Sam's strength. Sam had already grabbed his face and pinned him to the wall. Sam proceeded to search Jack's pockets.

"You ain't gonna get away with this," he groaned through Sam's boney fingers compressing his skull. Sam filled his pockets with money. Pulling out a bag of powder, he gave it a strong sniff, and the vinegar-like smell burned his nose.

That will get you to sleep at least.

He let Jack go and started to leave.

"You're going to regret this!" hollered Jack hunched over on the ground.

Sam turned around. "I've done a lot of things in my life. Regret ain't one of them." He took a long look at the limp Jack, huddled in a ball on the damp, dirty ground. "You dress like a nigger." Sam continued to leave, not thinking of the repercussions to come.

It took a lifetime to walk home. It had been such a long day. Sam's energy had drained from his body. All he wanted to do was lie down in bed, take a heavy dose, and get a fresh start in the morning. He dragged his heels up the front porch. He heard a faint meow behind him, but he was too tired to look back.

He scuffed his feet up the long staircase. Shouting coming from above.

"Let me in!" shouted a deep husky voice, followed by strong banging. "Come open the fucking door. I want to see her."

Again, more banging. It sounded like the door would fall off its hinges any second. Finally, Sam would see who had been making a racket until the early hours of the morning. *Of course. It had to be one of them,* Sam thought as he turned to face the noise-maker. The man with pitch-black skin was still bashing on the door.

"Open the door! You can't keep her away from me."

Just as expected, another loud-ass nigger. The man was a giant, standing a full foot taller than Sam. Even bigger as he was wasting away. The man would have had to duck under the doorway if whoever was on the other side opened it. His fists were the size of Sam's head, and could have easily ripped apart the door if he wanted. He stopped banging and shouting and stared down at Sam.

Sam looked back, straining his neck to see his face. Sam's eyes were heavy and exhausted but could have been mistaken for being timid and weak. He slid past the black man, who was taking up most of the hallway. The smell of alcohol was pungent. Sam stopped making eye contact, looking forward to getting his head on a pillow, and heroin in his veins.

His hand was an inch away from the doorknob.

"Fuck you looking at, boy?"

Sam stopped breathing. His hand started to spasm uncontrollably. He was no longer tired. His eyes bulged out of their sockets, almost grazing the door to his apartment. He awoke to endorphins of anger and violence; stronger than any drug he had taken. *Boy.* Sam was frozen. *Boy.* He needed to do something. *Boy! What is this fucking world coming to? Niggers talking back. Calling you bbbbooooyy!*

His open hand had contracted into a fist, a strong fist. He slowly turned back around; every muscle protruded and pulsed from under his skin.

The dead man had returned to hollering at the door. "Let me in! I'm her father. You can't stop me seeing her." Banging his fist on the dented door, he saw Sam approach. He turned to face him; a mass of pure strength. He should have been concerned, but his strength gave him a false sense of security. "You got a problem, bo–"

Sam struck the man in the throat before he could mutter the word. He fell to his knees, shaking the entire floor. The man grabbed his throat stunned.

Sam pulled his arm back and put all his strength into his punch. In the blink of an eye, he sent his fist into the man's face. The force was like a train hitting a mountain. It launched the man onto his back. Barely conscious, his arms and legs were spread out like a starfish. Sam climbed on top of him, pressing his knees onto the man's shoulders. He gave the man a left hook. Then a right. Then another left. With every punch that landed, Sam fractured every bone in his hands. The skin off his knuckles tore. It was astonishing how the man was still alive. Sam pulled him up by his collar. He could smell the alcohol on the man's faint breath.

"I used to own niggers like you." Sam's southern drawl flowed out. He let go of the man's collar, and his limp head dropped to the ground. Twisting at the hips, Sam selflessly gave him another right hook. The man's head almost came flying off his neck. Sam's bare knuckles connected with his cheek; bone ground against bone. His dark skin tore, exposing his pink flesh to the dingy hall light. His face purple; his eyelids almost completely swollen over. Sam raised his hand again, intending it to be his last.

———

The man looked up at his imminent death to see a blurry skull wrapped in skin, full of evil and hatred. Not the death he had expected for himself.

Sam went for his final strike.

"Daddy?"

Sam stopped. His hand rattled from the power stored inside. With his head still down, he hooked his eyes to see two small light brown feet stood in the open doorway. A pain grew in his heart. He wanted to kill the man. He had done worse. He lowered his fist and leaned down to whisper in the almost dead man's ear. "Call me boy again and I'll kill you."

Sam stood up keeping his face hidden from the little girl. He hastily walked down the stairs as screaming started to emerge from within the apartment.

It had been a bad evening. Sam wasn't sure where to go. He wasn't going back to the apartment. *Let time pass, like it always does for you.* He walked into the club with red neon lights outside, thinking he could drink and sleep at the bar. It wasn't going to be easy to relax with the eccentric singer blaring out his futuristic song, but he'd give it a shot. He bought a double whiskey with the stolen drug money and took it down in one like it was air.

He was about to order another when he saw it sparkle. A small silver tin at the other end of the bar and her. The inferno redhead from long ago. His cravings reemerged. He clambered off the stool.

His heart was pounding and sweat poured off his brow. He looked a mess. His eyes switched between the woman and the tin. His skin tingled as he stood just inches away. She looked at him. Her slim face showed recognition of his. Sam stood there swaying on his feet, and let her inspect him up and down. He could smell her perfume, infused with cocaine. He couldn't concentrate on what she was doing. She opened the tin he urgently wanted to get his hands on. She took out a small piece of colored paper and placed it softly on her tongue. She stroked the side of his face. He closed his eyes and embraced the physical human contact on his cold, loose skin.

Her hand moved to the back of his neck, grabbing a tuft of his hair. She pulled him close and slid her tongue down his throat.

He tasted her drug-infused saliva. His craving was quenched. A new desire emerged. He figured his life was about to get much better.

The next two weeks were heaven for Sam, or at least he thought they were. One substance or another was always being delivered into his body, clouding his mind. Time had no importance, and having the woman by his side made life even sweeter. He was bewitched by her. Wherever she went, he would follow. She was his and he was hers. He was extremely protective of her. If a man even went near her, he dropped him to the floor before they even opened their mouths. No man touched her. Sam would have killed them if they'd tried. He never wavered, even when standing in the middle of a bar covered in his own blood, and the men who he had rendered unconscious.

The violence only ever made the inferno woman more infatuated with him. Grabbing his groin, and sucking on his lips. She didn't know it, but she was out of her depth.

Sam would drive back to her apartment. He hadn't been back to his since that horrible night. The drive back was always exciting. The woman would either go down on him, or Sam would pleasure her with his fingers. The night wouldn't end there. He'd snort lines of coke off her naked body, or taste her addictive skin. His hands caressed her breasts and tickled her protruding ribs. The drugs magnified the intense sensation of being inside each other.

He'd heard that taking narcotics can soften such vigorous activities, but not for him. He was perfect in every single way and by the reaction on the woman's face, he was for her too. Her screams of pleasure rang unpleasantly in his ears. Placing his palm over her mouth sorted that small problem. She'd bite down. She would bite down until she could taste his spiked blood. Yet while being engaged in the unworldly pleasure, Sam knew he didn't have any real feelings for her. He didn't even know her name.

EIGHTEEN

A scrawny tabby cat patrolled around on a quiet, dark Manhattan night. It searched for rodents and rummaged through bins for food. It spent its time alone like most strays would, not getting friendly with other species. It strolled along the sidewalk with no plan nor knowledge of where it was going. A cat doesn't look to the past or think too far into the future. It was simply living in the moment, scuttling down the street, and seeing where its paws took it.

Finding itself in a dark alleyway, it clambered up onto some trash cans. The loosely fitting lid rocked when the cat perched itself on the edge. It stretched over the gap between another bin and the one it was sitting on. Sniffing at the open trash can, it batted and clawed at the bag where it had caught the scent. It shredded a patch of holes in the plastic. The cat drooled and licked its lips, seeing the oozing mess of a rotten chicken carcass. It wasn't fit for consumption by any species but the cat didn't mind. It just craved something to eat. It kept clawing at the sticky substance. It couldn't quite reach it.

It adjusted its footing. Wriggling closer to the edge, its backside almost hung off. Naive as it was, it leaped forward, planning on grabbing the bag. Its hind legs pushed down too hard and tilted the lid off. It fell to the ground and like all cats landed on its feet. The lid crashed on top of the distressed fur ball, almost trapping it under a dome of metal. It managed to get free and scattered away out of the alley. It made a beeline for the other side of the road. It only had a few more steps. It could have started its journey anew and continued its hunt for food. But it stopped in the middle of the road, blinded by a pair of bright lights.

The night was dark and quiet, and there were no other cars in sight. Sam was driving home at speed. The houses, the hospital, clubs, and bars flew past in a blur. His woman wasn't with him. She couldn't keep up with his pace and stayed in bed most of the day. Sam didn't care. He carried on as he had done for so long. He snorted a pinch of coke, holding on the steering wheel with one hand. It felt strange to him how much life had advanced forward. In a matter of minutes, he could travel the distance a horse and cart could in a day.

He realized something as his dilated eyes stared beyond the beam of the headlights. He had outlived everyone who'd been alive when he was born. *When I was born. Was I even born?* he asked himself. He wasn't expecting a reply. Life seemed to fall into segments. The earlier the segment, the further back in his memory they were to the point where he wasn't sure if they had actually happened. Like waking up from a dream and forgetting it in an instant.

Sam shook his head. *No point in dwelling on the past.* It wasn't going to affect his never-ending future. He pulled out a cigarette from his inner-jacket pocket. Wriggling around, he looked for his lighter while using his knees to hold the steering wheel straight.

"Get out of there," he said in frustration, rummaging in his pants pocket. Pulling too hard, it flew out of his hand and landed in the passenger's footwell. "God damn it." He laughed at his choice of words. He grabbed the steering wheel and gazed in front. Nothing could be seen, just his headlights blanketing the road. He quickly proceeded to stretch down, taking his eyes off the road.

That's it. Just a little further, said the voice.

The tendons in his arms burned as he extended them as far as he could. He pulled himself up, sparking his cigarette in accomplishment. Finally, he turned his eyes back to the road.

Time slowed to a crawl. The red eyes stared right into Sam's black soul. His cigarette dropped into his lap. He wasn't sure what to do. He just kept staring back into the hovering balls of red light that were getting progressively closer. He couldn't quite understand why he felt scared. There was no reason to. The scrawny tabby cat would have been no match to the force the car would inflict. He doubted it would even have scratched the paint. It would simply have hit the front grill with a thud and gone under the tires. It wouldn't have looked remotely like a cat; afterward only resembling a part of a war-torn corpse.

Sam gazed at the hunched over, long-legged silhouette, wondering why something would face its own death with no preservation of life.

You don't have any preservation either, said the voice in its gravelly drawl. Sam was almost upon the shadow. Still, it showed no urgency to move. Sam wrenched the steering wheel fully to the left, mere inches away from the cat. Tires squealed and burned into the road. Using all his strength, he tried to keep the car under control. A pair of white lights appeared in front of him. Screwing up his eyes, he pulled the steering wheel back to the right. He changed his gaze to his side window as the white light headed straight for him.

The lights went dark. The door started to crumble toward Sam. His lighter began to float and his hands rose up and brushed the cold metal roof. Time became fluid again. Sam's head smashed into the roof, and his body got compressed by the incoming metal. The car creaked and groaned while shattered glass twinkled in the air like stars. The car flipped several times. He had never been so out of control. Finally, the car stopped spinning and landed upside down. The dark four-legged shadow stepped onto the sidewalk and continued its search for food.

Sam rested his head on a pillow of shattered glass. He opened his eyes. His breathing was irregular. He couldn't move. His neck was definitely broken and so were his arms. He tried to wriggle, scraping his face over the shards of glass. It was no use. He started to panic. The fear of being trapped in a case of metal had become a reality. He wheezed and whimpered out of his collapsed chest. How pathetic and useless he felt as warm piss ran down his broken legs. He tried to move again, pushing his shoulder forward, but it was hopeless. One arm was contorted above his head, and the other was twisted behind his back. "Ughhhhh!" Sam let out a screen of desperation. The pain was horrific, yet he didn't care. He just couldn't bear being trapped. He sobbed and rocked his head across the broken glass and jagged metal. *Why can't I just die?* "Please, please, let it end!" He continued to sob.

"Meow."

Sam opened his eyes. They were red from broken blood vessels. There stood the tabby cat at the entrance of Sam's metal tomb. It didn't venture further in but just watched and sniffed with curiosity. With something to focus his mind on, Sam slowed his breathing. How he'd got in such a mess because of a cat was astonishing. He looked at the simple animal that didn't know what damage and havoc it had caused. Its matted fur still looked soft to touch; Sam would have given it a stroke if he could.

The plea of death disappeared and the voice inside emerged. *Come on. Get up. You can't lie here forever,* it chuckled.

Now focused, he wiggled and rocked his body. Short, sharp

breaths puffed out of his nostrils. "Ughhhhh!" he screamed, pulling his arm out from behind his back. Bone ground against bone. He left small strips of his shirt, skin, and flesh dangling on sharp, jagged metal. Falling out of the seat, he used his fingers to drag his limp arm to the crumbled door frame.

The cat sniffed his hand, getting the strong smell of blood and meat. He grabbed a tight hold of the frame and then with a quick jolt, he pulled the bone back into place. Phlegm sprayed out of his clenched teeth and hung off his lip. He could feel a slight tingle where the bone was fusing back together.

That's it. Just a little further, whispered the voice softly with its lips touching Sam's ear.

Then with all his might, Sam pulled himself through the shattered window; free from his claustrophobic living nightmare.

The cat scurried away, not looking back. By the time Sam had got to his feet, his wounds were healed. His bones solid; cuts and bruises vanished. The lacerations and draping flesh had fused back together. All had been replaced by raised silver scars, reflecting the moonlight through the tears in his shirt and pants. It was a somewhat majestic reaction to what had just passed.

He gazed at his former cherry-red Mustang GT. *V8 engine. 271 brake horsepower.* He wasn't disheartened at all. Nothing in his life lasted forever. He was just glad he wasn't still stuck inside it. He pulled out a cigarette, and found his lighter lying at his feet. Smoke escaped his lungs. Smoke was also escaping underneath the bonnet of a car several feet away.

Oh, the bright lights. That ain't good, said the smug voice. *Haha. No one could make it out of that alive*, it said through a cluster of cackles.

Sam wasn't sure how to react. He took a couple of weak steps toward the car.

You best get out of here. Some things ain't worth knowing.

Sam was glad he wasn't completely alone at that moment. There was the comfort of having the voice nibbling at his brain.

He tossed his cigarette onto his car, igniting it into a ball of flames. He then scurried off like the stray.

Sam walked the rest of the way to the redhead's apartment. Weaving through alleyways and using all shortcuts he could, he stayed out of sight as much as possible. He carefully and quietly opened the door, leaving the lights off so as not to disturb the sleeping red. She didn't need to see the dried blood and ripped clothes. He buried his clothes at the bottom of a trash can. Like many times before, he took a hot shower to wash away the blood from his scar-riddled body.

Naked and clean, he crept over to the bed and climbed under the sheets. He rubbed his hands over red's lukewarm skin.

"Hey, baby, did you have a good night?" she said. Her eyes were closed, and her voice was soft and fragile.

"It was okay. It would have been better if you'd been there," he replied, completely forgetting what had actually happened.

"Hmm, that's sweet," she mumbled, still half asleep.

He started to slide his hand down her body. Her breathing deepened. He slid his hand down even further. She opened her thighs inviting him in. She grew short of breath as he pushed two fingers firmly inside her. She grabbed hold of the sheets. He chewed on her neck and pinched her nipples. She became breathless when he thrust deep inside her.

Her body was tired and limp, barely able to move. Her heartbeat pounded out of her chest from the orgasmic adrenaline. Small whimpers and squeals came from behind her teeth as she bit down on her bottom lip.

Sam lay on top. She didn't seem as active as usual. Sam's temperature rose as he sped up his pace. As he penetrated harder and faster, the redhead opened her mouth and let out a silent scream. When he was finished, he stayed inside her and rested his head on her chest.

She used all her strength to wrap her arms around him, and stroked the back of his head.

He felt claustrophobic, but it wasn't as bad as the car.

Sam spent the time and took the care to prepare a syringe full of heroin, making sure to get the mixture just right. He was lying in bed with the woman between his legs leaning back onto his chest. Her hair tickled his chin. She groaned in an incoherent way.

Sam lifted her arm. "Here, have some of this. It will make you feel better."

"Yeah, everything will be better in the morning," she whispered.

Only Sam's strong hearing would have been able to hear her voice. He pressed the needle gently into her vein and pushed down on the syringe. She let out another groan, and this time with clarity in the tone. Sam pulled out the needle, placing his thumb on the puncture wound.

Lying naked with her kept Sam excited. With their skin sticky and the smell of her hair, Sam realized he felt something for her. Something he hadn't felt for anyone in a long time. He bent his neck down to whisper in her ear. Her hair tickled his cheek. "Hey, what's your name?"

She didn't answer. The drugs had already taken hold. Her face was at peace, and the faintest breath came out from her mouth.

Sam let her rest. He'd ask again in the morning. He pushed the other half of the addictive syrup into the vein in his neck, and then tossed the syringe onto the bedside table. He wrapped his arms around his inferno-haired woman so nothing could take her. His eyelids became heavy, and he allowed them to close. He let the drugs drag him away.

NINETEEN

Sam opened his eyes to a dark void. He perceived his body but could not see it. He felt like he was standing on something soft and spongy. "Not this again," he tried to say. But like before, nothing was audible. In a split second, his body erupted into dust. He let out an inaudible scream as he felt the incomprehensible pain.

Sam felt like he was standing on something soft and spongy. He was hesitant to open his eyes. Eventually, he did, seeing his legs and feet and the ground he was standing on. Earth. Freshly tilled soil, moist with dew, and ripe with snowy cotton. The plants were magnificent. It was the best crop he had ever seen. Growing tall, past his waist, with so many buds on each plant he could barely see the stem. He picked a bud, and it was the softest thing he had ever touched. It was like holding a cloud.

After he inspected the bud, he noticed the cuff of his jacket. It was a stone gray with handwoven, gold embroidery. *An outfit made for a god.* Sam looked around in amazement, thinking it was heaven.

Spinning around, he noticed a familiar figure facing away. He started to approach it. Its familiarity grew with each step closer. Finally, he realized who it was. It was his brother Marshall. Sam hadn't thought about him in so long, but it was definitely him. He hadn't aged a day. *This has to be heaven.*

Marshall still hadn't noticed his brother's presence. He just stood there peacefully staring into the endless fields of cotton.

Sam called out to his brother, anticipating an embrace from his older sibling. He didn't get it.

Marshall turned to face the caller, and the color drained from his checks. Marshall, big and strong, now trembled in his boots. It looked like he had seen a ghost. They both stayed silent for several drawn-out seconds.

"Marshall, it's me, your brother," Sam said, stretching out his arms. He took a step forward.

Marshall took two nervous paces back.

Sam stopped clueless. *Why is he scared of me?*

"Marshall!" shouted a voice from behind Sam.

He turned around, instantly forgetting the tension with his brother. His father and mother were approaching. His heart settled with relief. Both full of life. His father strong and mother with not a shred of sickness. "Father!" he shouted like a little boy, spreading out his arms for another embrace. They stopped in their tracks.

His mother started crying, covering her mouth, and hiding behind her husband.

Arthur became consumed by a protective rage. "Marshall! Get away from it!" he hollered.

Marshall obeyed his command, pulling further away.

"I don't understand," Sam said, his voice starting to crack.

Arthur started looking around the never-ending field, shielding his eyes from the burning sun. He turned his fearsome gaze back to Sam. "Where's William?"

Sam didn't know what to say or do. *This isn't heaven.*

"Where is my son!" Arthur's Colt appeared in his hand. Raising it up, he pointed it at what he feared.

Tears poured down Sam's face. "I am your son, Pa," he wept. He felt more pain from them not recognizing him than the Colt could ever inflict. Crying like the young boy he was, he wiped his runny nose. The outfit made for a god now soaked in tears and snot. He heard a familiar click. Arthur had pulled back the hammer. Sam looked at his father.

"You're not my son," he said before pulling on the trigger.

Before Sam could feel the shot, a boney, decaying hand grabbed him from behind and covered his mouth. A rotting corpse of a face leaned onto his shoulder, rubbing against his face, cheek to cheek. He could smell the decay from the hand under his nose and the warm moist breath when it spoke. In a gravelly southern drawling voice, it whispered, "Wake up, William."

Sam sprang back to life with sweat coming out of every pore. His strong heart pulsed as fast as it could, almost pushing out of his ribcage. The sun crept through the small gap in the drapes. He didn't feel like the nightmare could have lasted all night, but there he was, sweating in bed during the midday sun. He may have wasted the day, but waking up to reality, he knew he would have plenty more.

He looked over and saw his woman sleeping perfectly still. Her inferno hair just peeked out from under the sheets. He moved closer to wake her up.

"Hey, baby," he said softly, and gently rubbed her back. She gave no reply. He grabbed her by her shoulder and moved her on to her back. "Hey, honey."

Sam leaped out of bed, screaming as he went, and crawled up to the wall. She was dead and by the look of her, she'd been dead for a while. Her skin was dry and sagging, while patches of blisters infected her once-beautiful face. Mucus had foamed out of the mouth, run down onto her neck, and had become dry and crusty. Last were her eyes, gray and empty of life beside the maggots in the corners. He didn't want to know how long he'd been lying next to her while she decomposed. He couldn't ask her for her name anymore.

He crawled his way to the bathroom and vomited into the toilet, spewing out whatever had lain at the bottom of his stomach. He climbed to his feet, grabbing the sink for stability. Turning on the tap, he washed away his tears and the vomit off his face.

He stared at his reflection in the mirror. His skin, white as cotton, loosely fitted his sharp jagged skull. Purple veins surrounded his eye sockets and the corners of his mouth. His eyes showed no emotion. They were soulless. He figured if anyone saw him and the woman together, they would have been more frightened of him. He opened the bathroom door, and there she was, lying in bed with her beautiful hair. From that angle, she looked perfect, but the smell gave it away.

You better leave now, whispered the cautious voice. Sam agreed silently, believing he had thought of it first. Purposely avoiding the sight of his former beauty, he chucked on some spare clothes, a pair of pants, a jacket, and a creased damp shirt. *The drugs. She has no use for them now,* said the voice, so faint he barely heard it. He quickly grabbed all the drugs and money he could find and stuffed it all in his jacket pockets. He was going to need the gluttonous substance more than ever. With the clothes on his back and his pockets full, he left the woman's apartment. He didn't look back. He didn't forget her name. He couldn't forget something he'd never known.

The sun was already starting to set. It was obscured by the tall buildings, and yet the light still stung his eyes and the rays burned his delicate skin. *How long was I out for?* he asked himself, knowing it was of little importance. Left with nothing but a pocket full of drugs and money, he wasn't sure what to do. He saw the shocked reactions of people walking by. He was getting the wrong sort of attention. He knew he couldn't just stand there so, he decided to walk, keeping his head pointed down toward the ground.

The day got darker and darker. How long he walked for, he didn't know. Minutes? Hours? It was all a blur. A misty haze clouded his already scrambled mind. He was sad about what had happened to the woman, but he had become numb to such emotions. The same questions kept turning in his head. *Why is this happening? Why am I being punished?* He didn't answer them nor think about them. He had heard them plenty of times before. He had grown rather sick of it, like hearing someone tell a story and you already know what's coming next. Sam didn't know what was coming for him next. Not that he would have cared if he did. Nothing could harm Sam.

TWENTY

I t had got dark. Small droplets started falling from the sky. A young sickly looking man, who went by the name of Sam, walked slowly into an alleyway. He stopped and looked up at the night sky. The refreshing mist landed on his face. He was disoriented. His scrambled mind couldn't decide if the sky was ominous or peaceful. The clouds swirled around, and the colossal brick building soared straight up, capturing the night sky in a picture frame. If only his ability was to fly. He would have been able to float up there forever, lying on a soft bed of clouds alone. He liked the sound of being alone, at this moment in time. He stayed there a while and let the rain fall into his mouth. It was the happiest he had been for a while.

"Hey, you! Sam, isn't it?" shouted a man, interrupting Sam from his trance. Sam slowly turned around and saw three men blocking the entrance to the alley. They were all of different levels of familiarity with Sam. There were a short skinny man and a large bulky fellow. Both were drug dealers he had dealt with before; whose names were unknown. In the middle stood another man who Sam called Jackie, but preferred to be called Jack. He was still wearing his jewelry, yet now he was wearing a dark-green shirt.

"Jackie, how's it going?" Sam said with his crackly voice.

"It's Jack, asshole, but don't worry, that will be the last time you get it wrong," Jack snarled. The other two stayed silent. It was clear to Sam who was in charge. The three men all stood prepared and ready to fight.

"Whatever." Sam brushed aside the threat. His face glowed in the moonlight.

"I've been looking for you for over a month. You look like shit," Jack said, getting a glimpse of Sam's corpse-like appearance.

"I feel like shit." Sam was tired of talking. He wanted to be alone. "This isn't a good time for me. Come back in a couple of years. Haha."

Jack gave a swift nod to the two men. "It's too late to walk away now. Gotta finish this."

Sam cautiously watched as the other men circled him.

"I told you, you would regret what you did." Jack pulled out a pair of shiny unused brass knuckles from his pocket.

Now surrounded, Sam figured he wasn't going to have the peace he wanted. "Look, I'm sorry," he said, sounding truly sincere.

Jack and the others stopped, waiting for him to elaborate.

"I'm sorry. You don't dress like a nigger." He paused and started smirking. "You dress like a fag."

Jack gave another nod. The short man swung a baseball bat into the back of Sam's leg. With a loud crack, Sam fell to his knees. Other than a twitch of his lips, Sam showed little emotion.

Jack walked up and threw several punches to his face.

Sam's head rattled around on his neck with each hit. The cold brass tore through his thin skin, showing the layer of flesh underneath. He still didn't react or retaliate. He simply let the blows collide with his face.

Jack started to get fatigued. Having a few moments to catch his breath, he figured he would give Sam a break as well.

Sam spat out a mixture of phlegm, blood, and fragments of teeth. "You punch like a faggot too," he said, and laughed, his face looking like a bruised plum.

Infuriated, Jack continued the beating, throwing his punches erratically. He cracked Sam's cheekbone. A quick forward jap shattered his nose.

Sam still didn't react. He was unrecognizable; no longer looking human.

Jack swiveled his hips and threw a strong right hook to Sam's jaw, knocking him to the ground.

He started to groan, and struggled to pick himself up back onto his knees.

Jack stood in horror looking down at Sam's face. Sam didn't show much emotion, even with a completely dislocated jaw, saliva mixed with blood, and shattered teeth.

"You know, that actually hurt a little," Sam gargled.

Jack froze, looking into those evil eyes. "What the fuck are you?" he said under his breath.

"Jack, it's time to finish this," the thin man said, checking the entrance to the alley.

Jack nodded again and pulled himself back together. He placed the now blood-soaked knuckles back in his pockets. Then he took out a gun from behind his back.

The light mist had turned into heavy droplets, diluting the blood on Sam's face. He got a glimpse of the gun—wet and shiny—and started mumbling to himself, "Colt 1911. Semi-automatic. .45 rounds. Seven rounds per clip."

Jack cocked the gun that Sam was very familiar with and placed it against his forehead.

Holding the Colt in his hand gave Jack confidence. "Any last words?"

Sam rolled his eyes to the back of his head, trying to find the right words in his beaten brain. "Please, don't miss. Please," he said, pushing his forehead harder onto the barrel.

Jack couldn't understand what he'd said. It wasn't important. He was about to kill him. He pulled the trigger.

The .45 round entered Sam's skull. The metal electrified his brain as it passed through. Everything became vibrant and colorful. When the round erupted out the back of his head, he quickly snatched the gun out of Jack's hand. A fast punch into Jack's chest sent him flying to the wet ground. The mutilated Sam stood and pointed the gun back at him.

Jack looked petrified from what he was seeing, and thought his life was about to end.

Sam fired a shot but the short man had swung again, sending the slugger into Sam's face. He wasted the shot, firing it into the night sky.

The large fellow grabbed Sam from behind, pinning Sam's arms in the air. He tossed and turned trying to free himself. The man's fingers interlocked onto the back of his head. Several fingers sank into his exposed brain, which was extremely unpleasant.

The short man rushed over, having dropped the bat and now brandishing a knife. With a high-pitched growl, he lunged the blade into Sam's stomach.

Unphased, Sam kept trying to break free. The man behind him struggled to keep hold. The knife-wielder started to panic and stabbed Sam, again and again, severing arteries and slicing off chunks of flesh. The next thrust with the blade went in between Sam's lower two ribs, scraping the bone. It hurt. So much so that he let out a demonic, animalistic roar. He kneed the knife-wielder in the groin and kicked him away, smashing him into the wall.

Spitting and screaming, Sam pushed backward, pressing the larger man into the opposite wall. Finally, Sam was able to get his gun arm free. He fired four shots into his own chest. They passed through his black heart, stopping in the large man's chest with wet thuds. Both bodies dropped to the floor. Sam was the only one still alive, and just strong enough to fire his last shot between the thin man's eyes. Sam's arm went limp and landed on the ground. His heartbeat slowed and blood started pouring out of every wound, creating a lake of which he was an island in the center. His neck deliriously rocked from side to side.

He saw a blurry figure pick up the knife and take the gun out of his hand. He craned his neck. It was Jack. He couldn't see very clearly as the bat strike had shattered one of his eye sockets. He could still tell it was him by the color of his shirt.

Jack knelt down; his emotions encased in dread. "What the fuck are you?"

What remained of Sam leaned forward. Squelching sounds came from his oozing wounds. "See you around, Jackie," he said. The voice was clear and very sure of itself. A voice unlike his own. He smiled the best he could with his hanging jaw, showing the few shark teeth he had left.

A shiver crawled over Jack's body and lingered on his spine. He plucked up the courage to lift the blade and jaggedly ripped Sam's throat.

Jack left the alleyway alone, taking the Colt and knife with him. He left three corpses behind. He wasn't sure what had just happened, thinking it was all just a dream. He only knew that it had changed him. Nothing could have been as terrifying as what he had just witnessed. He lit a cigarette, too breathless to take in the toxic fumes.

He was about to walk off, but his curiosity got the better of him. *Just one more look.* He peered back into the long dark tomb. His fears weren't going away any time soon. The cigarette fell from his mouth. He sprinted off as fast as his feet could take him, taking the Colt and knife with him, and leaving two corpses behind in the alley.

Sam made his way back to his apartment, and hobbled up the front steps. He was too delirious to hear the meowing behind him. He just wanted it all to end.

Clambering his way up the staircase, his shoulder rubbed against the wall, leaving a trail of blood. With his poor vision, he could barely see in the darkness, which frustratingly made the journey longer. Taking care to feel for each step, he firmly trudged forward.

His wounds still hadn't yet healed, and gunshots and lacerations riddled his body. The blood had just started to coagulate, forming a gel cork that prevented his blood from spraying out. His face was unrecognizable, and not human. A color palette of purples, blues and reds, and a small glint of white, where his bone poked out of his skin. His eyes stained with blood, created crimson marbles. His nose was no longer there and, lastly, there was his jaw. The dislocated bone dangled, only staying attached by the flesh of his cheek. His elongated mouth was littered with razor-sharp teeth held loosely within his bruised gums. He had no interest in his wounds. He just wanted to get into bed and forget everything. Hopefully, never to wake up.

He was just a few feet away from his door. With the key ready in his hands, he was swaying in a figure of eight. His body wouldn't do what he wanted. With no light and the blood drying in his eyes, it made it impossible to unlock the door. He missed the lock and scratched the paint off the wood. He groaned and gargled, increasing the speed of his attempts.

The door to the apartment next to his opened. The light within began to illuminate the hallway. His punctured heart began to throb. He wouldn't have time to unlock his door. He dashed into the corner where the light stopped; next to the staircase to the floor above. He stood as silent and quiet as his body would allow, keeping his face pressed against the wall.

"Daddy, is that you?"

He didn't respond, hoping she would go away.

Come on, don't be rude. Introduce yourself, said the voice, squirming around his open skull.

He fought the urge to talk, but he could feel her tiny presence and knew she wasn't going to leave. He tried his best to speak softly and clearly. "I ain't your daddy, little girl," he said, wincing through the pain.

The brave young girl turned and faced the darkness. "Are you okay, mister?"

Sam really needed to get into his apartment, but it would be impossible without stepping into the light. He swayed, shifting his weight from each foot. He rested his forehead on the wall. "Why do you say that, little girl?"

"Your voice, mister. It sounds sad."

Sam smiled at the understatement. "You're a smart girl." He paused. His lungs deflated and his heart cramped. "Maybe I am a little sad."

"Why are you sad, mister?" the girl's squeaky voice stung his ears.

The hole in his head made him think more freely. "A lot of reasons. Some more than others." His heart started to beat more frequently, and, in turn, making him relax. It felt good to let his feelings out. Even if they were vague and told to someone too young to comprehend them. It made him feel normal, compared to how he looked. His heart beat even faster, making him groan as he spoke. "I've never talked about these things before."

"My mommy said if you're sad you should talk to someone about it," the little girl said with such confidence in her tone.

"She said that."

183

"Yes, mister. She said you shouldn't keep secrets all bottled up inside."

Sam chuckled and heard an echo of laughter inside his mind. "Well, I've got a lot of those. Someone would have to listen for quite some time for me to share them all."

A force pushed Sam against the wall. Using his hands, he braced himself.

Someone. Why do you need to talk to someone? You've got me. The voice sounded angry and irritated. *You don't need to talk to that girl.*

Sam tried to block out the voice, but it was too strong.

Go on. Step into the light. Show your face.

Sam ignored the request.

Do it! Scare that little nigger bitch! Make her shit herself!

Sam turned his neck, just enough to see her little brown feet.

It would have been easy and would have solved his problem. He imagined emerging from the shadow. "Do I look sad to you?" With his crooked ghoul mouth grinning at her.

The terrified girl would be screaming back inside and scurrying under her bed. She'd be feeling safer with the monsters there, compared to the one outside.

"No."

"What did you say, mister?"

"You best go inside, girl. There are dangerous people around. Close the door. Wait for your dad," Sam said, proud of his mental strength yet could still feel tugging on his skin.

"Okay. Good night, mister." She closed the door, taking the light with her.

Pathetic! said the voice enraged as it didn't get to have its fun.

"She was just a little girl," Sam whispered, knowing the voice could still hear. He stumbled back to his door, steadying the key in his hand. Then he remembered. He never locked it.

The apartment was exactly how he'd left it. He made his way to the bed, kicking the trash away from under his feet. He didn't waste any time tearing off his shredded and bloody clothes. He placed the mattress back on the bed and collapsed onto it.

Groaning and aching in pain, he mixed up all the heroin he had left, creating the strongest batch he could. He started injecting himself where possible. In his thigh, intact patches in his arm, between his toes. With shot after shot, he increased the number of puncture wounds he had accumulated. Finally, he stuck the now-blunt needle into the exposed flesh of his jaw. The cold liquid spread under his skin. A drop of the mixture fell onto his tongue making it flinch like it had received a static shock.

The intoxication began to cover every inch of his body. His heart slowed dramatically; a strong beat every ten seconds. His eyes rolled to the back of his head, showing the purest white sclera. His heart slowed even more. Then it stopped.

TWENTY-ONE

S am found himself in a dark empty void. But he wasn't alone. There was a sound coming from behind him. A gravelly rough sound, like something was struggling to breathe. Then came the smell; almost sour like gone off milk. It was so pungent Sam could taste it at the back of his throat. Finally, he heard a voice, a very familiar one. But it was not someone he knew. Crackly and damp, with a deep southern drawl. "Wake up, William."

Sam opened his eyes. He was hot and sweaty but relieved to be in his apartment. It was still dark. The moon was creeping in through the gap in the drapes. He rubbed the sweat away, slowing his movement down he checked his face in the darkness. He couldn't feel any wounds. All cuts were healed. The entry and exit wounds of the gunshots completely sealed. Even his jaw was pulled miraculously back into position.

Sam hadn't had any doubts. He'd never had any problems before. He wasn't going to start getting them now. Sliding his hand down to his chest, he felt the same occurrence. No cuts, no gunshot wounds, and torn-off flesh replaced with new. The only difference now was the silky soft texture of newly formed scars. He breathed a sigh of relief that he was back to his sense of normal.

He moved his hands off his newly formed body to grab the sheets, and then realized something didn't seem right. *Scars. I can only feel the scars.* Sam looked down at his chest, straining to see in the moonlight. *Where's the blood?*

He felt his body again. It was soft and clean. He scanned over the white sheets. Not a drop or smudge of blood on them. He could have sworn he hadn't taken a shower before climbing into bed. But it was all a little bit hazy. He needed to know what was going on. He was just about to jump out of bed and switch on the light but he stopped dead when he saw it.

The dark shadowy figure stood in the corner of the room, right next to the light switch. Sam's eyes had adjusted to the room yet the light and his vision stopped short, keeping the stranger concealed in darkness. Sam wasn't sure what to do. He felt vulnerable sitting naked in bed. He observed the curious silhouette that gently rocked from side to side. It felt like he'd been staring at it for a lifetime; never taking his eyes off it for a second. Finally, he initiated a conversation.

"Who's there? What do you want?" he said, demanding an answer, and hiding his fear from the unknown.

"William," it whispered after an irregular amount of time for a normal conversation. The shadow wobbled more dramatically, struggling to stay on its feet.

"I said, who are you!" Sam barked, irritated by its ineptitude.

A whisper came again from the shadow. It paused every few words, trying to catch its breath. "William. You hurt me, William. After all. We've. Been through. Together."

Sam was confused and distraught. *How does it know my name?*

Sam wasn't getting anywhere by asking for its name. "What do you want?"

The silhouette started darting around the room, too fast for Sam to keep his gaze on it. Still, it kept to the shadows. "What do I want? Question is... what do you want?" Its voice began to loosen.

Sam remained silent.

"Hahaha." A croaky laugh came from the darkness. "You don't know, do you, boy?"

"Don't call me boy," Sam snapped, tempted to pounce.

"Why?" The voice interrupted Sam from his action. "For it's the only title that ever evokes emotion out of you." The voice crackled as it spoke, seeming to be as irritated as Sam. "How many names have you gone by now, hey?" It paused. Disgusting sounds of cracking and squelching came from the direction of the voice. "Fuck, I bet you'll go by the name Jackie next. Haha." It gargled and sputtered with each laugh.

Sam was speechless and trying hard to hide his emotions. It seemed to know everything about him. "I'm not a boy."

"No, you are not," the voice said with such confidence in its words. "From the lust of the father's joy. To the anger of the fallen devil. When the treachery of grace comes. We both know you ain't a boy."

"Why the fuck are you talking all this religious shit for!" Sam shouted, grabbing fistfuls of the bedsheet.

"Haha, you and I both know there ain't no such thing." Again, with all the crackling. "Nothing of this had anything to do with religion. All of this is down to you."

"What?" Sam struggled to process all the words. "None of this was my fault." Sam tried to defend himself but the figure was too quick-witted for him, countering everything he had to say. Though it did let something slip. Its hand or what was left of it. Its nails long and brown stuck in old bone, wrapped in loose shreds of skin. With the sight of the hand came the smell; decaying meat, damp mold, and dead fish.

Sam covered his mouth to stop from vomiting. He grew cold. "What are you?" Sam asked.

"Not your fault, you say. Then answer me this," it grunted. "How many times have you passed by someone, minding their own business, then you decided to interfere with their lives– No." The figure paused, thinking over its choice of words. "Destroy their lives." It chuckled a mucus-filled laugh. "No, it ain't never your fault."

Sam's mind became a chasm, nothing fitting together, and jumbled into an incohesive mess. He shook his head mumbling. "No, no. People came into my life."

"Your life." The voice sounded surprised. "And what life would that be?" It continued to shift around the room. "A man with no life can only interfere with someone else's." Out of the darkness, it pointed its decaying finger at Sam. "You have no life. You lived long, but not lived a life."

Sam didn't take any notice of its words. His eyes twitched and swiveled in their sockets, trying to get a better look at what the hand was attached to. Wet and moldy, ripped, and moth-eaten, but the gray cuff was still prominent. The subtle glint of the once-golden stitching, reflecting in the moonlight. "You're the voice. The voice in my head."

It pulled its hand back into the abyss. "Well done there, young William, and you've dropped your fake accent. I'm so very proud of you. But that don't mean much does it. Haha."

"Where the fuck did you come from?" Sam said, spitting out his rusty southerness.

"Come from? William, I've always been here. It would have been impossible not to," the darkness said. Even behind the crackling and wheezing, it sounded confused.

"I was there when you took your first steps so long ago.

When you kissed your first woman. When you died the first time."

Sam knew the voice was trying to be comforting, saying he was never alone. But it just disturbed him even more. Something so vile lurking inside him. "Died the first time," Sam repeated. "How is it possible? Why am I like this?"

The shadow sighed in disappointment. Two people were talking, yet they were having separate conversations.

"How is life possible? Beginning and ending so quickly. It doesn't end for you." Its voice started to tighten. "Life begins for some many, then you take it away."

"It's not my fault!"

"Again, you shift the blame off yourself, passing on the judgment," the voice spoke its undeniable truth.

Sweat started pouring off of Sam's healed face. "I never asked for this shit. I never wanted it; never needed it. I never asked for you. I never wanted you. I don't need you."

A horrifying crack came from the darkness, making Sam flinch backward. He knew the sound came from the figure's neck, and could feel its concealed eyes staring deep within his soul.

The voice let out a wheezing growl. "You don't need me." In a heartbeat, the monstrous figure pounced toward Sam. Leaping onto him, it held him down by his shoulders.

Sam cowered in terror at the sight of the creature. Its elongated neck contorted out of the Confederate jacket like a snake. Its soggy decomposing skin hung from its cracked and shattered skull. Long jagged black teeth sat fragile in its drooping jaw.

"You don't need me!" it said in a violent rage. "I'm the one who keeps the darkness at bay gripping you to the fields. I'm the one who gives you wings when you fall and softens the ground when you land."

Sam couldn't move, too terrified to even try. He couldn't even avert his eyes from the monster's gaze. The thin line of the green iris was enlaced with the strongest evil he had ever seen.

Its rage grew. It stabbed its serrated nails into Sam's chest.

"I'm the one who keeps your heart pumping." It grabbed Sam's arm in a vice-like grip, cutting off the circulation. "Your bones from breaking." Releasing his chest, it fish-hooked its nails into Sam's head. "Your brain functioning." The face leaned in, close enough for Sam to feel the moisture on its breath. "Without me, you would have died in the war before you saw your brother's head get blown the fuck off."

Its rage started to subside. "Without me, you would have died of a stroke when you woke up in a blind sweat. Shit, without me, you'd be dying of an overdose right now." It released Sam from its force and stood up from the bed. "It's your choices that keep me here, and you will live with that." It started to shift back into the darkness.

Sam pulled himself up. The pain of the monster still consistent in his mind and body. "Then it's your fault. It's your fault I'm like this. What I've done," he said, clutching his chest.

The monster let out a long, tired, and breathless sigh. Then turned and stared into Sam's green eyes. "You still don't get it, young William. I am you." It raised its crippled arm and flicked on the light.

Sam woke up with a scream. The faint moonlight had switched to bright sunlight. The room was fully lit and the monster, fortunately, wasn't there to welcome him. His body was covered in sweat and blood; a relaxing sight for him. *Was that all just a dream?*

He rubbed his hands over his face. It was fully healed but he could feel the roughness of the dry blood. He climbed out of bed. His limbs were sore.

Taking the hottest shower he could muster, he pondered over the figure's words. *I am you. Could that be true?* He tried to decipher the words; too deep in his thoughts to feel the water scalding his skin.

Stepping out of the steaming shower, he moved over to the sink. Steam rose off his body. The cupboard door was open. *Must have been when I was searching for a fix.* He placed his trigger finger on the frame about to close it.

I am you.

He hesitated. He wasn't sure what he would see when he looked in the mirror. He slowly pushed the door shut. The hinges creaked when they closed. His heart sank.

He stared at his fresh face. His wounds had completely vanished. There was not even a new scar, and he didn't see the drug-addicted skin. His flesh was healthy and pure of toxins. He didn't even crave the substance anymore.

He felt dirty and a cheat. He had avoided death again, and lost his addiction. Yet those weren't the reasons why he felt so terrible. Looking into the green eyes behind his own, there was the ill, rotten monster staring back at him.

I am you.

Sam quickly struck the mirror, shattering it into tiny pieces. As the shards fell, a faint laugh echoed out.

Sam realized acting out in violence wasn't going to make it go away. He walked out of the bathroom, got dressed, and left the apartment.

He knocked on the neighbors' door. It seemed the little girl knew Sam the most at that moment. He started to squirm, expecting the man he had beaten half to death would answer.

"Can I help you?"

Sam stumbled and stuttered when a white-skin man he had never seen before answered the door. "Umm. Yeah. A dark family was living here. With a little girl."

The man grunted, "I moved here three months ago. The owner put it up for sale after their wife died or something like that. Why do you want to know anyway?"

Sam wasn't paying him any attention. *Three months*. He didn't know what was worse, being dead or talking to that thing for so long.

"Hey, why do you want to know? You slow or something?"

"Uhm no, I own the apartment next door. My name's..."

The man who went by the name Sam couldn't finish the sentence. He could feel the monster scratching at the back of his neck. He didn't want to prove it right.

"Jack. The name's Jack."

The newly named Jack sighed. His heart sank to his stomach.

"Hmm. I didn't know anyone lived in that apartment."

"They don't." Jack nodded. He quickly proceeded down the stairs.

"I wouldn't have bought this place if I'd known a nigger owned it first!" the man blurted out.

Jack raced down the stairs and out the front door. With the little girl gone, he felt compelled to do what she said.

TWENTY-TWO

Joanna thought a change of scenery would do Adam some good. They went out onto the front porch. Adam sat on the bottom step.

"Schizophrenia."

"What was that?" shouted Adam back to Joanna who was leaning on the wall, not able to hear over the busy New York streets. Engines roaring, bellowing horns, and screaming people. It all made Adam feel uneasy.

"Schizophrenia," Joanna repeated, walking down the steps and taking a seat next to Adam. She gritted her teeth as she bent down. Her body wasn't as strong as it once had been. "*Auditory hallucinations* is the term used when someone can hear voices in their head. You have mentioned having some visual hallucinations several times now," she said, her mouth close to his ear. She continued but moving out of his personal space. "Well, that would be my explanation for simpler cases."

"So, I'm not a simple case?" Adam said, wanting acknowledgment.

"You and I both know there is nothing simple about you," she replied.

Adam started to fidget. His voice was shaking. "I know you may think this could be boiled down to a couple of mental disorders but I heard that voice, felt its skin, and tasted its smell." He sparked up a cigarette; the flame shook as cars drove by. "I know who it was now. I didn't believe it, but I know now. It was me talking. My true self talking back." He placed his head in between his legs, filling up the space with smoke. The tar vanished from his lungs as fast as he could breathe it in.

Joanna placed her hand on his shoulder; it was a cheap tactic to keep him talking.

"I never did find out the woman's name. She died because of me. I never saw that little girl again either." Raising his head, he took in a lung full of clean air before the smoke clouded his face. "The next part of my life got surprisingly better."

"How so?" Joanna said, her eyes widening.

Adam turned to face her. "I met you."

TWENTY-THREE

1979. The newly formed Jack had a new, unfamiliar goal in his life. Listening to the unexpected advice of a little girl, when he had only seen her little brown feet. He felt like he owed it to her. He had lost everything once again and had nothing better to do. Besides, he had done worse things in his life. *If you're sad, you should talk to someone.*

Jack barged his way into the front door of a psychiatrist's office. It wasn't the first he had walked into, but it would be the last.

The others had either sent him away or wanted to lock him up. That wasn't going to happen. He wasn't going to spend endless days in a padded cell, being prodded and poked. He'd be out of their offices as soon as they said something along the lines of *"I would like to observe you for a few days,"* or *"I can recommend a great place that deals with your symptoms."*

He didn't fall for it, and would leave with or without force. He figured that keeping things vague would be the best bet from here on out.

"Anyone here? Hello!" he shouted at the top of his voice,

standing in the middle of the waiting room. The door opened to the neighboring room. The woman peeking out was about to become a distant but long-term friend.

"Can I help you?" squeaked a timid and nervous voice.

Jack looked over to see a young brunette. He thought she looked scared. Of course, she was. A large man was shouting at her. Jack tried to calm down, but his patience had worn thin. "Yeah, I'm looking for the doctor," he said.

"Well, I'm not a doctor, but this is my practice."

Jack stood in shock and doubt. Maybe he had walked into the wrong place. "If you ain't a doctor, then I don't think you can help me." He started to walk back out of the building to continue his search for help.

"Yet. I'm not a doctor yet," she replied, regretting it instantly, thinking he could be trouble and she should have just let him go. But it was too late now. With butterflies in her stomach, she opened the door fully. "I'm a psychologist, not a medically trained doctor. Please, come take a seat."

Jack walked over, leaning his head through the doorway and checking the layout of the room. Two brown leather chairs pointed at each other. One against the window and the other looking out. A desk covered in paperwork was in the far corner, and an oil painting was mounted on the wall behind it. The smell of mahogany went up to his nostrils, softly sweet like unripe cherries. Finally, he stepped in.

He jumped out of his skin when the woman closed the door behind him. Her sweaty palm slipped off the brass doorknob. "Like I was saying, I'm not a doctor yet. But I will finish my doctorate in the next year or so." She started stacking all the paperwork scattered on her deck. "I study psychology, in which I study human behavior."

Jack's face went blank. Her words went over his head.

"Mrs. Joanna Chambers," she said, walking over to him and offering her hand.

Jack stood a foot taller than her. He could feel her hand trembling, under his loose grip. "Jack."

"Anything else to go with that?" she asked.

His eyes darted from left to right. "No, just Jack." They let go of each other's hands.

"Very well. Please, take a seat," Joanna said, gesturing to a chair against the window.

Jack pulled out a cigarette.

"I'm afraid there's no smoking in here. I quit a couple of weeks back and don't need the temptation."

Jack rolled his eyes and put the cigarette away. He sat down on the squeaky leather, burning his skin as it had been baking in the sun.

Joanna sat in the chair opposite, holding a pen and pad of paper. "So, what can I help you with?" She looked down at her blank sheet, ready to write what he said.

Jack kept to his plan. "I'm tired of this life."

Joanna lifted her head and looked him up and down. He was young. By her guess, he was a good ten years younger than her at least. "What do you mean by that?"

"I'm tired of everything. Everything I have done boils down to nothing. Then I end up with nothing." She quickly jotted down his words, then read them back to herself. "Uhm, I'm still not quite sure what you're telling me?"

Jack's brow pulled closer to his eyes. "You're the doctor. You tell me. Oh wait, you're not a doctor yet."

Joanna's stomach kept on churning and wasn't going to stop. His words hurt. She wanted to make him leave, but her need to help was stronger. "You're still young, you've got plenty of time to figure things out. You don't want to be making any rash decisions."

"I'm a lot older than you think," Jack muttered through his gritted teeth.

"How old are you?"

Jack quickly snapped his head to the floor, suddenly remembering his plan. "It's not important."

"Well, let me ask you this. Why did you come to me?" Her voice cracked with emotion. "There are many other professionals around who would happily help you."

"I know. I've been to them already. They weren't as helpful as you'd think."

"How long did you talk to them for?"

Jack shrugged. "Half an hour, I guess." He had no clue, barely knowing what a minute was.

"What happened? Didn't they want to work with you?" she asked, writing down everything that was said.

"No, I walked out."

"Any particular reason?"

Jack started to dig his nails into the armrests. "I didn't like what they had to say. They were wasting my time."

"Well, let's hope we'll last a little bit longer." She cleared her throat. Leaning back in her chair, she scanned over her notes. "You say you're tired of life. Anything specific? Family, friends, work?"

Jack stared blankly past her. His vision focused on the

painting on the wall. Two brown adult horses, exactly like the one he used to ride. The third was a gray foal, speckled with black spots. They were running together in a valley; the clearing was surrounded by trees. They were happy. A family. Unlike Jack who was alone. "I haven't got any of those," he said.

Joanna leaned in. "You have no family?"

Jack shook his head. His face was tense with anger and a teardrop was caught in his eye. He tried to picture his family at the dinner table, but all he could muster was a blurry reflection in a dirty puddle. He quickly wiped away the tear feeling embarrassed. He wanted to get up. "This is a waste of time. I am not here to think about my past. I want to know my future."

―――――――

"Future," Joanna said, raising her pitch. "You're young and you're tired of life. Yet you care so much about wasting time." Joanna felt surprised, holding in a smile about what she had said. She glanced at her wristwatch. They may not have been talking the whole time, but an hour had already passed. "I'd like you to come back tomorrow. Would you do that for me?"

―――――――

Jack was about to turn her offer down. Then realized why he was there in the first place. He could see the little girl's feet in his mind, as clear as the painting in front of him. He gave Joanna a nod and stood up from the chair.

―――――――

Joanna grabbed him by the arm. Her heart started to pound, waiting for the repercussions of touching him. Yet he just looked back at her with dead eyes. "You may be tired of life, Jack, but life isn't tired of you. Don't hurt anyone."

Jack nodded again. He didn't want to explain what that meant. *I've only ever hurt people.*

He left the building and lit up a cigarette. He felt different, relaxed like he had woken up from a long sleep. He wasn't sure what to do, but he didn't mind. He just started walking back to his apartment. He figured he would have to buy another car. He had walked over forty blocks, getting lost within the labyrinth of buildings.

He started to ponder what it would be like to jump off the top of one of the colossal rooftops. Falling through the cold wind, the people and cars getting closer and closer. Then the inevitable stop. Craning his neck to see the top of the building, he had forgotten that that had already happened to him.

A warm breeze infused with music came blowing past. He had heard the sound before. Searching his stretched-out mind high and low, he spun around, trying to pinpoint where the sound was coming from.

He stood outside a bar. The music radiated out of the bricks. The building stood smack bang in the middle of the avenue. It was painted matt black. The name was written in large gold calligraphy above the door, spanning the length of the building. *The Palace.*

Jack must've passed the place a dozen times, but never noticed it. With a smile on his face, he opened the first set of doors, heavy and strong. Bushing his feet on the mat, he gazed through the murky glass of the second set of doors. His smile diminished seeing a room full of white teeth.

"Well, that's fucking great," he muttered. He moved his head around to get a better look. The band on the stage was playing the sound that had got him there. People were drinking, smoking and laughing, and not a white person in sight.

A slightly heavyset fellow limped over to the bar. He took a seat on a stool, taking the weight off his legs. He waved over the woman behind the bar, pointing at some liquor on the shelf and speaking some meaningful words. In return, she gave him an appreciative smile.

Jack felt a peculiar sensation, knowing she was about to look in his direction. He quickly made haste out of the first set of doors before she could meet his gaze. He only let her see the back of his head as he left.

The next morning, Jack entered Joanna's building for the second time. He was feeling more at ease since he didn't have to introduce himself again.

The door to her office crept open.

"Oh, I'm glad to see you've made it," Joanna said politely. "I'm afraid I've already got a client at the moment, but you're more than welcome to wait."

Jack nodded and took a seat.

He sat there quietly. He had nothing to say to himself. He simply stared at the wall in front of him. There was nothing interesting about it. There were another couple of chairs pressed up against it. It seemed they weren't used much, compared to the side he was sitting on. Jack guessed it was because people wanted to look at the door to Joanna's office, perhaps thinking they would be picked next if they were seen first.

A few paintings of landscapes scattered the wall he was staring at. He thought they were there to relax any waiting patients. Intrigued, he turned to check the wall behind him. It was littered only with medical advice and articles. *Perhaps that was the reason people choose to sit on this side.*

"I'm sorry. I should only be a few minutes longer," Joanna

said, peeking out the door. She closed it again before Jack could reply. He turned back and faced the more appealing wall. He started to wonder at the reason why he was there. The little girl, or the monster?

"I'm ready to see you now. Please, come on in," Joanna said opening the door.

He got up and walked into the other room. He searched around but there wasn't anyone else in there. "Please, take a seat."

He sat down waiting for her to join. "What's this, some kind of joke?"

"No, it's not a joke." Joanna settled in her chair. "That was a little test, to try and figure you out."

Jack wasn't amused and screwed up his face. "I don't like being made a fool of," he muttered.

"Well, then there's no time to waste," she said, fluttering her eyelashes. She looked down, scribbling small circles in the corner of her notepad. "You waited very patiently out there," she said, jotting down her words.

Jack shrugged. "It was alright. I wasn't out there long."

Joanna lowered her paper and rested it in her lap. "I made you wait out there for three hours." She waited a moment to let the notion sink in. "It seems apparent to me that you don't mind wasting time if you're on your own," she said, looking at the blank expression slapped across his face.

Her stomach started to feel empty like she hadn't eaten in days. All the thoughts in her head still kept telling her to turn him away. But she couldn't. For some unknown reason, she felt fixated with him and needed to help. She shook her head, dismissing her prognosis. "It's something else, isn't it? The fear that you'll lose someone. You don't want to waste time when you're with them."

———

Jack released a deep sigh. He found it crazy how someone could understand him better than himself. *Maybe she has some unseen ability too?* he thought. Still, he remained quiet, thinking it would be best not to ask. "It's pointless being with people. I always end up alone."

Joanna leaned back in her chair, scanning her notes. "Do you think being alone would be better or easier?"

Jack didn't answer.

"My father, God rest his soul, said that the harder things in life always end up being better." Joanna averted her gaze away from Jack. "I assumed he was referring to fear during the war, but I feel it works in day-to-day life as well."

"Your father was in the war?" Jack said, finally having a subject he knew very well.

"Yes, before my time. Back in England. He landed on the beaches at Normandy." Joanna's bottom lip started to quiver.

It had been a very long time since Jack had felt fear. He was never scared during the war, yet he could still remember marching in the fields in Jackson before any of this had started. That was when he felt the terrifying fear inside. "Hard thing to do, to run toward your own death. Your father was a brave man."

———

Joanna turned away, kicking herself inside. She shouldn't have been letting her emotions go like this. She was feeling extremely unprofessional. "I think we should leave it there for today, we've made good progress."

"Progress to what?" Jack asked.

Joanna didn't reply. She quickly tossed her paper on the desk and showed him the door. Again, she grabbed his arm. "If you could do one thing for me."

"What would that be?" he asked.

"Don't be alone. Find someone to talk to. Come back when you want."

Jack nodded and left the building.

Jack stood right outside The Palace doors. It was the only place he could think of going. He took short, sharp breaths to prepare himself for what he was about to do. Never would he have imagined he would step foot in a place with so many colored people in it. Taking large strides, he made his way in. He figured he could easily burn the place down if he needed to.

Avoiding looking through the glass, he pushed the second doors open and they swung shut behind him. Reddish-brown varnish covered all the surfaces. Tables and chairs covered most of the floor; they were all filled with dark-faced people.

To the left of him stood a rack to hang hats and coats. To the right were several photographs mounted neatly on the wall. Beyond the photo frames, the L-shape bar jutted out. A small stage was in the far-left corner. Even with just a quick gaze, Jack noticed how much of a struggle it must be for the band members and their instruments to fit on it. They managed it, however, without causing a fuss.

Being the only white person in there, was like being a grain of rice in sand. Jack assumed they would all stop and look at him. It certainly would have happened if their skin colors had been reversed. He wasn't sure what to do. He didn't feel unwelcome, but nor did he feel at home. He took a seat on a free stool at the corner of the bar.

Everything started to move slowly. He observed the patrons, the barmaid, and the jazz band playing their song. Talking, smoking, and drinking. Everyone would pause to listen to each of the musicians' solos. Jack couldn't take his eyes off of them. He could see the patience in the drummer's hands. He could hear the strength in the trumpeter's lungs; the skin of the bass player's fingertips ripping. Finally, he could feel the pain in the singer's voice.

"How'd you like those cool cats?" said a slightly heavyset man, interrupting Jack with his deep soulful voice. His eyes were soft and his smile shone from his dark face.

Jack had never been enticed into conversation with a man such as him. Tingles spread over his arms and neck.

"I hate cats," he whispered.

The man was sitting so close he was still able to hear. He let out a deep chuckle.

Jack's piercing eyes didn't move or flinch. Showing a toothy smile, he laughed with the clueless man.

"I like you. Hey, Catherine." The man waved the lady behind the bar.

"How are you, Jerry?" she said, a tone of appreciation in her voice. "What can I get for you?" she continued with a polite hostess smile.

"I'll take a whiskey. Make it a double. My leg is playing up something furious." He started to rub his right knee cap like a crystal ball. "And get one for my friend here."

Jack looked at Jerry out the corner of his eye. He presumed Jerry was using the term friend loosely. Catherine evaluated Jack, looking him up and down.

He kept his head down staring into the shiny polished bar top.

"Ain't you a little young to drink?"

Jack let out a deflated sigh, already starting to lift himself off the stool.

"Oh, get the man a drink, Catherine. He looks like he needs it more than I do," Jerry said, giving a tweak of his neck toward Jack.

She reluctantly agreed with Jerry. She walked over to the counter and poured two double whiskeys. Jack looked at Jerry again, a warmth building up inside him. No money exchanged hands when she served them across the bar. She gave Jerry a quick smile and another glance at Jack, before leaving. "*Tenez vos chevaux, je viens,*" she growled, walking over to an impatient customer at the other end of the bar.

Jerry grabbed his glass firmly and took a small sip. He savored the rich flavor in his mouth.

Jack stared into his glass and swirled it around. It appeared he had lost his thirst.

The band had finished their set, and another started to take their place. They were juggling around the cramped stage. To Jack watching, it seemed to be a nuisance. The band didn't seem to care at all. They seemed more than willing to have the annoyance. The honor of playing was worth it. It reminded him of Joanna's waiting room.

The next few hours drifted slowly by. The bands swapped. People came and went. Jack still sat at the bar, talking to his new acquaintance Jerry, who was doing most of the talking. He was very open to sharing every detail of his life with Jack. He talked about past relationships and up to his present wife. From stories of other bars to the one they were sitting in. He appeared to know everyone in there, giving them all a wave or a firm handshake. A few people even sat down and joined the conversation. Jack only ever gave short, closed replies, subtle smiles, and occasionally said his name. But only when they asked.

Catherine served drink after drink, topping up Jerry's from

time to time. Jack still hadn't touched his. He was too busy listening to the music and the conversations.

The Palace audience started to dwindle. The bands had packed up and gone. Only Jack, Jerry, Catherine, and a few stragglers remained.

"So, Jack, what do you do?" Jerry said, his voice sore and scratchy.

It caught Jack by surprise. Not knowing how to answer it, he swiftly downed his drink. "That was nice," he said. The whiskey burned the lining of his throat. He hopped off the stool. His legs were weak and wobbly. "Thanks for the drink, by the way."

"Don't mention it," Jerry replied. They gave each other a smile and a nod, then Jack quickly left through both sets of doors.

Catherine walked over to Jerry. She leaned on the bar, taking the weight of her feet. *Chi era quell'uomo?*

Jerry screwed up his face. "Why you do that? You know I don't know what you're saying."

Jack stepped out into the dark but still busy street. He lit a cigarette. A strange restless feeling of mystery coursed through his body. He wasn't sure where his life was heading and he kind of liked it. Some things are best left unknown, he supposed.

After a few days, Jack visited Joanna for the third time. He was mildly relaxed with the new fresh experience in his life. Both of them sat in their designated chairs. Jack slowly began to share what he had been up to. He'd been meeting new people and had a newfound taste in music.

Joanna listened so intently she didn't get the chance to write any words down. He didn't even care to mention the color of their skin.

"What about you? How'd you end up here?" Jack asked, starting to get tired of his own voice.

"Well, uh..." Joanna rummaged around her mind.

Jack hid that he was annoyed by the fact she was taking too long. It should have been easy for her.

Eventually, Joanna started to explain how she had traveled from England and come to America. She'd arrived as a little girl with her parents after her grandmother had passed. Joanna was stronger today, and able to keep her emotions at bay. She could barely remember her grandmother. "My father always said I reminded him of her," she said with a wistful smile.

She could recall arriving in New York by ferry, and their luggage being piled up on the docks. Her father kept a cautious hold on a large brown paper package under his arm. "The painting of the horses behind me," Joanna said, gracefully pointing her index finger toward it.

Jack noticed the glint of her wedding ring.

She had been married for several years. He was also a doctor. "We met at university. Love at first sight," she said. Her eyes reflected her words. They had one child. "My daughter started school a year ago, so now I'm able to continue with my doctorate."

Jack with some discretion was envious of what she had. He was also intrigued to know more. "Your father's dead. What about your mother?"

With a soft exhalation, she responded. "She's gone too. She died a few days after my father finished his painting actually. At least she got to see it." Joanna shifted her body to look at the painting. "It took him so long to complete. He changed it so many times." She started to explain to Jack that it had begun as a simple landscape. Every few weeks while she played or read in his study, she would notice the trees that were once there had been painted over. "I have so many versions of that painting in my head." Then on one occasion when a young Joanna went into the study, a gorgeous, majestic horse had appeared. The purest white coat with the bluest of eyes. "I believe he was imagining his mother."

Joanna had become obsessed with it, just as much as her father. Resting on his shoulders, watching every brushstroke, and falling asleep on his lap. When they left England, the horse left the canvas, fading back into the lonely valley.

"Eventually, my father added the three horses, our family." She took a long hard look at the trio, running in unison. The gray foal at the front being watched over by the other two.

Jack leaned to the side with a curious squint. "What about the fourth?"

Joanna turned back completely lost.

"The fourth horse, in the top right, on the ridge of the valley," Jack said, guiding Joanna's gaze.

She turned back to the painting, shifting her eyes to where Jack instructed. She didn't take her eyes off it when she stood up and slowly wandered closer.

―――――――

Joanna was terrified; of what, she didn't know. Suddenly she started to gasp in convulsions. Her eyes drowned in tears. There it was. It was standing on the ridge, looking down into the valley. It was certainly intended to be there, and not just an accidental brush stroke with excess paint on the bristles. A dark black stallion, watching over the other three. Joanna bit her bottom lip, keeping back the tears. She raised her shivering hand and attempted to touch the canvas but resisted, not wanting the oils on her skin to damage it. "I've stared at this painting for so long. Countless hours. I could have recreated it myself by memory alone." She closed her mouth. Short sharp breaths shot out of her nostrils; shivers crawled down her neck. "But I've never seen that horse before."

The stallion had been coated with a dark black, but years of being in the sun had faded it to a dull gray. It had never been painted over. Never been replaced. It had been there since the beginning. Joanna gave in to temptation softly stroking the horse with her fingertip. "How have I never noticed you?" she asked it with a smile. She tried to wipe away the tears, yet they just kept flowing. A mixture of sadness and joy.

Jack had silently approached her from behind. Attaching himself to her like a shadow, he gently placed his hand on her shoulder.

Without warning, she twirled around and squeezed him tight.

He wasn't sure how to react, so he just kept his arms open.

"Thank you so much," she said muffled by his shirt.

"Uhm, that's alright," Jack said with a blank expression across his face, feeling extremely uncomfortable.

Jack was eventually able to leave, getting out quite late. He felt good about himself for helping Joanna. Even though he had no idea what he had done. It was just a painting to him. But he had enjoyed the conversation nevertheless. His throat was dry. He knew where to go.

His mood was deflated stepping into The Palace as his new acquaintance wasn't there. He didn't feel keen on starting again. Just the thought of introducing himself to someone new sounded exhausting. He took the same stool he'd sat on the night before. It was a slow evening with only a dozen people scattered around, but still, they enjoyed each other's company and music.

The man on the piano was practicing more than actually playing. He paused after each line, changing its tone and rhythm. He seemed content in the moment all alone, similar to Jack. Jack liked the sound of having some alone time after what had happened. He was hoping to simply listen to the blissful music with a drink.

The same lady who served Jack the other night was behind the bar. Jack observed her peacefully cleaning glasses purely out of boredom, and conversing in a deep conversation with herself. Her black curly hair and brown eyes matched the color of her skin. He figured she was definitely in her late sixties.

"Can I get a drink?" Jack said. The Palace was still surprisingly loud, even with the minute amount of people. He needed to speak louder if he was ever going to be heard. "Hey!"

She still didn't notice.

"Hey, lady!" he shouted, visualizing his voice flying toward her.

She stopped polishing the already clean glass and looked in Jack's direction. Her eyes were wide yet she still didn't respond.

"Can I get a drink?" he said again, his voice sharp and scratchy. His patience was getting thin.

"*Mœurs blanches,*" she mumbled under her breath. "Hi, what can I do for you?" she asked, a painted polite smile on her face.

"Whiskey," he snapped.

The woman didn't flinch at Jack's bark. With her face muscles taut, she slowly walked over. "Whiskey? I've got a lot of different whiskeys. What would you prefer?" she said, her sarcasm overflowing from out of her plump lips.

"Look, lady, all I want is a drink."

"Lady?" Her eyes widened. "Thank you, but I'm not royalty and don't deserve such a title. The name's Catherine."

Jack didn't want to play her little game. "Miss, I've done enough talking for one today. So, I'll just have a drink and sit here quietly."

"Oh, it's *miss* now. I'm flattered, but I'm already taken."

It became clear that she wasn't finished playing, so Jack planned to win. He slid the stool closer to the bar. "You're married. So where's your husband?"

Catherine's eyes let out several rapid blinks. "Well, he's passed. But I'm still married in my heart," she replied, still quite upbeat. A large smile grew on her face, and her heart pumped warm blood to her rosy cheeks.

Jack thought she was too happy for someone who had lost their husband. He admitted silently to himself that she was very attractive for her age but far too optimistic for him. "Hmm, that was the biggest amount of bullshit I've ever heard," he said, inhaling the first drag on his cigarette.

"Oh, I've definitely heard worse." Catherine pinched the cigarette from between his fingers and placed it between her lips.

The tension was so getting thick, even the smoke had trouble dissipating. She passed the cigarette back to Jack. His eyes engulfed in fury, like a lion stalking its prey. The cigarette was passed back and forth like a flirtatious, but spiteful baton.

"You seem awfully cheerful for someone alone," Jack said.

She tilted her head to the side. "You assume I'm alone. Why is that?"

"No husband. You got any other family?" Jack replied, tracking the scent of his prey.

Catherine's mood started to deteriorate, and her smile disappeared from her face. She stubbed the cigarette in an ashtray. "Well, that's enough talking for one day. Let me get you that drink."

Her attempt to leave ended in failure. Jack had found his prey. "You got any children?"

Catherine froze. She bit down on the plump lip, her eyes glistening with moisture. She shook her head.

Jack could tell it was excruciating for her to do so. He rubbed the stubble on his chin. "Hmm, just in your heart, I suppose."

"*Hurensohn!*" Catherine raised her hand, and with lightning-fast speed, struck Jack's cheek.

His rage exploded when her black skin touched his. The lion pounced off the stool, slamming his hands on the bar. He could have killed her with one swipe of his claws if he so desired.

He caught a glimpse of his reflection in one of the photographs beside him.

The photo was of a group of people standing in a row, posing for the camera. Catherine stood in the middle with a large smile on her face. It wasn't the expression she was giving Jack now.

It took him a moment to see past the darkness of her skin and see the pain she was concealing. He slowly lowered himself back onto the stool.

"*Wie kannst du es wagen,*" she snarled, her voice cracking and tears forming in her eyes. She walked over to the liquor shelf, and back to Jack. Placing a full bottle of whiskey and the mirror-finished glass beside him. "Pour your own goddamn drink." Catherine walked away, clutching something tightly in her hand.

What it was didn't matter now. Jack was left on his own, just like he'd wanted. He didn't feel like he'd won the game.

The hour was solemn with no one to talk to. He slowly made his way through the whiskey bottle. Finally taking the whiskey past the bottom of the label, he felt it was time to leave. With his head down, he calmly pulled himself off the stool. Reaching into his pocket, he pulled out enough money to cover the entire bottle.

He tried to resist but couldn't stop himself glancing at Catherine. There were only a few people in the world who would raise a hand to Jack, mostly fools. Jack knew Catherine was no fool. After several very uncomfortable seconds of eye contact, Jack broke the silence. "Thank you for the drink, Lady Catherine." He slipped away.

He didn't see the small smile appear on her face. She'd accepted his unconventional apology.

Joanna was sitting at her desk, reading and signing off paperwork. They were some of the more mundane parts of the job. It was almost time to leave. She couldn't wait to put her feet up when she got home and was looking forward to having a nice meal with her family and cuddling up together next to the fireplace. She paused for a moment, dropping her pen, and stretching out her arms. Closing her eyes, she let out a loud yawn. She adjusted herself in the chair and continued with her work.

———

"Hey, Joanna."

"Jesus Christ!" Joanna jumped out of her skin. "Jack, I didn't even hear you come in."

"Sorry about that." Jack's voice was soft and slow.

"That's alright," she said, flattening her jacket and tidying her hair. "What can I do for you? I haven't seen you in a while."

Jack stepped into the office, scratching the back of his head. "That's the thing. I'm just here to say that this is the last time you'll see me."

Joanna stood up from her desk, again straightening her clothes. "Okay. I don't quite understand," she said, walking over to him.

"You've helped me sort some things out in my head." He kept things vague. He didn't mention the fact he had locked himself away for the past week in his apartment. For what he guessed was a week anyway. He thought having some solitary time would be a good idea after what had happened the other night at The Palace. Similar to not driving a car after having an accident. It was difficult, after letting himself be connected with human interaction, yet it had to be done. He knew it wasn't about locking him away.

Joanna tried to speak, but he didn't give her a chance. He had already made up his mind. "I just came to say goodbye. And thank you. I've been saying that a lot lately," he said, his eyes not focusing on their surroundings.

"You're welcome," Joanna said with a sympathetic smile.

"Goodbye, Joanna." Jack returned the gesture and proceeded to leave the room.

"Jack." Joanna stopped him for the final time.

He turned around and looked at her.

"It's very late. Get yourself a watch," she said with a cheeky grin.

Jack nodded. He hesitated before leaving. "Maybe I'll come back." He paused, not knowing where the idea had come from. "In a few years. See how things are going."

"That would be nice," she replied, excited at the thought. "I'll see you then."

TWENTY-FOUR

It got too loud outside to stay on the porch, so they both went back to Joanna's office. Adam had taken up his original seat. Joanna sat at her desk with her back toward him smoking a cigarette, and silently gazing into the oily brush strokes of the painting. She had appreciated what he had done for her but now she couldn't shake the feeling of being manipulated for all these years.

"When you said a couple of years, I didn't think you meant two decades. You should have told me," she said, still facing away.

"Like I said, you wouldn't have believed me if I'd told you," Adam replied to the back of the leather chair. "I didn't actually think I'd come to see you again. But something unexpected has happened. I thought you'd be able to help."

Joanna kicked her heels, spinning the chair around. She was sick of his vague and poorly spoken excuses. "What is it? Tell me!" she said, slapping her hands on the desk.

Adam remained silent.

"Is it something to do with Catherine?"

Adam lowered his head and looked down at his shoes when

she said Lady Catherine's name. He shrugged. "Sort of. It's quite complicated."

Joanna nodded and gave him a piercing stare.

Adam took a deep breath. "I'm sorry to hear about your husband by the way."

Joanna's gaze softened and her eyes began to glisten. "Thank you. Wait." She paused. "He died a couple of months back and I never told you."

Adam looked away again. He knew she wouldn't like what he had to say. "I found out by reading a paper. I had to check on you."

Joanna was confused, wondering what he was on about.

"I wanted to make sure you weren't alone or doing anything stupid," he said, looking back at her. His eyes were drained, leaving only a serious glare.

"You were there." Joanna's voice started to crack. "At my husband's funeral. I knew I saw someone skulking around in the distance." She attempted to light another cigarette, but she couldn't get the lighter to spark. "Damn thing!" She slammed it on the desk, flattening the cigarette. She walked away from her desk and started pacing around the room. "How long have you been spying on me?" she yelled, rubbing her head. "I'm not just a small part of your life, Adam, Jack. William. Whatever you want to call yourself. I have my own. I've loved and lost more than you will ever know."

Adam stayed silent again. Her words dug in deep.

"You said you didn't plan this, but all I'm hearing is planning. So why are you here?" She crossed her arms, avoiding the temptation to lash out.

Adam stayed slouched in the chair. His chest kept jumping up and down. He looked like a little boy being interrogated for breaking a lamp.

Joanna relaxed her imposing posture. "I'm sorry," she said, her emotions had got the better of her.

"I'm sorry too. I've been saying that to myself a lot recently," Adam muttered. "I didn't mean for this to happen, and I don't deserve it."

Joanna approached Adam, knelt beside him, and grabbed his hand. "What is it? What don't you deserve?"

He closed his eyes, concentrating on slowing his chest. He felt the sun warming his neck and gestured to the chair in front of him. "How long has it been since we last saw each other?" he asked.

Joanna lowered herself onto her seat and recited his words. "Twenty years, give or take a few days."

Adam took hold of his watch. The time had just passed ten. "They were some of the best years of my life. Then I had my worst day."

TWENTY-FIVE

I t was a simple but fresh time for Jack, spending most nights in The Palace. The cushion of the stool he sat on began to mold to the shape of his backside. It was almost tailor-made for him. It was a shame the cushion was made of cherry-red velvet, making the hairs on the back of his neck stand up. The frame was made of polished oak. Jack would have preferred steel; something more permanent. Slowly drinking and listening to the bands, and joining conversations when he deemed fit, he was always content with eavesdropping on everybody's tales.

He was reluctant to talk to Catherine; not wanting to repeat the past. Yet her being the person who served him drinks made it mandatory. The exchanges were distant but civil, and he would always finish with the words. *Thank you, Lady Catherine.* He said it often enough that it stuck. Eventually, everyone was referring to her as Lady Catherine. Especially after Jerry got wind of it.

Jack thought it was just another regular night, yet the havoc made it stand out more than the rest. He took his tailored seat at the bar. Lady Catherine was managing the bar like always, marching up and down relentlessly. She didn't seem to mind, being the gracious host she was. They were all oddly appreciative of her. The men would give her a soft handshake and a kiss on her cheek. The women would lean across the counter and grab her in a loving embrace.

"Hey, Lady Catherine," hollered the grisly voice of Jerry, weaving his way to the bar.

"Hello there, Jerry. How are you?"

"Not as good as you on this fine evening. Happy Birthday." He leaned in closer. "What's the magic number this year?" Jerry asked.

Catherine began her usual sarcastic quip. "Jerry, you should know better than to ask a lady her age."

"He doesn't know much. He even leaves his wife to put her coat away alone," Jerry's wife said, appearing from the crowd. She was a bubbly, short woman with short natural brown hair. "Happy birthday, Catherine."

"Thank you," Catherine replied.

Jerry's wife grabbed him by his arm. "Come on. You invite me out, then vanish. I'm keeping my eye on you. You don't need to wear your hat inside either."

With them departing, Catherine had an opening to breathe. She looked to her left to see Jack sat down, quietly sipping his drink.

So many people visited The Palace that night. It was the busiest time of the year for the place, even surpassing New Year's. Still, Lady Catherine managed the entire bar single-handedly.

"So, Lady Catherine, the big seven zero," Jerry said, making his way back to the bar with his wife in tow.

"How did you find out?" Catherine retorted.

"Ohh I have contacts who get me information."

"Contacts. Information," his wife interrupted with her eyebrows high and with a patronizing smile on her face. "It was me, Lady Catherine. I knew the year you were born and worked it out," she said, grinding her teeth in frustration. "Foolishly, I let it slip next to my big mouth of a husband."

"It's why you married me."

Catherine gave her a forgiving smile. "It's alright. It's just a number. Just another year without my husband." She froze, not having intended to say the last part.

Jerry stayed quiet for a big-mouthed man. He knew when to stay silent and let his wife do the talking.

"He was a brave man," she said, squeezing Catherine's hand.

"Thank you. But let's not dwell on the past." Catherine's smile grew wider with warmth.

"Hey, let's make a toast!" shouted Jerry. Feeling confident that it was alright to speak, he raised his glass. "To husbands."

The two women raised their glasses, merely humoring him. "To husbands."

Suddenly, everyone else followed. "To husbands!"

Jack kept his head down and remained silent.

"I'm going to powder my nose," Jerry's wife said. She kissed him on the cheek and headed to the restroom.

"Seventy years old. I'm going to be sixty-eight this year," Jerry said, panting and sweating over all the excitement.

Catherine took a small rationed sip of her drink as she needed to stay sharp. "Where does all the time go?" she said.

Jerry gulped down his drink, polishing it off. "What I'd give to be young again," he said, his vision blurred as he fantasized.

Catherine's eyes glimmered and twirled around. "I'll drink to that." She filled his glass and they clinked them together. Then both took large swigs.

Catherine looked back over in Jack's direction. His head was still down. He was running his index finger along the grain of the counter. Catherine had refilled his drink several times throughout the night. He never asked her to do so. She did it anyway, being the generous host that she was. She knew he would pay at the end of the night, and say the four simple words.

She also thought he would be more comfortable not having to ask. He appeared to be lonely. Catherine couldn't help. She found it just as difficult to talk to him as he did to her.

"Hey, Jack!" Jerry hollered, noticing what Catherine was looking at. He didn't take notice of what Jack was doing, nor how he appeared to be feeling.

Jack lifted his head, taking his finger out of the wooden maze he had created.

"When's your birthday?" Jerry asked.

Jack nodded. A simple question to answer after all. Taking a quick sip to moisten his mouth, he opened his lips to speak. Catherine and Jerry watched patiently for several drawn-out seconds. He could feel their eyes burning into him. He started to sweat. For all his effort, no words came out. He couldn't even fashion up a lie. He began to squirm in his seat. His jaw jerking from side to side. He had never felt so small, foolish, and pathetic. In his long life, he couldn't remember the day he was born. They were still staring at him. Jack was too lost in mind to see they weren't judging. Eventually, he shamefully started to shake his head.

"Well, at least you don't need to worry about getting old," Jerry said with a warm optimistic grin.

Catherine admired Jerry's passion to keep people's spirits alive. She wasn't blessed with such a gift. She was sympathetic toward

Jack, seeing the pain he had buried inside himself. They shared something in common. She knew too well how to bury pain.

Jack lowered his head and placed his finger on the starting position of his maze.

"Speech, speech, speech!" the crowd yelled. This was followed by a round of applause as Catherine made her way to the stage.

"Alright. Alright," she said, trying to calm all the excitement. Standing at the microphone, she shrugged and started to blush. "I'm surprised I'm still here."

The crowd cheered and chuckled.

She placed her hands on her hips and frowned. "I'm even more surprised all of you are still here."

The laughter increased, littered with whooping.

"Anyway, all jokes aside." Catherine tried her best to express how she felt in words. "I'm so thankful to have you all here to celebrate this day with me."

The crowd clapped in admiration.

She carried on talking about how she could see old familiar faces and regular faces. "Some of the regulars I wouldn't mind seeing less off. I'm just saying."

"Not gonna happen," Jerry shouted, raising his glass.

His wife kept him restrained but laughed beside him.

"I can also see some new faces here." Catherine lowered her tone. It was not the time for jokes.

Jack listened intently from his distant seat.

"The new faces are even more important. For everyone starts as a new face." Catherine raised her glass and forty reflections did the same. Bar one. "*A nuovi volti*. To new faces."

"To new faces!" The crowd smacked their hands together and stomped their feet, rattling the floorboards.

Jack could see the love they had for each other, embracing and smiling together. He looked down at his glass. It was full. Catherine must have filled it when he was lost in his mind. He lifted it up an inch off the counter. His reflection emerged in the brown liquid. "*A nuovi volti.* To new faces," he muttered to himself.

The crowd started stirring and repositioned itself by the bar.

Jack grabbed onto the counter, watching the ruckus.

"Everyone, squeeze in," Catherine said.

"Come on, get close!" Jerry shouted.

Everyone huddled together, with the people at the front taking a knee. Lady Catherine stood in the center and Jerry embraced his wife.

"Is that everyone?" Jerry's wife asked.

Catherine looked over her shoulder. "Jack, are you getting in the picture?"

By the seriousness of her voice, he didn't think she was giving him a choice. He slowly moved off his stool, making his way to the group. He felt uncomfortable in his skin like he was wearing a costume.

"Ten seconds," said a guest on the stage. Scurrying back to the group, he knelt down at the front.

"Okay, everyone. This is the only present I ask for so, big smiles," Catherine said, stretching out her lips.

Jack was still confused, having no idea what was going on. He was watching everyone stare at a strange object on the stage. A blinding flash appeared out of the lens and stunned him. Everyone else cheered and applauded. Jack still didn't quite know what had just happened, all dazed with white spots etched in his eyes.

Strolling into The Palace a couple of weeks later, he saw there was a new photograph added to the wall. Everyone had been captured in a single moment in time. The only person not smiling was Jack. He was standing alone, a foot between him and the next man. He thought he looked like a ghost, and that he shouldn't have been there.

Lady Catherine's birthday came around and around. The time in between was just a blur. With a second photo on the wall, Jack began to feel like a part of The Palace. A minute part at least. He would engage in conversations now. He started to recognize faces and, in turn, they recognized his. Still, they were only acquaintances, compared to a familiar face. He never ventured far from the confines of the short side of the bar, matching the separation within the picture frame.

Catherine sat at one of the tables, tapping her foot along with the beat of the music. Jerry took hold of the bar for a while, letting her take a break. Much to her reluctance to do so, she was relieved to take the weight of her feet. She had already made her speech and had everyone participate in a photograph. For the third time, she had to tell Jack to join. Observing him at the bar, he looked more relaxed than ever before, chatting with Jerry and a few other guests. She couldn't recall the last time he wasn't there, thinking it would feel a little less full without him. She had a hunch that they had something in common, just couldn't quite place what it was. She could tell he had secrets and so did she. Her eyes drifted down to his feet, tapping in time with her own. She had already received her present this year, but there was something else she would enjoy. Even if it would make her feet sore.

"Jack."

Jack flinched on his chair, balancing on two legs. So engrossed in his conversation with Jerry and the others that he hadn't seen her creep up. "Uh… Lady Catherine," he stuttered. Jerry and the others continued on without him. "Happy birthday." He was hesitant when speaking to her directly. It was like he was standing on eggshells. The fear he would unintentionally upset her again plagued the back of his mind.

"Thank you," she said with a smile. She couldn't but enjoy watching him squirm. "*Les jeunes hommes n'ont pas de manières de nos jours.*"

"I don't understand." Jack's heart beat faster, his temperature rose, and he could feel the sweat building up in every pour.

"When music is playing, you ask a lady to dance." She cleared her throat. "I've been waiting for almost an hour and I'm not getting any younger. So, I've come to get you to dance with me."

Jack had nothing to say in response to her request. He just stayed sitting there with his mouth open wide.

"So, you going to escort me to the dance floor?"

Again, it didn't sound like Catherine was giving him a choice; similar to her request for him to join the photo. "I don't know how to dance," he said, hoping he could stay seated on his tailored chair.

"Rubbish. You're never too old to learn."

The thought of being alone with her made his heart flutter. "I don't think that's a good idea," he pleaded.

"If I could interject." Jerry had been listening in the whole time. He leaned over the counter and whispered his words of wisdom in Jack's ear. "Son, if a lady asks you to dance, you get up and dance." Jerry shrugged and gave an expression of tough love.

Jack reluctantly stood up, shuffling his feet.

Catherine had a smug grin on her face as she interlocked her arm with his.

Jerry helped himself to a glass of whiskey for a job well done. He liked seeing them both get along.

The tables and chairs had been moved to make space near the stage. Catherine escorted Jack to the middle of the dance floor, passing everyone else already dancing in synchronization. Standing face to face, Catherine took the role of the teacher. "First, take my right hand," she said, opening up her palm and showing the lighter variant of her skin.

Jack quietly pondered why it was the case, taking her hand with a soft grip. Her palm was cold to the touch. But it was the smoothest hand he had ever felt, creating tingles up and down his spine.

"Very good. Now, put your other hand on my waist." She took Jack's caution as prudence. She tutted at the distance he had kept between them, which made it impossible to dance probably. She yanked his wrist, pulling them together.

The tingles in Jack's body intensified.

"That's better," Catherine said, smiling at how uncomfortable he looked. "This is the easy part. Just move your feet and I will follow," she instructed, confident in his ability.

The second she stopped talking, Jack dropped his head and looked at his feet.

"Don't look down!" Catherine snapped.

Jack obeyed her command and met her gaze.

"That's the hard part. Now we dance."

Taking slow and short steps, moving backward and forward, Jack tried his best to keep in time with the music.

Catherine had her eyes closed, swaying her head side to side. She was at peace; forgetting all her losses and regrets. Simply living in the moment.

"Hmm…this is nice. Tell me about yourself, Jack," she whispered.

"There's not much to tell," he replied, keeping his focus on his footing. Besides, he had already said all he wanted to Joanna and didn't feel the need to do it again.

"Oh, tell me something, Jack. Where did you grow up? Why do you come to my bar every night?"

"I've only ever been in New York," he said, convincing himself he was speaking the truth. He quickly glanced at her face. He couldn't shake the feeling that she didn't care what he said but just wanted to hear his voice to prolong the moment. He didn't want to trust his gut, yet having her body pressed up against his, he too didn't want it to end. Feeling more at home than ever before, his movement became automatic. "I feel I fit in here. The music. Jazz. I've never heard anything so beautiful."

"Hmm, it's lovely isn't it?" she whispered, her lips sticking together as she spoke.

Jack could feel her relax all her weight onto him. He was almost carrying her entirely.

"It was my husband's and my dream to get this place. At least one of us was able to see it." She rested her head on his chest, feeling the inconsistent heartbeat.

"I'm, uh, sorry. For what I said. When we first met," he said, a ball of ice forming in his stomach.

Catherine looked up and gave him a warm smile, stretching out her plump lips. "*Grazie*. But that was a long time ago." She closed her eyes and continued to sway. "I'm not one to dwell on the past."

They danced through the rest of the band's set, but eventually and regrettably they had to separate. "Would you look at that. You're a natural," Catherine said. Blood rushed to her cheeks as she smoothed down her dress. "Thank you for humoring me."

Jack shook his head. "No, thank you, Lady Catherine."

TWENTY-SIX

Another year passed just as quickly as the last. Jack had a new lease on life, existing in Catherine's palace. He initiated conversations now, not merely joining in with them. If music was being played, he would ask a lady to dance before they asked him. On one occasion, he even stood behind the microphone and participated in a song, with Jerry on the piano. Jack wasn't very good. Stuttering and spluttering over the lyrics.

"You should stick to dancing," Catherine said and Jack agreed. Time was going fast. He started slowing down to grab every moment. He had no fear for the future anymore. It was a shame his past was about to catch up from behind him.

Jack was walking the several blocks from his apartment to The Palace. He had intended to buy himself a car but hadn't got round to it. Besides, his money had started to dwindle again. It's what always happens when you spend every evening in a bar, not having an income. He would have run out a lot earlier if he'd had to worry about food and water. He'd spend all his time in The Palace. Drinking and listening to soulful music made him forget about the mundane responsibilities of money and getting an automobile. He started increasing his strides, needing to get to The Palace as quickly as possible. He was going to get there early.

An unsettling sensation started forming in his stomach when he grabbed the handle of the first set of doors. Something felt wrong. He didn't quite know the time but knew he was early, and he'd expected the doors to be locked. The sickening feeling only intensified when he got to the second set of doors. He couldn't see past the beautiful reflection of New York shimmering in the glass.

As he walked through the second set, his shoes made ripples when he stepped on the floor. It was covered in liquid and broken glass. It was fortunate he hadn't been smoking when he'd entered. The smell of alcohol infused the air. The tables and chairs had been thrown onto their sides. His stool now lay in a puddle of whiskey that was being absorbed into the red velvet. The door to the ladies restroom swung open. Jack's neck pivoted in the direction, ready to attack the culprit of the destruction.

It was Catherine barging her way out the door, carrying a mop and bucket. She was struggling with the bucket full of water. He heard the clanking sound of the metal handle as it hit the door frame.

"Ohh." She jumped, sloshing the water when she saw Jack standing in the middle of the liquor lake. "Jack, I didn't hear you come in," she said, pulling out the mop and getting started on the mess. She pretended to be oblivious to the broken glass she was crushing under her feet.

"So, what happened?" Jack asked, picking up his stool and shaking off the glass and alcohol.

"How did what happen?" Catherine replied, keeping her head down and mind focused on the mopping.

Jack shrugged to himself. He should have known by now that she wasn't going to open up so easily. He took a seat at his old spot by the bar. "Could you get me a drink please, Lady Catherine?" He showed Catherine the smug grin slapped on his face, hiding the fact his pants were getting wet.

Catherine wasn't pleased. She knew what he was doing. Not having much of a choice, she quickly walked behind the bar, splashing alcohol up the back of her legs as she walked. She impatiently grabbed an intact bottle and poured Jack a glass, then proceeded to wipe down the counter.

Jack let out a loud gasp, letting the whiskey burn his throat. He could tell she wanted to clear up before anyone else arrived. Yet he did like giving her a taste of her own medicine. He could understand why she did it so much. "What happened, Lady Catherine?" he said, his voice straight and direct.

"Ohh, just another person wanting something and taking it if there's any resistance," she replied, brushing the shards of glass to the floor where they tinkled like little gemstones.

"What did they want?" he said, gripping the edge of the counter.

"Oh, money." She exhaled. "Funny how they always destroy the expensive stuff, when that's what they're after." She wrung out the towel into the bucket. A smile of desperation grew on her face. "If they wanted to hurt me, they should have destroyed something I care about." She gestured to the photographs on the wall. She stopped talking and quickly turned to the shelves. Her whole body trembled, searching through the many drawers that laced the counter. She let out a loud sigh of relief when she saw it hadn't been taken.

Jack finally caught a glimpse of what she was worried about

losing. A pocket watch. A softly colored silver watch connected with a long chain and clasp.

Catherine could barely hold it all in her delicate hands. She closed her eyes and brought it close to her chest. She could feel the vibration of her heartbeat through the precious metal. She took several deep breaths, remembering her past.

"Who were they?" Jack interrupted her peaceful trance.

"*Der übliche weiße Mann*," she whispered in frustration. She took a second to calm down and refrain from her anger. "Ohh, simple men. One of them loved telling the religious tales of their boss," she said. Her sarcastic tone emerged once again.

"Where are they?" Jack took another sip of his whiskey.

Catherine stopped what she was doing and faced him. A cold feeling began growing in her gut. "Look, I know you're just trying to help but you don't need to worry about little old me."

Jack felt that she was treating him like a child, not seeing that she was concealing her feelings. "It's not right," he muttered, blocking his mind from the wrong he had done in his long drawn-out past.

"Not right," she said as she continued with her cleaning. "Honey, what's not right is a man being beaten for the money in his pocket. Now Jerry can barely walk ten feet without suffering." Finishing the counter, she wiped her brow, and placed her hands on her hips. "There's a lot of pain in this world, baby. I just got to deal with it. If Jerry can deal with his, I'm damn sure going to deal with mine," she said, sharing her words of wisdom.

Jack remained silent, feeling the alcohol soak into his underwear.

After a few minutes of silence, Catherine opened her mouth. "Well, would you look at the time," she said, breaking the silence with her uplifting spirit. She opened the cover of the silver pocket watch. It was a quarter to five and counting. The second hand rotated with a strong firm tick. "Well, if you're so eager to help, you can grab that mop and bucket."

Jack smiled and shook his head, amazed at how cheeky she could be. It was one of the many things he admired about her. He pulled himself up, peeling his pants off the sticky red velvet in the process. "Very well, Lady Catherine."

To her surprise, The Palace was back to its original form. The glasses and bottles had been replaced with others stowed in her office. The floor was mopped but remained slightly sticky, they had propped open the front doors to let out the stale odor of beer and whiskey.

"Ugh," Catherine groaned, finally tucking in the last chair. She flicked open the watch. "Well, would you look at that. We've still got five minutes to spare," she said, fanning herself down.

"We didn't do too bad," Jack replied, tucking in his shirt and walking to her side.

"I think I owe you a drink." She turned and looked deep into his eyes.

"We make a good team."

"That we do. Maybe I should hire you." She chuckled.

Like everything else in Catherine's life, after a couple of days, she had put the ordeal behind her. She placed it on a shelf to gather dust, not to be disturbed ever again. However, the more she added to the shelf, the harder it was to keep secret. Inevitably, something had to fall off.

A month passed, sweeter than the one before. Tucking in his shirt and fastening his belt, Jack headed toward a basin of The Palace's restroom. He took care not to slip on the recently mopped floor. He didn't have much going on in his mind. He was simply being in the moment. He felt the cold water flow between his fingers. He gazed into the mirror and barely recognized the reflection before him. His soft smile and tired eyes. His hair was long enough that little curls had begun to grow. His skin looked fresh and new; the best it had ever felt. If he could have remembered at least. He did see some distinctive and familiar features. Green eyes, strong jawline, and a small scar on his chin. He tried to recall the memory of the scar. It was more like a dream, with everything slightly out of focus. Yet he could still smell the embers in the fireplace and hear the ticking of the longcase clock. He splashed his face with water, washing away his memory. A new song started. He turned off the tap and headed out, his head bobbing to the beat of the music.

Something caught Jack's attention. The band was playing, and people were dancing and talking. It seemed normal as usual. But leaning over the bar talking to Catherine was a white man he had never seen before. Jack observed the stranger for a moment. Even Jerry seemed to take notice and was watching from his table. It wasn't odd to see white people in The Palace; everyone was welcome. But besides Jack, they were few and far between. He didn't take note of everyone who entered. However, like a black person stepping into a sea of white, white people stood out here.

This man was different. He wasn't there for the music or the pleasant company. He was wearing a black shirt that matched his hair, goatee, and a bruise on his left eye. His arms were folded and leaning across the counter. He was slightly overweight but trying to fool people it was muscle. He kept his lips pinched as he spoke to Lady Catherine.

"Can I help you?" Jack said, interrupting the man from his muttering.

His brow lifted surprised to see someone like him. "No. Me

and the lady are just talking business," he said with an unpleasant tone and rolled his eyes over to Catherine.

"It's fine, Jack. Don't worry," she said.

He had become an expert at reading her body language. She was standing straight, her muscles were tightened, and her hands closed and quivering on the counter. Jack could just make out the glimmer of the pocket watch she was squeezing. Jack respected her but he wasn't about to leave her alone. He wasn't going to obey her tonight. "Lady," he said, cracking a smile. "Since when did you become royalty?"

Catherine shook her head and buried her face in her hands.

Jack smiled, seeing her reaction to his remark, then turned back to the man. "Her name is Catherine. Lady Catherine to her friends. You don't get to call her either," Jack said, his smile vanishing from his face.

The man straightened himself up, tilted his neck back, looking past his nose and lifting his heels. He was trying to match Jack's height. Inflating his chest, the man thought he was invulnerable. "You got some crazy nerve. I can smash a bar up alright but you gotta have some sort of death wish to interfere with my boss. Not a good idea to mess with someone who's fought the devil."

The band carried on playing, but the interaction had started to gain more attention. A couple of men came over, Jerry being one of them. Jack didn't take any notice of the man's rambling but one part did catch his attention. "You trashed the bar?" he snapped.

"Not my best work but I'm here to prevent such things happening. My boss's services don't come cheap, however," he replied in a salesman's manner.

Jack turned to Catherine. Her skill at hiding her feelings was fading. He could see her eyes glisten with undropped tears. Her hands rested on the counter, shivering and shaking. She was squeezing her watch so tight, the crown cut into her palm.

He knew Catherine would hand the money over if he told her to. That was never going to happen. She never asked for his help but she was going to get it.

"That ain't happening. It's time for you to leave," Jack ordered. He got straight to the point with no more pleasantries. The muscles in his face contracted. He was prepared for whatever might come next.

"Haha," the man chuckled. "I don't think you understand."

"Oh, I understand. The answer is still no. Tell your boss not to come back."

"Haha." The man gave another artificial chuckle. "Or what?" He gave Jack a firm shove. His eyes widened when Jack only swayed gently backward.

The tendons in Jack's neck started to twitch. "Let me show you how a devil fights." Jack punched him in the chest. He hadn't used his strength for so long, he'd forgotten how strong he was. Intending the punch to be weak, he sent the man tumbling backward into Jerry and the others, knocking them all to the ground.

Catherine placed her hands on her mouth, holding in her screams.

Jack stayed quiet. It did feel good to use his strength again.

"Get your hands off me!" the man shouted. He was tussling and waving his arms, not wanting to be touched by their dark hands. Struggling to pull himself up, it became obvious he was more fat than muscle.

"I think it's time for you to leave," Jerry said. His eyes were drained of joy, hating to see trouble in the place he cared for and the people he loved.

"Yeah, I'll leave," the man snarled. He brushed himself off and put his hands in his pockets. "But I'll be back to deal with you all. First, I'm gonna deal with this nigger lover!"

The man lunged at Jack, flicking out a knife.

Jerry and the others couldn't stop him in time. Their fingertips grazed off his black shirt.

Jack watched the four-inch blade being thrust toward him. He could have easily pried it out of the man's hand, grabbed his hair, and smashed his face repeatedly on the bar. He'd have sprayed the man's blood across the surface of the counter and on the silver watch that lay there. It would have solved his problems. It's what he wanted to do. But after the man uttered those words full of anger and violence, his face became all so familiar.

Jack was frozen, seeing himself brandishing the blade. The monster swimming in his veins. A toothy grin appeared on the second Jack's face as it plunged the knife deep into the stomach of the first. He could feel the flesh being torn, and the cold smoky air touching his organs.

Catherine screamed, not being able to contain it any longer.

"I'll take that as payment." The man snatched the pocket watch off the counter, right before Jerry and the others dragged him out.

Jack came out of his hallucination dazed and confused, seeing blood oozing from his white shirt. He quickly covered it from any prying eyes. Keeping pressure on the wound, he made his way back to the restroom. He hadn't been hurt for some time. The pain was intense and vibrant. The rapid loss of blood made him light on his feet. Dragging his toes, he stumbled through the door.

Blood began to weep between his fingers, dripping onto the freshly mopped floor. He steadied himself with the basin. Little specks of light sparkled in his vision. He pulled up his shirt and tucked it under his chin.

The blade had cut deep. The wound was three inches deep and six inches wide across his abdomen. The flesh was torn at either end, resembling scrambled egg. He used his shivering fingers to poke his intestine back in and pinched his flesh back together.

He hadn't been injured in some time, and his ability was slow to start its magic. His heart was heavy and sluggish. The lack of blood and displacement of organs was taking its toll.

The wound was deep, but the man's words cut deeper. Jack had uttered the same hateful words himself and now he had been on the receiving end. He couldn't imagine what it must have felt like for someone like Catherine or Jerry to hear those sorts of words, for so long. By so many people.

He switched his attention to the problem under his hand. The blood was still dripping. It was everywhere, the floor, sinks, and mirrors. Using his free hand, he began frantically wiping down all the surfaces. Pins and needles started to form in his wound. No longer needing to hold it, he focused on the floor. He flushed away paper towel after paper towel desperately trying to get rid of the unnatural amount of blood he had excreted.

"Jack, you okay?" said a husky out-of-breath voice, creeping open the door.

"I'm fine, Jerry," Jack replied, back at the basin washing his hands. He thought he was standing in a spotless restroom.

Jerry could tell the room had been cleaned. There were pink smears on every surface. He was beginning to get queasy watching Jack wash his hands and arms, his shirt stained a cherry red like it had been bought that way. "You sure you're alright?"

"I said, I'm fine!" Jack gnarled, unable to look Jerry in the eye.

"I'm just worried, son. I'm sorry." Jerry's soulful voice smashed its way into Jack's weak heart.

He stayed focused on scrubbing the crystalized blood to keep the tears at bay. "Don't ever apologize to me, Jerry."

"It's not your fault, you know. I could have done more. I

should have grabbed him sooner," Jerry replied, reassuring Jack not to blame himself.

Jack nodded. "There are a lot of bad people in this world. You're not one of them," he said, finally connecting with Jerry's dark brown eyes.

Either the choice of words or the iron in the air, made Jerry's stomach drop. "Take your time. I'll wait outside. We're all here for you, son," he said, leaving his jacket on the doorknob and closing the door.

Jack looked back into the mirror disgusted with what he saw. His tucked-in red shirt covered his new horizontal scar, shinny like fish scales. Another one to add to the collection.

Half an hour later, Jack finally resurfaced from the restroom, wearing Jerry's oversized jacket. Hunched over, this new scar pulled tight as he walked. Jerry had told everyone to give him some space. They just gave him positive smiles when he passed. He walked up adjacent to Catherine, and kept his eyes trained on the exit.

She wiped the tears off her guilty face, but with a glimmer of relief at seeing he was unharmed.

Jack lit a cigarette. Coagulated blood still lodged in the webs of his fingers and under his nails. They stood silently listening to the music playing like a soft breeze. Nothing had to be said. They both knew what the other would say.

When the song ended, Jack asked one question. He wasn't giving her a choice in answering. "Where are they, Lady Catherine?"

TWENTY-SEVEN

Jack found himself in an alleyway and facing a bar with red neon lights. It was a place he had visited before. Butterflies fluttered in his stomach, bouncing off his sealed wound. He knew what might happen if he went in there, but he didn't care about that. *A little violence would hurt everyone but me.* The reason the butterflies were flapping their wings was because he didn't want to fail. Finally, he was fighting for someone else and it terrified him.

Taking a deep breath for composure, he readied himself for what was to come. He needed the darkness he had buried. When he got his act together, he took wide strides across the road. He skipped the line, ignoring the groaning from the crowd. He approached the two bouncers. "I'm here to see your boss."

"Fuck off," snapped the first bouncer.

With a calm, relaxed face, Jack nodded and punched the other. His arm stopped rigid when it struck the man's nose. The man fell backward through the doorway with blood gushing out of each nostril. Jack quickly dragged his hand through the air and grabbed the first bouncer by the neck. He lifted him six inches off the ground. "I'm here to see your boss," he repeated.

The man tussled and turned but couldn't break out of Jack's grip. "What do you want with him?" He struggled to speak and was already starting to turn blue.

Jack looked up to the night sky. The neon lights were illuminating everything with a reddish hue. Staring deep into the luminescent bulbs made his pupils contract to pinholes. The sign had changed. He couldn't recall what it used to say. Yet now it was very recognizable. *Jackie's.*

"He's expecting me," Jack whispered.

"I'll take you to him," the elevated man said with his last breath.

Jack lowered him back to his feet and released him from his vice-like grip.

Coughing, sputtering, and gasping for air, he helped the other man up, still clinging onto his broken nose.

They escorted Jack across the main floor. The smell of alcohol, sex, and drugs was pungent in the air, reminding him of pleasant and unpleasant memories. The bouncers pushed the dancers out of the way, making a clear path. Some of the women took a shine to the handsome, mysterious Jack. They groped him and whispered sweet temptations in his ear. He squeezed his way past them, being cautious not to return any affections. This wasn't the time for such activities. He had to keep his mind focused on his goal.

Walking through a door and with it closed behind them, the music diminished into a subtle heartbeat. Jack found himself following the men down a long, dark, and narrow corridor. Several paintings were mounted on the walls. They were religious in nature; winged and horned beasts were fighting in a bloody battle. Jack even recognized one painting. It was Dante and Virgil standing before the gates of hell. *He's really exaggerating this devil story,* he thought. Getting to the end of the hall, there stood another door. Groans could be heard from behind it.

The two men looked at each other with hesitation. Taking the plunge, the man with bruises pressed on his neck turned the handle.

"Four! Five!" Jackie shouted, counting his punishments. A man sat bound to a chair. Jackie had got stronger, with muscles to boot. A darkness had grown inside him. He had no need for brass knuckles anymore and, to top it all off, he had a thick bushy beard. He took no notice of the three men entering. He was too busy inflicting pain on the restrained man.

"You shouldn't have stolen from me. It never works out," Jackie said, picking the dead skin off of his knuckles. "Six!" he shouted, lunging forward with a right hook. The man was knocked out cold as Jackie's fist struck his jaw. Jackie walked around him and headed to his desk. "Get rid of him," he ordered, wiping his blood off of his hands.

Two of his subordinates untied the man and dragged his limp body out of a back door. This left five men in the room. The large metal desk made a permanent structure, being bolted to the ground. A bookshelf across one wall and a private bar on the other. Lastly, disguised as a private dance floor, a large space where Jackie could pass his judgment.

The strangled bouncer nudged the other with his elbow. "I opened the door," he whispered, flicking his head and rubbing his neck.

"What are you here for?" the other asked Jack. Sweat was profusely pouring off his forehead, and mixing with the blood on his face.

Jack could feel the man's fear radiating off of him.

Stepping over the smears of blood, the bouncer approached Jackie who was still wiping his hands. "Uh, boss, there's someone here who wants to speak to you," the man said, keeping his distance. The fear inside him made his blood thin and nose pour.

After a couple of unbearably long minutes of silence. Jackie acknowledged the whimper. "What the fuck happened to you?"

he snarled after cracking a glance over his shoulder. Jackie handed him his towel.

Placing it over his nose, he scurried off to the far corner of the bookshelf. The strangled bouncer walked over to the other.

"That was a very foolish thing to do," Jackie said, acknowledging his visitor, yet refusing to face him; too concerned about cleaning the grime from under his fingernails. He was comfortable in his surroundings and too confident he couldn't be harmed. "You must have a death wish or a damn good reason to come in here." Jackie finally turned around.

Silence fell as two men going by different names stared into each other's eyes. Jackie's bulged out of their sockets, seeing the man his stories had been born from, while Jack's were soft and sympathetic, watching the monster he had created. Knowing he wasn't going to have to fight, brought him a small amount of comfort at least.

"Fuck! I know you," said the last man in the room, breaking the intense silence. He was perched on a stool at the private bar. "He's the one who wouldn't pay up at the nigger bar," he said, hollering his big mouth at Jackie. "I'm surprised you're still standing. I cut you pretty deep," he said, spitting saliva as he spoke.

"It was just a scratch," Jack muttered.

Jackie flinched, stepping so far back he was almost sitting on his desk. He felt the cold grip of his Colt 1911 graze the side of his hand. Glancing down then back to Jack, he moved his hand away, having the realization that he would have had to keep one bullet for himself. Not wanting to shed his own blood, he decided to use his words. "That bar. Is that why you're here?" His voice trembled as he squeezed the words out of his mouth.

"Yes," Jack replied, still as calm as before.

Jackie nodded a fraction and began to plead his bargain. "Forget what has happened. Forget me and no one will set foot in the place again."

"Boss, what are you doing?" the loud man shouted.

"Shut the fuck up," Jackie interrupted. "Do we have a deal?" he said, his voice cracking in anticipation and holding on to the edge of the desk.

Jack felt relieved but kept his expression blank. That was until he got a glimpse of what the man at the bar had in his possession. A silver chain dangling out of his pocket. He blew a puff of air out his nostrils and his lips started to twitch. "I want the watch back too," he said, directing his words at Jackie and gesturing to the man on the stool.

Jackie took the words as gospel. "Give him the watch," he muttered, sweat dampening his collar.

"Fuck that," the man shouted, hopping his heavy frame off the stool. "Jackie, boss, why don't you just kill this man already?"

Jack shrugged, wondering the same.

"Ha! Good one," Jackie replied, blurting out a chuckle as he attempted to bring humor into the intense situation.

The loud man wasn't amused. He was confused and frustrated by his boss's unfamiliar submissive nature. He pulled out his gun.

"Maybe I should just do it myself?" he snarled, spitting over Jack and pointing the gun at his right eye.

"Stop! Don't do anything!" Jackie screamed, holding out his hands. The two men who'd escorted Jack into the room remained quiet, standing sheepishly in their corners.

Jack looked down the short barrel of the handgun, seeing the rifling inside. "I've never been shot in the eye before. I'm gonna be upset if it doesn't go the way I expect," he said, feeling surprisingly curious and slightly tempted to let the man pull the trigger.

"What the fuck are you?" the man whispered.

Click.

Jackie grabbed his gun, pulled back the hammer, and aimed it at his employee. "Give him back the fucking watch."

The man wasn't scared of Jack, but he was terrified of Jackie and what he was capable of. Feeling things had got out of hand, he lowered his gun and submissively handed over the watch.

The heavy, full Hunter silver watch fit neatly in Jack's palm. It was the first time he had seen it up close. Flipping it over, he saw some words engraved on the cold silver. *To Adam. Always in my heart. From your loving wife.* It made more sense to him now why Catherine cared for it so.

"We're done here?" Jackie asked, hoping that he had remembered the deal.

The man who went by the name of Jack nodded. "You were right by the way. I'm starting to regret. Goodbye, Jack." He quickly turned and left the room, walking back down the long corridor. He didn't want to witness what came next.

Jackie exhaled. He had survived his dealings with the devil a second time. With each step away that Jack took, the monster he had created began to re-emerge. Anger and violence erupted inside of Jackie. "You two!" he shouted. Pointing at the men skulking in the corners. "Get this loudmouth son of a bitch out of my sight."

"Jackie! Boss, wait!"

"I told you that a big mouth of yours would get you killed. You could have killed us all!"

The man stood in the middle of the dance floor, watching the men he called friends and boss surround him and draw closer.

Jack exited the bar with the red neon lights. With his ears pounding and stomach churning, he hastily made his way back to the alley. The shadows concealed him. Slumping over, he started to vomit. He puked up everything he had stored in his stomach. He was a fraud. He was trying to help someone when he was the reason for her misfortune. He really wanted to be a good person but didn't believe he could be. Wiping his mouth, he had a glimmer of hope. If he was already a fraud, he could at least pretend to be good.

The next morning came, like many mornings before, and just like many other times, Jack walked into The Palace. However, he had a better reason for being there. It was comforting to be surrounded by the familiar four walls again. He didn't want to be anywhere else. He could see movement coming from Catherine's office.

She was sorting through boxes, stacking them into piles. Her office was cluttered and cramped. There was a small desk covered in papers and documents. Crates of liquor and other supplies were stacked all around. A shelf stacked with upside-down photo frames, and a cot bed, again covered in a blanket of papers.

"Lady Catherine," he said observing her for a moment from the door frame.

"Jack," she said, quickly standing up. Crawling over the floor wasn't how a lady should be seen. She gave him a look up and down, making sure he was all in one piece.

"It's done. You won't have any trouble again." His voice cracked and hands shook when he took hold of hers.

She gripped on tight and felt the cold silver warming up between their palms. "You didn't have to do that. It's just a watch."

Jack could feel her heart pounding in her chest. He looked into her dark brown eyes, glittering with joy. "Not to you it ain't." He paused. An idea popped into his head. He never wanted to leave The Palace walls again, and it was the perfect place to hide as a good person. He swallowed hard. His voice swelled up with hope. "Can I have a job?"

TWENTY-EIGHT

Jackie was true to his word and never bothered The Palace again. It was unsettling for Jack, seeing what had happened to him, which had then altered Lady Catherine's life, who he cared for so much. At least the ordeal was over.

Lady Catherine and he had become inseparable, spending all their time together in The Palace. He would help behind the bar, and talk to each of the faces he saw. He would tidy up when they left and restock the alcohol they had consumed—anything to make Lady Catherine's job that little bit easier. Getting paid to be in the place and around the people he loved, made it all the sweeter.

Every night, he would watch the musicians struggling and clambering to fit on the stage. They never complained once. Even when the equipment veered too close to the edge and crashed to the ground. Jack insisted that it should change.

"Just what on earth are you doing?" Catherine said, entering through the front doors. She was reacting to the mess of Jack kneeling, surrounded by piles of timber.

"We've got too much empty space. I'm making the stage bigger," he said, continuing to pry up the broads. "Where have you been? You normally get here before me," he asked as he measured out the replacement boards.

"*Wie unhöflich.*" She tutted. "Haven't I taught you anything? Never ask a woman what she does in her spare time," she said, avoiding the question. She walked over to her office, being careful not to trip over the mess he had created.

Making more noise than he was, Jack was curious about what she was up to.

"Here you go." She placed a small metal toolbox down by his side.

Jack took a look. Clawhammer, hacksaw, and an assortment of nails; a simple collection.

"You are not going to be able to do it with your bare hands." Catherine smirked and headed back into her office to make a start on all the paperwork. "You better have that finished before we open!" she shouted from the open door.

"Yes, Lady Catherine." He kept his eyes on the doorway while he pulled the old boards with his hands. Positioning the new boards, he pushed in the nails with his thumb.

The finished product went down extremely well. The bands were now able to come and go off the stage as they pleased. Seeing larger smiles on the customers' faces, which, in turn, made Catherine's more prominent; that's all he wanted. It made the splinters worthwhile.

1983.

"Late again, Lady Catherine," Jack said, a greeting he had started using on a regular basis. "I almost thought you weren't going to make it to your own party," he continued, sarcasm oozing out. He had already set everything up for the event and was now just drying off the last couple of glasses. He looked over at Catherine who still hadn't responded.

She seemed deflated for some unknown reason. She had her

head down and shoulders slumped forward. It wasn't like her to be quite so dejected. Jack knew by now not to ask. She would tell him in her own time. He made the glass he had just cleaned dirty again by pouring her a small drink. He secretly observed as she placed her lips on the rim and delicately took a sip.

"*La mia bellissima nipotina. Ti amo.*"

Jack couldn't hazard a guess what she had just whispered. Yet figured that in her own little way, she had shared what was troubling her. She finished her drink with a satisfied sigh.

"I hope you're not intending to be at my birthday party dressed like that," she said with an enormous tut.

"What's wrong with what I'm wearing?" Insulted, Jack looked down. White shirt, tucked into black slacks with sleeves rolled up. He didn't see the frays around his ankles, nor the creases in his shirt that was more of a dull yellow.

Catherine shook her head in despair. She hadn't even begun to comment on his hair. "Come with me," she said, striding to her office.

Jack stayed still with his mouth open.

"Well, come on then," she said again, waving her hand and beckoning him to follow. "We haven't got long until our guests arrive. I'm not allowing you to be late for my party."

She trimmed Jack's hair and let him change into the clothes she had laid out in her office. The office was still cramped. Crates of booze partially obscured the mirror he was using. Stacks of boxes littered each corner, almost like pillars holding up the roof. Shelves with more dust on them than the picture frames that all lay face down. It was unlike Catherine to have such an unorganized area. The only thing that had been cleared was the cot bed on the far wall. *Maybe she is beginning to sort the mess out?*

The outfit she gave him was more suited to her lifestyle. The brown, tweed, three-piece suit was carefully laid out for him on the bed. She had obviously taken great care of it. It fit him quite well, apart from the arms. Being slightly too long, they grazed his palms.

"Well, don't you look handsome?" she said, fastening her earrings by the door. She gracefully walked in front of him, her heels tapping against the floorboards. She inspected him up and down, screwing up her face when she saw the state of his tie. "Come here," she said, pulling him by his tie. Their lips merely a few inches apart.

He could smell the sweet perfume on her neck. The hairs on his neck stood up as she brushed her fingers, remaking his tie.

"Close your mouth, Jack," she said, pulling the knot up to his throat. "Now, let's see how that looks." She turned and stood by his side, linking her arm around his and sharing the space in the mirror.

He thought the haircut made him look younger, but the outfit made him look old. He looked like a man.

"Hmm. Something is missing," she pondered. She walked over to the shelves, covered with upside-down picture frames and dust.

"Here, take this," she said, offering out the pocket watch.

Jack could see how tight she was gripping it. "I can't accept that, Lady Catherine."

"Rubbish." Not giving him a choice, she was already fastening the chain to his waistcoat. "It was my husband's."

Jack listened intently. Her eyes filled with tears with each word spoken.

"He didn't want to take it with him. Wasn't sure if he'd bring it back." She opened the front, stroking the crystal. "It was intended to be passed down but…" She hesitated. She closed the front and slipped it into his pocket. "Anyway, he would have wanted you to have it."

Jack wondered what man could affect Catherine's heart so deeply. He wished he could have met him.

"Now, that's much better," said Catherine approvingly, taking hold of Jack's arm once again. They stayed silent and watched their reflections. "The party will start soon," Catherine said, placing a soft peck on his cheek and leaving the room. Jack carried on looking into the mirror. He stroked the tweed and patted the watch in his pocket, adapting to its weight. He was rather pleased with his new look.

The Palace thronged with people; more than Catherine had ever witnessed. The tables had double their capacity of people sitting around them. They were rubbing each other's shoulders with any kind of movement. Jack and Catherine were behind the bar, serving the many patrons overflowing the counter. It was non-stop but never felt like hard work.

Everyone was patient, waiting to be served. They passed the time talking or listening to the unique singer who was on the stage.

The singer was a white skinny fellow. Long brown hair and a wiry beard that concealed most of his features. The impractical amount of jewelry that laced his fingers and neck only exacerbated the untidiness of the rest of his outfit. It looked like he had worn it for weeks. His checkered shirt was scruffy with the creases permanently woven in. His slacks were worn thin and a layer of sand covered his shoes. He seemed obsessed with the lady playing the guitar, giving her intense glares on a regular basis. The woman was definitely welcoming to his advances, always returning the gestures with a smile. She had an extremely slim figure, glimmering black skin, and a large afro. Jack thought she was quite pretty dressed in her gold sequin top, and a very talented guitarist. No matter how peculiar the man looked, he sure could sing.

The song wasn't something Jack had ever heard before, yet the fast tempo of the jazz beat enthralled everyone. The stranger's voice burrowed deep into the souls of everyone who could hear.

The music seemed to be playing from behind the eardrums of the listeners. They all danced like they were all stuck in some sort of trance.

"He's a very good singer," Catherine said, putting her mouth next to Jack's ear.

"He sure is. Where did you find him?" he said, keeping his eyes on the stage.

A soft frown grew on her face. "I thought you'd hired him."

They stopped what they were doing and continued to listen.

Catherine had just finished her speech and was busy thanking the guests for coming, leaving Jack alone to tend the bar.

"Hey, can I get a drink?" the singer said, taking a seat at the bar and stretching out his arms.

Jack approached the man with caution. "Sure, what can I get you?"

"Something strong, but keep it short," he replied. His bottom teeth were crooked and yellow, peeking out from behind his wiry beard as he spoke.

Jack poured him the strongest whiskey he had and slid it across the counter, keeping as much distance between them as possible.

He quickly necked it down and passed the empty glass back to Jack.

"You're very talented," Jack said, trying to stop any awkward silence before it started. He fought against the nerves he felt talking to the man.

"Well, that's nice of you to say," he replied, curling up one corner of his mouth. Then he tilted his neck and chucked his next shot down his throat. "You look oddly familiar." The man leaned across the bar glaring with his intense bug eyes.

Jack nodded. "I get that a lot. So, what's your story?" Jack asked, avoiding eye contact and pouring him another drink.

The singer let out a long sigh. "My story is just patches of time, stitched together with music."

His reply just created more confusion for Jack, who was subtly checking him up and down. His rolled-up shirt sleeves and several undone buttons made the tattoos on his skin visible. Black and gray, all different shapes, overlapping each other.

Jack didn't understand why anyone would mark themselves like that; scarring their flesh out of their own free will. It was too permanent in his opinion. Apart from one, he could barely make any of them out. Embedded in the indent of his jugular was an upside-down black triangle. Jack didn't have the faintest idea of why he would have that.

"It's Jack, isn't it?" the man asked, sparking up a cigarette. "So, what's your story?" His eyes peered into Jack's soul.

Jack hesitated, feeling a gentle melody flickering in his head. "Long," he replied, taking a shot for himself. He wasn't about to share anything with such a suspicious person.

The man closed his eyes for a moment and swayed from side to side. The other side of his mouth began to rise, creating a large clown-like smile. "I don't doubt that." Opening his yellowy-green eyes, he once again sent out a piercing gaze.

Jack took a step back. "What's your name?"

The man chuckled and then his smile vanished from his face. "Some things are best just not knowing. Cheers." Taking his final shot, he stood up and walked over to be with his guitar woman.

"Did you just make a new friend?" Catherine said, coming over, and wiping away tears of joy from Jerry's overwhelming jokes.

Jack shook his head. "No, I don't think so. He's a bit too lively for me."

Catherine scoffed. "Jack, baby, sometimes you sound older than me." She crouched down and looked at her reflection in a nearby glass. She tidied up loose hairs and thoroughly checked for any grays. "Anyhow, time for the photo."

Catherine took center stage with Jack holding on to her waist. He couldn't help himself. His eyes were always wandering over to the strange man. He was standing at the end of the group; too busy groping the afro woman to pay attention to the camera. The woman seemed to be enjoying herself even more. Jack started to feel guilty. He was in no position to pass judgment. He brought his thoughts back to Catherine, who had gradually rested more of her weight onto him. He grabbed her firmly and squeezed her tight.

"Thank you for today," she said, stroking his cheek and kissing the corner of his mouth.

"Anything for you." He looked down into her eyes. They were glimmering like she was staring into a memory.

"Ten seconds everyone," hollered Jerry, who insisted he should be in control of the camera. He quickly hobbled back to the frontline before the blinding flash went off, capturing the memory forever.

"Ugh," Catherine groaned. She clenched her eyes shut, and rubbed her head.

Jack supported her on her feet. "Are you alright?"

She held onto his shoulder. "Ohh, I'm fine. Just got over-excited for a moment." She pulled herself up. "Never mind all that. We've still got work to do."

Jack's stomach began to stew. However, he had learned her talent. He gave a subtle smile and replied, "As you wish, Lady Catherine."

TWENTY-NINE

1984. Jack unlocked The Palace doors. Flicking on the lights, he watched how the entire place lit up. He picked up the scattered post and noticed how unnaturally quiet it was. He opened his watch and checked the time. Five past ten, the hands showed; always moving forward.

He began setting out the tables and chairs, the same as the day before. He was calm and content with his task at hand. He wiped the counter, cleaned the glasses, and restocked the shelves. He walked into Catherine's office for more supplies, stepping over all the boxes that only ever seemed to increase in number. He did notice that the camping cot had been cleared. It looked like she had stayed overnight recently.

Jack stood behind the bar, leaning on the counter and tapping his fingers. Waiting in a silent Palace, he took out his watch. Five past twelve. It felt like the hands hadn't moved at all. "Where is she?" he whispered, not wanting to wake the sleeping Palace. He scratched the back of his head and started looking through the post. There wasn't anything special just bills on top of bills. He still found them fascinating to open. He had only ever received one letter.

He got to the last letter in the stack. It was thick and dense. Catherine's name wasn't on it. It was simply addressed to The Palace. Tearing it open, he began to scan through the layered document. It took him a while to comprehend what it was about. Too many long-winded words; the kind that would be used in a business contract or court of law. Finally, he was able to understand what it was about. Apparently, Catherine hadn't paid the bills for some time. The word *foreclosure* stood out.

Catherine finally arrived, using her shoulder to push through the heavy door. "Good morning," she said, her voice surprisingly upbeat.

"Good morning, Lady Catherine. Late again, I see," Jack replied, giving her a nod and raising his eyebrows. "Since you're here, do you want to explain this?"

Catherine quickly glanced at the letter Jack was waving in the air. "Oh, that's nothing," she said, walking past and going behind the bar.

"It doesn't seem like nothing. It says you're behind on your payments. It says they're going to close you down." Jack paced toward her, trying to get her attention.

She kept herself busy, grabbing a glass to clean.

"Lady Catherine, it says they're gonna take the bar."

"Oh, people say a lot of things. Only half of it turns out to be true."

Jack's lip started to twitch. "I already cleaned that glass five times!" he snatched the glass out of her hand and looked down at her. "You don't have to pay me if you're behind on the rent, Lady Catherine."

Catherine stroked his face and shook her head. "You know you don't take that much." She walked over to the counter and searched through her handbag, impatiently pushing the clutter aside. She pulled out a lighter and cigarette and sucked in a mouth full of smoke. "I'm dying, Jack."

Jack had a blank expression. Again, he couldn't comprehend what he was hearing.

***

She started to explain how she had been going to the hospital most mornings. She'd been having test after test, hoping something could have been done. She failed to mention the pain or medication being pumped into her. "I can't understand the nonsense the doctors say. But that Dr. Chambers, he's nice."

Catherine was calm, indulging in a cigarette, and feeling relieved one of her secrets was out in the open.

***

"No. There's gotta be something that can be done," Jack said, slamming his fist on the counter. Catherine settled him down, brushing away his pleas and bargains.

"It's alright, Jack. I sold my apartment and I have no more money. I've spent it all on the doctors and treatment available. I can't avoid the inevitable and I'm going to lose the bar." She took her hands and cradled his closed fist. "None of that matters. I've got other things to care about."

Jack didn't want to look at her. He kept his head down, scanning over the letter.

She squeezed his hand tighter and smiled. "Everyone dies eventually, baby."

Jack's eyes started to bulge. The name on the bottom of the letter caught his attention.

The cogs in his head started to turn as he etched out a plan. "No, they don't." He looked back up at Lady Catherine, seeing her puzzled expression. Her confusion only grew as he kept on talking. "I gotta go. I'll be back in a few days." He headed toward the doors.

"Where are you going?" she asked, lighting another cigarette.

"I need to buy a car."

Catherine scoffed at his oddness. "What the blazing hell do you need a car for?"

"I'm going home."

THIRTY

Jack had saved enough money to get himself a car, but he needed more. The car wasn't anything special. Silver in color, two seats. As long as it traveled the 2400 miles there and back, he didn't care. It was going to take a lot of gas and a lot of cigarettes.

He kept driving through the nights not entirely sure which way he should be heading. It had been a while since he'd last read a map. After driving aimlessly throughout the night, he decided to pull over and get some sleep.

He woke up feeling worse than before—mouth dry, suit chafing, and the midday sun glaring through the windscreen. He climbed out of the car to stretch and light a smoke, and wait for his sweaty back to dry off. He checked his surroundings. He had an odd feeling of deja vu. He slowly strolled down the road and took in the scenery. Eventually, he recognized where he was. He was standing in front of the main gates of Camp Moore. The feeling of nostalgia was ever-present.

Lost in his own mind, he kept getting in the way of the groups of people. He didn't know why, but he had an urge to follow. The groups grew larger with each step and finally merged into a crowd gathering together. They were morbid but consoled each other with comforting support. The route became even more familiar, walking the same path that led to the dreaded Mile Hill. The land around had been converted into a home for the dead. There were a lot of them.

Two ranks of soldiers emerged facing each other. The crowd walked between them. Jack hesitated but followed suit. He concealed himself at the back. The crowd went silent apart from the faint murmurs of sobbing. All the elderly men sat at the front, with some frailer than others. They were all dressed in their best Sunday suits, and clad in medals they had earned.

Jack didn't know if he had ever earned any. He certainly didn't think he deserved any.

The ceremony began. It was beautiful. Elegantly formal soldiers carried a coffin under the arch of the weapon-drawn soldiers. The ceremony went on for some time. It felt longer for Jack as he had an unwelcome feeling inside as if he was going to be spotted.

Once the ceremony was over, people started to disperse. Jack held off and approached the grave. He wondered who he had just witnessed being laid to rest. A wheelchair clipped the back of his heel.

"I'm so sorry. Dad! Why did you do that?" said the man pushing the wheelchair along.

"Don't worry about it. It didn't hurt," Jack replied, feeling the skin on his heel had ripped.

"Well, I've got to get the car. Would you mind waiting with my father? I won't be long."

Jack shook his head. "No, that's alright."

"Thank you. I won't be long, Dad. Just stay here," he said, placing his hand on his father's shoulder before walking off.

Jack knelt in front of the man in the wheelchair. He must have been in his seventies. His body looked strong, with distinguished muscles imbued under his thin skin. Jack assumed it was something in the man's mind that kept him confined to a chair. The old man's face grew familiar as he noticed the scar splitting his right eyebrow in half.

"Fletcher, is that you?"

His wrinkled skin hung loose on his face. His tired eyes wandered around aimlessly. Nevertheless, Fletcher's boisterous attitude reflected out.

"Fletcher, you in there?" Jack snapped his fingers, trying to get Fletcher's attention. Their pupils met the best they could. Fletcher's hawk-like eyes stared right through him. Jack wasn't a fan of Fletcher but it pained him to see him like this. He wouldn't wish it on anyone.

"I don't like you," Fletcher groaned, his strength vibrating inside him. "I don't know. There's something about you," he muttered. As he twitched in his chair, his body tried to make sense of what his mind couldn't.

"It's okay, Fletcher. I don't like myself either," Jack replied.

They remained silent for the rest of their time together. Jack contemplated how different things would have turned out if his and Fletcher's roles were reversed.

"Sorry to keep you waiting," Fletcher's son said, returning with the car.

"Don't mention it. It was nice to catch up," Jack replied.

The son looked puzzled. Jack had let too much slip. He quickly elaborated, stitching together a lie. "Uhm, I mean my grandfather served with your father." He was surprised he could still lie so naturally. "Oh, I see. He must have known Sergeant then."

"Sergeant?" Jack said, keeping his confusion hidden.

"Yes, that's why we're here. My father served under him at Normandy." The son continued to explain with gratitude how if it hadn't been for the sergeant, he might not have been standing there today. Jack listened intently, but it wasn't anything he didn't already know.

"That's why we're here."

Jack didn't contain his confusion as well this time.

The son elaborated thinking Jack was slow, similar to his father. "He died a week ago. This is his ceremony."

Jack gazed at the grave. The large array of flowers that lay beside the sergeant covered the tombstone so much that the inscription couldn't be seen. He would have continued staring if Fletcher's son hadn't interrupted.

"Well, we best be going. It was nice meeting you. Say good-bye, Dad."

"Urgh," Fletcher grumbled.

"Dad! Don't be rude."

"It's alright," Jack said, not taking it to heart.

He looked down at Fletcher's wandering eyes. "Thank you for your service, Corporal Fletcher." He helped get Fletcher into the car and waved them goodbye.

Two men began to fill in the sergeant's grave and conversed in a deep conversation.

Jack took another look at the tombstone. *What would have happened if our roles had been switched?* he thought. After a couple of minutes, he walked away and headed back to the car. He didn't look at the inscription. *Some things are best just not known.*

He got back in his car. Feeling overwhelmed, it felt good to be encased in metal again. He opened his cigarette carton. *Empty.* He screwed it up and threw it on the passenger seat. He picked up the map. The perfect route back to his home was already marked out for him. He figured he had written it last night but was too tired to remember. He twisted the key in the ignition and headed home.

The drive back was hazy, like a forgotten dream. He still couldn't shake the sense of deja vu. Everything looked familiar but also different at the same time. The signs were modernized, and the roads resurfaced and made wider. But when the sun began to set and he took the last turn, everything went back to how he remembered it. The gravel road kicked up dust as he drove on the uneven surface, punishing the suspension. He drove up the hill and reached the peak, and then he saw his home.

Nothing had changed. It had stayed untouched in its own location in time. The cotton field looked like it had been picked yesterday. The chain on the barn was now covered in a thick layer of corrosion. Yet it still held the doors tightly enough that even Jack would have struggled to break in. He walked up the front porch; each step let out its own personalized squeak. The door opened smoothly. The hall was dark, only being illuminated by the remaining orange in the sky.

Jack peeked his head into the living room. Dust particles floated in the warm air like the fire had been lit recently. A short length of fabric still hung from the cross beam in the center. Dry and moth-eaten, but it had more motion than the longcase clock that stood dormant in the corner. A baseball bat covered in dust rested against it. It looked as if once it had been wiped, the polished wood would shine again.

He walked to the kitchen, stopping at the doorway.

"Arthur, Marshall, William. Dinner's ready."

"Thank you, darling. Come on, boys. Get in here."

"Out of the way, little brother. Men go first."

Jack couldn't sense his family, smell his mother's cooking nor see their faces. It was just an empty kitchen. The words were being made up in his head; he assumed it might all be something that would be said when dinner was ready. He exhaled out of his nostrils and went to find what he'd come for.

He pried open the door under the stairs. Dust and cobwebs shook off the ceiling and stuck to his face in that unpleasant way. He knelt down and unlocked the safe. The metal had warped. It took all his strength to open it. The dry air hit him in the face and made his eyes sting. He took hold of his mother's wedding ring, pushing it onto his little finger. He faced it inwards, not wanting to lose it on the journey back. His father's Colt lay on top of what he wanted. He carefully picked it up; keeping his fingers as far from the trigger as possible. He laid it on the bottom shelf. He wouldn't be needing it.

He could finally get what he wanted. The deed to the farm. He thought it was amusing, having to travel all this way for a scrap of paper, but he would travel the depths of hell for Lady Catherine. He pinched the corner and pulled it out. Then he added two more names. *Sam Jenkins. Jack Fletcher.*

It was a tranquil journey back. He knew where he was going; all he needed to do was keep his eyes on the road. The headlights remained enveloped by the darkness. He wasn't sad about the farm. He was numb, not feeling much of anything. He hadn't been home since he'd died the first time. Before he'd left, he'd added a fourth grave.

With William buried with his family, Jack went to see another man. The one whose name was on the foreclosure papers.

"Matthew Cale will see you now," the secretary said.

"Thank you," Jack replied, walking into the office, deed in hand.

"You're Mr. Fletcher, I presume," Matthew said from behind his desk, too engrossed with his work to look up. "You're here on behalf of one Miss Catherine. Uhm, I can't recall her last name."

Jack was listening but was more interested in looking around the office.

Matthew continued with his work while speaking. "If the reason you are here has anything to do with that bar, I'm afraid you're too late. She's six months behind on the payments and I can't wait any longer."

Jack couldn't hazard a guess how many times Cale had muttered the same speech. "I'm not here for the bar. I'm looking to sell," Jack said, slipping the deed under Cale's line of sight. Finally, Cale acknowledged Jack's existence. He then proceeded to examine the document.

Jack looked around the office again, checking out the newspaper cuttings that had been framed on the walls. Business deals and buyouts; a couple of articles on racing events. Jack would have never guessed that Johnathan would become one of the largest real estate owners in New York. Selling cotton would have been beneath him if he'd still been alive.

"This barely makes any sense," Cale croaked, thoroughly inspecting the document's authenticity. "If this is real, why hasn't anyone bought it and built on it already?"

"No one knew or cared it was there," Jack answered, still with his face pressed against the wall.

"Arthur Lake," Cale read off the previous owners.

Jack's attention was taken by a framed black and white photograph.

It was Jonathan Cale, his partner, and him shaking hands in Jackson after the cotton deal. Pale and skinny, but unmistakably him. He was even wearing the handkerchief around his neck. Through his own fault, he hadn't finished on good terms with Jonathan. Jack still appreciated how he'd kept the photo all this time.

"Matthew Cale?" Cale said. His voice escalated in pitch reading his own name.

"No relation," Jack replied, turning his body to block the photo. "But Ethan Chaplin knew your grandfather."

Cale finally began to look interested. He leaned forward on his desk.

"They did a good deal together, your grandfather and him. I was hoping to do a kind service for someone else."

Cale glossed over the document again, scratching his chin with his pen.

Waiting for him to make a decision, Jack saw another photo

on the table. "You like your cars, Mr. Cale?" Jack asked, seeing the photograph of him looking enthusiastic with a woman in a very extravagant car.

"Yes, I do. Why do you ask?"

"No reason. Other than the fact there's a 1919 Paige roadster locked in the barn."

Matthew's ears perked up and his voice rattled. "1919 Paige roadster. That's a very expensive car."

Jack smirked. "Yes, it is."

It only took ten minutes for Cale to get all the paperwork and payment together. With a firm handshake, he signed his name on the deed.

"Lady Catherine!" Jack shouted, unlocking The Palace doors. "Catherine!" he shouted again, barging into her office.

"Jack! What's the meaning of this?" she shrieked, dropping her book and concealing herself with the blanket. Definitely not how a woman should be seen.

"I've got the money you need for the treatment."

Catherine began shaking her head, dismissing his enthusiasm.

"Come on, get dressed. We got to get you to the hospital."

"I'm not going anywhere. Besides, I haven't done my hair," she replied.

Jack clenched his teeth, scraping together some of her things. "You're dying, Catherine. We haven't got time for your sarcastic games."

"It's the perfect time for games!" she snapped, her voice cracking under the pressure.

Jack turned to face her. He had never felt so scared.

"It's late and I'm tired. But, more importantly, I've already made up my mind."

"How can you just lay there and give up on life."

"I'm not giving up on life," she retorted, talking to the inexperienced young man he was. "I'm giving up on fighting the inevitable. I'm going to enjoy the time I have left and not spend it in a hospital." She coughed and sputtered, placing her hand on her chest. She tucked herself in and reopened her book. "When your time comes, you'll understand, Jack."

Jack slumped forward, dragging his feet to the door.

"Jack," she said, not lifting her gaze from her reading. "I'm very comfortable here. It would be nice not to have to move."

Jack nodded and opened the door to leave.

"Where did you get the money from?" Catherine asked, placing her book back on her lap.

Jack looked back at her. Her nighty barely stayed on her frail figure. The straps gently graced her protruding collar bones. The dark bags highlighted her bloodshot eyes, while her wig was placed neatly on her desk.

"I let go of something I didn't need. Goodnight, Lady Catherine."

THIRTY-ONE

Jack did what she asked. He used his money to pay off her debt. Cale was very understanding and sorted out all the necessary paperwork. With the rest of his money, Jack bought himself a studio apartment, only a few blocks away from The Palace.

He offered Catherine the chance to move in. But she politely declined, spending her nights in her office. Jack would spend most nights at The Palace as well, persistently refusing Catherine's request for him to leave. "I don't need to be looked after," she would say in between retching.

"I'm not going anywhere," Jack would reply.

He fed her when she was too weak to move. He supported her when she vomited. Bathed her when she soiled herself. He helped her get dressed and disguise her frailness with makeup. Lastly, he waited. Perched on his tailored stool outside her office while she slept. The illness took a toll on both of them. Jack didn't care or complain. The honor of her presence was worth it. When Lady Catherine knew her time was coming to an end, she finally asked Jack for a favor.

· · ·

"Which way now?"

"Take the next left."

Jack didn't know where he was taking her. It was only eight in the morning and they had already been driving for an hour. It seemed important, and that's all that mattered.

"Pull over here," Catherine said, slouched in the car seat.

Jack took a look around but nothing stood out. Simple houses and apartments, and a small park. It looked like a nice place to live. Jack started massaging his chest. "So, what are we doing here?"

"Shh. Over there," she whispered.

Jack squinted trying to track where Catherine's boney finger was pointing.

About fifty feet ahead was a bus shelter. A teenage girl sat inside, with her head down, minding her business.

"Who is she?" Jack asked, keeping his voice to a minimum.

Catherine's emotions started to escape her fragile posture. "She's my granddaughter."

Jack remained silent, sensing her urge to share.

Filling her lungs with her weak shaking breath she finally spoke. "I raised my daughter alone. I was thirty when I had her. All the women in my family have children then." She rested her head on the window, her eyes beginning to weep. "I was heartbroken when my husband died. He was the only man I had ever loved." She began to fidget in the seat, screwing up her face. "When my daughter fell in love, I was…I disapproved. To put it lightly. She must have got tired of arguing with me. She left with the man and never looked back." Catherine turned to face Jack and pleaded her defense. "I didn't want her to end up like me."

There was no judgment from Jack, just a sympathetic smile.

"I kept everything from her. Never talked about her father. Of course, she didn't want to end up like me. I was meaning to get in contact with her again, but I kept putting it off." She smacked her fist into her thigh. "Then all of a sudden it was too late." She looked over at Jack. A waterfall of tears gushed down her face. "I lost my baby."

Jack grabbed her tight. Her salty tears soaked into his jacket, making contact with the watch.

After all the tears she had bottled up had been expelled, she let go of Jack. She blotted her damp face and looked back at her granddaughter. "I've been coming here for several years now. Never plucked up the courage to talk to her. The school bus will be here soon."

Catherine sorted herself out, straightening her hair, and making sure her make up wasn't ruined. She didn't want all the time Jack had spent doing it going to waste. "How do I look?"

Jack was in awe of her complete royal form. "Like a queen."

She smiled and used all her strength to climb out of the car and walk over to the bus shelter.

Jack cracked open his window, getting some fresh air for when he lit a cigarette. He could faintly hear Lady Catherine introduce herself. He waited peacefully, listening to her speak in her other languages with her musical voice. When the girl got on the bus, Jack stepped out of the car. "Lady Catherine, are you alright?"

She slowly craned her neck up at him. "Yes. I'm ready to go now, Jack."

He took her back to The Palace. He carried her to her bed and tucked her in. The Palace stayed closed that night, even after Catherine insisted under her slurring. He sat watching her sleep. The sound of her breath barely made it to his eardrums. He felt useless and insignificant. His ability wasn't of any use at this point. He held the pocket watch in his hand. Seeing the minute hand tick forward, he wondered how many Catherine had left.

Movement came from the bar. Taking his gaze off Catherine,

he went and took a look. It was Jerry, pouring himself a drink. "You alright there, Jerry? Little late to be drinking."

"Oh yeah. My wife got sick of me stirring." He shook the bottle.

Jack nodded and sat down on his old stool. There was a somber mist in the air. It was unlike Jerry to be so quiet. He kept fidgeting and blinking.

"I really do admire this place," Jerry said, gurgling through the satisfying burn of his whiskey.

Jack was grateful Jerry had started talking but he kept his head down, swirling his glass and nursing it occasionally.

"This is where I met my wife." Jerry's joyful spirit started to shine out of his newly born smile, reflecting off every polished surface illuminating the room. "That was before Lady Catherine took over. It was so different back then." His smile subsided, taking the light with it. "This isn't how I imagined she would go," he said looking over at her office door. He tapped his fingertips on the bar, trying to wake up the dying Palace. "It's gonna be different when she's gone."

Jack nodded and poured the dizzy whiskey down his throat.

Jack went back into Catherine's office. Catherine was still asleep; Jack could sense the soft tremor of her heartbeat. He took a look around the room. So many memories, all cramped in such a tiny space. Noticing the face-down picture frames, he gently lifted one and took a peek. He snapped it back down and walked over to the bed. "Lady Catherine. Lady Catherine," Jack whispered in her ear. There was no response. "Lady Catherine!" he shouted, shaking her shoulders.

"Ugh," she squealed, clutching her chest. "Jack, you almost gave me a heart attack."

He smirked, "I wouldn't know what they feel like. I've never had one," he said, scooping her into his arms. She was light as a feather and cold to the touch.

"Where are you taking me? What's that sound?" she asked, looking through the slits of her eyelids.

Jack headed toward the door. "When music is playing, you ask a lady to dance."

He stepped into the bar. The warm melody Jerry was playing on the piano crept up the wall, concealing the room with a bubble of affection. His stronger fingers made the keys bounce with every push, giving the chords a ghostly echo.

Jack took to the middle of the dance floor. He slowly spun and swayed with Catherine cradled in his arms.

"Hmm, this is nice," Catherine said, burying her head in his chest. Her pulse was faint. She didn't have long left.

"It is. But you've got to stay awake for me, Lady Catherine," Jack replied clinging on tight.

"Hush now. Don't go ruining this perfect moment."

Jack's bottom lip began to quiver. "I need you, Catherine. The Palace needs you." Catherine smiled. Her eyes were closed, yet Jack could feel them looking directly at him.

"Oh, honey. The Palace is yours. I made the arrangement the day you paid off the debt." Her voice was barely audible. "You keep it going. Make it your own. Take care of yourself."

Tears poured down Jack's face. His stomach had been turned upside down and his heart torn from his chest.

"There's something I need to tell you, Lady Catherine."

Lady Catherine grabbed the back of his head. Using her remaining ounce of strength, she lifted herself up and laid a kiss on his lips. "It's okay. I know." She dropped her head back on his chest, making herself comfortable. Moments later, her movement stopped. Jack continued to dance, long after Jerry had finished his soulful song.

It took him until the morning to convince the broken Jack to finally let Lady Catherine go.

. . .

Lady Catherine's funeral was extravagant. Not in the sense of money, but from the many people who'd come to say farewell to such a beloved woman. The man who went by the name Jack Fletcher didn't feel welcome. The sad yet content faces that surrounded him weren't the problem as they didn't know what he knew. His skin irritated and itched in a suit that wasn't his, and on the chair he didn't deserve. He'd been trying so hard not to be a monster that he had forgotten that he already was one. It was clarified when the pastor spoke.

"We are here to say goodbye to someone who has touched so many hearts in her life. A lover of music and language. Cherished by all. A wife, mother, grandmother, and a friend. Joining her husband Adam in heaven. We wish you an eternity of happiness. Mrs. Catherine Hallis, may you rest in peace."

The man who called himself Jack sat on a box in the late Catherine Hallis's office. He clutched the pocket watch. The chain was wrapped so tight around his hand, it cut off most of the blood to his fingers. He was surrounded by photos. The first was of Adam and Catherine on their wedding day. There were myriad other events, including one with a newborn baby, which he assumed was their daughter. Yet Adam Hallis was abruptly left out of them. Adam never got to see his daughter. The man who went by many names had made sure of that.

There he sat, listening to the photos' silent judgments. He couldn't comprehend what Catherine would have said if she'd known. His limbs were heavy. His blood was so cold it barely moved through his veins. He was alone again. Yet he wasn't alone. The voice was burrowing its way between each segment of his spine.

"Jack? You there, Jack?"

Jack could hear it but was too afraid to answer.

"Oh, there you are," Jerry said, shuffling into the office. His voice was surprisingly upbeat.

"Yeah, I'm here. You alright, Jerry? What can I do for you?" Jack replied, not reflecting Jerry's cheerful tone.

"Well, I was wondering when you planned on opening The Palace."

Again, Jack remained silent, failing to avoid the stares from the photographs. "Some other time. Not really feeling it."

"It's been almost a month. Don't you think it's about time? Besides, it's a good day."

"How so?" Jack asked, lowering his head. His brain was throbbing and pounding out of his skull as he finally broke the gaze of the photos.

"On the way here, the wind blew my hat clear off. A young man picked it up and handed it back to me."

"Is that so."

"Indeed. I'm never gonna forget his face."

"There are some good people in this world."

Jerry gave a hearty sigh at Jack's reply. "Why is it, Jack, that when you say things like that, you're not referring to yourself?"

Jack looked over at the picture of Adam Hallis in his pristine uniform. Never changing. Never aging. Finally, Jack knew what he had to do. He was going to be lost without Lady Catherine around to guide him; no one to drive him forward. She had given him the bar and he would honor her wish to keep it afloat.

"Can you do me a favor, Jerry?"

"Anything you need, Jack."

The man who went by Jack clipped the silver chain to his waistcoat. Each link bore down on to the next, and all the way down to the bow, which held the entirety of the silver full Hunter pocket watch. He looked at the face, and the hands always moving forward. "Call me Adam."

THIRTY-TWO

Adam leaned back in his chair, feeling exhausted with the guilt he had finally released. He couldn't bear to look at Joanna's reaction. He already despised himself and didn't need to see it in anyone else's eyes. "I've been keeping that a secret for more than ten years," he blubbered and spluttered. "Over fifty when I didn't know myself." He rubbed his face and blocked Joanna from his vision. "I didn't know the reason why I'd killed him at the time. I guess I didn't want him to know my secret."

He found himself back in the farmhouse. It felt cold and empty, no one had lived there in decades. Specks of dust floated motionlessly in the air. The color had been sucked away, like a painting basking in the sun. Finding himself standing over Adam Hallis, who laid propped up in the corner clenching his wound. Wearing a uniform too short for him, the cuffs stopped an inch before covering his wrists.

"I know why I did it now," Adam said while Adam Hallis remained silent, patiently waiting for his fate. "It was your eyes. Even when you lied there dying. You still hoped to see your wife again and meet you, daughter for the first time." Adam clenched his first until they started to tremble. "I hated you for that!" He relaxed his hands and his body became numb and limp. "Now I hate myself. What kind of person stops another from ever holding their child in their arms? No one deserves that." Adam looked deep into Adam Hallis's glistening eyes. "I'm sorry."

Adam Hallis said nothing in return.

Adam was sat back in the leather chair, rubbing his wrist against the armrests and eyes pointed toward the floor. "Black people. No matter how bad it gets for them. Whatever they endure. They can still find light in the darkness. It's how they survived for so long."

He shuffled back up in the chair, rubbed his face, and wiped his damp eyes. "Thank you for letting me share this with you. I know it couldn't have been easy to hear. Until last night I didn't think I needed to. But everything in my life catches up with me eventually." He took a large breath, expanding his chest.

"I lived such a long life. Too long. From one war to another, all the way up to the moon landing." Adam let out a soft chuckle. "It's funny. Humans haven't even sorted out the problems on earth, or found out it's mysterious. Yet they're already trying to leave it." Adam sparked up a cigarette and sucked in the toxic fumes. "I'm almost finished with my story and the reason why I'm here. The next few years were simple enough. I only had one thing on my mind. That is until I met an angel."

THIRTY-THREE

1997. It was just past midnight. Adam was busy signing paperwork in his office. His wrist started to ache with bone grinding on bone. The side of his finger had become red and spongy. He still hadn't got used to the amount of paperwork needed to run a bar. Electric bills, stock check, wages; the pile never seemed to go down. He contemplated getting a computer that everyone seemed to be raving about. He never went through with it, however.

Technology kept changing. Televisions got bigger and louder. Telephones had become something that you could store in your pocket. Every year, another car came out, claiming to be the next step in automotive history. The old was always being replaced with something newer and faster.

Time had taken its toll on Adam; he wasn't as fast as he once had been. His voice was calm and precise. He now took a moment to think before he spoke. His movement was slow and steady, especially with the watch weighing him down. He was able to keep a happy face for others but he couldn't forget what he had done for more than a couple minutes, like someone was reminding him to blink. After a few years, he stopped trying to forget. Similar to having a toothache and learning to eat on the other side.

The years after Catherine's departure weren't all bad. He kept The Palace going as she wished. Always full of faces, new and old. Turning more profit than ever before. Not that he cared. It just meant there was more paperwork to do. Even with The Palace full to the brim, there was always something missing. The radiant glow of Catherine's face that used to brighten The Palace, more than the lights ever could. The bar was under his name. After all, he had done, he knew he didn't rightfully deserve it. At least he had found it a suitable purgatory to serve his sentence. He kept everything how Catherine had left it. It was her dream. Her vision. Though he did replace the stools with something more permanent.

Adam looked down at his watch. It was coming up to one in the morning. He stretched his neck from side to side, giving out a tired crack. His eyes stung from the superficial light that hung above. The paperwork he had finished looked insignificant in comparison to the unstable stack that towered beside it. With an exasperated sigh, he grabbed another handful. Right before putting pen to paper, he heard a loud bang come from the bar. He was confused about what it could have been. The bar had been closed for over an hour. He put his pen down and curiously headed to the door.

"God damn it. What are you still doing here?" Adam shouted.

Jerry was slouched over, holding himself up by the table. One of the chairs lay sideways on the floor. "Sorry, boss. I'm almost done. My leg is getting the better of me today," he said, rubbing his knee cap.

Adam cleared his throat. "That's not what I meant, and I'm not your boss. You do the work without me asking, and I pay you the same way." Adam walked over to Jerry and helped him to his feet. "Go home, Jerry. You should be resting in bed and taking care of your wife."

Jerry nodded. "Then who's gonna take care of you?"

Adam looked around and gently tapped his pocket. "I've got this place to keep me company." Dormant and lifeless, The Palace stayed silent.

Adam began getting Jerry ready for his walk home. He took great care that he wasn't scruffy when his wife saw him. He tucked in his shirt and guided his arms into his coat. He picked out any loose threads and stray hairs. He was meticulous, making sure nothing was out of place. He still hadn't got the knack of doing up ties, and putting it on someone else's neck was especially difficult. "You got something to say, Jerry?" he said, feeling Jerry's intense gaze burning him.

"Hmm," Jerry grumbled. "You've been here quite some time."

"Your point is?" Adam replied, his concentration still focused on the tie.

"You ain't got no older," Jerry grumbled out of his dry plump lips.

Adam had known this time would come eventually. He was even surprised it hadn't come sooner. He still wasn't quite sure how to explain it unless he sat down and told his entire life story. He couldn't blame Jerry for asking. For the past ten years, he had been referring to him as Adam without hesitation or reason. Adam respected Jerry too much. He couldn't suffocate his joyful spirit with his troubles. "How old are you, Jerry?"

"Eighty-six," he answered firmly, shoulders back and head up high.

"And how old do you feel?"

Jerry's top lip started to twitch. "Eighteen."

They both chuckled, and the sound absorbed into The Palace walls.

"Well, I may look young," Adam said, finally meeting Jerry's gaze and finishing the tie, pushing the knot gently to his throat. "But I feel old," he said, with tired eyes and exhausted breath. He picked up Jerry's hat, giving it a quick brush, and perched it on his head. "So, who's got it better?"

Jerry's eyes rolled around, pondering the question. "Well, when you put it like that."

Adam smiled. He knew Jerry wouldn't press the matter any further. Another one of his brilliant and joyful traits.

"You gonna be alright?" Adam asked, seeing the cold night air hit Jerry's face.

"I'll be fine," he replied with a small amount of hesitation as the cold filled his lungs. He grabbed both sides of his coat and wrapped them around himself. "Besides, I'm eighteen years old." Jerry chuckled to himself and began to walk home. "I was right you know," Jerry hollered back.

Adam stuck his head out of the door.

"It is different. A good different." Jerry tipped his hat and continued his limping walk home.

Adam went back into The Palace. The open doors had sucked all the air out, leaving a thinning chill. Yet the words Jerry spoke kept Adam warm. Too warm apparently. Using his index finger to pry his collar from his expanding neck, he massaged his chest and with sweat pouring from his brow, he managed to pick up the fallen chair. He set it back upside down on the table.

Suddenly, a jolt of energy pulsed through his heart. Staggering backward, he managed to grab hold of the bar. Wheezing and groaning, his arm began to throb. His heart felt like stone. Heavy and brittle, each new pulse made the earthy mineral crack. The shearing pain went up to his neck and into his jaw. With vision blurry and disoriented, he stumbled his way into the restroom. The door swung wide, smashing into the wall and bouncing shut. Adam plummeted to the floor, hitting his head on the basin as he fell.

As he convulsed on the floor, blood dripped out his ears, and he choked on his tongue. He remembered joking to Lady Catherine about never having had a heart attack. Now he wished he'd kept his big mouth shut. The crushing sensation of his heart felt like it was being held by two large strong hands, much stronger than his own. They squeezed his heart tight, crunching and crumbling the rock, and letting the remains flitter between their fingers. Adam guessed it was his time to go.

"Argh. Hurry up already," he gargled, banging the back of his head on the floor. Quite ironic after all he had been through and everything his body had endured. People would think he had tripped and hit his head on the sink. It definitely wouldn't have been his first choice. With a loud sound of stone shattering, he stopped moving.

The room was cold. The only sound was coming from a leaky faucet. Each drip echoed exactly the same when it fell into the sink. Adam lay motionless on the floor, mouth ajar, and eyes drying out with every second that passed. What could have been an eternity felt like a few seconds. Color brushed his skin, his eyes blinked, and he closed his mouth.

He calmly pulled himself up, breathing gently out of his nose. He felt refreshed like he had just woken up from an afternoon nap. His mind was clear. Other than a mild disappointment at the final outcome, he didn't want to overthink about what just happened. He cleaned himself, tucked in his shirt, and straightened his collar. He washed his hands and face. The cold water rehydrated his skin. He felt somewhat foolish for getting his hopes up. He was back to his normal state. The watch was already bearing down on him.

He heard the high-pitched whine of the front doors swing

open. In frustration, he shook his hands dry and walked out of the restroom. "Jerry, I thought I told you—" Adam paused. A young woman stood in the corner of the room, admiring the photographs. Adam approached slowly, stopping at the corner of the bar.

"Sorry, Miss, but the bar's closed."

The woman was so engrossed in the photos, she hadn't heard him join her. She nearly flinched out of her skin. Her cheeks turned red. "Oh, I'm sorry. The door was unlocked. I didn't know." She made sure she had all her belongings and scurried to the exit. "It's just that my grandmother owned this place. Again, I didn't mean any offense."

"Wait!" Adam hollered.

The woman froze. A nervous expression settled on her face. One hand gripped the door handle, waiting curiously for the stranger.

Adam was mesmerized, looking her up and down. Her slender figure, and the long, black straight hair, which was the darkest he had ever seen. The whites of her eyes popped in contrast to her soft brown skin. Her warm matte lips were as smooth as silk. Adam smiled amidst the nostalgia. "Catherine Hallis was your grandmother?"

The woman loosened her grip, and any negative thoughts fizzled away. "Yes. How did you know her name?"

"Everyone knows Lady Catherine. She owned this place before me." He hesitated, his eyes twisting from left to right. "Before me and my grandfather, that is," he quickly interjected, not thinking if it made sense at all. "Please, stay, have a look around," he said waving a hand.

"Are you sure? I don't want to be any trouble."

"It's no trouble. Any friend of Lady Catherine is welcome here. You're family. Well, that's more important."

"Lady Catherine?" she said, walking back toward the photographs.

Adam paused for a moment. He hated the fact he was lying, especially when it involved Lady Catherine, but figured it was for the best. He missed talking about her. "It's what my grandfather used to call her. Guess it stuck." He leaned on the bar and he pointed at the photos, getting the attention off of his lies.

———

She marveled over each and every one, resisting the temptation to reach out and touch. They were well looked after in their matching frames as if they had only recently been put up. She gazed into the first photo. Her grandmother stood glamorously in the middle of a small group of people, all with smiles on their faces. The collection of people grew, the further she moved across the row. When she reached the second row someone else stood out. A young man pale as a ghost, standing at the end of the group. He didn't match the other people in the frame; he was like an accidental brush stroke on a canvas. She leaned in, nose to the glass. The young man looked lost in his own mind, somehow regretting a secret he didn't yet know. The woman turned and saw the same man standing near her.

———

"Uh, that's my grandfather," Adam said, trying to reassure her confusion.

She took another glance. "You look exactly alike."

Adam tried to act nonchalant about the situation, lighting a cigarette before speaking. "Some would swear we were the same person."

The woman smiled with pursed lips and continued looking at the photographs. She was in awe of her grandmother's beauty, surrounded by her guests. "She must have been loved by a lot of people," she said, her gaze fixed on the photos.

"She was one of the best," Adam replied, stubbing out his cigarette.

The woman noticed how the pale man in the photographs had moved ever closer to the middle of the frame. His smile grew with each change in position; eventually embracing center stage with her grandmother by his side. "They seemed very close," she said, raising her eyebrows.

"They were but nothing like that. Lady Catherine's heart belonged to your grandfather."

The woman nodded. "I don't know much about him."

Adam's head sloped, running his finger across the grain of the counter. "Me neither," he whispered.

The final photo had a row all to itself. Once a strong vibrant woman, now weightless. The joints on her wrist and collar bones protruded from under her frail skin. She was barely able to lift her head in the chair she was sitting on. No matter how bad she looked, it didn't take away the large smile on her face; matching all the photographs before and the man's who knelt beside her. Love and affection forever saved in the flash of the camera.

"The doctor gave her less than a year, she held on for three," Adam said.

"There are no more pictures?" the woman eagerly asked.

Adam shook his head. "My grandfather didn't think it was right without Lady Catherine."

The woman turned away, gently wiping her eyes. "I should go. Thank you for letting me look around."

"Please, wait one second," Adam said. He put his index finger and thumb into his waistcoat pocket and unclipped the chain. He bundled the chain neatly in his hand, with the watch resting on top. "Lady Catherine gave this to my grandfather. It belonged to yours." He straightened his arm. "Here, take it."

The woman blinked several times and tilted her head, astonished by the man's generous and selfless gesture. "Thank you, but I can't accept that," she said, edging closer to the door.

"Please." Adam lunged forward, his voice cracking with his plea. He tried his best to keep his arm from shaking. "They would have wanted you to have it." The woman stretched out her arm and with a sigh of relief, Adam released the watch into her palm. The absent weight immediately felt off his shoulders, making him feel light on his feet.

"Are you sure?" the woman asked.

"It deserves to be with its rightful owner. Besides." His eyes drifted down to the dark worn silver, beckoning him back. "It's just a watch to me."

The woman took a moment to admire the watch in her possession, stroking the clear crystal. "Thank you. This means a lot. My name's Grace by the way."

"Adam. Nice to meet you."

Grace fluttered her eyes. "Hmm. My grandfather was called Adam."

Adam gave her a quick sharp nod. "Who do you think I'm named after."

———

Grace had nothing to say in response. She just blindly stared at the mysterious man who seemed to know more about her family than she did.

———

"Good night, Grace," Adam said, guiding her out of her starstruck gaze.

She held open the door, smiled, and gave him a small wave goodbye. "Good night?" she scoffed. "That's a strange thing to say past noon." She walked out and closed the door behind her.

Suddenly the midday sun glared through the windows, lighting up The Palace and blinding Adam. He scratched the back of his head. He sensed he had lost something important and forgotten something even more so. He staggered back to his office, bewildered by the unexpected events that had happened throughout the night. To top it all off, he was now behind on the paperwork.

THIRTY-FOUR

A few weeks later. Yet again, another busy night at The Palace. The new band had brought in a large crowd. Adam was sprinting up and down the bar, serving drink after drink. He was light on his feet, weaving between the other staff.

"What can I get you?" he asked a customer while pouring the drink for the customer before.

"I'll just have a beer," a soft voice said, drowned out by the band.

Adam looked over. It was Grace. He became short of breath, seeing how beautiful she looked in her black floral dress. "Grace, nice to see you again." He grabbed a beer and popped off the cap. "There you go. It's on the house."

"Really? Are you sure?" Grace said, holding out the money.

Adam nodded, refusing to take it.

"Well, thank you," she said, taking a sip of the beer and was about to take a seat at the corner of the bar.

"No, don't sit there."

"What? Why?"

"It's a lonely spot. You won't make any friends there." Adam gestured over to Jerry, sitting at a table with his wife. "See the couple near the stage? Introduce yourself to them. They'll make you feel right at home." The naive Adam watched her stand up and approach the table, then continued serving the other customers.

"Thanks again. See you soon," said one of the last remaining guests.

"Thanks for coming," Adam replied, his cheeks sore from all the smiling. He wouldn't have had it any other way. He let the other staff leave and started to close down the bar, assuming no more drinks would be served that night.

Jerry hobbled over. "How's it going, Adam?"

"Alright. How was your evening?"

"I'm with my wife listening to good music. What's not to like?" Jerry replied with an inquisitive look about him. "We made a new friend as well. Young Grace over there." Jerry craned his neck back. His wife was getting ready to leave, and giving Grace a loving hug goodbye. He turned his head back, twitching his smirking lips. "We had a nice long chat. Talking about Lady Catherine. And your grandfather."

Adam pretended not to notice Jerry's blues-soaked eyes peering into his mind.

"We best be off, honey. See you again, Adam." Jerry's wife said, taking hold of her husband's arm.

"You best go talk to her now," Jerry said.

His wife chuckled behind her hand, seeing the puzzled look plastered on Adam's face.

"Why do you think she's still here? It's almost closing time," he explained. "She didn't come here just for the music."

"We were talking about Lady Catherine. She was more interested in hearing about you," Jerry's wife interjected.

Jerry shuffled on his coat and took his wife's hand.

"What do I say?"

"You'll figure it out. Besides, you're the one who looks young," Jerry said, tipping his hat and bellowing with laughter as they both left.

Adam looked over at Grace, watching her trace the grain of the table with her finger and listening to the band's final song. He wasn't sure what to do; the butterflies were too distracting. "Hey, I got you another beer. Mind if I sit down?"

"No, not at all," Grace said, taking the beer from his shaking hand. "Oh, that's good," she said, taking a swig of the amber liquid.

Two empty bottles became eight as they talked. Adam continued where Jerry left off; keeping in mind to change some of the facts.

Grace gripped her ribs, holding them together, while she cried with laughter. "That can't be true."

"Honestly, she slapped him right across the face." They both laughed uncontrollably. Continuing with his stories, he started believing them himself. Like the moving pictures he used to watch, now he was simply describing them. Adam finished off his beer, sliding it into the cluster. "They became good friends after that."

Grace took a look around. Only them and one band member remained. A huge contrast from the beginning of the night. "It would have been nice to see this place when my grandmother was around." She smiled and closed her eyes, imagining what it must have been like. "I wish I could have met her."

Adam sighed and rubbed his sweaty palms on his pants. "When I was younger, I used to have nightmares," he said, scratching his head and rolling his eyes. "Usually about war. Death. A monster standing in the corner of my room."

Grace leaned forward, putting her elbows on the table and resting her chin in her hands.

"To get me back to sleep, my grandfather used to tell me stories about a palace made entirely out of music, and a queen of many languages."

The more Adam continued with his story, the more Grace's smile resembled Catherine's.

"The queen had lost something dear to her heart. With her time running out, she searched for the long-lost princess."

Grace was completely enthralled by the fairy tale, almost believing it was true.

"Eventually the queen found the princess. Then the queen said her magic words, hoping to find some peace."

"What did she say?" Grace asked, sitting on the edge of her seat and pinching her bottom lip.

Adam rubbed his chin and cleared his throat. "*Sembri tua madre. Così bella.*"

Grace gasped and covered her mouth, her tears rejuvenating a forgotten memory.

Adam smiled. "I always fell asleep by that point."

Grace wiped the steady flow of tears away. She glanced back up at the stage, observing the lonely guitarist. Mid-twenties, buzz cut, and light brown skin. Sitting on an old wooden stool with a faded red velvet cushion. He gently plucked the strings so only he could hear.

"Do you do any of that?" she asked, waving her finger at the stage.

Adam laughed, having the lost memory push its way to the front of his head. "Once. It didn't go well." Grace smiled and started tapping her feet, copying the guitarist. Adam could hear the faint plucking of the guitar strings. He sensed Lady Catherine's voice tutting and telling him to get up. He nodded with compliance. "But I can dance. Excuse me for a moment," he said, getting up from the table.

"Hey there," Adam said, disrupting the guitarist from his trance. The strings clashed together, echoing a loud twang.

"Oh hi, I didn't see you there. You want me to leave?" the young man replied, standing up and leaving the guitar propped up against the stool.

"No, it's not that," Adam said, trying to dismiss any offense that may have been perceived. "I was hoping you would sing us a song."

The young man didn't seem too pleased with Adam's request. He squirmed around and looked at the exit. He wondered if he could just make a break for it. "I don't think that's a good idea."

"Please? It's for the young lady over there. I want to ask her to dance. But I need music to do so."

"Sorry, I can't help you," the young man urgently said, about ready to hop off the stage. He froze, then took a step back.

He glanced at the woman and then back at Adam, inspecting him all over. A look of bewilderment on his face, similar to the one Grace had a moment ago. "Have you known her long?" he asked.

Adam shook his head. "No, we only just met. But hopefully, that will change."

The man took a deep breath. "Alright, I'll do it," he said staring into space.

Adam could see the man had some uncertainty. "Thanks. I really appreciate it. If you ever want to sing again, then you're welcome back anytime." Adam offered out his hand.

The man let out a discreet mixture of laughter and sobs. "I hope so." He smiled. With the light brown skin on his hand, he gripped Adam's, squeezing it tight. After staring out of his soft green eyes for a moment, the man took his rightful position at center stage.

Adam walked back over to Grace; the hum of the guitar simmered in the air. "May I have this dance?" Adam asked, holding his breath and offering out his hand. The butterflies flapped so hard they created a miniature hurricane in his stomach.

Grace took hold of Adam's hand. His rough dry skin was almost painful to touch. They took their positions on the dance floor. Holding her hips, he pulled her in close.

The guitarist plucked the strings and began to hum. His sweet song echoed and bounced off every surface. The one man sounded like an entire band blooming within their eardrums and crawling down their spines, cradling Adam's heart and blossoming in Grace's womb. Mere moments felt like an eternity. Time became anchored to that specific memory. An entire audience watched them dance. When they finally finished dancing, the guitarist was already gone, disappearing from existence.

Adam continued the perfect moment, stroking Grace's cheek. "Can I kiss you?"

Grace smiled, nodded, and closed her eyes, anticipating his lips touching hers.

They almost didn't make it to Adam's apartment; barely able to keep their hands off one another. They kicked off their shoes. Adam unbuttoned her dress and Grace ripped off his jacket. With her legs wrapped around his waist, and their lips pressed together, Adam blindly carried her to the bed. He caressed her perfect skin. He slid his hands lower and lower, watching her stomach collapse as she gasped. Grace frantically grabbed his shirt, pulling the buttons from the holes. So engrossed was he that he almost felt human. The feeling changed when he saw Grace's reaction to his multiple flaws.

She was stunned. She scrolled her eyes around all the stories he hadn't told her; all written on his skin. She had a thousand questions but didn't need any answers.

Adam tried to button up his shirt, yet Grace stopped him and pulled it down off his shoulders. She ran her soft fingertips across the long scar on his abdomen. Around all the small tears, cuts, and holes and finally rubbing the two stars where his story began. She pulled him in close, resting their foreheads together and massaging the back of his head.

Adam leaned in to kiss her. Thinking if heaven was real, this must be it.

Grace became a regular part of Adam's life. A familiar face he never didn't want to see. He felt so free with her by his side as if wings had sprouted from his back.

Even Jerry could see the newly born spark in his eyes. All Adam could think about when working was her; hoping she would be the next person through The Palace's doors. He never had to second guess her. If there was anything she needed, wanted, or was bothering her, she would say. She was the most honest person he had ever known and she encouraged him to be the same. After six months, he asked her to move in with him. She accepted.

THIRTY-FIVE

"Hey, Grace. Wake up," Adam said, kneeling at her side by the bed.

"Oh hi, baby. Everything alright?" she asked with a croaky voice and eyelids still partially closed. Adam couldn't contain his smile, brushing the hair from her face.

"Everything's fine. Just going out. I got a funeral to go to." Adam wasn't one to read the obituaries. But someone had left the newspaper on the counter in The Palace and it had caught his attention.

Grace sat up, rubbing her eyes. "Do you want me to come with you?"

Adam shook his head. "It's alright. I'm not gonna be long. What are you doing today?"

Grace paused. Looking around, she contemplated her plans for the day. "Well, I was thinking of seeing my dad," she said with hesitation in her voice, and shrugged. "I doubt he will even notice. He's not all there."

A distant memory came to the front of Adam's mind. A memory from when he went by a different name and was attending another funeral. Adam shook his head. "He knows. Might not show it but there's no way he could forget you."

Grace smiled while sucking her bottom lip, then leaned over to kiss him. Her lips were soft and sweet, the notion of ever letting them go seemed insane. But alas, every good thing had to end and their lips separated. "See you later?" she asked.

Adam stumbled; the question only had one answer. "Definitely."

Months passed, yet seeing Joanna at her husband's funeral put things into perspective. Adam had never really intended on seeing her again. He also couldn't have guessed how his life would have turned out. However, he knew what it was like to lose someone close and had to see that she was alright. He decided not to go talk to her. Knowing how she was in her time of grief, seeing him would have made it worse. She had been married to her husband for over thirty years. A minuscule amount of time for Adam, yet still noteworthy. Must be different for a regular person. He hadn't thought of being married, not since he was a young man. Have a simple life, meet a girl, and have a few children. A ridiculous concept. But then he'd hold Grace in his arms, and sway on the dance floor while celebrating her thirtieth birthday. He had finally met his girl. All he needed now was a ring.

He stepped out of the jewelers with his mother's wedding ring now fitted for Grace's finger. New York, the busiest city in the world, no longer affected Adam. He was too fixated in asking Grace a question. He weaved in and out of people as if it was normal. Grace's face wouldn't leave his mind. To call her his wife would have been unbelievable or too good to be true.

He turned the corner. "Woah, sorry there," Adam said, almost butting heads with a man walking in the opposite direction. Fortunately, they didn't collide. Adam's unnatural strength would have knocked the young man out cold, messing up his swept-back hair and dirtying his suit.

Adam gave an apologetic smile that quickly disappeared when he saw the terror in the man's reaction to him. An unworldly cloud of gloom covered the man. His pale skin twitched, and bottom lip quivered. The thousand-dollar suit he was wearing soaked up the beads of sweat that poured from his brow. He stared at Adam, peering deep inside. Adam had never been looked at like that; like someone seeing what he truly was.

Adam's skin began to crawl. Something balanced on the tip of his tongue; something lost and forgotten. His mouth began to dry up. His tongue was rough and sticky, making it difficult to swallow. "You okay?" Adam croaked. He opened his palms, showing he meant no harm. Adam glimpsed his reflection in the nearest window. He wasn't sure what the man was so scared about. He didn't look very threatening in his waistcoat and tie.

The man, muttering incomprehensible ramblings, wasn't looking at Adam's clothes. He saw something deeper; something Adam couldn't. Past the suit and under the flesh.

Adam took a step forward.

"Get the fuck away from me," the man spat, edging closer to the road. "You're not real." Covering his ears, the man shot off across the road before Adam could speak. He took no caution about the moving cars that sounded their horns. On the other side of the road, he took a look back at Adam. Shaking his head, he scurried off into the nearest alleyway and continued his chaotic life.

Adam was left shaken. He could hear the overlapping voices of passers-by when they twisted their bodies to get past him; the howling construction and screaming traffic. His walk back home wasn't so peaceful anymore.

· · ·

Two long weeks passed. The encounter with the well-dressed man constantly tapped on Adam's mind. He carried out his duties at The Palace yet he was distant. He rarely smiled and never joined in with conversations. He was only doing what an employee would be contracted to do.

Jerry hobbled over to him near closing time. He had taken notice of Adam's newly strange behavior. "Hey, Jerry. How's everything going?" Adam said, looking down at the glass he was pretending to clean.

"I was going to ask you the same thing." Jerry leaned on the counter, taking the weight of his leg that had been bugging him all night.

Adam looked up, his wandering eyes catching on the few customers he had left. "What was that? Oh yeah, Jerry. I'm fine, thanks," he said, grabbing a glass he had already cleaned. "Just been having this strange feeling, that's all," he continued. Adam shifted his gaze and then leaned in close. "I don't belong here," he whispered.

Jerry had to squint to get him in focus. "Why is it, when you speak, you always say something to put yourself down."

Adam shrugged. "People don't seem to notice me."

Jerry stood up straight and gritted his teeth. "I noticed you the moment you stepped foot in here."

Adam didn't know what to say. He just stood motionless in a daze with his memories merging together. Wind blew on his face. The taste of iron in his mouth and the smell of freshly picked cotton stuffed his nostrils. "I think my name was William," he said, remembering the murky remnants of his past.

Jerry raised his hand and for the first time, stopped someone from speaking. "It doesn't matter who you were. It's who you are now that counts." He leaned in even closer, their noses nearly touching. "You're a good man, Adam."

Adam closed his eyes, repeating the words over and over in his head.

The Palace door swung open. The moment he saw her, he stopped worrying about the past. He started thinking about the future and wanting Grace to be a part of it.

"I'm gonna head out. Leave you two alone," Jerry said, popping on his hat at an angle.

"Thanks, Jerry."

"Don't mention it. Besides, my leg doesn't hurt that much." Jerry let out a massive heckle as he hobbled away, giving Grace a polite nod when he passed.

"Hey," Grace muttered, taking over Jerry's spot.

"Hey. You want a drink?"

"No. I'm fine, thanks."

Adam gently rubbed the back of her hand. "I know I haven't been myself lately," he said.

Grace grabbed his hand and gave it a tight squeeze. "Oh, it's okay. I've been feeling really strange too."

Adam leaned in and placed a soft kiss on her lips. The only lips he'd want to touch again. "You want to do something tomorrow night?" he asked quickly, not able to contain his excitement.

Grace nodded. "What did you have in mind?"

Adam sorted himself out in the bedroom mirror, checking over his pristine gray suit. He took a step back, standing central to the mirror. He didn't have a speck of hair on his face. Nevertheless, he enjoyed the few minutes it took to shave his bare skin. Grace had already done his tie for him and was now getting ready in the bathroom. He was content with the way he looked. He constantly tapped his inner pocket, making sure the small velvet box was still there. He was ready to go. A slight fluttering in his stomach covered any feeling that he was forgetting something.

"Well, don't you look handsome," Grace said, leaving the bathroom and fastening her earrings.

"Wow!" Adam gasped, seeing her in her green silk dress. Cut off just above the knee, it tightly caressed her luxurious figure. Her hair gently stroked the nape of her neck. Her bare shoulders and back shimmered with a radiant glow. Adam could swear he could almost see a halo floating above her head. He was so tempted to skip the pleasantries and present the box right there and then.

"Close your mouth, babe."

"Oh yeah, sorry." He was so stunned, he couldn't stop rambling on. "You look amazing in that dress. Not that you don't look amazing without the dress, or any other dress."

Grace laughed, watching him squirm. "Thank you. I figured I'd wear it now, before." Picking up her purse she checked she had everything. "Anyway, you ready?"

Adam nodded, giving his pocket another subtle squeeze.

Dinner was pleasant and sweet. Especially with the desired company. They talked and laughed while enjoying the delicious Italian food and wine. Grace sipped on water as she had offered to drive. Their conversation swayed back and forth; some topics were more important than others.

It was almost time to leave, and Adam thought it was now or never. "It's been a good night, hasn't it?" he asked, secretly taking the box out of his pocket.

"Yes, I'm glad we did it," she said, taking hold of his hand. They were so fixed on each other's eyes; no ordinary force could tear them apart.

"It's getting late but I was wondering–."

"Oh, that reminds me," Grace interrupted. She took her hand back and plunged it into her purse. Adam waited, frantically tapping his foot and peeking down at the open box in his lap.

"Here you go."

Adam looked up. What he had forgotten and what he was missing became very apparent. *To Adam. Always in my heart.*

From your loving wife. The words he feared to read. The ones that kept him up at night. Forever engraved into the back of the silver full Hunter pocket watch. The ticking of the second hand rang out with a repetitive thud. He couldn't hear what Grace was saying with the ticking filling his eardrums. He smiled and prepared himself for the weight to bear down on him as he shackled it to his waistcoat. He closed the box and slid it into his pocket. He knew she would say yes, and didn't want to ruin the night. But he couldn't ruin Grace's future either. His attire was complete again. Wearing such a pristine suit and the watch, at least he could enjoy pretending to be a good person.

Grace pushed him through the apartment door. She'd pulled off his jacket and whipped out his belt. Pressing her against the door, Adam threw his keys in the bowl, and quickly dropped the box in the drawer. Their lips stayed connected the entire time. His neatly pressed shirt now lay screwed up on the floor. He lifted her onto the back of the couch and rolled up her dress. The soft silk didn't compare to the purity of her skin. He pulled her underwear down and tossed it away.

She wrapped her legs around his waist, pulling him inside her. She bit down on his shoulder, conserving the sensation for as long as she could.

Her warm sticky breath on his skin sent tingles down his spine. They folded their arms around each other, bringing themselves closer into the fleshy embrace. Adam didn't believe in heaven. He certainly knew he didn't deserve to be there. But if it was real, this would be it.

Grace lay in bed, unconscious to the world around her. Her brown naked body barely covered by the sheet. Adam sat on the couch. The newly opened bottle of whiskey was nearly empty. Staring into space, he played his life back in his head like a movie reel. It was faded and stuttering, worn by time. He chuckled remembering the tomfoolery Charlie Chaplin had got up to. He laughed throughout the entire movie. Sadly, he didn't feel like anyone would be laughing at his moving picture. Besides, he was alone on stage. The only person to see it in full.

He picked up the phone and punched in the number he didn't know he knew. "Hello," Adam said, replying to Joanna's croaky and disoriented voice. "Sorry to call you. I doubt you remember me." He sniffed and wiped the tears from his eyes. It was good to hear her voice. "Yeah, I know what time it is," he said, the full Hunter watch reflecting the moonlight from his other hand. "Anyway, the reason I'm calling is that I need your advice again. So, I would like to book an appointment. As soon as possible." Adam's heart bounded, waiting for her response. "Nine o'clock. I can do that." He let out a sigh of relief. "What's my name?" He paused, a simple question for most people. He poured another drink. "Adam. Adam will do. Okay. Thank you. I'll see you then. Goodnight, Joanna."

He quietly placed the phone down, finished the whiskey, and gently rested the watch on the table. He stood up, rubbing his tired eyes. It had been a long eventful night and the morning would be no different. He slowly climbed under the sheet and rested his head on the pillow. He glared at the digital alarm clock on the bedside table.

Adam was awake.

THIRTY-SIX

"That's it? The reason you're here?" Joanna said, leaning on the edge of her chair. "You're wondering if you deserve to marry the granddaughter of the man you killed?"

Adam slowly but surely nodded his head. His emotions erratic after sharing most of his story. "There's one more thing."

Joanna turned in earnest.

"Grace is pregnant." Adam seemed quite calm. All his nerves were concentrated into a rapid tapping of his foot. "She told me last night. I smiled. I didn't really understand what she meant. It never occurred to me that I could be a father." The responsibility of raising a child felt foreign to him. Teaching them how to walk, talk, even breathe. He wasn't sure how he did all of those himself.

His temperature began to rise. His skin became tacky, and clung to his clothes. "Everything was going so great. Jerry's words guided me through. But then I saw that fucking watch." He coughed and spluttered. "I realized I'd be raising a child in a world with people like me in it." His nose continued to pour, no matter how many times he wiped it. "You know what the worst thing is?"

Joanna shook her head.

Adam was broken. Tears ran down his face; a river of secrets he had finally released. "I know I don't deserve them but I can't imagine my life without them." His salty tears continued to drop, burning his eyes. "I'm sorry." His voice cracked. "All I can think about is when they die, I'll be left here all alone again." Adam buried his head in his lap, finally finishing his story.

Joanna leaned in and stroked the back of his head. The mysterious man who had come to her twenty years ago needed help again. Yet this time, he could help himself. "Listen, no matter your name; no matter the wrong and good you've done, they will die. Whether you're with them or not." She placed her hands on his face, lifting him up so she could look him in the eyes. "They will grow old and eventually die. It's what happens before and after that's important."

Joanna pulled him in closer. "Do you love Grace?"

"I do," he said without hesitation.

"Do you want to marry her?"

"Yes." He felt somewhat better already saying it out loud.

Joanna leaned back in her chair. Slowly and calmly as she could, she asked her final question. "Grace will grow old, while you stay the same. Then eventually she will die and you'll carry on. What will you do?"

Adam closed his eyes. He saw Grace's face light up the darkness. She turned and looked at him. Her eyes widened and her smile grew. A loving warmth pulsed through his body. A tingling sensation blanketed his skin. "I'd still be married in my heart."

Joanna nodded. A different man sat in front of her from the one she had met this morning.

"The child," Adam said, forgetting about his upcoming fatherhood he was about to adventure on. "What if they are like me?"

"Then you'll be able to show them what's right, and tell them what's wrong."

Adam stayed silent. He wanted to remember those words.

They walked to the front door, past the secretary who didn't even lift her head from the computer. Walking down the front steps, Adam glanced at his watch. It was almost noon. He let out a sympathetic chuckle. "Well, that didn't take long," he muttered. Dropping off the bottom step, he turned to face Joanna who stood two steps higher. Now at eye level, they both stared cluelessly at each other, not knowing how to say goodbye.

"Well, I guess I'll see you around," he said, then was caught by surprise when Joanna dove in for a hug. Her bony elbows stabbed his shoulders and her wiry hair scratched his face. He wrapped his arms around and firmly squeezed, protecting her like a father would a daughter.

"Don't wait twenty years next time."

Adam smiled and they parted ways. With a soft sigh, Adam took out his packet of cigarettes, ready to spark one up. The streets were as busy as ever, but that wasn't going to detract him from what he needed to do. He crumbled the pack up in his hand and threw it into the open trash can.

Adam unlocked the door to his apartment. The keys clanged together when he dropped them into the bowl. The place was a mess, exactly how he'd left it. The sun blared through the small slit in the drapes. A long narrow bulge lay under the sheets. Grace was still unconscious to the world and lying in bed. Her head was buried under the pillows as they shielded her from the glaring sun.

Adam knelt beside her, taking away the pillows to see her angelic face.

Delirious and disoriented, Grace woke up from her peaceful slumber. She squinted and licked her dry lips. She smiled when she saw Adam smiling back. A burst of adrenaline pulled her up when she saw the small velvet box open in his hand.

THIRTY-SEVEN

"I can't stop looking at it," Grace said, flaring out her arm. She'd get the light to flicker on the elegant green stone. Bringing her arm in close, she twirled it around her finger. She was getting her skin used to the metal rubbing against it. "It's so beautiful," she said, flaying out her arm again.

"I'm glad you like it, but I'm trying to concentrate," Adam said, moving her arm from his view and keeping his eyes on the road.

"Sorry."

"It's okay." Adam Interlocked his fingers with hers. "Which way now?"

"Take the left here."

Adam pulled through the gates of a very fancy nursing home. The place was well-maintained. The windows were clean, trees and bushes trimmed, and the grass cut. Residents walked around the garden with enough staff to care for them efficiently. Adam thought it was quite a nice place to be when or if you got old.

Adam's perception changed when they got inside. Cautiously trailing behind Grace, he observed all the old and frail, simply waiting to die. It felt alien. Why would anyone want to visit such a place, just to be reminded of the future that awaited them? He shuffled closer to Grace's side, avoiding the thoughts of her inevitable future.

"Hey, Dad," she said, crouching down by an elderly man slouched in a chair.

Adam kept twitching. His vision snapped left to right, attempting to make sense of his surroundings.

Grace continued to talk to her father, but she only got grunts and gurgles in return. Nevertheless, it didn't take away the smile on her face. He was the first man she had ever loved. "Dad, there's someone I'd like you to meet," she said, gripping his shoulder and with her other hand pulled Adam out of his trance.

"Dad, this is Adam."

Silence persisted for the longest time. The man wasn't as old as Adam had first thought. He slowly pulled himself up straighter in the chair. His muscles were rusty with years of neglect. Yet the strength remained between the fibers, hibernating, waiting for a moment like this. Specks of gray littered his hair. His black skin was dry and flaky, with wrinkles burrowing themselves deeply. The most notable thing Adam could see was a geometric-shaped scar. Bleached pink, torn into the man's left cheekbone.

"Could you stay with him? I'm going to talk to the nurse for a moment." Grace had already walked off before Adam could reply. Not wanting to stand awkwardly in the middle of the room, he took a seat on the couch opposite the man.

Staring face to face, Adam kept his movements to a minimum. Grace's father wasn't able to reflect Adam's posture. Panting, shaking, and digging his nails into the arms of the chair. "What are you, some kind of devil?" the man garbled with a petrified, yet scolding glare.

Adam sighed and let out a pathetic chuckle. "Well, I ain't no angel."

The man nodded. Hearing the familiar voice was confirmation enough that it wasn't just a figment of his imagination. His eyes widened with a sudden realization. He frantically craned his neck to check on his daughter.

Adam looked as well and saw her leaning on the counter.

She turned around and gave them a quick wave.

"You're not going to–"

"No, never," Adam interrupted.

Hearing the honesty in the stranger's voice, the man began to relax.

Adam looked around. He checked they were far enough away to have a truthful conversation. "I seem to bump into the same people." He paused and scratched the side of his face. "It's funny. Never thought I'd run into you."

"I bet," Grace's father replied, wiping the sweat from his forehead. He let out a large breath, deflating his puffed-out chest. "I wasn't a very nice man back then."

"Me neither," Adam interjected.

The man lifted his hand and looked closely at the calluses on his knuckles. "Never been one to back down from a fight. If anyone pushed me, I pushed back faster and harder."

Adam remained silent. His role had changed. It was his turn to listen to a very familiar story.

"Things got worse coming back from Nam. I'd push people before they could push me." He shrugged and cleared his throat. "It's all a blur now. All I really know is if I couldn't find a fight, I'd start one at home."

The old man shuddered. A deep fear kept him awake at night. "The night I met you was a bad day. I was drunk, like most days. The wife locked me out. Not the first time she had done it." He raised his hand and rubbed the scarred tissue on his cheek with his thumb. He began muttering under his breath, not intending to be heard by Adam. "I've never been hit so hard in my life. I'm strong and I've seen stronger but nothing compared to you." He raised his head and voice. "You could have killed me if you wanted."

"I was going to."

"Then why didn't you?" the man spluttered. The answer to the question had been playing on his mind for so many years.

Adam opened his mouth ready to speak. He had a sudden change in emotion as he pieced together the missing parts of his life. "The girl with the little feet," he whispered.

"What was that?" the man barked with short, sharp breaths.

"I couldn't kill you in front of your daughter," Adam stammered as he continued. "I didn't want to be a monster."

The answer was difficult for the old man to swallow. It wasn't what he'd expected, but it filled the void. "My wife could have done the same. Left me out there for my body to rot." The man closed his eyes, remembering the few memories he had of his wife. "After all I had done, she still dragged my sorry ass in and patched me up. I never deserved her. She should have listened to her mother and kept the hell away from me. I quit the drink and managed my anger." Long overdue tears began to run down the man's face. "She died two weeks later. I hope she knew I had changed before she went." The man rubbed his burning red eyes and pulled himself back up in the chair. He exhaled a large puff of air. He was finally released from his heavy burden.

The tone in his voice shifted. It was now driven and precise. "The passion I didn't show to my wife, I gave to my daughter." His tired eyes were focused and unflinching.

However, Adam could see the uncontrollable twitching and spasms of his limbs. "Don't you pity me," the man snarled.

"When my mind and body started playing up, I put myself in here. Not making my daughter look after a crippled old fool."

Adam gave him a swift, respectable nod.

The man gave himself a few minutes to calm down again. "I guess I should thank you."

Adam tilted to the side, lowering his brow.

"If you hadn't put me on my ass that night, I wouldn't have changed my life around. I'd hate to think what life would have been like if you hadn't." The man shivered, shaking the terrible thoughts from his head.

"Thank your daughter," Adam said. "She saved your life. Mine too."

The old man closed his eyes. His breathing became deep and methodical. His limbs stopped shaking. He no longer needed to fight. "Best feeling in the world, being a father," he said with a soothing voice.

"You're gonna be a grandfather. Grace is pregnant."

The man raised his eyelid making a small slit, just enough to see Adam. He tried to hide his flickering smile the best he could. "Of course, she is. She turned thirty a month back. Don't tell her you told me. She'll kill you."

Adam chuckled along with the man. Any onlookers would have mistaken them for old friends.

"You told her yet?"

Adam shook his head. "I'll tell her everything in time."

"Time." The old man coughed. "All anyone ever wants. Never can have enough."

"Agreed."

They remained silent for the rest of the time they were alone. Their eyes fixed together.

Grace walked back over. "Hey, Daddy. You alright?" she said, taking a knee by his side.

"Oh, hey there, darling. It's good to see your face."

Grace almost fell back in astonishment, wide-eyed, mouth gaping, and cheeks red. "Hey there, stranger," she squealed, with a warm smile growing from ear to ear on her face. She glanced at Adam with a bewildered look.

Adam raised his shoulders and eyebrows in unison.

Grace moved her attention back to her father. She gently placed her hand on his unscarred cheek. "It's good to see your face too."

Adam waited patiently, listening to father and daughter talk for the first time in a long time.

"Haha!" the old man bellowed. "Well, now. I've taken up enough of your day. You go enjoy your freedom. While you still have it."

Grace frowned, trying to interpret his strange phrase. But she let it go, assuming she was just being paranoid. "Okay, Daddy. I'll see you next week," she said, her voice several pitches higher than usual. Then she kissed him on the top of his head.

Adam walked over to her side. Again, there was a moment of silence. This was different, however. It was peaceful and content. Another piece of Adam's life had fallen neatly into the rest of the puzzle. "It was nice to meet you, sir," Adam said, offering out his hand.

"The name's Ethan," he replied, firmly grabbing hold of Adam's hand. "It was good to finally meet you."

With a final wave, Adam and Grace headed to the exit. Adam looked back. With each further step, Ethan sank deeper into the chair.

They got back into the car. Adam was busy clipping in his seatbelt and looking through the assortment of keys for the right one.

Grace leaned in, twisting her body, to lay a long, soft kiss on his lips.

"What was that for?"

"No reason," she said, running her fingers through his hair. "Your eyes," she mumbled, getting lost deep within them. "Thank you for coming with me today. I haven't seen my dad like that in a while."

"Thank you for inviting me. What about my eyes?"

Grace lifted her head; dizzy and disoriented by the colorful maze of his iris. "I feel them. I can't explain it. They mainly feel sad."

Adam held the back of her head pulling her in close. He pushed their lips together. Her hair looped around his fingers. Clenching his hand into a fist, he never wanted to let her go. "Never when I look at you," he said, finally releasing her. He found the correct key and they went home.

THIRTY-EIGHT

Grace sat on the couch, rubbing her now bulging belly, and giggled every time the baby kicked. The nine months had passed fairly quickly. Quick even for Adam. "We still need to think of a name," she said.

"Is that really important," Adam replied while clearing the table.

"We can't keep calling them the baby."

"Why not?"

Grace tutted at Adam's response.

She moved her attention over to her engagement ring that sparkled in the reflection of the window. *It's a very beautiful ring,* Grace thought to herself. *Adam's mother must have been truly loved to have been given such a ring.* "You've mentioned your mother, but never your father," she said. The man standing in front of her was still a mystery.

"My father was an asshole," Adam quickly blurted out.

He froze solid, catching a glimpse of his reflection in front of the night sky. He wasn't sure why he'd said it. Force of habit maybe. He had been lying about his past for so long, he had started to believe it. He didn't know which part of himself he was referring to. What he did know was that he wasn't talking about his father. He couldn't remember a thing about him. Just an ancestor who had died a century ago with Adam being the last evidence of his existence. Adam figured that should change.

"My father," Adam started to say, trying to think of the right words. "My father was a cruel and heartless man." He nodded his head. "But he loved his family. He would've done anything for them. Even if that meant doing the wrong thing." The watch became weightless in his pocket; no longer holding him down.

———

Grace nodded with acceptance. She sensed it was difficult for Adam to have shared that with her. A small pain in her side made her think the rest should remain unknown. A quick glance back at the ring made her gasp. Bringing her hands to her mouth, her cheeks flushed red with embarrassment. "I don't know your surname," she said, her voice flooded with undeserving guilt.

———

Adam took another look at his reflection. A small smile appeared on his face when he saw his reflection smiling first. "Lake," he whispered.

Grace lowered her arms. Looking down at the ring and straightening it with her thumb. "Mrs. Lake it is then," she said with a smile of her own.

. . .

A stray tabby cat wandered down the dark New York streets. Its fur was damp and matted together in clumps. Scrawny and slender, its ribs and shoulder blades protruded from under its fur. Time had taken its toll on the feline. It never looked back. The past was unimportant to a cat. No strong ambitions for where it was headed. Scurrying down the cold sidewalk, it lived in the moment. It did not worry itself with the uncontrollable and unknown future that awaited it. Its only goal was to find its next meal.

It was a shame it didn't look slightly to the future or at least left and right when it scurried into the road. It only needed to take a few more steps. It straightened its legs and hunched its back, blinded by the pair of white lights bearing toward it.

Adam woke from his relaxing slumber. A pain was starting to simmer in his chest. It had been occurring more frequently in the past few months. Grace wasn't having a comfortable sleep either. She had been tossing and turning throughout the night, stealing all the covers and wrapping herself into a cocoon. Adam stared up at the ceiling. He really couldn't be bothered to get up. He carefully listened to the faint echo of music playing outside. He knew the pain would get worse before it got better. Not wanting to disturb Grace, he reluctantly pulled himself out of the bed.

Shivers brushed over his skin followed by a cold sweat. He slowly stumbled his way to the bathroom, trying to stay as quiet as possible. He knew Grace would only worry if she woke. He gritted his teeth to hold in the pain as he closed the door behind him. His anxiety dropped when he felt the lock engage. Taking in a couple of long deep breaths, he prepared himself for the pain that clamped ever tighter on his chest. He grabbed hold of the side of the basin. This pain felt different.

What usually made his heart feel hard and cold like lead now burned, making it soft and malleable. The fiery organ pulsed, sending boiling blood into his veins. His other organs couldn't take the heat any longer. They squirmed around frantically, wanting to escape their environment.

Adam broke the tortured silence by letting out a weeping groan. His teeth and the ceramic of the basin began to crack under the immense pressure they were under. "Ugh!" he groaned again. He didn't think the pain was ever going to end.

"Adam!" Grace shouted from the other room.

"Fuck," Adam mumbled frustrated with his failure. He spat the phlegm, blood, and fragments of enamel out his mouth. "I'm fine, Grace. Go back to bed. I'll be out in a minute."

"Something's wrong with the baby."

The hairs on his neck stood up, sharp and prickly. The pearls of sweat stopped moving after hearing those words echo from behind the door. He ran out of the bathroom. The pain erupting inside of him was no longer his concern.

Grace stood in a puddle of blood, grasping her swollen stomach. Tears ran down her face as she trembled in terror.

"What happened?" Adam shouted, trying to determine where the blood was coming from.

"I don't know," Grace squealed. "The pain just started suddenly, and then the blood." She stood there petrified, watching the blood trickle down the inside of her legs. The puddle increased in size with every drip. "There's so much blood," she said.

"It's alright. I'll grab some clothes and we'll head to the hospital." Adam squeezed her shoulders. Grace shook her head.

"Everything will be okay, Grace. I'll make sure of it. Aghh!" Adam screamed once again. Searing hot pokers plunged themselves into his heart. Collapsing onto the floor, his hands splashed in the warm excreted plasma.

"Adam, what wrong?" Graced groaned, the intensifying pain still rolling around in her womb.

Adam's teeth squeaked from his clenched jaw. "I'm gonna get

you to the hospital." He pulled himself up off the slippery floor. He washed the blood from his hands the best he could. He scrambled to put on some clothes, and carried Grace to the car.

Grace kept screaming, "It really hurts!" The baby felt like it was being ripped out of her stomach.

"I know, honey. We'll be at the hospital soon," he said, pushing the gas pedal to the floor. "Just try to relax. Think about something else."

———

Grace winced and shifted her body to rest her head against the window. She watched the blurry lights rush past. It was unusually quiet. She saw a building that resembled the apartment she'd lived in when she'd been a child. She braced herself to stop her stomach from churning when Adam took the next left. She'd had a hunch he was going to do so.

———

Adam kept his focus on the road, occasionally giving her a quick glance. Her eyes flickered between different thoughts. Adam wiped the mixture of tears and sweat from his eyes. He was shaking and stretching his fingers to stop the trembling. His clothes were irritating his scars. They were sticky and cold as if they were bleeding again. He could feel something pushing on his chest, making it difficult to breathe. Panting away, he placed his hand on his chest. He let out a soft sigh of relief when he figured out it was just the pocket watch. It was lying in his jacket pocket, tangled up in the chain. All of a sudden, his focus was drawn to the ticking; irregular and pulsating. It took him a moment to notice the ticking was matching his heartbeat. His anxiety increased. He thought it was impossible. Thinking he was just delirious and paranoid, he tried to convince himself that his heart was matching the watch.

"The next right," Grace whispered.

Adam turned right.

"It's funny."

"What is?" Adam asked with a begrudging look on his face. He didn't know what could possibly be funny at this moment.

"You must be taking the same route my mother used to. She was a nurse at the hospital."

"You've never mentioned your mother," Adam said with bated breath. The pain inside reached up and squeezed on his windpipe.

———

"She died when I was young. I don't remember much about her. I think she used to say if something was bothering you, you should share it." Grace sighed. A warm invisible embrace comforted her. "Something along those lines anyway."

———

All of a sudden, the road became strangely familiar to Adam. Feeling an ancient memory curl its way out from the depths of his mind. The girl with the little feet sat beside him. All grown up and carrying his child. He decided to take her advice again. Yet some things are best left unknown.

"How did your mother die?" he asked, staring into the darkness in front of him.

"She was a nurse. She was on her way to work. There was a car crash."

Grace's words faded away like a cloud after a storm. Adam had only ever visited one doctor and only one nurse.

He could see her face. Beautiful and pretty, just like her daughter.

Adam's past had finally caught him. It left him to face his treachery alone in the dark.

Every ailment, wound, and scar he had endured erupted in unison. He screamed in agony, losing control of the car.

"Adam, what's wrong?" Grace yelled, grabbing hold of the steering wheel.

"I'm sorry," he whimpered.

"Sorry for what? You're really scaring me," Grace said, crying in fear for the man she loved.

Adam's pain froze. He unknowingly took control of the steering wheel again. Time slowed to a grinding halt. He was blinded by the pair of neon red eyes that lingered in the distance. "I didn't expect to run into you again," he said.

The floating emeralds didn't reply. Staying perfectly still, they waited patiently for the future.

Adam shook his head. "No, no. Not again. Not now," Adam pleaded.

The eyes remained silent.

Adam growled in anger, screaming at the future that awaited him. Then he realized. Taking a deep breath as time pulled back. "No, not this time."

"Baby, you're not making any sense. Please, just pull the car over!" Graced screamed.

"It's alright, honey. Everything's going to work out fine," he said, his voice aimed and precise. He sat up straight and gently gripped the steering wheel. He kept the car centered on his side of the road. "Let's get you to the hospital."

A pair of white lights burrowed toward a stray tabby cat.

With a dull thud, the cat hit the front fender, rolling under the back wheel and barely leaving a mark. Adam jolted in his seat and his body became numb. He no longer felt pain. He no longer felt anything. Finally, he had finished his journey, arriving at the front doors of the hospital.

"Someone, please, help!" he shouted, walking through the doors with Grace held in his arms. Everything moved so fast, he couldn't concentrate.

A swarm of doctors and nurses took Grace from him and placed her on a gurney.

"No, help him!" she protested as she was trolleyed down the hallway to the delivery room.

"Don't worry," Adam said, slurring his words. He squeezed her hand. "You'll see me when you come out. I'll wait for you. I love you so much."

Grace nodded, smiling away the tears.

Adam released her hand and gave her a wave as she was taken to the next room.

"No, Adam, please! Don't leave me." Her voice became inaudible when the door closed behind her. Yet her screams could be felt vibrating through the walls.

Adam sat down on a chair against the opposite wall. He was unusually calm. Bystanders would have mistaken it for a lack of personality. They would have been wrong. He knew exactly who he was.

It had been a very revealing night, yet none of it mattered now. Too late to dwell on the past. He looked over at the small window in the door.

He imagined walking over to it, light on his feet. Peering through the glass. Seeing Grace with her angelic glow, and holding their baby in her arms. This wasn't the way he expected to go. After all that had happened, he was just thankful he could save two. A small piece of heaven that he truly deserved.

A man who went by the name of Adam Lake sat in a chair in an empty hallway of the hospital. A silver full Hunter pocket watch in his hand. He listened to the ticking that matched his heartbeat. *Tick-tick. Tick-tick. Tick.*

William was dead. This happened to him often.

Printed in Poland
by Amazon Fulfillment
Poland Sp. z o.o., Wrocław

61999644R00197